11/4/2020

D0977062

Love

Is a

Rogue

Love
Is a
Rogue

🌹 A Wallflowers vs. Rogues Novel 🌹

LENORA BELL

AVONBOOKS

An Imprint of HarperCollinsPublishers

First Avon Books mass market printing: November 2020
First Avon Books hardcover printing: October 2020

Print Edition ISBN: 978-0-06-303553-9
Digital Edition ISBN: 978-0-06-299335-9

FIRST EDITION

20 21 22 23 24 LSC 10 9 8 7 6 5 4 3 2 1

*For Brian. Because you gave me that
beat up old tool belt as a courting gift.
Because I like the way you use
your Leatherman.*

Love Is a Rogue

Chapter One

Cornwall, 1830

LADY BEATRICE BENTLEY was meant to be researching word origins for her etymological dictionary, not making a study of wild rogues.

One wild, untamed rogue in particular: Stamford Wright.

Carpenter. Distraction. Bane upon half-finished dictionaries.

How could she concentrate on scholarship with such an overbearingly virile specimen of manhood disturbing her tranquil literary idyll?

All summer long, and well into autumn, she'd watched from behind the safety of the library curtains as he hammered, heaved, and dominated her brother's Gothic mansion in Cornwall into submission.

The crumbling crenellations and bricked-up windows of Thornhill House proved no match for Mr. Wright. By sheer force of personality and person, he'd helmed a group of workmen in the rapid renovation of the great house's facade.

While Beatrice had only managed the woefully inadequate addition of two hundred new words to her dictionary.

Her brother Drew, Duke of Thorndon, was traveling with his new bride, Mina, on the Continent. They should have arrived back in England by now, but had been mysteriously delayed. When her brother finally returned to Thornhill, he'd be thrilled with the progress Wright had made.

Beatrice was less than thrilled—in fact she was livid. She'd bargained with her mother for these precious months of blissful solitude in which to be as scholarly as she pleased, without fear of her mother's scolding or London society's ridicule. Was that too much to ask?

Apparently.

At every turn she'd been perturbed, nay, overset by the ungovernable force of nature known by the name of Wright.

She'd tried stuffing cotton batting in her ears. Humming to herself as she wrote. Swathing the library in thick velvet hangings.

Nothing made a jot of difference. Even if she couldn't *see* him, she could still hear his gruff, commanding voice, and that was enough to shatter her peace of mind.

Take today, for example.

Wright and his men were building a pergola in the gardens. She could hear him barking orders and whistling jaunty melodies—quite tunelessly, she might add.

And when she gave up on studiousness, crept to the window, and shifted just an inch of curtain aside, the sight of him immediately unnerved her.

He stood with his leather boots firmly planted, shouldering the burden of a heavy length of timber as one of the workers, the giant one they called Tiny, maneuvered the log into place.

"Hold her steady," Wright ordered. "A little to the left. Your *other* left. Steady on . . ."

His wavy dark brown hair gleamed in the late afternoon sun. He wore no coat, and his shirtsleeves were rolled to the elbows. Sweat-dampened white linen did nothing to hide the outline of his bulging arm and shoulder muscles.

"Easy does it, now. Nearly there." Wright released his hold as the beam was nailed into place. "Well done!"

An odd little shiver traveled the length of her spine. He was so very commanding, so unquestioningly confident. Even though the air was brisk and cool, he tugged his shirt free from his trousers, fanning the fabric away from his torso.

Her breath caught in her throat. She stared, transfixed, as he lifted the hem of his shirt and used it to mop his brow. The newly revealed landscape of his abdomen rippled with ridges of muscle. A dusting of brown hair trailed down the center of his stomach, disappearing into his trousers.

He couldn't mop his brow with a handkerchief like other people. Oh no, he must display his uncommonly flat and finely sculpted abdomen for everyone to see.

For her to see.

She covered her eyes with her hands to block out the discomposing sight. Her spectacles fogged over and she wiped them clean with her skirts, setting them back in place, unwilling to miss a ripple or a ridge because . . . because she was making a list of Wright's infractions to present to her brother upon his return.

Tuneless whistling. Ribald jokes. Flagrant displays of sculpted musculature. Refusal to modulate or modify his work habits to suit hers.

When she'd instructed Gibbons, her brother's land agent, to request that Wright work more quietly, Wright had sent back a brief, impolite missive informing her that he had a job to finish, limited time with which to accomplish it, and that the noise and debris simply couldn't be helped. He'd then suggested that she might wish to repair to the comfort and luxury of her London townhouse until the work was complete.

Thornhill House was meant to be her sanctuary *from* London.

Beatrice had work to complete as well, but Wright couldn't care less. All he cared about, besides finishing the renovations at a breakneck pace, was gulping pints of ale and striking manly poses for the benefit of the housemaids.

He was the most maddening of men.

Another infraction to add to her list: transforming sensible housemaids into breathless scatterbrains.

She overheard them twittering about Wright's handsome face and brilliant blue eyes. They all fancied themselves in love with him. They said that he was a ship's carpenter with the Royal Navy and was only here because his father, the duke's long-term retainer, had suffered an injury falling from a ladder.

The maids opined about the hearts that Wright must break at every port he visited. Their fondest hope was that he would decide to stay in Cornwall, marry a village girl, become the lead carpenter at Thornhill upon his father's retirement, and settle down to raise a large and happy family.

All the man had to do was flash that roguish grin and level-headed maids melted into quivering puddles of ninnyhood.

Ninny. Late sixteenth century, English, meaning simpleton, or fool, possibly derived from innocent, or the Italian ninno, *"baby, child."*

It was a very good thing that Beatrice had not one ounce of ninny in her.

"I could use a frothing pint about now," Wright said, restoring his person to a semblance of civility by tucking in his shirt and donning a coat.

"All this heavy lifting makes a fellow thirsty," agreed one of the younger workmen, a wiry fellow named Preston.

"Reminds me of the load I 'ave to lift every time I take a piss," said Tiny.

"Got a big tallywhacker, have you?" asked Preston with a cheeky grin.

"Naw, lad. Got to move me stomach out of the way first."

Wright broke into loud laughter.

Beatrice rolled her eyes. *Men.*

What she'd gleaned from eavesdropping on several such exchanges was that they had an inordinate preoccupation with their . . . with the aspect of their anatomy that differentiated them from females.

Wright squinted at the sky. "Light'll be gone soon." He glanced toward her window.

Beatrice stepped backward, nearly stumbling in her haste to hide. She flattened against the wall, her heart attempting to leap into her throat. Had he seen her?

The lonely spinster in her tower, watching life pass beneath her window.

She knew how the world saw her. But she wasn't a spinster, at least not yet. She'd promised her mother that she would go back to London for her fourth and final attempt at the marriage mart. Mama was determined to find her a brilliant match.

Beatrice was determined to remain a wallflower.

All she had to do was endure one last wearisome round of social engagements, grating gossip, and insincere suitors, and then she could return to the magnificent library at Thornhill House. For good this time.

She'd be well and truly on the shelf by next summer.

And what was so bad about being on the shelf? Most of her dearest friends lived on shelves.

Her gaze swept the library's vast expanse of bookshelves, punctuated by sliding wooden ladders.

She'd learned very early in life that books were her most trustworthy companions.

Books never stared. Never whispered or snickered.

Never called her Beastly Beatrice.

You're beastly inside and out.

Pushing away the unwelcome memory, she feasted her eyes on the library instead. Mahogany shelves hugged every wall and rose to embrace a domed ceiling painted with scenes from Greek mythology. Every available surface was piled high with books and papers, filling her mind with the soaring promise of endless possibilities.

All of those new words just waiting to be discovered, mapped to derivatives and cognates, defined and annotated.

Words were her sole passion in life. She explored their origins in the way a painter mixed pigment to render a stormy sea, or a symphonic composer chose reed instruments to re-create birdsong.

She explored words in the way that lovers explored love.

There'd been a time when she'd entertained foolish romantic notions about true love and fairy-tale endings, but she'd discarded her girlhood dreams after they'd been dashed against the rocks of reality.

This was her future: this library, and her dictionary, which might very well take decades to complete. The most comprehensive and well-researched etymological dictionary of the English language ever compiled by man . . . or wallflower.

The dictionary that, once again, she was sadly neglecting. She settled back at her writing desk determined to make some forward progress. Regrettably, the desk was situated near the open windows and she could still hear Wright and his men talking and laughing.

She dipped her pen resolutely in ink.

Let's see; she'd finished *intercede* and *interim*. Now on to *interloper. Late sixteenth century*, she wrote, *a hybrid of Latin* inter *and the old Dutch* landloper, *or vagabond*.

She tapped her chin with the feathered quill. *Mr. Wright is an interloper upon my peaceful countryside retreat.*

Thump. Thump. Thud!

The hammering sounded as though it were inside her head.

Stamford Wright, she wrote. *See* Rogue. *Born and bred in Cornwall. Ship's carpenter in the Royal Navy. Heavy of hammer and brawny of shoulder. Characterized by excessive virility and boundless arrogance. Believes he's God's gift to womankind. Highly distracting and irritating to the scholarly female.*

Well *that* wouldn't be going in her dictionary. She drew a line across the page.

"Oh, Mr. Wright," Beatrice heard a lilting female voice call. "Would you care for some cider?"

"You go on ahead to the pub, lads," she heard Wright say. "I've something to take care of first."

"Oh, aye," came Tiny's answer. "Something by the name of Miss Jenny."

More guffaws. Probably some thumping of shoulders and winking.

They must be talking about Jenny Hughes, one of the kitchen maids.

"You're a sight for sore eyes, Jenny," said Wright, much closer now by the sound of it.

"I thought you'd be thirsty, working so hard and so long," Jenny replied.

The sound of cider being gulped. A soft giggle.

"Mmm. Exactly what a man needs after a hard day's labor. Did you sweeten this cider with your smile, Miss Jenny?"

"Go on with you now." Said in a tone that conveyed precisely the opposite instruction.

Of all the infuriating occurrences.

Instead of going to the pub and giving Beatrice a well-deserved respite from his outsize presence, Wright was flirting shamelessly beneath her window.

Beatrice pushed her spectacles up the bridge of her nose. Enough was enough.

You've met your nemesis, Wright. From the Greek for retribution. The goddess of vengeance. The personification of divine wrath.

She marched to the windows and opened them wider. She'd drop an inkpot on his head—that ought to douse his ardor. Better yet, a flowerpot.

She peered over the ledge. Divine wrath had carried her thus far, but the sight of Wright's massive shoulders scrambled her thoughts and sent them running in opposite directions.

He stood directly below her, one dusty black boot propped on a stair to better display his heavily muscled thighs. His white shirt was open at the collar, revealing a triangle of sun-kissed chest.

If he untucked his shirt from his trousers at this moment, she'd have a direct line of sight down his . . .

Lady Beatrice Bentley! exclaimed her mother's scandalized tones in her head. *Stop gawking this instant. He's not an eligible gentleman. He's not a gentleman at all and therefore far beneath your notice.*

True. But he was also beneath her window and she couldn't look away.

Not now. Not when he was cradling the cider mug in one of his huge hands, stroking a finger around the rim.

Watching him gave her the most unsettling tingling sensation in her belly. Must have been something she ate for luncheon. There'd been a rather questionable leek and cod pie.

Jenny took the empty glass from him. "Will you be wanting more refreshment?"

There was no mistaking the suggestive inflection in her words. She wasn't offering cider; she was offering kisses.

Beatrice peered over the ledge. Wright had moved closer to Jenny and away from Beatrice's line of vision. All she could see was the taut curve of his backside and his long legs.

Whispers and . . . smacking noises? Were they kissing? And, incidentally, what would a kiss from him be like?

She stuck her head farther out the window.

Too far.

Her spectacles slipped off her nose and plummeted straight for his head.

She dropped into a crouch beneath the window, cheeks flaming and heart thudding. She could only hope that he was too occupied to notice a pair of spectacles falling from the sky.

Silence from below. She risked a quick glance out the window.

Egad.

She dropped back to a crouch.

Wright had found her spectacles, and apparently he meant to return them to her.

He was climbing straight up the rose trellis like a pirate scaling the rigging of a ship, making a beeline for the library window.

He couldn't climb the stairs like other people. Oh no, he must display his brute strength by climbing hand over hand.

Mortification. Noun. Late fourteenth century. From Late Latin mortificationem, *"putting to death."*

Could she make a dash for the library door? Not without her spectacles.

Nothing for it but to face him.

She'd faced humiliation before. Stared it down. Dared it to break her.

This would be a very brief interaction. He would hand over the spectacles; she would thank him, and then send him on his merry way back down the trellis.

"Greetings, princess." His voice was velvet-wrapped gravel.

Beatrice rose on wobbly knees. He was fuzzy without her spectacles, a huge shape blocking out the sunlight, a hulking blur with azure eyes.

A blue to drown in, she'd heard one of the upstairs maids say swoonily. Beatrice's brain sank beneath water. Her thoughts went *blub, blub, blub*. Which wasn't like her at all. Words were her stock-in-trade, were they not?

Apparently, when confronted by the sudden appearance of a far-too-handsome rogue at her window, she lost the ability to form words into sentences . . . or even to speak at all.

Pull yourself together. Not an ounce of ninny, remember?

He balanced easily on the trellis, gripping the wood with one enormous hand and dangling the wire loop of her spectacles from the fingers of his other hand.

"Good day, Wright." She spoke in the most nonchalant and unconcerned tone she could summon. "Lovely day for climbing rose trellises, what?"

He dangled the spectacles closer to her. "I presume these are yours?"

"Er . . . yes. I lost them while"—*trying to see down your trousers*—"watering the roses."

Ludicrous. If she'd been watering the roses, she would have poured water on his head.

"Really?" His voice dropped to a rough, conspiratorial whisper. "Because I thought you might have been spying on me."

"Don't be silly. I needed a breath of air. I opened the window and I . . . I don't have to explain myself to you. Hand over my spectacles immediately."

His laughter was low and intimate. "A lofty lady would never spy on a carpenter, is that it?"

"I wasn't spying."

"I see," he said with a smirk.

"I don't." She held out her palm.

Instead of giving her the spectacles, he reached forward and set them on her nose, using one thumb to gently hook the wires over each of her ears in turn. She was so startled by his touch that she froze in place.

His thumb brushed her right ear. Somehow the tip of her ear was connected to the pit of her belly. Which was connected to . . . *everything.*

His face sharpened into focus.

She'd known his eyes were blue. What she hadn't known was that his left eye contained an uneven patch of golden brown, like a sunflower silhouetted against a summer sky.

His chin was hard-angled, and there was a cleft slightly to the left of center. Dark whiskers shadowed his strong jawline.

Don't do it, Beatrice. Do not *melt into a puddle of quivering ninny-hood.*

She took a steadying breath. "You'd better climb back down before that trellis breaks under your prodigious weight."

"Don't worry about me, princess." He winked. "Repaired this trellis myself. It's built to last."

"Do stop calling me princess," she said irritably, the nonchalance she'd been striving for making a fast retreat.

"You're imprisoned in a tower."

"I'm here quite by choice. I'm writing, or I would be if you weren't making so much noise."

"Is it the noise that distracts you?" He flexed the muscles of his free arm. "Or the man."

Beatrice gulped for air. Why must the man incessantly call attention to his physical endowments? "Such an ostentatious display might be efficacious where housemaids are concerned, but it has no effect whatsoever on female scholars."

"You're not fascinated by me." His voice swirled from velvet to smoke. "You never watch me from behind the curtains."

He caught her gaze and held it.

He'd seen her watching.

A fresh wave of mortification washed through her mind. "If I happened to glance out the window from time to time, it was due to sheer frustration. You've ruined what was meant to be a tranquil literary haven."

"And here I thought I'd been inspiring you."

"Inspiring? Hardly!"

"I was sure you were scribbling away at a romantic novel and needed inspiration for describing your hero. That's why you were always gazing at me from the window." He gave her a smoldering look. "I'd be happy to provide a more up close and personal study."

"You conceited peacock!"

"Admit it. You enjoyed the view."

"I'll admit nothing of the sort."

He plucked a single red rose and offered it to her through the open window. "For you, princess. It matches your cheeks when they're flushed from my proximity."

"You . . . you . . ." Beatrice sputtered.

"Scoundrel?" he suggested.

"Malapert rapscallion!"

He tilted his head. "That's a new one."

"Have you considered that your renovations might progress more swiftly, Mr. Wright, if you did more carpentering and less flirting? First Jenny and now me—don't you ever exhaust your store of vexatious trifling?"

He propped his elbow on the window ledge and leaned closer. "I thought you weren't spying on me."

"I wasn't. I was watering the roses."

"I think you were watching." His gaze dropped to her lips. "Because you wanted to see what a kiss from me would be like."

Beatrice wasn't accustomed to men perusing her with that hooded, hazy look in their eyes. She was no beauty. She never incited desire.

She never experienced desire.

And yet . . . the glow in her belly was spreading. She still felt the soft brush of his fingers along the edge of her ear.

"This conversation is over. Be on your way."

"Not yet." He wrapped his hand over the window ledge. "I have a question to ask you."

"Well?"

"I don't want anyone to overhear me ask it."

"That doesn't sound proper."

"I'm never proper. Don't even know what the word means."

"It's from the Latin *proprius* meaning 'one's own, particular to itself.' It's not until the mid-fourteenth century that we see the usage meaning 'by the rules' or 'correct and acceptable.'"

"I don't play by the rules, either." He slid one knee onto the ledge. "I'm coming in."

"No. Wait—!"

Too late.

Her sanctuary had been invaded by a rogue.

Chapter Two

FORD JUMPED DOWN onto the library's expensive imported carpet. Life was always attempting to bring him to his knees, but he always landed on his feet.

The duke's sister had retreated to a shadowy niche between two bookshelves. She stood there, half-hidden, all glinting spectacles and glowing red hair.

The new-minted copper of her hair never failed to strike his mind and reverberate like a ship's bell tolling the hour of the watch.

She was dressed in a simple blue gown, unadorned by frills and ribbons. Her gown might be plain, but there was no mistaking that she was highborn. Sister to a duke. Blazing intelligence in her eyes and finishing school in her posture. Privileged, cosseted, and raised to believe she was a superior being.

He'd never entered the library before. It looked like an explosion had occurred in the center of the cavernous room, scattering books and papers over every surface.

Ford flung the rose he was carrying onto a table. "Now you can have a better look at me, princess."

"I don't want a better look. Leave, please."

Stay away from the noble house. That's not your place. No trespassing, do you hear me, son?

The warning had been drilled into his head over and over when he was a child. Thornhill House and its noble part-time occupants were off-limits.

Well, here he was breaking the rules. Would the gods painted on the ceiling smite him down?

Lady Beatrice looked like she wished she had a spare thunderbolt to hurl his way. Her expression was distant and forbidding. Her slender arms were crossed over her chest in a gesture that clearly said *no trespassing*.

All summer long she'd watched him from the library windows, but they'd never exchanged a word in person, communicating instead through a brief exchange of notes. He'd glimpsed her walking along the path that led to the sea, her long curly hair escaping from the hood of a gray cloak. Walking alone.

Always alone.

She kept herself apart, isolated in her tower, too superior to fraternize with those beneath her elevated social standing.

His mother was sorely disappointed that there was a lady living at Thornhill House who'd never once paid a visit to any of the cottagers, or hosted any kind of festivities. Not many elegant ladies from London visited these parts.

Ford didn't give a damn about social standing or the rules of propriety. He needed information and he would have it. "When will the duke return? I can't seem to get a straight answer from anyone."

"I don't know. I haven't heard from him in weeks. I expected him home well before now."

"Is he stopping in London first, or coming directly to Cornwall?"

"He planned to spend several weeks in London to visit with family."

"I have to speak with him on a matter of urgency."

"Why don't you speak with Gibbons?"

"Absolutely not," Ford said vehemently. He suspected Gibbons, the duke's land agent, of embezzlement on this estate, and possibly on the duke's other properties. He'd uncovered a series of troubling discrepancies in the receipts for timber and other goods. He didn't want his father, or himself, to be blamed if the theft came to light.

"And why not?" she asked.

He glanced swiftly around the room. They were still alone. She hadn't rung for a servant.

"Because Gibbons is the problem."

"Really? He's a distant cousin of ours."

"Just because he's related by blood doesn't mean that he has your best interests at heart. I can't discuss it here. These walls have ears. I'll need to speak with the duke in person."

"I'm not sure when you'll be able to do that. He's gone missing. I haven't heard from him in weeks, though that's not unusual for my brother. He must have his reasons."

"I'm sure he's only delayed by weather and his letters were lost. He'll be home soon enough, and I'll have my chance to speak to him before I go back to sea."

"You're leaving, then?" She kept her face turned so that all he saw was her left profile. "There seems to be some debate on the part of the housemaids as to whether you'll stay here or return to the navy."

"There's not a chance in hell that I'd stay in this provincial little village. I prefer broader horizons."

And he would be no duke's servant. At least as a ship's carpenter he commanded the respect of a crew that knew his skill with his tools was the bulwark that stood between them and a watery death.

"The maids will be so disappointed to hear that you're leaving."

"And you'll be devastated, I'm sure."

"I'd be delighted, if I weren't returning to London soon."

"I was wondering why you were here instead of waltzing around ballrooms with foppish dandies."

"I already told you that I'm here by choice. Why is that so difficult for you to comprehend?"

"Because no one chooses to spend their summer in the wilds of Cornwall with nothing but books for company."

"I'd stay here forever if I could." She caressed the bindings of the books on the shelf next to her. "This library is my happiest of places."

"I've seen your lamp burning at all hours of the evening."

"I have to work at night because it's the only time when you're not banging, hammering, whistling, or telling naughty jokes."

"I'm not going to apologize for doing my job."

"Well, you could have done it with more sensitivity to my exigencies. When I see the duke next, I'm going to present him with a long list of your infringements."

Wonderful. That's all Ford needed. "I may have inconvenienced you, but the duke won't be able to deny that I accomplished more in these past months than most men could do in a year."

"I'm not debating that, Wright. I only wish your visit hadn't coincided so disharmoniously with mine. I only achieved a paltry number of pages."

He removed the top paper from a stack on the writing desk. "Is this your novel?"

She startled, moving into a shaft of sunlight. "Don't read that."

Which, of course, made him have to read it. He held the sheet to the window. "'Stamford Wright,'" he read aloud. "'See *Rogue.*'" He grinned. "'Heavy of hammer and brawny of shoulder,' eh? So you *have* been writing about me."

She rushed forward. "That's not for your eyes."

"Clearly. You wouldn't want me to know that you find me excessively virile."

"And boundlessly arrogant." She was close enough to reach out and touch. Her cheeks were pink, and her hazel eyes sparked with indignant light. "Give it here."

"'Thinks he's God's gift to womankind,'" he read. "True. Because I am."

"Humph!" She reached for the page and lost her balance, tumbling against his chest.

He folded his arm around her small waist. "Steady there."

"You are . . . not . . . a gentleman," she accused, her breathing ragged.

"Far from it." He was the furthest thing from a gentleman that dainty, delicate, sheltered Lady Beatrice Bentley would ever come into close proximity with.

And she was close.

Plastered against him, her soft breasts rising and falling against his chest. Her dress was buttery soft beneath his arm. Her hair smelled like apple blossoms floating in honey.

One of the maids had told him that she'd been born with palsy, which had given her face a distinctive asymmetry. The right side of her lips curved downward and her right eye drooped at the corner.

There were ink stains on her fingers. A smudge of ink on her cheek. He wanted to wipe it away with his thumb, just to touch her soft skin.

Stay away from the duke's sister. That's not your place. No trespassing.

"Ruffian rogue. Scurrilous scoundrel." She glared at him but made no move to distance herself. "Climbing trellises and reading a lady's private papers."

"You like scoundrels. We're far more interesting than other men. We're highly distracting to scholarly females. Might I suggest a few edits to your novel, though? Excessive virility is a promising beginning, but I would add 'handsome as sin' and 'completely irresistible.'"

"No, you may not. And I'm not writing a novel. I'm compiling an etymological dictionary."

"Featuring rogues."

"What you read was a symptom of extreme discomposure caused by your loud disturbance beneath my window."

"And inspired by my brawny shoulders."

"My dictionary will be a comprehensive exploration of the origins of the modern day English language."

"Is that all?"

"It's a formidable undertaking. It will be my life's work. If I complete it before my demise, I'll progress to a study of female authors."

"There's a large market for etymological dictionaries?" He'd dropped his arm from around her waist, but she stayed within touching distance.

"I don't expect it to sell particularly well outside of scholarly circles."

"Then where's the profit? Don't you want it to go into a second printing and be rudely reviewed by all of the most sarcastic critics?"

"Just like a rogue. Always thinking of profit. It's not about monetary reward, Wright. It's about intellectual curiosity. Awakening minds. Expanding vocabularies." She brushed a lock of hair over her right cheek. "I find that people are bafflingly incurious about the origins of the words they use. Take the word *oxymoron* for example. It's contradictory in itself. *Oxy* comes from the Greek word for sharp and *moron* from the word for dull or foolish."

"Scintillating."

"It *is* scintillating. It excites me to no end to uncover these elegant origin stories. There are many words that contain two conflicting ideas, like *chiaroscuro*, light and dark, and *pianoforte*, soft and loud."

"I think maybe you need to leave this library more often."

"I was sickly as a child, Wright. I spent my days in isolation from other children, alone in my room, and I started memorizing dictionaries. Words are living things. They must be treated with respect. They're born, they live and grow, and change, just as we do."

As she spoke, her entire face changed. She lost the distant and disapproving look, and her hazel eyes lit with emotion. Her cheeks flushed a delicate pink, her hair glowing in the fading sun like a candle flame inside amber glass. Her long, slender fingers waved through the air, illustrating her meaning.

"Sometimes words fall out of fashion and wither and die, never to be used again. I find that dreadfully sad. I make it my mission to use as many lost, arcane words as possible in an attempt to imbue them with new life. I don't expect you to understand my obsession."

"I read the occasional book. Time passes slowly at sea."

Or sometimes it passed swiftly in a deafening blaze of cannon fire and shouting. The dull smack of bodies hitting water.

The backhand of fate across a man's back. Or his belly.

Blood frothing in the wake.

But he wasn't supposed to think about the battle in Greece. The Admiralty had pinned a medal on him for bravery and told him to turn his gaze firmly forward, never backward.

"The occasional book . . . ?" She shook her head. He'd disappointed her. "I'm a *logophile*, a lover of words, as well as a book-devouring bibliophile. One might even say I suffer from bibliomania. Reading keeps the mind nimble and gives me fodder for my dictionary. Reading is my greatest pleasure in life."

Now that was just too easy. "Spoken like a lady who hasn't experienced real pleasures."

"Spoken like a rogue who doesn't read enough books. You could impress your sweethearts with a larger, more varied vocabulary at your disposal."

"My sweethearts are more impressed by the size of . . . other things."

She rolled her eyes. "Oh come now, Wright. Wouldn't you like to learn some impressive new words for wooing? Your paramour's voice could be *canorous* and *mellifluous*, her eyes *pellucid* and *lambent*. Her lips might be *ambrosial* or *sapid*, and her figure *pulchritudinous* and *lissome*."

He didn't know about pellucid, but the lady's eyes were a lovely light brown color with sparks of gold that flashed when she talked about words.

She really, *really* loved words.

It was plain to see that this prim and proper lady had passion simmering inside her, waiting to be unleashed by some lucky sot with a large vocabulary. He'd never be the one to bring her passion to the boiling point, but he could have a little more fun lighting those sparks in her eyes.

"Now you've got my attention, princess. Teach me some more words to use for wooing."

"You should purchase a volume of Shakespeare's works. He was a master of ingenuity when it came to wordplay. I have a fascination with archaic words, ones that we no longer use in conversation or in our written texts. I have lists and lists of them. I'd like to bring some back into circulation."

"Such as . . ." He wanted to keep her talking, if only to watch her eyes blaze and her lissome bosom heave.

"We used to embellish our speech with *flosculations*, and condemn deceitful *fallaciloquence*. If the moon slipped behind a cloud, we were left *murklins* and a slothful person was filled with *pigritude*. A prickly lady such as myself might have been referred to as *senticous*, and a rogue like you as *cockalorum*. And after a night at the pub you might be *crapulous*."

He quirked his head to one side. "That doesn't sound very pleasant."

"It's from the Latin for intoxication and from the Greek word meaning the headache one gets from drinking."

He grinned. "I've definitely felt crapulous upon occasion."

"It's a delightfully descriptive word. It just sounds so unpleasant. I do love words that make their meaning known with only a few short syllables. Like disaster. The hard 'd' and the expansive, merciless 'a.' Did you know that disaster originates from the Latin for 'ill star'? And then there's tintinnabulation. What a word! Why you can hear the bells ringing within it!"

He'd bet he could teach her a few new words. He'd acquired quite a colorful vocabulary living on a ship full of sailors.

Enough words. There would be no unleashing of passions this afternoon. He'd received his answer about the duke's whereabouts, and it was time to leave. He hadn't liked the answer, but there was nothing he could do about it. His orders from the Admiralty would come through any day now, and he'd sail at their pleasure, on a ship of their choosing. If he didn't have a chance to speak with the duke before setting sail, he'd have to find another safe way to give him the evidence of embezzlement that he'd uncovered.

Dallying with the duke's precious, cosseted sister wouldn't help his case.

It was past time for him to leave.

The lady, whether she was aware of it or not, was attracted to him—he knew it as surely as he knew the sun would rise tomorrow and his arms would ache from all that pounding and timber framing.

He might have believed she was unmoved by his presence and only passionate about the words, if it weren't for the way she swayed toward him, unconsciously reaching her hands close to his. The little surreptitious glances she kept darting at his open shirt collar. The pink flush across her high cheekbones, a lovely contrast to the mass of curly copper hair piled into a messy bun with tendrils framing her oval face.

There was no harm in just a little more teasing banter. "You make words come alive in a unique way, but I can think of hundreds of things more pleasurable than *logophilia*. Kissing, for one."

"You mean *osculation*, the place where two curves or surfaces come into contact?"

"I mean kissing." He dropped his gaze to her full pink lips. "What happens when lips meet, and converse, and learn a few things about each other. Wouldn't you agree that kissing might be slightly more pleasurable than archaic words?"

She lifted her straight little nose so that her spectacles reflected his face. "I would not."

"Spoken like a lady who's never been kissed, or not properly kissed, at least."

"Osculation could never be as thrilling as discovering a new word."

"Is that a challenge, Your Ladyship?"

"It's a certainty."

AT LEAST BEATRICE was fairly certain that it was true. She had vast experience with the discovery of new words, and none whatsoever with kissing.

Certainly, if she were going to gain such experience, she might very well consider Mr. Wright as a prime candidate for osculatory experimentation.

He was obviously very confident in his abilities. And the smoldering light in his azuline eyes was disconcertingly effective, if one was to judge by the weakening of knees and the persistent flutterings in one's stomach.

Don't let it go to your head. It's not for you.

Beatrice was quite certain that he stared at every young woman with the exact same smolder in order to inspire feelings of adulation. She was nothing special to him, only an unmarried female to flirt with; a game he played every day.

But he played it so well, so masterfully.

She wanted to join in the game. Trade ripostes for sallies, become one of the vivacious and coquettish heroines of the Gothic romances she loved to read.

If her name were Amaranthine, and she were a violet-eyed beauty imprisoned on the windswept moors by this enigmatic and darkly handsome man, she would be in danger of a thorough kissing.

He was standing very close. She hadn't moved away very far after she'd fallen against him while attempting to retrieve her manuscript. Tumbling against his chest had been like falling into a massive oak tree that had suddenly pushed through the floor of the library, spreading its branches and knocking books from shelves.

He occupied so much space, filling the library with his presence, making her life seem tame and lacking in kisses.

All summer long she'd watched him outside her window and here he was within arm's reach, pulsing with life and confidence. There was such freedom in his movements. She thought so carefully about her every move, her every utterance, and he just did as he pleased.

If she abandoned that carefulness, if she were Amaranthine, a feisty, headstrong heroine, she might pound her fists against his chest in a fit of pique until he had no choice but to capture her in the steel band of his arms and kiss her breathless.

Would she remove her spectacles first? Probably prudent. They might get in the way.

It would be a glorious kiss. A kiss worthy of her favorite novels. His lips against her lips. A sunrise in her body.

Golden warmth spreading from where their lips met, suffusing her body, pooling behind her knees and in her belly, and . . . lower.

A kiss he'd remember when he was sailing at sea, far from land. He'd recline alone in his narrow berth and remember the moment when her lips sought his. When she taught him how transporting a kiss from a bookish wallflower could be . . .

"Lady Beatrice?" His voice broke the spell.

She crashed back into the pragmatic, nonwhimsical body she normally inhabited to find one truth confirmed without a shadow of a doubt: she, Lady Beatrice Bentley, was a prize-winning ninny.

One who indulged in fictitious kisses with handsome, arrogant rogues.

"Oh, so you do know my name," she said tartly. She was upset; she must return everything to rights.

"Are you feeling quite right? You stood there staring for quite some time. I was beginning to think that the etymologist had run out of words."

"Never better, Wright. And I never have an insufficiency of words, thank you very much." She walked briskly to the bookshelves and began ordering books with no regard to alphabetical or subject order.

He knew that she'd been thinking about kissing him. Of course he knew. She'd been staring at his lips. What had come over her?

"There's much work to be done before I depart for London." She grabbed a cloth and started dusting the shelves. "I must put this library to rights, decide which books to bring with me, gather my papers. I won't have much time for writing dictionaries in London. It will be balls and operas and musicales. Oh, how I detest musicales."

She was gabbling nonsense.

"Lady Beatrice . . ." His voice rumbled, shaking her to the core.

Don't turn around. Don't stare into his eyes.

"Are you sure you're all right?"

"Quite. Now if you'll excuse me . . ."

He didn't leave.

She plucked a book from the shelf at random and gave it to him, keeping her gaze on his large hands, rather than his sensual lips. "Here's something to read on your next voyage, Wright. I hope it may expand your vocabulary."

He tucked the novel under his arm. "I'll be going then."

Yes, Lord. Let him leave.

"Will you inform me if you hear anything from your brother?"

"I promise that I will. Good day, Wright. I do hope you'll take the stairs this time."

"Now where would be the fun in that?" He bestowed one last disarming grin on her before disappearing over the windowsill, descending back to his adoring kitchen maid.

She rested against the solid bookshelf, the smell of parchment and ink surrounding her in a familiar and comforting embrace.

There was no going back for her. She'd turned a shadowy corner in her mind and found something she'd never expected.

Irrational desires. Swooning tendencies. A bad case of quivering ninnyhood.

She couldn't go back; all she could do was move forward armed with this new information.

The most annoying thing about all of that practiced charm was its effectiveness. She'd never considered herself to be a girl who might be susceptible to good-looking, arrogant rogues with bulging biceps.

Who could have predicted such a nonsensical development?

Certainly not her small group of friends in London. Sensible, pragmatic ladies, all—fellow members of the Mayfair Ladies Knitting League. Not that they did much knitting. Theirs was a society secretly dedicated to the advancement of women's goals and achievements in nontraditional roles.

Her friends would be quite disappointed to learn that Beatrice had succumbed to such giddy imaginings, especially after he'd insulted her dictionary by inferring that no one would want to read it.

The red rose he'd offered her languished on a table, its petals beginning to wilt. She brought it to her nose and inhaled the faint, sweet odor.

She set it between the pages of a little-used copy of *Debrett's Peerage.*

She'd keep this rose as a symbol of what the ancient Greeks would have termed her *hamartia,* her tragic character flaw: a heretofore unsuspected susceptibility to the appeal of charismatic rogues.

She would henceforth be on the strictest guard against all handsome rogues. All she had to do was survive one last Season in London and she could return to Thornhill House, and stay forever. The old maid in her library tower, surrounded by books, and probably some cats.

Wright would be long gone, and Beatrice could resume progress on her dictionary unimpeded by such virile distractions.

She slammed the book shut, covering the ruby red rose, a symbol of weakness. She must shore up her defenses and her determination in order to survive the trials of London and return to Cornwall as swiftly as possible.

Spinsterhood was going to be glorious.

Chapter Three

"LADY BEATRICE BENTLEY! Do you *want* to become a spinster?"
Why yes, mother, yes, I do. "Of course not, Mama."

"Then please pay attention when I'm speaking to you."

"Yes, Mama." Beatrice had decided that in the interests of survival she would simply agree with everything her mother said.

"Put that book down."

Reluctantly, Beatrice lowered the Gothic novel she'd been reading while being fitted for a new gown. The dressmaker, Mrs. Adler, a thin woman with a blade for a nose and a mouth bristling with pins, tugged at Beatrice's hem under her mother's watchful eye.

Since returning to London, Beatrice had managed only a few pages of research notes for her dictionary. It was exactly as she'd feared: too many fittings, tedious shopping excursions, and awkward morning calls.

She hadn't even been able to see her friends Isobel and Viola yet, but they were coming over this afternoon for tea. She couldn't wait to see them.

"That's better," said her mother. "If you'd only make an effort, you could make a brilliant match. I feel that this is your year, Beatrice, I truly do."

The dowager duchess was all softness with her round face, full lips, and generous figure, but her ambition to marry Beatrice off to a duke, a marquess, or, at the very least, an earl, was as hard-edged as a cut diamond.

She had launched into the "if you'd only make an effort" speech, which Beatrice had heard many, many times before. She knew exactly when to murmur "yes," and "of course," and "quite right, Mama," all while allowing her mind to roam free.

Usually her mind ran to the book she was reading, or to her dictionary, but lately her mind had been roaming to one topic and one topic only: Wright. More specifically, their encounter in the library at Thornhill House.

She'd left days after their exchange, so she'd never had to face him again. She doubted that he'd spared her a moment's thought since he'd climbed down from her window, while she had thought about him almost constantly.

She must stop thinking about him. About how close their lips had been, and the uncharacteristic urge that had gripped her, the mad desire to kiss him.

Thinking about kissing him made her breathing shallow and her heart speed.

She couldn't blame it on the new gown, though the bodice was so tight around the ribs as to induce breathlessness.

It was all Wright.

His mismatched eyes and large, capable hands. The way he'd humored her, asking her to teach him more words, all the while seducing her with that disarming grin.

Why couldn't she marshal her thoughts to order? It was most disconcerting. She supposed that time would be the only panacea.

She'd changed during her sojourn in Cornwall; London had stayed the same.

Her chambers were still decorated in the discordant combination of blush pink and pale blue that her mother considered pleasing.

Her mother, the dressmakers and milliners, and the lady's maids were still trying to accentuate what they considered to be her best features and hide what they thought of as the worst. They drew attention to her slim waist with brightly colored sashes, and covered the right side of her face with thick spiral curls of hair, cascading silk ribbons, and veils.

In London, she was something to be concealed and camou-flaged.

In Cornwall, at least she'd been free to wear simple, practical gowns of her choosing and pencils as the only ornament in her hair.

All of that temporary freedom was the only explanation for her unforgivable lapse of sense and that fictitious kiss.

She recalled with an inward groan the bemused look on his face. He'd known exactly what she was imagining. Dizzy-headed females must throw themselves at him all the time.

She'd made a narrow escape.

Mrs. Adler pulled the bodice even tighter and pinned it in place.

"Ouch!" Beatrice exclaimed as a pin jabbed her rib cage.

"Apologies, my lady."

"If you didn't fidget so, Mrs. Adler would be finished more swiftly," said the dowager duchess, who must have concluded her speech some time earlier.

Beatrice should pay closer attention or she'd be subjected to more speeches. The "woe is me my daughter lives to give me gray hairs" one was particularly trying.

"Repeat the rules to me, Beatrice."

"Er . . ."

"Oh, Beatrice." Her mother heaved a sigh. "You haven't heard a word I've said. I was explaining the rules."

"The rules?"

Another exasperated sigh. "I have four simple rules for you to follow. The first is no hiding behind potted ferns."

"Of course, Mama."

"You must remain visible for the entirety of every ball."

"I'll do my best, Mama." Hiding behind potted ferns was the best place to read during social engagements; everyone knew that. She always had a slender novel secreted in her reticule. Sometimes, if the event were held in a location such as her own home or the home of an acquaintance, she'd even gone so far as to hide books in the ballroom and retrieve them after the event was underway.

"The second rule, and I know you'll find this one very difficult, is this—no reading in public."

"Mama! You know I can't promise that." Reading was as essential as breathing. Without books, there could be no joy in life. "I must be allowed at least a little respite from the vacuous confabulation of London's dunderhead dandies."

"Which leads me directly to rule number three—no using archaic or nonsensical words and no explaining the origins of words. Under no circumstances are you to so much as mention your etymological dictionary. Such antics are the quickest way to dissuade potential suitors. No one likes a know-it-all, Beatrice."

That was another one of her standard speeches.

"Gentlemen don't want ladies to display an overabundance of intelligence, or to appear as though they believe themselves to possess a superior intellect."

"But Mama—"

"We made a bargain, Beatrice. I upheld my end and suffered all alone in London with none of my three children for company for months while you scribbled to your heart's content in that moldy old library in Cornwall. Now it's your turn to follow a few easy rules."

"Very well, Mama. I shall refrain from all intelligent conversation." That wouldn't be difficult given the paucity of intellect among the bucks of London.

"And you must dance with at least seven eligible gentlemen per ball."

Beatrice narrowed her eyes. "Five. I'll dance with no more than five gentlemen."

"Six."

She and her mother locked eyes. "Five," said Beatrice.

Her mother nodded. "Five, then." Which was probably the number she'd wanted in the first place. "But you'll give the first dance to a gentleman of my choosing."

"Do you have a gentleman in mind?"

"I might have." Her lips curved into a beaming smile. "I have it on good authority that a certain handsome earl might finally be ready to tie the knot."

Beatrice flipped through London's eligible earls in the picture book of her mind. None of them were particularly handsome . . . except . . . "You want me to marry Mayhew?"

Her mother's smile widened. "You've always been such a clever girl."

"I thought he was promised to Lady Millicent." At the mention of her name, Beatrice's throat constricted.

She'd known Lady Millicent since finishing school. Lovely and gregarious with honey-colored ringlets and emerald eyes, Millicent had decided that silent, bookish Beatrice had "airs" and thought that she was above everyone else. Because of this perceived fault, she'd made Beatrice's life miserable with her taunts, tricks, and derogatory nicknames.

You're beastly inside and out.

Beastly Beatrice.

"Not promised, precisely," said her mother. "No papers were signed. The families have close ties, but there's still hope that he might make a different choice. He's kept everyone guessing long enough. He's made some bad investments lately and his coffers need filling."

"If he's joined the ranks of genteel impoverishment, he'll be after my dowry."

"Not impoverished, only not so well off that he can afford to keep all of his properties. Economies have been made, and his mother and sisters haven't taken kindly to them. If you follow my rules, your reward could very well be a proposal."

Oh joy of joys. A proposal from a man who saw her as a money-bag with arms and legs, if he saw her at all.

Whenever Mayhew spoke to her, his eyes were always searching the room as if looking for someone more worthy to bestow his attentions upon.

All the eligible gentlemen of London desired was her dowry,

and she wasn't about to hand it over to them in exchange for a lifetime of humiliation and unfulfilled dreams.

"That's four rules," she pointed out. "Am I finished now?"

The dressmaker was consulting with one of her assistants about ribbon choices. She seemed to be nearing the end of her ministrations.

"I just thought of another. Rule number five—you must avoid the company of wallflowers. Their society can only diminish your luster."

Beatrice gave a short laugh. "You do know that I'm considered to be a wallflower?"

"You won't be when I'm finished with you," said her mother with grim determination. "Your wardrobe will be the envy of every lady in London."

Beatrice had never understood what all the fuss was about. Her mother and her mother's friends discussed hairstyles and gown designs for hours on end. To Beatrice's mind, clothing was what separated man from beast. A gown was a necessary covering for one's naked form.

The more comfortable and serviceable the better.

She'd had three gowns made before she left for Cornwall. All exactly the same, with sleeves loose enough to allow for reaching books on the highest library shelf, but not so voluminous they made one's arms feel like the clapper inside a bell.

She'd had pockets specially sewn into the skirts for the storing of books and papers. Her one concession to luxury had been the fabric—brushed cotton that flowed almost like silk, in a lovely blue color that put her in mind of a summer sky.

"I'm afraid I can't agree to the last rule, Mama. Most of my friends are wallflowers. Miss Mayberry and Miss Beaton should be arriving any moment, in fact. May I be excused?"

Beatrice couldn't wait to reconnect with her friends.

Her mother pursed her lips. "Not until this gown is perfectly fitted."

"If it fits any closer, I won't be able to breathe. Isn't that generally a requirement for dancing?"

"A lady doesn't need to take deep breaths. Gentlemen prefer to be the robust and lusty ones, while ladies should take small sips, shallow breaths, and dainty steps."

Beatrice groaned. "You don't truly believe that tripe, do you, Mama?"

Mrs. Adler returned with several lengths of ribbon. "The white or the yellow, Your Grace?"

"The yellow, I think," replied her mother.

"I'll sew the ribbons to the bodice myself. I can't entrust the task to anyone else."

"Thank you, Mrs. Adler." Beatrice's mother clasped her hands together. "It's simply perfect."

Beatrice glanced down at the layers of ruffles rioting down to the carpet. "It's extremely stratiform."

"What was that, Your Ladyship?" asked Mrs. Adler.

"Layered. It's very layered."

"It will put Mayhew in mind of a wedding cake," said her mother.

"You want him to think about eating me?"

"That's the idea." Her mother and Mrs. Adler exchanged cryptic glances.

"The bonnet you ordered arrived," the dressmaker announced. She snapped her fingers, and a maid arrived bearing an enormous hatbox.

Mrs. Adler unwrapped the bonnet reverently and held it up.

"Ooh!" exclaimed the dowager duchess.

Zounds, thought Beatrice. *It's hideous.*

"What do you think? Isn't it the very height of fashion?" asked her mother.

It was the height of *something*—a towering mishmash of yellow straw, red ribbons, white feathers, and . . . what were those scrunched-up round things? "What have you trimmed this hat with, Mrs. Adler?"

"Poems," announced Mrs. Adler, permitting herself the ghost of a smile. "Your mother told me that you are known as a bookish lady, and so I fashioned roses from verses."

Beatrice squinted at the paper roses. "'Shall I compare thee to a summer's day . . .' You desecrated a volume of Shakespeare for my millinery?"

"It's utterly ingenious," said her mother. "Everyone will want to copy this design."

"What if it rains?" asked Beatrice. "Paper doesn't do so well in a downpour."

"Don't be so prosaic," said her mother. "I'm sure they are treated with a fixative."

"Of course, Your Grace. These paper roses are as durable as any stiffened cotton."

"If I agree to wear this bonnet trimmed with sonnets, may I leave, Mama?" She always had to bargain for any precious moments of freedom.

Her mother nodded her assent, and she and the dressmaker moved to the wardrobe to discuss other gown options.

A maid helped Beatrice into a frothy day dress. At least she could breathe in this one. She filled her lungs with air. "I daresay I'll even be able to eat a ham sandwich," she mused.

"Lettuce, not ham, dear," called her mother. "You must forego ham in the pursuit of the greater prize."

Mrs. Adler and her wedding cake gown departed. Unfortunately, the sonnet bonnet remained.

The dowager duchess handed Beatrice an envelope. "This came by post for you today. It's about the property."

"What property?"

"Didn't I tell you? It must have slipped my mind. While you were in the country, your Aunt Matilda bequeathed you a property."

"I've never heard of an Aunt Matilda."

"She was your father's eldest sister. No one spoke of her."

"Why? What did she do?"

"She married a bookseller."

"Is that all?" Beatrice had been imagining scandalous liaisons, or secret babies out of wedlock.

"That's more than enough," said her mother with a frown. "Your father, may he rest in peace, was furious. First, his sister married a shopkeeper, and then, when Mr. Castle died and she inherited the shop, she refused to sell. She continued to run the shop herself. The sister of a duke engaged in commerce. It used to keep him up at night and give him terrible dyspepsia. He tried to run her out of business, but the woman was very stubborn."

"Did you say Mr. Castle, as in Castle's Bookshop on the Strand?"

"That's the one."

"I visited it once. I remember it very clearly. He had a marvelous collection of antiquarian volumes. Did I inherit his inventory, as well?"

"I've no idea. All I know is that the building has fallen into disrepair lately, and there's been quite a generous offer on the derelict bookshop and I told your brother's solicitor to accept it."

Beatrice regarded her mother with disbelief. "Are you telling me that I inherited a bookshop, and you've already instructed Greenaway to sell it?"

Why should she be surprised? This was only the latest rung on a long ladder of indignities stretching back to her childhood.

"That's right, now come along. I want you to try this darling pair of slippers I found in the window at—"

"Mother."

"Yes, my dear?"

"You can't make decisions like that on my behalf without consulting me."

"Well!" Her mother picked an imaginary speck of lint off Beatrice's gown. "I don't know what you're so cross about. It's best to let the men of business deal with these things, and if it's a derelict property, we're best rid of it. I thought you'd be pleased with the profit from the sale."

"But the books. What about the books? I must go visit the shop to see if the rare and ancient volumes and manuscripts are still there. May I go with my friends this afternoon?"

"I suppose you may go for a brief visit to view the inventory. I believe there was a small inheritance, as well, though Greenaway will have the details."

"Did I inherit a leasehold, or the property outright?"

"Outright, I believe, though I've really no idea. I don't concern myself with such things, and neither should you. As I recall, there's some scandal attached to the shop. I think your aunt Matilda was not a virtuous or pious woman. There are . . . *rumors.*"

Beatrice waited for her mother to elaborate. "Rumors of . . . ?"

"Lovers," her mother whispered. "After Mr. Castle died."

So that was it—Aunt Matilda had been scandalous because she'd been a merry widow. Men were expected, even encouraged, to have their diversions, but Lord help a woman if she decided to pursue diversions of her own.

"Now you see that it's quite impossible for you to keep the property," said her mother. "So do come and see these darling slippers. Every detail must be perfect."

Beatrice followed her mother out of the room, her mind still reeling from the news of the inheritance. Wait until she told Isobel about this; she'd be so excited.

Her mother stopped and placed her hand on Beatrice's arm. "I'm simply determined that you'll conquer society this year. Though I'd settle for you conquering one eligible earl."

Unfortunately for her mother, Beatrice had no intention of conquering anything other than etymological dictionaries.

"Now that you're a warrant officer, with the blue coat to prove it, it's your solemn duty to marry, Mr. Wright," said Mrs. Meade, Tiny's sister, passing Ford the butter dish.

Ford normally took lodgings in a boardinghouse for sailors while in London, but this time he'd traveled to London with Tiny, and his friend had insisted that he stay with him at his sister's home.

Ford only had a fortnight in London before his new ship, the HMS *Boadicea*, arrived in port. Tiny had traveled with Ford to London to pick out a promise ring for his intended, a Miss Eliza Broome.

"He's only five and twenty," said Tiny, through a mouthful of sausage.

"He's not getting any younger," Mrs. Meade replied. "And what would happen if he were killed in battle?"

"I should think that'd be a reason *not* to marry," said Ford.

"Don't you want to leave a son behind to carry on your line?" asked Mrs. Meade.

Her three daughters, ranging in age from thirteen to nineteen, leaned forward, eager to hear his response. He couldn't keep their names straight. The youngest one was Dinah, and he thought the eldest was Martha. The middle one he couldn't recall.

"I'm not the marrying kind, Mrs. Meade. I treasure my freedom too much."

And he never stayed in one place long enough to be tied down.

"All bachelors say that until they find the right girl," said Mrs. Meade. "Love will find you yet, Mr. Wright, mark my words."

If Tiny's sister had her way, love would find him right here in this breakfast room. She'd been pushing her daughters in his path ever since his arrival yesterday.

Ford wasn't looking for a bride. Finding female companionship was easy enough. He preferred experienced women with healthy appetites for carnal adventuring and no expectations of anything beyond a mutually pleasurable and finite liaison.

He never put down roots anywhere; he stayed adrift.

"Love found you, John, didn't it?" asked Mrs. Meade.

Tiny, whose real name was John, ducked his shaggy head. "Eliza's a sweet lamb of a girl."

Ford had met Eliza and he wouldn't describe her as sweet or docile, but perhaps Tiny wanted someone to rule his roost. The big lug was clearly besotted.

More fool, him.

"Still no word of Thorndon?" Tiny asked, mercifully changing the subject.

"I visited his solicitor yesterday, and the man practically begged me to send word if I heard anything about the duke's whereabouts. He's gone completely missing. Last time anyone saw him was in Naples at the Hotel Royale where he was staying with his new bride. They left there and haven't been heard from since. Never showed up to board the ship back to London."

"Strange, that. A duke and his bride going missing," said Tiny.

"Maybe they've been kidnapped," said Dinah.

"I hope not," Ford said. "I need to speak to him before I ship out. I'm going to visit his townhouse today to see if the family has any more recent news."

"You're going to the Duke of Thorndon's townhouse in Mayfair?" asked the middle niece, her eyes widening. "You must tell us every detail."

"Lady Beatrice Bentley is rumored to have the most beautiful gowns in all of London," Dinah said with a sigh.

"And she's bound to marry a dashing duke or a handsome earl this Season," said Martha.

Ford set down his fork. "How in the world do you know all of this?"

"We read the society pages," replied Dinah. "If you see Lady Beatrice you must tell us what she's wearing. We want to know the color of her gown, the pattern of the cloth, how her hair is dressed, we want to know *everything.*"

"Men don't notice details like that," said Tiny.

Ford was fervently hoping not to see Lady Beatrice. He'd been seeing far too much of her in his memories. The copper of her hair, the glow in her eyes as she taught him new words.

"I'm due at the jeweler's at nine," said Tiny.

Ford rose with the rest of the group. "Thank you for breakfast, Mrs. Meade."

"Don't forget the details," said Dinah.

Ford and Tiny left the house and headed toward Covent Garden.

"If you stay at my sister's house much longer, she'll have you married to one of my nieces," Tiny remarked.

"Your nieces are safe from me."

"Martha's taken a shine to you. She'll be heartbroken when you leave."

"What about you? You're actually going to go through with it and tie the noose around your neck?"

Tiny ducked his head. He was so large that passersby stared at him. "Reckon Eliza's the girl for me."

"She's got you wrapped around her finger."

"I don't mind."

"Love makes fools of us all."

His parents had married for love and paid a high price. His mother had been disinherited by her wealthy father for choosing a mere carpenter when her father had wanted her to marry into the aristocracy and increase their social standing.

London never felt welcoming to Ford. This was his estranged grandfather's city—a cold and pitiless place where gold was king and thousands of unfortunates were left to rot in the poorhouses, workhouses, and rookeries.

"I hope you have the chance to talk to the duke before you leave London." Tiny frowned. "Never did like Gibbons, that close-fisted windbag. What if the duke doesn't return before you leave, then what will you do?"

"Then I'm in a bad spot. If the embezzlement comes to light, I know Gibbons will try to pin it on my father—or on me. I must warn the duke about him in person, or find another trustworthy method to warn him before he leaves London for Thornhill."

"I wouldn't want to visit the duke's townhouse without an invitation."

"Dukes don't intimidate me. A title doesn't make them any better than you or me. Noble blood is only a lie passed from generation to generation, a way of keeping all of the power in the hands of the few."

"Well, Thorndon's not a bad sort, as far as dukes go. I think he truly cares about the fortunes of his crofters."

They walked through Covent Garden—the bustling heart of London, teeming with taverns, theaters, brothels, and coffee houses. Tiny stopped outside a jeweler's shop. "This is me."

"There's still time to reconsider," Ford said jokingly.

"And you still have time to find yourself an Eliza."

"Small chance of that when I'm always at sea."

"Good luck at Thorndon's." Tiny had to duck to enter the shop doorway. He was soon swallowed by glittering displays of nuptial shackles, taken in hand by a gatekeeper of hell disguised as a jolly salesman.

Ford shook his head and continued on his way to Mayfair. He wished Tiny the best. He could be happy for his friend, even if Ford would never marry.

He walked along Piccadilly and headed into Mayfair. Here the houses stood in rows of imposing stone facades and orderly windows. Massive iron gates set close to the buildings stood at attention to keep the riffraff away.

Lady Beatrice had grown up in this exclusive neighborhood, protected by guards and governesses, blinkered to the harsh realities of London's poorer areas.

He couldn't seem to shake Lady Beatrice and her slender waist and oversize vocabulary from his mind. He kept thinking about that near kiss in the library. If they'd actually kissed, he probably would have forgotten about it by now, but an almost-kiss was a memory that could be expanded and elaborated upon in endless variations.

She'd wanted him to kiss her.

There'd been no denying her intentions when she stared, unmoving, at his lips for such a prolonged length of time. He'd almost convinced himself that she was about to kiss him, and he'd been so close to making the first move.

But reason had prevailed. It hadn't mattered if the lady wanted kissing. What mattered was that her brother was a duke, and his father's employer, and she was an innocent lady.

They were from two different worlds. Kissing was forbidden.

In reality. Fantasies were another matter.

There was nothing stopping his mind from reliving the moment, and making a very different choice. Gently removing her spectacles from her aristocratic nose and setting them aside.

Cupping her face with his palms.

And giving her one unforgettably passionate kiss.

In his fantasies it lasted a long time, that kiss.

He teased her lips open with his tongue, swallowing her soft, startled cry. He deepened the kiss and moved his hands to her softly rounded breasts, brushing her nipples through the buttery fabric of her gown until she moaned . . .

He stopped walking and muttered an apology as a man swerved to avoid running into him.

He had to stop thinking about the kiss not taken. Especially because he might very well be granted an audience with her mother today, who would be horrified, outraged, and quite possibly litigious if she knew the things he'd done to her daughter in his mind.

Bad, bad things involving sturdy desks.

He had the book she'd given him in his coat pocket, and he planned to leave it with the butler. He was certain that Lady Beatrice hadn't meant to give him this particular book. It was a Gothic romance, *The Mad Marquess's Secret* by Daphne Villeneuve.

It was about a blonde with the silly name of Sophronia who kept getting chased around the grounds of the castle while wearing a diaphanous nightgown by the mad marquess who may, or may not, have murdered his previous wife.

He'd read it in secret, of course. Hadn't wanted the boys to rib him about it.

He'd read it at night by the light of a candle. He'd never admit it to a soul, but he'd enjoyed the book. It had been a page-turner.

He'd been halfway through the story when he'd found the note tucked between the pages. Written in Lady Beatrice's precise lettering, it appeared to be an entry torn from a diary in frustration.

What she'd written had tugged at his heart, and made him want to relive their encounter in the library again, but in a different way.

He'd tell her that not all men were repelled by intelligence in a woman.

That she was uniquely attractive, and if the mean-spirited ladies and empty-headed fops of London couldn't see that, then they were idiots.

Which was also a conversation that would never happen.

No doubt the lady was out on the town being courted by barons and earls. Who knew, perhaps she'd even become a princess in truth. There were plenty of impoverished European royalty hunting for fortunes.

Ford shouldn't care where she was, or by whom she was being courted. He was only visiting her house for news of her brother.

Warn the duke, ensure his father was above suspicion, and ship out. That was the plan.

The duke's bookish sister was one buttoned-up bundle of simmering passions that Ford would never, ever unwrap.

Chapter Four

BEATRICE AND HER two friends, Miss Viola Beaton and Miss Isobel Mayberry, were ensconced in the drawing room, devouring thick ham and butter sandwiches and talking over one another while they caught up on everything that had transpired during her absence.

"I *have* missed you," said Beatrice to her friends, through a mouthful of ham. Her mother's lectures on proper diet and etiquette for young ladies always made her want to eat everything in sight.

"We missed you, too," said Viola, her green eyes sparkling. "When we held meetings of the Knitting League at the Duchess of Ravenwood's apartments, everyone talked about how it wasn't the same without you there to expand our vocabularies and teach us the origins of things."

"Is the duchess back from Egypt yet?" Beatrice asked.

"Not yet," Viola said. "We expect her in the coming weeks. We may need to find another house for our meetings."

"Your brother and Mina haven't returned from Italy yet?" Isobel asked.

"No, but I'm not too worried. As you know, Mina had some rather interesting activities planned for them on this honeymoon, including matters of"—she dropped her voice to a whisper—"espionage. If they don't want us to know their whereabouts, I'm sure they have their reasons."

"Weren't you lonely in Cornwall with Thorndon and Mina off traveling?" asked Isobel.

"I could never be too lonely surrounded by books."

"And carpenters," said Viola, with a warm smile. "Your letters had quite a lot to say about your brother's carpenter."

Isobel made a motion as if she were donning a pair of spectacles. "'Wright is repairing the rose trellis outside the library window today,'" she said, imitating Beatrice's crisply enunciated way of speaking. "'He refuses to wait until I leave for London. He's an infernal nuisance.'"

Viola pretended to dip a quill in ink. "'Wright is the most maddeningly arrogant man in the world.'" She set down her imaginary pen. "Wright *this*, and Wright *that*. You wrote more about him in your letters than about the progress on your dictionary."

Beatrice brushed a crumb away from her chin, careful not to betray any emotion. "That's because he hampered my progress. The accelerated pace at which he attacked the renovations on Thornhill House directly correlated to the decreased progress on my dictionary. He was excessively loud and distracting."

"I had the distinct impression from your letters that he might also be excessively handsome," said Viola.

"I suppose some might think so," said Beatrice carefully. "But enough about me. Didn't you win a prize while I was gone, Viola?"

"She won second place in the Royal Society of Musicians' contest for new symphonic works," Isobel proclaimed.

"I didn't have the courage to go through with the plan to reveal my identity," said Viola, her eyes solemn. "They thought the score had been composed by a Mr. Beam, who mysteriously never appeared to collect his prize."

"We all know you won the prize, and that's enough," said Beatrice. "I'm bursting with pride. Have there been any other developments?"

Isobel adjusted an invisible cravat and cleared her throat. "I'm studying the history, principles, and practice of the Law of England relative to real property. An abstruse, yet endlessly fascinating, system."

Beatrice gave a little laugh. "I still can't believe the deception is working."

Isobel was the most daring member of their secretly subversive league of ladies. Her brother was a homebound invalid and had given her permission to attend a School of Law using his identity.

"I've had some close calls." Isobel glanced down at her chest. "This flat bust of mine does help, and my mannerisms are already mannish—or so my aunt delights in telling me."

"And how is Ardella?" asked Beatrice.

Viola leaned closer. "She's working on something highly secretive in that makeshift laboratory of hers. She says it might very well change the world as we know it."

Miss Ardella Finchley, the only member of the League who actually knew how to knit, was also an experimental chemist.

"Intriguing." Beatrice was proud of her friends' talents and goals.

"And your dictionary?" asked Viola.

"Will have to be put on hold for the moment. My mother presented me with a social calendar and a list of rules today. She's planned out every second of every day." Beatrice took another defiant bite of ham instead of lettuce. "I'm afraid I'll have no time for my own pursuits. I had to go all the way to Cornwall to find some room to breathe."

"In fine fettle, is she?" asked Isobel.

"The finest. *Fettle* is a wonderfully descriptive noun, isn't it? I wonder if it's from the Middle or Old English?"

Viola gave her an affectionate wink. "I'm sure you'll inform us the next time we meet."

"I did notice that your hair is dressed in rather a singular style," said Isobel.

"Singular is one word for it." Beatrice sighed. "Does anyone except my mother think this style is flattering to me?"

Isobel and Viola perused her hair, which had been piled on top of her head with the aid of wires and padding, and stuck all over with beads and feathers. Two very long, very wide, curls framed her face, falling against her cheeks. She kept seeing them out of the corner of her eye because they quivered when she spoke. It was most distracting.

"I cannot tell a lie," said Viola. "It's not a good look. It's somewhere betwixt a bird's nest and the leaning tower of Pisa."

"I can lie with impunity, since I'm going to be a solicitor," said Isobel. "It's most becoming, Lady Beatrice. You might add a few more feathers. Or perhaps some common household objects? Forks! Why not a few judiciously placed silver forks? It would make you even more unique and could be quite useful for an impromptu luncheon al fresco."

"Stop." Beatrice chuckled. "Today she promised that if I follow her rules, which, I might add include an injunction against associating with wallflowers, I would have my reward in the form of a proposal from the Earl of Mayhew."

"First of all," said Viola, "you can't follow the rule about wallflowers because . . . *us.* And Mayhew? Absolutely not. He's no one's prize except for Lady Millicent's, and they deserve each other. The venomous gossip and the vain coxcomb."

"I know my mother loves me, and she thinks she's acting in my interests, but her love isn't unconditional. It's as if she sees me as an extension of herself—another limb—and she can't conceive that I might have my own separate will and my own desires. We're almost opposites, really." Her mother thought that Beatrice's entire future rested on the perfect collection of gowns. She wanted her to emerge as this Season's social butterfly, but Beatrice was firmly encased in a cocoon of her own design, and she had no intention of spreading her wings until she returned to Cornwall.

"I wish I had known my mother," said Viola.

"Oh, I'm sorry, here I am going on and on and you never even knew your mother." Beatrice smiled at her friend.

"It's all right." Viola shook her head and the sparkle returned to her eyes. "Tell us more about your mother's plans for your time. We'll have to find some way to steal you away from her."

"There is something else. She gave me this letter." Beatrice pointed at the envelope sitting on a nearby table. "While I was in Cornwall, I inherited Castle's Bookshop on the Strand. Do you remember when we visited it several years ago, Isobel? It's where I purchased my *Whyter's Etymologicon Magnum*."

"You inherited the bookshop?" asked Isobel.

"Mr. Castle left it to his wife, my aunt Matilda Castle. I never even knew I had an Aunt Matilda. She was my father's eldest sister and was disinherited for marrying a shopkeeper. She owned the shop outright and bequeathed it, and a small inheritance, to me in her will."

"How extraordinary!" Isobel moved to the edge of her seat. "I can count on the fingers of one hand the number of females I know who've inherited real property."

"Don't get too excited. Mama decided that owning a bookshop was unacceptable for a lady, and she already instructed our solicitor to sell the building to a London property developer who sent in a report that the bookshop was in a dangerously derelict condition."

"She can't do that, Beatrice," said Isobel, her voice deepening. "If you've inherited the property, you're the only person who can legally sell it. And I wouldn't trust a report from a property developer. They are notoriously avaricious and would say anything to purchase a property cheaply and resell it for profit."

"She'd never let me keep the bookshop, but I'm overjoyed by the prospect of owning the collection of antiquarian books. I want to visit the shop immediately to see if the collection is intact."

"Let's go today!" said Viola. "I want to see it."

"We should go," agreed Isobel. "I refuse to let you sell a property that you inherited without at least viewing it first, or having an independent inspection conducted. This developer may be unscrupulous and attempting to bilk you out of your inheritance."

"I hadn't thought of that."

"I'm studying inheritance laws. One of my future goals will be to assist ladies in the ownership and retention of real property.

As your future solicitor, I strongly encourage you to have an independent appraisal performed."

"The property might be too derelict to be salvaged," said Beatrice. "When I visited it several years ago I noticed a decidedly musty odor. There's nothing worse than the presence of moisture or mold for rare books."

"Properties can be repaired," said Isobel.

"Indeed," said Viola. "By *carpenters*. Don't you know one of those, Beatrice?"

Beatrice tensed. "If you're referring to Mr. Wright, you can forget that notion immediately. He's not available. He told me that he's going back to sea with the Royal Navy as a ship's carpenter."

"That's too bad," said Viola.

"And even if he were available, I'd never consider hiring the man. He's overconfident and arrogant."

"Confidence is generally considered to be a good trait in a builder," said Viola.

"I have a long list of his transgressions to present to my brother Drew upon his return, chief amongst those being that Wright derided my dictionary."

"Well then, that's different," said Isobel. "We can't have males tearing down our achievements. What did he say?"

"He said that it wouldn't be a financial success, and that not many people would want to read it."

Her friends exchanged glances.

"He's very wrong to have said it, I'm sure," said Viola.

Beatrice studied her friends. "Wait. You don't . . . Do you agree with him?"

"Darling, the merit of your dictionary has nothing to do with profit," said Viola soothingly.

"Of course not," said Isobel. "A very small and highly selective group of people will be ecstatic about your dictionary. I, for one, intend to purchase as many copies as I can get my hands on."

Beatrice groaned. "You think it won't be a success. That I'm laboring for nothing."

"What, precisely, defines success?" asked Isobel. "If you're proud of your work, then it's successful."

"I can't believe this—my friends siding with an arrogant male."

"I gather that Mr. Wright hurt your feelings," said Isobel.

"He did more than that," said Beatrice. "He made me think the most uncharacteristic thoughts."

"What kind of thoughts?" asked Viola.

"Ninny-ish thoughts."

"Define ninny-ish," said Isobel.

Beatrice glanced at the footman standing by the door and lowered her voice. "I kissed him."

"You *what?*" exclaimed Isobel with a look of astonishment.

"Kissed him?" cried Viola at the same time.

"Hush, please," said Beatrice. "That came out wrong. I didn't *actually* kiss him. I thought about it. I imagined a scenario in which I was the heroine of a Gothic novel and we met on a dark and stormy night in a haunted castle and I kissed him."

"Well then," laughed Viola. "That's quite harmless. I kiss handsome men all the time in my mind. One in particular." She blushed. "One whom I would never consider actually kissing. It doesn't mean anything."

"It means that I have a tragic flaw that I didn't know about, but now I'm on guard against it ever happening again. I'll never fall prey to such maudlin meanderings of the mind again."

"Beatrice, just because you live most of your life inside your mind doesn't mean that what happens there should be confused with reality," said Isobel gently. "You're so very intelligent and cerebral. Believe me, you haven't committed any crime of character."

Then why did Beatrice feel so shaken by her encounter with Wright? What had happened in the library was the antithesis of everything she believed herself to be: self-sufficient, independent, and impervious to sentimental longings and foolishness.

It was her childhood that had set her apart, molded her spine of steel and replaced her need for love with a craving for solitude and privacy.

Too many specialists and physicians in and out of her chambers with their ghoulish treatments, their supposed cures for her palsy.

She'd always known that she was different.

She'd never be her mother's perfect little girl.

And so she'd given up trying to please her mother and had plotted a different course for her life, one that she'd thought out carefully and set in motion with great deliberation.

That's why the fictitious kiss had shaken her to the core. A longing for physical intimacy wasn't in her vocabulary. She'd exorcised any such need long ago.

"He climbed through the library window, handed me a rose, and I . . . I had some preposterous idea that he was wooing me because I was special. He woos every female he meets. It's what he does. He's a rogue of the first order."

"Climbed through your window? How very Shakespearean of him," observed Isobel. "Did he compare you to a summer's day?"

"I dropped my spectacles on his head. He climbed up the rose trellis to return them."

"I'm even more confused," said Viola. "Why did you drop your spectacles on his head?"

"The *why* doesn't matter." The hot flush of humiliation had crept back up her neck. "What matters is that it will never, ever happen again. I will never succumb to irrational imaginings about handsome rogues ever again. I'm quite impervious now."

"Oh, Beatrice," said Viola with a tinge of sadness in her voice. "Only you would castigate yourself for something that never even happened."

They didn't understand. To her it had been real. Vividly, exquisitely, real. So exquisite, in fact, that an actual kiss from Wright could never possibly live up to the imaginary one.

"One imaginary kiss is hardly a reason not to—" Isobel was interrupted by a light knock on the door.

"Yes, Hobbs?"

"There's a gentleman here to see you, my lady," said the butler.

Beatrice sighed. "I suppose my mother has already arranged a call from Mayhew."

"I don't believe the person is in possession of a title, my lady. He's a Mr. Stamford Wright. Shall I tell him you're not at home?"

Wright. Here? The air left Beatrice's lungs. How could that be?

Viola clapped her hands together. "Tell him she's at home and receiving visitors, but only if they have offerings of roses and have composed at least three sonnets to her amber eyes."

"Viola!" Beatrice remonstrated.

"You're not frightened of him, are you?" whispered Viola with a scheming glint in her green eyes. "You're not afraid that when you see him you'll immediately imagine *you know what?*"

"I'm not the least bit frightened. I'm perfectly in control of my thoughts." The idea that she might succumb to such witless wanderings twice was unthinkable.

"I'd like to have a look at your Mr. Wright," said Isobel. "Why don't you invite him in? Aren't you curious about why he's here?"

"He's not mine," Beatrice replied indignantly. "And no doubt he's here to see my brother. He kept asking when he'd return. He has some matter regarding the duke's land agent to discuss with him."

"Then you have to invite him in," said Viola. "It could be important."

"He wouldn't tell me what it was in Cornwall. I don't know why he would tell me now."

"But I want to see the good-looking rogue who gave our sensible Beatrice such longings," said Viola. "You just said that you were impervious to rogues so what can be the harm in a brief conversation?"

Quite right. She had nothing to fear from seeing Wright again. This was her chance to prove to herself how unaffected she was by him. She had her friends by her side. Their presence would stop her from succumbing to any ninny-ish impulses.

With that comforting thought, she shook the bread crumbs from her skirts. "Send him in, Hobbs."

"Mr. Stamford Wright," the butler announced. "Of the Royal Navy."

Ford had never been announced before, not that he'd ever wanted to be, though it did add a certain amount of swagger to his stride.

He'd told the servant that he wanted an audience with the dowager. When he'd learned she wasn't at home, and that only Lady Beatrice was here to receive him, his heart had done a suspicious little jig in his chest.

He hadn't come all this way not to have his questions answered by someone.

He entered a large, airy room done up in clashing shades of pink and burgundy.

She wasn't alone.

She sat on a sofa flanked by two other young ladies, one with pronounced, angular features and the other all dimples and sweet smiles.

Lady Beatrice eyed him with a fleeting flare of some strong emotion, and then, as if a screen had been drawn over her eyes, an impassive expression of studied disinterest.

Her hair still glowed like a new copper piece in the noonday sun streaming through the windows, but the rest of her looked . . . different.

In Cornwall she'd been dressed simply. Something blue and soft that he'd approved of, even though the bodice could have been cut lower. Today she was trussed into enough ivory frills and lace that he had difficulty discerning the natural shape of her.

The diamond drops at her ears were obviously real, and probably cost more than he'd see in a lifetime.

He cleared his throat. "Lady Beatrice."

"Wright," she replied, with a frosty little nod.

Damn, he should have made a bow. No matter. He wasn't a bower. No need to start now, just because she wore diamonds.

"What have you done to your hair?" There were two plump curls hanging down on either side of her face, and the rest of it was piled up and towering so high above her head that it must set her off-balance when she walked, like a ship listing under a heavy cargo.

She touched one of the spiral curls against her cheek. "This, I'll have you know, is the very latest fashion."

"It doesn't suit you."

Sweet Smiles smothered a giggle with the palm of her hand.

"Why thank you so much," replied Lady Beatrice. "What a pretty compliment."

He'd already offended her. Nothing to be done about that. He'd already made it clear that he never followed the rules of propriety. But he was here to ask her about her brother and therefore he shouldn't be insulting her. "What I meant to say was that such a towering coil of hair doesn't look like *you*. The lady I knew in Cornwall—the one with ink-stained fingers."

The one he'd imagined kissing so thoroughly that she forgot every word she'd ever entered in that dictionary of hers.

"That lady isn't allowed to live in London," she said.

What did she mean by that? "I'm sure the young bucks of London love the style of your hair. They'll be showering you with proposals."

"Don't assume I wish to receive proposals."

Ford cocked his head. She couldn't be much more than twenty. "Isn't that the usual goal for young ladies?"

"You presume to know the goals of young ladies?"

"Er . . ." He scratched his head. "One generally assumes that all of the dancing and opera-going and folderol that happens in London this time of year is for the sole purpose of matrimonial arrangements."

"I thank you *not* to assume that all young ladies wish to be married."

"If you say so, it must be true. Young ladies can have other goals."

"Oh we can, can we? How good of you to give us permission." She pushed her spectacles higher on the bridge of her nose. "I see you've finally learned how to tie a neck cloth and put on a coat."

"I'll take off this noose of a cravat if you tumble that

uncomfortable-looking tower of hair. It must be giving you a headache."

"Humph," replied Lady Beatrice. "You're giving me a headache."

At this, Sweet Smiles giggled, and the one with the angular cheekbones wagged a finger at him. "Living up to your reputation already, Mr. Wright."

What reputation? Had Lady Beatrice been telling her friends about him?

Not that he cared. Ask his question and leave. "Have you had word from your brother, Lady Beatrice? I've been making inquiries and no one knows his whereabouts."

"I've still heard nothing, I'm afraid," she said frostily.

Damnation. "I won't trouble you any longer then."

"Oh don't leave yet, Mr. Wright," said Sweet Smiles. "Aren't you going to introduce us, Beatrice?"

"This is Miss Viola Beaton," Lady Beatrice said, gesturing at her friend with the dimples, "and Miss Isobel Mayberry. They are fellow members of the Mayfair Ladies Knitting League, a charitable organization."

"You're eyeing the sandwiches rather hungrily, Mr. Wright," said Miss Beaton. "Wouldn't you like one?"

"No, he wouldn't," said Lady Beatrice, glancing pointedly at the door.

She obviously wanted to be rid of him. Ford didn't like being dismissed by the high-and-mighty princess. He'd leave when he was ready to leave. The sandwiches did look tempting . . . and so did the lady.

His fantasies made flesh. Though in his fantasies her hair was loose and cascading over her shoulders, and she wasn't wearing much more than a pair of stockings, some silk garters, and, perversely, those glinting spectacles.

He hadn't eaten since breakfast. May as well get something out of this visit.

"Don't mind if I do, Miss Beaton." He settled warily onto a spindly chair covered in rose-patterned silk and accepted a delicate china plate piled with sandwiches from a footman who magically materialized to serve him.

"What are your plans this afternoon, Mr. Wright?" asked Miss Beaton.

"I'm going to the docks to help my friend with some repairs on his boat."

"Do you have an hour to spare?"

Lady Beatrice glared at her friend. "He's very busy."

"Do you have experience inspecting buildings to determine their worth, Mr. Wright?" asked Miss Mayberry.

"No," said Lady Beatrice.

"No, what?" asked Ford.

"Just no," repeated Lady Beatrice firmly.

The sandwiches were too dainty and delicate, just like the ladies. He was outnumbered. He felt like a lumbering bear paraded before an audience at a menagerie. "I should be going. If you'll excuse me, ladies I—"

"We wish to hire you," said Miss Mayberry.

"We do?" asked Lady Beatrice.

"We do," said Miss Mayberry with a firm nod. She turned to Lady Beatrice. "Well, he's here, isn't he? And he's someone your brother trusts. We can be sure that his assessment of the property will be honest. You may as well make use of him."

"Er, make use of me for what purpose?" Ford was completely lost.

"To inspect the condition of a property Lady Beatrice inherited. We'll leave immediately. There's no time to be wasted." Miss Mayberry handed his plate of dainty, half-eaten sandwiches to a footman.

"I meant only to return this and be on my way." He pulled the novel from his pocket and handed it to Lady Beatrice.

"Oh. I didn't mean to give you that one. I just grabbed the first book my hand found."

"That Sophronia could use a few lessons from you in how to send a man packing. She was far too meek, if you ask me."

"You read it?"

"Don't look so astonished. I can read."

"We don't want to send you packing," said Miss Beaton. "It's all settled. We'll proceed to the property immediately. It will be a quick carriage ride to the Strand." The ladies rose.

Ford hastily stood. He'd follow that much etiquette, at least. "I really do have to—"

"Come along, Mr. Wright," said Miss Mayberry, moving to stand next to him. "We require an expert opinion."

Miss Beaton dragged Lady Beatrice, who appeared to still be adamantly against the idea of his joining the party, out of the room.

Miss Mayberry laid a hand on his arm and lowered her voice. "We've heard so much about you. But I'm watching you." She fixed him with a stern look. "I won't have you toying with Beatrice's affections."

"Pardon me?" What, exactly, had Lady Beatrice told her friends about him?

Miss Mayberry herded him toward the door. "I know your kind, Wright. You're a rogue. But you're also a builder, and we happen to be in need of one of those. Come *along*."

Ford watched as Lady Beatrice's maid stuffed her hair into the most enormous brimmed bonnet he'd ever seen. It covered her face almost completely.

She gave him a sidelong glance, those hazel eyes beckoning him like a warm fire on a cold winter's day.

More like the glow of a lighthouse, warning him away from dangerous reefs.

Ford had no choice but to follow. What else could he do?

He'd been outmaneuvered.

Press-ganged by a league of lady knitters.

Chapter Five

*I*T WAS A gray, drizzly day, and Beatrice shivered despite the warm woolen spencer she wore.

The bookshop stood on the Strand, its entrance decorated with a leaded glass window in a webbed design and flanked on both sides by multipaned windows. The buildings bracketing the shop looked vacant, their facades darkened by soot and their windows coated with grime. A narrow lane to the right of the shop had cobblestone terraces leading downward, presumably to the Thames.

Rain dripped from a wooden sign hung from an iron framework. The words *Castle's Bookshop, Dealer in Secondhand Books and Antiquated Manuscripts, By Appointment Only* were painted in courtly gold script over a picture of a fairy-tale castle with a blue pennant flying from its ramparts and a dark forest surrounding its walls.

There was a sign that read *Closed for Business* in the window.

"How quaint," said Viola, her dimples appearing as she examined the wooden sign.

"When I made an appointment to visit several years ago, I remember it had only one small showroom piled with books." Beatrice peered in the glass; she couldn't see anything inside.

Wright rapped on the building with his knuckles. He wore no gloves. "Stone facade," he said. He craned his neck backward. "Slate roof. It's a good thing it's not a wooden facade like the shops on Holywell Street. Stone weathers better, and is much more attractive and solid."

He could be describing himself, thought Beatrice. He was certainly attractive, and very solidly built. He looked different in London, even more imposing, as if one of the Cornish cliffs had suddenly risen on the cobblestone streets of London.

Rugged and out of place.

He had an expression on his face that said he was humoring them and would bolt at the earliest opportunity.

She hadn't expected to ever see him again. Her gaze wanted to rest on the inviting contours of his face, the strong jawline and interesting shadows of his whiskers. He hadn't shaved today. He probably didn't even have a valet.

Of course he didn't have a valet. Carpenters didn't have valets. And why was she thinking about such things?

"Was that a movement in the upstairs window?" Isobel asked, pointing upward.

Beatrice glanced up. "The solicitor's letter said that two family servants had been given annuities by my aunt with the stipulation that they would continue keeping up the premises for one year past her demise, or until the shop is sold, whichever comes first."

Wright rang the bell. When no one answered, he tried the brass door handle. "It's locked. Did the solicitor send a key?"

"No. How disappointing. I so wanted to go in and see the books."

"And ascertain the condition of the building," Isobel reminded her.

"You own this building?" Wright asked.

"I do," Beatrice replied.

"Then wait two seconds." He reached inside his coat and pulled a palm-size elongated oval of wood out of an inner pocket. He flipped the wooden casing open to reveal several protruding metal implements, before selecting the one he wanted. He bent down in front of the door and inserted a thin piece of metal into the keyhole.

"He's very resourceful," whispered Viola in Beatrice's ear.

"Or possibly criminal," whispered Isobel.

Wright paid no attention, intent on his task. He moved the tool around inside the keyhole, gently turning and prodding until they heard a click. "There." He rose and turned toward her, and all Beatrice could see for several shaky breaths was his mismatched blue-and-gold gaze and the satisfied quirk of his lips.

"What's that tool you're using, Mr. Wright?" Isobel asked. "I've never seen anything like it."

"Something of my father's invention." He held up the wooden oval and showed them how the various metal tools folded out, and then back into the curved frame. "There's a turnscrew, a blade, pliers, a wrench, a file, and even a pick, which is what I just used."

"That's quite extraordinary. I wonder that he hasn't tried to patent it." Isobel was also studying patent law.

"My father's always inventing some fantastical gewgaw or other. But this one happens to be quite useful, though he can't find anyone willing to finance a patent application."

"What does he call it?" Beatrice asked.

"Wright's Versatile Ten in One Master Tool."

"Oh no," said Isobel. "That won't do. Far too long and complicated. You need a short, memorable name. Let's see . . . what about Wright's Versatile Tool?"

"Or you could combine the words," said Beatrice. "Wright's Versa-Tool."

"That's not bad, I'll write to my father and tell him that the lady knitters have a new name for his invention." Wright opened the door with a flourish of his arm and an exaggerated bow. "Your castle awaits, princess."

Something inside Beatrice's chest clicked open and her breath caught in her throat. *Beatrice, you ninny. It doesn't matter how many locks he picks or roses he plucks, it's only what any charming rogue would do.*

Viola laughed softly. "A princess for a castle."

"Don't encourage him," Beatrice muttered, as she brushed past him into the shop.

It was dark inside and took several moments for her eyes to adjust. Dust motes danced in the watery sunlight allowed through the paned glass windows. A dark wood staircase with scrolled balustrades curved upward at the end of the entrance hall. "The showroom's through here," she said, leading the way through the doorway to their right.

"Careful!" Wright caught her arm as she nearly tripped over a wooden crate on the floor. "Stay here until I open the curtains." He disappeared into the room and moments later, streaks of light illuminated their way. There were crates stacked over the entire floor, some of them open and spilling forth piles of books.

"What a frightful mess!" exclaimed Viola. "Why, it looks as though it hasn't been occupied in years."

"My beauties." Beatrice hugged a stack of manuscripts piled on the shop counter. "Just look at you. Left here all alone to molder. Someone should be taking care of you."

More curtains were opened, and someone lit a lamp. Beatrice was only dimly aware of the activity in the room. She gravitated to the bookshelves lining the walls and began reading spines and greeting old friends, and new.

Viola sneezed. "It's ever so dusty."

"I fear the solicitor may have had the right of it—this is most dilapidated," said Isobel.

"My delectable darling." Beatrice cradled an early etymological dictionary in her hands, reverently opening it to the title page. "You're here. You're still here. And you're all mine!"

"Should we give you some privacy with these books?" Wright asked with a sardonic smile.

"Beatrice loves books," said Viola.

"So I've gathered." His gaze made the back of her neck feel hot, so she concentrated on the book she held. "This is the original folio of Skinner's *Etymologicon Linguae Anglicanae*. I've only seen copies. This is the very first etymological dictionary produced in England."

"That's excellent, Beatrice!" enthused Viola.

"And you own it," said Isobel.

She did. She owned this folio. These shelves. This bookshop and everything in it.

The thought settled in her mind, unfamiliar but not unwelcome. She'd never owned anything before. Not truly. She owned nothing that hadn't been purchased for her by a family member.

These books were hers. Not her brother's, or her father's, hers alone.

"Have you noticed the buckets?" Wright called from the far end of the room.

Beatrice followed the line of his finger. Several buckets were lined up against the side of the room, collecting drips that gathered on the ceiling and then splashed down with a *plink, plink, plink*.

"Leaky roof. That's not good." He bounced up and down a few times. "Floor's like sponge cake in places."

The roof might be leaking but the folio she held was intact, even though it had been written over one hundred and fifty years ago.

"Unhand that folio, you knaves!" A tall shape brandishing a heavy silver candelabra charged into the room.

"Out, thieves!" a plump woman shouted, waving what appeared to be a rolling pin.

Wright placed himself between Beatrice and the ladies and the two people with their strange weapons.

"Put down that candlestick," he growled, "or I'll be forced to take it off you."

The tall thin man shook the candlestick. "I'd like to see you try!"

"You don't want to test me. Trust me on that."

Beatrice shivered. Wright's voice was menacing and low and brooked no argument.

"We're not intruders," she said, attempting to come out from behind Wright, but he spread his arm to prevent her from walking any farther. "I'm Lady Beatrice Bentley, the new owner of this bookshop."

"Oh!" The woman lowered her rolling pin. "Oh, it's *her*, Coggins. The one Mrs. Castle told us about. Well, why didn't you say so in the first place?" She dropped the rolling pin onto a chair and hastened toward Wright. "Come in, dearies, come in and make yourselves comfortable."

Wright maintained his protective posture. "The candlestick, if you please."

"Could be a trick," Coggins grumbled. "Says she's Lady Beatrice but could be anyone."

Wright folded his arms. "She's Lady Beatrice and your new mistress. Put down that candlestick and show some respect."

"I'm Mrs. Kettle, dearie. And this is Mr. Coggins. He's quite harmless, really. Relinquish that candlestick, Mr. Coggins."

Coggins finally lowered the candelabra. The old servant had a suspicious look in his eyes, but a rather whimsical curled mustache. Beatrice didn't detect any true menace from his presence.

"These are my aunt's servants," Beatrice whispered to Wright. "We'll be safe with them."

Wright finally relaxed his protective stance, allowing Beatrice to circumnavigate his imposing frame.

"Mrs. Kettle, Mr. Coggins, this is Miss Mayberry and Miss Beaton, my friends, and this is Mr. Wright, my . . . consultant."

"Very pleased to make your acquaintance, though I do wish we'd known you were coming. We've let things run away from us, I'm afraid," said Mrs. Kettle, who was shaped like her namesake, a comfortable, cozy figure with wisps of white hair escaping her lace cap.

"Why are there so many unopened crates?" asked Beatrice.

"Mr. Castle only had this small showroom for the public, and it was by appointment only. His clients were mostly eccentric collectors of antiquities."

"I visited the shop once to view this folio."

"He kept the most precious manuscripts and books in a warehouse, but there was no money to pay the rent for them and so Mrs. Castle used the last of the funds to bring all the books here.

She was very ill at the end." She blotted at her eyes with a handkerchief. "We haven't unpacked them all because we don't know where to put them."

"Footstools," said Coggins. "Firestarter."

"Coggins!" Mrs. Kettle huffed.

"Mr. Coggins," said Beatrice. "That is not even remotely funny. These books are precious. They must be protected and stored properly. Mrs. Kettle, I remember that there was a catalog published twice yearly?"

"There used to be, my dear, but we fell behind and it's all in a jumble now. We're still under contract for several months yet, by the provisions of Mrs. Castle's will. Some of the books are quite valuable, as you know. Why, before he died, Mr. Castle sold a medieval illuminated book for five hundred pounds."

"How long have you been in my aunt's employ?"

"Nigh on forty years now. I started as a maid and worked my way up to housekeeper. Mr. Coggins is the man of all work."

"And you live on the premises?"

"Mr. Coggins does. I live with my daughter, Ann, and my granddaughter, Kit."

"And when did the bookshop close?"

"When Mrs. Castle became too ill to meet with customers. That would be a year ago. Poor thing. She loved this shop and wanted nothing more than to carry on her husband's business."

"I own the Skinner folio," Beatrice said wonderingly. "Who would believe it? I own one of the most rare and most sought-after dictionaries in the world. It's a dream come true."

"If you say so," said Wright with a smirk.

"Do you have any idea how much this dictionary is worth?"

"Ah, so there are authors of etymological dictionaries who turn a profit in their lifetime?"

"It was published posthumously," she admitted.

"Shocking," said Wright.

Isobel and Viola had matching smiles as they witnessed the interchange.

"It's a phenomenal collection, Mrs. Kettle," Beatrice said firmly.

"It's all yours, my dear, all of it. Why, you could even open the shop again! That is, if you wanted to, you being a fine lady and all . . ."

Beatrice's mother would never allow her to engage in trade. That would definitely be the straw that broke her mother's back.

"My mother wouldn't approve. She wants me to sell it immediately."

"What a pity that would be."

"See, Mrs. Kettle?" said Coggins. "She'll evict us early, she will. Time's run out for us. We're for the scrap heap. It won't be long before we freeze to death in a doorway."

He was a ray of sunshine, that one.

"Don't make any decisions just yet, dearie. I've always said never to make up one's mind about anything until you have a nice steaming cup of tea in your hands. Everyone come into the parlor and I'll make a nice pot of tea, shall I?" She bustled away, glancing back over her shoulder to make sure they were following her.

"She might have sandwiches," Isobel said, giving Wright a wink.

Mrs. Kettle ushered them through the showroom and into a parlor crowded with mismatched and overstuffed sofas and chairs.

"And there's a letter for you from Mrs. Castle, Lady Beatrice. Now where did I put it?" She hastened out of the room. "Help me in the kitchen, Mr. Coggins."

Coggins backed out of the room, eyeing them suspiciously, one by one.

"Well, it's a little run-down and it's overcrowded and overstuffed, but isn't it an enchanting place?" Beatrice couldn't stop the excitement welling in her heart. If she could move her writing supplies here, she could work in a house filled with books.

A house blissfully free from mothers.

Wright leaned back in his chair, looking as confident and at ease in this frowsy parlor as when he was constructing pergolas on her brother's estate. He carried his confidence with him every-where.

"Your aunt definitely knew what she was doing when she left you this shop," said Viola. "She knew that you would love these books as family."

"From a bibliophile's perspective this house might be enchant-ing, but from a carpenter's perspective it's a serious project," said Wright. "The roof leaks, I saw evidence of rats—they're probably running amok in the basement, coming up from the river. The floors in the front room need to be completely replaced, and there are probably more issues on the upper floors."

"Make a list, Wright. I'll hire someone to do everything," Bea-trice said.

"But Beatrice, will your mother allow you to keep the shop?" Viola asked.

Isobel tsked her tongue against her teeth. "It's not a question of allowing. Beatrice is a grown woman. If she wants to keep the property then it's hers to keep."

"She'd never allow me to enter into trade, but I can't just leave these books to rot, or to be disposed of by the new owner. I'll need time to inventory the books and manuscripts and decide what to do with the collection."

"I was thinking . . ." Isobel glanced around the room. "I was thinking that we'll need a new place for the Mayfair Ladies Knit-ting League to meet once the Duchess of Ravenwood returns to London. Perhaps the bookshop might serve as a temporary meet-ing space?"

Viola drew a sharp breath. "Isobel—what a splendid idea! Why shouldn't we have our own clubhouse?"

"A clubhouse," Beatrice mused. "I hadn't thought of that."

"Do you know what London has far too many of?" asked Isobel. "Exclusive gentlemen's clubs."

"That's true," said Beatrice. "And they're all very close to here on Pall Mall and St. James's. There's White's, Boodle's, and Brooks's."

"The Athenaeum and the Travellers Club," Viola said.

"And do you know what London has none of?" Isobel asked.

"Ladies' clubhouses." Viola grinned. "This could be our clubhouse! Though we wouldn't be in Mayfair any longer and we'd have to change our name."

"A clubhouse for lady knitters?" asked Wright with a puzzled expression.

"And why not?" Beatrice rounded on him. "We have more than ordinary goals."

Ford wiped the smile from his face. "Of course you do."

"No, we actually do. We can't tell you about them or we'd have to kill you," said Miss Mayberry with a severe expression.

Ford laughed. All three ladies glared at him. He transformed his laugh into a cough. They were deadly serious about these goals, apparently.

Ford tugged at his cravat. "As delightful as all of this sounds, for lady knitters, that is, I'm due at the docks today." He had a few hours before he was supposed to meet his old navy friend, Timothy Griffith, at the docks. "I'm afraid I'll—"

"Do you think it would work, Mr. Wright? Could we renovate this property into a clubhouse with a dining room, a reading room, and other facilities?" asked Lady Beatrice.

Ford considered that question. "I suppose it could work. I'd have to tour the upper floors to make a final determination."

"It could work." Viola danced in her seat. "Wait until I tell Ardella and our newest member, Lady Henrietta Prince."

"How many of you are there?" asked Ford.

"We're recruiting new members every day."

"You couldn't fit more than twelve members at a time, unless you expanded to an adjacent property, as well."

Miss Mayberry raised a glove-clad fist. "We'll take over the Strand."

"Revolutionary lady knitters?" asked Ford.

"We prefer 'bluestockings who knit stockings,'" said Miss Beaton.

Ford considered that. "I thought bluestockings was a derogatory term."

"We've reclaimed it, Mr. Wright." Lady Beatrice made that little gesture with her chin and eyebrows—everything winging upward—that meant she was about to lecture him about something.

"We proudly call ourselves bluestockings. A term originating in the last century to describe a group of ladies who hosted literary salons for men of letters. They admitted all true scholars, regardless of their social standing, overlooking the inexpensive blue worsted stockings of the more insolvent of their guests. Hence the origin of the derisive term Blue Stocking Society. Though the ladies cleverly adopted the epithet and began referring to themselves proudly as bluestockings."

Ford wondered what color her stockings were under those long skirts. White, most likely. And did she wear silk garters, or plain cotton ones? She had lovely long limbs and elegant, expressive fingers that she waved about while she was lecturing a fellow.

And . . . he should leave now. Too much imagining of underthings. Desks were next; he knew that from experience. Desks and the decidedly objectionable uses he'd like to put them to with bookish ladies. "I should be on my way, ladies."

Mrs. Kettle returned with the tea and placed an enormous pile of sandwiches in front of him. Maybe he could stay just a few more minutes. These sandwiches looked much more substantial than the paltry offering he'd been served at the duke's townhouse.

"You're a ship's carpenter with the Royal Navy, Mr. Wright?" asked Miss Beaton.

"I worked my way up from a floating apprenticeship to carpenter's mate, and now I've been promoted to warrant officer, with responsibility for the maintenance of the HMS *Boadicea*, a seventy-four gun third-rate ship of the line. She's being refitted in Bristol and will arrive in London for coppering soon. I'll have to wait for the shipwright to sheath her in copper to protect her against the salt water, and then we'll follow orders to wherever she's wanted."

"The HMS *Boadicea*," said Lady Beatrice. "Named after the legendary Celtic warrior queen, I presume?"

"How romantic," said Miss Beaton.

"Not very romantic, Miss Beaton. There will be hundreds of sailors living on that ship. With all of those men in such close quarters you can imagine the . . ."

"Odiferousness?" supplied Lady Beatrice.

"I was going to say challenges, Lady Beatrice. But yes, it doesn't smell like a ship full of roses."

"A navy man," said Mrs. Kettle, pouring him more tea. "And so handsome. Are you married, Mr. Wright?"

"I'm not, Mrs. Kettle."

"You should be."

"You're the second matron to tell me that today." And he hadn't changed his mind on the subject in the length of two hours.

"I don't wish to be unmannerly, Mrs. Kettle," said Lady Beatrice, "but I was told there was some scandal attached to the bookshop?"

"There's nothing scandalous about our little shop, nothing untoward whatsoever. Isn't that right, Mr. Coggins?" Mrs. Kettle glanced at Coggins, who stood beside the doorway studying the ceiling, his hands behind his back.

"Erm," he replied noncommittally.

"So those double-sided, revolving bookcases don't hide anything?" Ford had noticed some interesting shelves in the front room.

"Pardon?" Lady Beatrice caught his eye.

Mrs. Kettle poured more tea, her hand trembling slightly.

"Hidden bookshelves?" asked Miss Beaton. "How intriguing!"

"Nonsense. They're just ordinary bookshelves," said Mrs. Kettle.

"Shall we go and look?" asked Ford.

As the party rose from their chairs, Mrs. Kettle began fluttering around them, emitting reassurances that there was nothing to see.

Lady Beatrice entered the front room of the shop first. "I don't see anything out of the ordinary."

"I know a swiveling shelf when I see one." Ford ran his fingers over the seams of the wood. "There." He pressed a hidden button and the shelves began to swivel, revolving a full turn and presenting an entirely new set of shelves.

"We're done for," said Coggins with a fatalistic shrug. "He's on to us."

"More books?" asked Lady Beatrice, moving closer. "How clever. Twice the space for storage. *Sins of the City. The Further Adventures of a Gentleman Scholar. Memoirs of a Madam.* These aren't antiquarian titles. *The Dairy Maid's Dilemma.*" She opened the book.

He approached and bent his head over her shoulder. The illustration on the frontispiece left no doubt as to the nature of the book.

"Oh. Oh *my*. So it's *that* sort of dilemma." She slammed the volume shut. "Mrs. Kettle," she said severely. "Please tell me what is going on here."

Chapter Six

❧ ✿ ❧

"*I*'LL BE HAPPY to explain what's going on." Ford pointed at the illustration. "This buxom dairymaid is attempting to choose between two virile young suitors, both of whom have the most enormous—"

"Not the illustration!" Lady Beatrice cut in. "The bookshop. Mrs. Kettle, what is the purpose of this bookshop? I was under the impression that it sold only antiquarian books and manuscripts."

Lady Beatrice's cheeks had gone scarlet again. That illustration had probably been the most scandalous thing she'd ever seen in her life. It was all well and good for a proper lady to study the etymology of off-color words, but to see them illustrated in garish detail—now that was something to make a lady blush.

And she did look so fetching when she blushed.

Mrs. Kettle groaned. "Oh dear, oh dear. We should have been rid of these titles but I couldn't bear to throw them all out, not the bestsellers. We still have customers, you know. It's only a very small and selective collection of popular novels."

"Popular with lonely men," said Ford.

"And some women," said Mrs. Kettle. "Profits plummeted after Mr. Castle died, Lady Beatrice. We had to find a way to appeal to a new clientele since there are so many bookshops and book dealers nearby. Stocking these books meant enough profit to keep the shop open. Please try to understand."

"Do you mean to tell me, Mrs. Kettle," said Lady Beatrice, speaking very slowly and clearly, "that I have inherited some manner of . . . that is to say, a bookshop that secretly specializes in . . ."

Ford waited for her to supply the words. She was an etymologist, after all. When she just stood there, her cheeks stained with pink and her lips pressed together, he came to her rescue. "Obscene books. Naughty scribblings. One-handed reads."

Miss Beaton giggled and Lady Beatrice glared at her. "Thank you, Wright. That will do."

"It's only a very small collection, and we only ever sold them to a small and discerning clientele who could never reveal the secret for fear of being exposed themselves. It was Mr. Castle's private interest and he . . . oh dear. Please don't let this affect your decision to keep the property. Now come back to the parlor and finish your tea. It's getting cold."

"Weren't you worried about being closed down by the authorities, Mrs. Kettle?" asked Miss Mayberry.

"Not a bit, love. The authorities placed special orders, they did. Our constable has a taste for the memoirs of saucy serving maids."

Lady Beatrice groaned. "Alack. I fear this changes everything."

"It does complicate things," said Miss Mayberry. "A bookshop of this nature isn't the most ideal location for a respectable clubhouse."

"I'd be happy to take a few of the books off your hands," Ford offered. "Those sea voyages can be long."

Lady Beatrice gave him a murderous look. "You're not helping, Wright."

"You're the one who invited me."

Miss Mayberry fastened her bonnet over her dark blond hair. "This has been a most interesting and edifying afternoon, I must say, but I have an appointment to keep. Wright, I look forward to reading a full report on the feasibility of renovations, if Beatrice decides to keep the property."

He bowed and she gave a little mannish bow in return, instead of curtsying.

Lady Beatrice pulled her aside, and Ford couldn't hear what they whispered, except for the words *scandalous, naughty, and carpenter*.

He approved of that combination of words.

Miss Beaton thanked Mrs. Kettle for the tea and said that she was expected at music lessons very shortly and she would accompany Miss Mayberry out. "I might just take one of these, for research purposes." She plucked a naughty book from the shelf and slipped it into her reticule.

The two ladies left, the shop bell tinkling as it closed again.

"Do you want me to finish the inspection, Lady Beatrice?" he asked.

"Yes. I'd like to make an informed decision."

"I have an appointment on the docks, but I'll take a quick look around." They made their way to the staircase. "Why were your friends looking at me like that?"

"I don't know what you mean."

"They were staring searchingly. As if they knew something about me, as if you'd already described me to them."

"I may have mentioned you in my letters from Cornwall."

"You told them how handsome I was."

"More like how arrogant and obstructive to my work."

"Admit it, you told them I was distractingly virile."

"Humph. You have an inspection to make, Wright." She walked ahead of him up the stairs, and he couldn't tear his gaze away from the curve of her backside—well, at least he imagined her curves under all those layers of petticoats.

Duke's sister. No trespassing.

"I hope your brother returns soon," he said as they climbed the curving central staircase. At least the staircase was in good repair. "My ship leaves in a fortnight, and I must speak with him in person."

"You said it was something about Gibbons?"

"I believe he's embezzling from your brother."

She stopped walking at the first-floor landing and faced him. "Really? That's a serious accusation."

"I have proof." He patted his pocket. He'd pilfered a receipt from Gibbons's desk that showed the discrepancies in the bookkeeping.

"Then my brother needs to know immediately upon his return. He trusts Gibbons completely and has granted him wide latitude to make decisions on his behalf."

"I don't want my father implicated in any way when the theft is uncovered."

"I'm sure my brother will return any day now and you may present your evidence."

The landing led on one side to a drawing room stuffed with mismatched furniture, and on the other to a small back room with well-scrubbed walls, sparse furniture, and several bookshelves. The room was light and airy with none of the clutter evident in the rest of the house.

Lady Beatrice entered the room, her eyes lighting with approval. "A reading room. This must be where Mr. Castle kept the more rare volumes of his personal collection."

Ford bounced on a few floorboards. "Seems safe from damp."

She walked to the window, the light teasing the flames in her hair to life. "And there's a view of the Thames!"

He moved to stand beside her. "A view of coal barges."

"You see coal barges, I see a river undulating into the distance. The perfect view for writing. I'd place my desk right here by the window."

Please don't talk about desks. "So you will keep the property?"

"My mother told me that she'd heard rumors of scandal attached to the shop, and she assumed it was because Aunt Matilda had taken a lover. She has no idea about the bawdy books, or she never would have allowed me to visit the shop."

"But that's exactly what your friend Miss Mayberry was saying—*you* own it, not your mother."

"You don't know my mother, Wright. When I'm in London she controls what I wear, what I eat, what I think, everything. If one word of this reached her . . . let's just say that hell hath no fury like a Mayfair mother protecting her daughter from scandal."

"She sounds quite formidable."

"She's not to be crossed, not in matters of propriety or taste. When in London, I'm under her rule. She's obsessed with finding a brilliant match for me. But here . . ." She spread her arms wide as if she wanted to hug all of the books to her bosom. The movement lifted her breasts, giving him an enticing hint of lush curves. "Here I could be as bookish as I please. This could be my literary haven. My little slice of freedom."

"You must be thrilled to inherit this collection."

"It's like a dream." Her face fell. "But I can't possibly read all of them. It keeps me up at night sometimes, knowing that I can't read every book I own. An unread book is a terrible thing. You should see how many books are stacked beside my bed just waiting to be read. And I don't have time to read them all."

Her gaze caressed the books lovingly. "Don't worry, my beauties. We'll patch the roof and keep the damp away from you and build you a nice safe home," she crooned.

The attention she was lavishing on the books made him feel restless and . . . jealous?

He was jealous of a bunch of old books. He must be losing his mind.

He cleared his throat. "If we're finished with the tour, then I'll be on my way."

"Oh, no, we must see the bedrooms. I want you to assess any structural damage."

"I think I've seen enough to make a report," he began, but she was already out the door and heading upstairs.

The two small guest bedrooms were unscathed by damage of any kind. They moved to the master bedroom.

Take a glance at the walls and be on your way.

Ford turned his back on the spacious bed festooned with pink velvet curtains and peeled back a section of blue paper from the wall. There was a faint line of water, just as he'd known there would be from the condition of the paper. "If I trace this water upward, I'll find the source of the leak, but it will often be in a different location than one would think."

"I don't understand. If the roof is leaking, can't you just walk around up there until you find the loose tile?"

"Sometimes it's that simple, but other times not. When slate roof tiles become cracked or dislodged, it's often too minimal to see, but the water enters nonetheless. And water will always follow its own path throughout the frame of the building. In order to find the source of the breach, someone will need to translate this course upward through its pathway."

"Within the walls?"

"In the walls, beneath the floor joists, under the beams." He grabbed a pencil and notepad from a table beside the bed. "I'll draw it for you."

She stood closer, watching as he sketched.

He pointed at his drawing with the pencil. "When water enters through the roof, rather than flowing straight down it first follows beams horizontally, then flows down the rafters until it comes to a wall plate, flowing down the interior of the wall cavity and pooling in the base, or following the floor joists until it settles at the lowest point. That would be the leak in the showroom. I don't think the damage has moved past the ground floor."

She bowed her head to study the drawing. She smelled differently than she had at Thornhill. Instead of sweet and fresh, like apple blossoms after a rain, this was more of a city scent, heavily floral—a costly eau de toilette that her mother had chosen for her to dab behind her ears.

Ford had preferred the simple scent. As he'd preferred her hair loosely knotted with unruly curls escaping and framing her face, instead of this elaborately constructed tower.

She tilted her head and caught his eye. "You're a talented draftsman. I wonder that you didn't become an architect?"

Ford laughed harshly. "You make it sound easy, princess, as

though I had all of the opportunities in the world. I'm the son of a carpenter who rents a cottage, and whose livelihood is dependent on the largess of a duke. First your father, and now your brother."

He wasn't ashamed of his humble origins. He wouldn't pretend to be something he wasn't.

"Oh." Her pale lashes fluttered closed for a moment. "I didn't think about what I was saying."

"In case you haven't realized, Your Ladyship, you and I are from two vastly different worlds."

She inherited bookshops and treated it as a fun little diversion. *Let's transform this bookshop into a clubhouse for lady knitters!* Only a pampered and privileged lady would ever have a notion like that.

To own property, to own land, was to have power in this world.

Ford was an exile—from Cornwall, from London—his place was on a ship, drifting across oceans and touching land only briefly. But even so, his goal since he joined the navy was to earn enough money to purchase land near London and build a house. He wouldn't live in the house very often, but his mother could use it when she visited, and it would be a symbol that he'd escaped the yoke of servitude his father wore.

"And yet the circumference of your life is wider than mine." She traced her finger down the lines of his sketch. "My mother narrows the scope of my experience as much as possible. I can only follow prescribed, preapproved paths through life. While you've explored the world with the navy."

"Mostly the Mediterranean. I was stationed off Greece for several years."

"I've never left England's shores and I probably never will." She turned to study the portrait hanging over the bed. "This must have been Aunt Matilda's bedchamber."

The portrait showed a young woman with bright red hair sitting on a bench heaped with gold velvet cushions and reading a leather-bound book.

"I wish I'd known my aunt," she said with a wistful expression.

"Why didn't you know her?"

"She was my father's eldest sister. She fell in love with Mr. Castle and was disinherited by the family for making an imprudent marriage with a shopkeeper. It's nearly unfathomable to me that she lived so close by and I never even knew she existed." Her brows knit together. "It's not right."

"No, it's not right, but it's common practice. My mother, Joyce, was born into a wealthy tradesperson's family and fell in love with my father, a mere carpenter. She was cut off and disowned for her choice. She and her father have never reconciled."

"I'm sorry to hear that."

It made him furious that he would never know his aunt, or his nieces. His mother only visited her sister once a year, in utmost secrecy, for fear of retaliation from his grandfather. She would arrive in London for their yearly meeting soon, and then she would bid Ford farewell.

He threw the pencil down. "I always laugh when I hear people express the sentiment that our world should live in peace and harmony. How can we achieve peace between nations when families are torn apart so easily and so often?"

Lady Beatrice nodded her agreement.

"I've seen enough of war," he said bitterly, "to know that men thirst for it, that they say they want a diplomatic solution, but instead they charge toward it, guns at the ready, pointed straight for hell. Families are no different. One transgression and a beloved daughter, or a sister, becomes a stranger, an enemy."

"It's tragic. How I should have liked to know my aunt. Anyone who reads a book while having a portrait painted would have been a bosom friend of mine. She was very beautiful, wasn't she?"

"You look like her," Ford pointed out. "The same red hair and slender figure. The same pale brows and straight little nose. And definitely the same expression of pure bliss when you're turning the pages of a book."

Lady Beatrice stared at him. "Don't be silly. I look nothing like her."

"You don't see it?"

"Mr. Wright." She turned fully toward him, into the light from the windows. "I was born with palsy of the facial nerve caused by damage from the instruments the doctor used during my birthing. I speak plainly of it, using none of the euphemisms my mother employs. It's become more manageable and less noticeable over the years, but there's no use attempting to ignore the condition, hide it, or pretend that it doesn't exist. This is my face. Nothing more, nothing less. And I'm no beauty."

Her vehement denial gave him pause. He'd read her diary entry, but that had been written by a young girl in a fit of passionate humiliation. Surely she'd realized by now how lovely she was.

"Clearly, you won't believe anything I tell you. You should have your portrait painted. Maybe then you'd see the resemblance."

She turned away. "I've no interest in having my likeness painted."

And he shouldn't have any interest in telling, or showing her, how attractive she was. This conversation was far too intimate for a simple business transaction. It was time for some lighthearted banter, to regain the earlier footing of their interactions, and then it was past time for him to leave.

He framed her face with his hands in the air. "If I were an artist, I'd paint you reclining on a velvet divan with your hair unbound. Rather like that dairymaid we saw earlier. I think your hair is long enough to have much the same effect."

"Wright!" His name came out somewhere between a laugh and a snort. "I'm not having my portrait done and certainly not in the style of that most objectionable frontispiece."

The dairymaid had been reclining on a bed, her hair streaming over her bare breasts, and her arms outstretched to test the girth of the two enormous pricks being offered to her by the two farmhands.

Her gaze dropped to the bed and then lifted to him. "Perhaps . . ." Her voice had gone throaty and soft. "Perhaps we should go back downstairs."

There was nothing between him and Lady Beatrice except some teasing banter and professional services rendered.

And a bed.

A large, comfortable-looking bed. Her coppery hair would look stunning spread across that coverlet.

Don't look at the bed.

He'd had enough fantasies about her involving desks. He didn't need to replace those with images of her on this enormous bed hung with a very suggestive shade of pale pink velvet.

He cleared his throat. "I think that would be a good idea."

He waited for her to flounce toward the door and out of his life.

She stayed. "Do you want to know the real reason that my friends were staring at you like that?"

Don't answer that question . . . "Tell me."

"I told them about our conversation. How you insulted my dictionary and said it wasn't much fun."

"I don't think that's the reason they stared. I think you told them that you thought about kissing me."

"That's preposterous. I'm not a ninnyhammer. I've never imagined kissing you. I'm not imagining kissing you right now."

The last said in a husky whisper accompanied by a heated gaze upon his lips.

"You're *definitely* imagining kissing me right now."

"Don't you wish that were true?"

This conversation was all kinds of wrong and veering toward wicked.

Somehow the distance between them had melted away. It would be so easy to tumble her down upon the bed and set to work destroying that carefully constructed tower of hair. His fingers itched to unravel her copper curls and test their silken texture between his fingers.

"If I kissed you right now, princess, it wouldn't be a safe little taste. I'd kiss you so well that you'd remember it for the rest of your life."

"Does that line usually work?"

"I've been remarkably successful. We all have our skills. I repair ships and houses . . . and I give unforgettable kisses."

"So do I," she whispered. "Hypothetically. But I know you would never take advantage of me."

"How can you be so certain? You're alone in a bedchamber with a notorious rogue."

"A rogue with a moral code. I asked the housekeeper at Thornhill about you, and she told me that you were an incorrigible flirt, but an honorable one. As far as she knew, you'd debauched no innocents at the estate. Therefore, I'm quite safe with you."

"Is that a challenge, princess?"

Damn it, he was going to have to kiss her now. He needed to kiss her so that he could forget about her. Because now, with this new episode of almost-kissing in front of a big, soft bed, he'd have fodder for years of fantasies to come.

He cupped her chin and tilted her face toward him and . . . the shop bell rang, a faint tinkling sound.

A warning bell.

He dropped his hand.

"We should go downstairs," he said gruffly. "I thought the bookshop was closed."

Her hand rested against her belly, her bosom rising and falling rapidly. "Perhaps Isobel or Viola forgot something and they are back to collect it."

She walked swiftly to the door.

The moment was gone. The danger had been averted. He could make his escape, and not a moment too soon. What was it about this prim, bookish lady that ripped his resolve to shreds like a gale tearing at a canvas sail?

When they reached the showroom, Mrs. Kettle rushed toward them. "They just entered the shop without warning. I tried to ask them to leave, but they began walking around as if they own the place."

"Where's Coggins?" Lady Beatrice asked.

"He went to buy more candles," said Mrs. Kettle, her eyes worried.

"I'll handle this, Mrs. Kettle," said Ford. "You may go back to the kitchens."

Ford approached the gaunt, tall man, made even taller by a black top hat, who stood with his back to them, discussing something with a shorter man wearing workman's coarse woolen clothing.

"Now, guvnor, I'd knock out this back wall here, and I'd connect the two houses with a walkway, see?" Ford heard the workman say.

"What's this?" Ford asked. "Who are you?"

"Who are *you*?" asked the gaunt man disdainfully, turning to face him. "I own this bookshop."

"Pardon me, you do not own this bookshop, I do." Lady Beatrice stepped closer. "I'm Lady Beatrice Bentley. Your name, sir?"

"Richard Foxton, at your service, Lady Beatrice. I didn't expect to find you here."

Ford stopped in his tracks. He'd only been eight when his mother had taken him to London with her. He recognized the hooked nose and the deep-set gray eyes, but his hair had gone snow white.

This was the villain from his youth. The big bad ogre in all his mother's stories.

The man his mother had made him swear never to contact, never to claim a connection with, never even to name.

Richard Stamford Foxton.

His grandfather.

Chapter Seven

FORD CAUGHT A flicker of unease in Foxton's hard gray eyes.

"The duke's solicitor, Mr. Greenaway, informed me that the property was for sale, Lady Beatrice. The terms have been decided."

Lady Beatrice regarded him with the icy, aristocratic stare Ford recognized from their first interaction in the library at Thornhill House. "Mr. Greenaway acted without my knowledge or consent."

"Do you mean that you don't wish to sell? How odd. As you can see, the shop has a leaky roof and hazardous flooring. The building is unstable and would require expensive renovations to make it habitable."

"That's only partially true, and you know it." Ford puffed out his chest. "This building is structurally sound, and the repairs won't be extensive or costly."

Foxton glanced at him dismissively. "That's your opinion, Mr. . . . ?"

"Wright. John Wright." His middle name. He wasn't going to announce himself to the man he'd promised his mother never to contact. He looked evenly into Foxton's eyes, daring him to recognize his own grandson, to make the connection and acknowledge him, but Foxton's face remained blank and hostile.

This was the cruel and ruthless man who had torn apart his own family to satisfy his pride.

Ford had made a discreet study of him. Foxton's property empire was built on similarly heartless principles. No tenant had ever received leniency during lean times from his grandfather.

No bricklayer down on his luck with a sick wife and child at home was ever given a loan to tide him over to the next payday.

Foxton lived for the god of profit alone. He didn't care about the backs he broke or the lives he ruined in his quest for the almighty gold.

"You may have knowledge of structural integrity, Mr. Wright," Foxton said. "But Mr. Brown here has been employed by my firm for ten years now, and he says the building's in dangerous disrepair."

"That's right." Mr. Brown walked toward them, nearly stumbling over a crate of books.

"Be careful of those books, Mr. Brown," said Lady Beatrice.

"Apologies, milady," mumbled Mr. Brown.

"I don't want the books, of course, Lady Beatrice. I'll pay to have them delivered to a warehouse of your choosing." Foxton attempted to soften his voice, but the result was more grating than empathetic. "Aren't you in the midst of preparing for the whirlwind of the social season? Surely you don't wish to trouble yourself with these matters. Allow our solicitors to work out the details and then—"

"Do you presume to know the goals of young ladies?"

Uh-oh. Ford knew where this conversation was headed.

"Er." Foxton's bony fingers tightened around the gold knob of his walking stick. "I meant no offense. It pains me to speak so bluntly, but Mr. Greenaway did lead me to believe, in essence, did *guarantee*, that you were amenable to selling this property. For a handsome profit, of course."

Ford delighted in bursting his grandfather's soap bubble. "This property will soon house a clubhouse for bluestocking lady knitters."

"For *what*?"

"For *whom*, Mr. Foxton." Lady Beatrice pursed her lips. "The Mayfair Ladies Knitting League, though we shall have to change our society's name once we occupy these premises."

"These lady knitters have goals," Ford said with relish. "Deadly serious ones."

"But Lady Beatrice, you can't seriously be considering such a thing. You do know that this bookshop, besides having fallen into disrepair, was . . . is . . . not a fit place for any lady to enter, much less own or gather inside? Genteel ladies would never patronize a bookshop with a less than savory reputation."

Lady Beatrice smiled, but her eyes remained as cold as wintry wind blowing over the ocean. "Are you referring to the hidden bookshelves, Mr. Foxton? Because I know all about them."

"But . . . but Lady Beatrice," sputtered Foxton, looking like a man who was rarely thwarted and was at a loss as to how to proceed. The purple veins in his temple protruded.

Ford rejoiced at the sight of those protruding veins. He'd promised his mother he'd never seek out his grandfather, or attempt to exact revenge, but if his grandfather walked into his life, he'd damned well do his best to see that he got a taste of his own bitter medicine.

In that moment, Ford decided that he would do everything in his power to help Lady Beatrice keep this property, achieve her goals, and thereby ruin his grandfather's plans.

"You haven't thought this through, Lady Beatrice," said Foxton. "You're only a girl. You must think of your reputation, of your mother. Please be rational."

Now he'd done it.

Lady Beatrice advanced on Foxton. "Only a girl, did you say?"

"Well, that is, you're very young . . ." Foxton mumbled.

"Mr. Foxton," said Lady Beatrice, pronouncing the name as if it meant *putrid pestilence*. "I have reached the age of majority and I'm fully capable of administering my own fortune. I'm not helpless, brainless chattel with no will of my own."

She truly was a splendid sight when she was reprimanding a man. Her eyes became crystallized amber, and she held her neck at such a proud angle she appeared much taller than she was.

"Apologies, Lady Beatrice. I never meant to suggest such a thing."

"You didn't have to. It was evident in your tone of voice."

"I'm merely relaying what was told to me by your brother's solicitor."

"And I'm telling you that I was not consulted on the matter."

"If I may, Mr. Foxton," Ford interjected, "don't tell the lady what she can and can't do. It never ends well."

"The building is not for sale, Mr. Foxton," said Lady Beatrice.

"Then I must inform you that I own the properties on either side."

Damn his hide. "Then you want to own the block. What are you planning to build? A hotel, or a factory?"

"Not one of those foul, polluting factories that employs children I hope," said Lady Beatrice. "I read a report of a boot blacking factory near here and it was most inhumane."

"A shirting manufactory. I need this building for its access to the steps leading to the Thames. I assure you, Lady Beatrice, that any workers I employ will be treated fairly."

"Ha." Ford laughed bitterly. "That's a lie. I know all about your gunpowder mills in Leigh and your other moneymaking ventures. You don't care about poisoning the water or protecting your workers from harm."

"Hearsay, Mr. Wright," replied Foxton with a small shake of his walking stick. "Slanderous hearsay."

"You won't be purchasing this property, Mr. Foxton." Lady Beatrice squared her shoulders. "Good day."

Foxton was not a man who was accustomed to being dismissed by a woman, even if she was sister to a duke. His expression went from sour to vengeful. "Unfortunately, you'll never find a carpenter willing to perform the repairs necessary to transform this into a clubhouse, Lady Beatrice."

Ford raised his eyebrows. "Is that a threat, Foxton?"

"I could easily use my connections to have this building declared a public safety hazard. Instead, I've made the lady an extremely generous offer, one which I'll only extend for the next week."

This man had cast Ford's mother out of his life like soiled laundry and run her, and Ford's father, out of London.

Foxton thought he could buy or control everyone and everything. He didn't control Ford, and he had no business attempting to control Lady Beatrice.

Ford would do everything in his power to help her win this battle.

Although he was probably going to regret it.

He felt the warning in his bones, like the ache in his old elbow injury when there was a storm brewing on the horizon. He didn't stop to consider impossibilities or timelines. "As it happens, Mr. Foxton, the lady has already hired a carpenter."

"I have?" asked Lady Beatrice.

"She has?" Foxton echoed.

"Yes." Ford moved to stand next to Lady Beatrice. "Me."

BEATRICE GAPED AT Mr. Wright. What on earth was he saying? He couldn't be her carpenter. He was leaving England. He *must* leave England so that she would cease having these maddening urges to kiss him.

He truly was a breathtaking sight standing with his muscular arms crossed and boots planted firmly on the floor, skewering Foxton with a thunderous glower.

Standing up for her—for her dreams.

He may as well have come galloping into the room on a spirited stallion and swept her up onto the saddle in front of him.

Beatrice, you ninny. You don't require rescuing.

But there was no point in contradicting him in front of Foxton. "Indeed. I've hired Mr. Wright. All of the arrangements have been made."

Foxton glared at Wright. "You obviously have no idea who I am, or the influence I possess in this city, Mr. Wright."

"I know exactly who you are."

Foxton looked him up and down. "I don't know you. Never seen you before."

"You'll just have to build your factory elsewhere, Mr. Foxton." Beatrice struggled to keep her voice calm and even. She drew courage from Wright's imposing presence at her side. "The lady knitters are moving in and there's nothing you can do to change my mind or wrest this property away from me."

"We'll see about that, Lady Beatrice." Foxton headed for the door. "Come along, Brown. Your services won't be required until later."

Mr. Brown trailed after him, looking confused, hat in hand.

At the door, Foxton turned back. "I trust you'll reconsider this rash decision upon submission of further evidence and discussion between our solicitors. I would hate to have to take this matter to the courts. Good day, Lady Beatrice." He bowed and left.

Wright closed the door behind him and locked it.

"Cozening fox," Beatrice muttered. "Jeering goosecap."

"I couldn't agree more," said Wright.

"He can't take my bookshop!"

"We won't let him."

Mrs. Kettle popped her head around the doorframe. "Well done, Lady Beatrice and Mr. Wright. Well done, indeed! You were both magnificent."

Wright had been rather magnificent, thought Beatrice.

"Wait until Mr. Coggins hears about this. He'll be so pleased that you're keeping the bookshop. He's a little gloomy, Mr. Coggins, but he has a most noble heart."

"I'm not certain that I can keep it yet, Mrs. Kettle."

"Where there's a will there's a way, Lady Beatrice. Or, should I say, where there's a Wright, there's a way." She giggled at her joke, beaming at them. "This calls for a fresh pot of tea." She left, humming a happy tune.

"Why did you tell Foxton that your name was John?" Beatrice asked.

"It's my middle name. I don't want him knowing my full identity if I go up against him in this matter." He removed his coat, flung it over a chair, and began rolling up his shirtsleeves. "Let's get to work. You can sort through those crates. Coggins can help once he reappears. I'll go examine the basement. I don't have all the tools I need but this will help." He brought out the tool he'd used to break into the shop.

"Mr. Wright, I think I gave you the wrong impression. I haven't agreed to hire you."

"You need a builder." He removed his waistcoat and laid it over his coat. "And as your wise friend Miss Mayberry said, I'm here and so you may as well make use of me." He unknotted his cravat and opened the top button of his shirt.

Make use of him. Her treacherous mind began inventing uses. Those sensual lips of his could be used for kissing. Those wide shoulders and strong arms for lifting her and carrying her up the stairs . . .

"Mr. Wright! Do stop disrobing."

"Why?" He stopped midbutton. "This is my only suit of decent clothing. I'm not going to get plaster and dirt all over it."

"I don't have the permission or the means to hire you at the moment."

"I need to speak to your brother. If I'm helping you, I'll know instantly when he arrives." He cocked his head. "And you'll put in a good word for me, instead of giving him a list of everything I did to annoy you at Thornhill."

So that's why he was so eager to help her with the building. "I don't require rescuing, Wright. I'll find a way out of this mess on my own."

"I think you do need a little rescuing. I think Foxton is going to make good on his threat, and you won't be able to find another carpenter willing to help you."

She removed her spectacles, which had gone a little blurry, and wiped them clean. Happened every time Wright stripped to his shirtsleeves. "But your friend is waiting for you at the docks."

"Old Griffith? He can wait. He's only hiring me as a favor. He can easily find someone else."

"The HMS *Boadicea* is arriving soon."

"I have a fortnight. It should be enough time to make decent progress on the renovations if I work night and day. You've already seen what I'm capable of, Lady Beatrice." He spread his arms wide. "Make use of me. I'm yours."

She wished he'd stop saying things like that. It made her brain fog over just like her spectacles. He wasn't hers and he never would be.

"There's the matter of the paperwork," she said crisply, trying to keep this conversation impersonal and businesslike. "I'm not entirely certain yet of the details of my inheritance until I meet with my brother's solicitor to review my aunt's will and . . ." *Every time you roll up those sleeves and expose your forearms, I become so flustered that I can't even remember how to form complete sentences.* ". . . I'm not ready to begin renovations. Foxton knows about the bawdy books, and he threatened obliquely to use it as leverage to force me to sell. He knows my mother would never tolerate me owning a shop with such an objectionable past."

"You can't let him win. He thinks he owns everything and everyone."

"I agree. I want nothing more than to foil his plans for that awful factory."

"You could sign the property over to your society for use as a clubhouse, and that way it wouldn't be your family name associated with any past scandals. You keep the books but the society owns the property."

"That's actually a very good idea."

He grinned. "I have a few good ones from time to time."

His smile was a weapon employed to scramble the minds of sensible ladies. The teasing curve of his lips, the laughter dancing in his eyes, the way he proffered such ingenious solutions to her problems in that gruff voice of his . . . everything about him disarmed her and made her feel off-balance and not at all like herself. "Even so, I'm not at liberty to employ you at the moment, Mr. Wright."

He strode toward her, throat exposed, the white of his shirt contrasting with the uneven blue of his eyes. "Could there perhaps be another reason for your reluctance to hire me?"

She backed away from all of that too-vivid virility. "Frankly, yes." She might as well be honest. "After what happened upstairs . . . I don't think it's prudent for us to be alone together. Especially in the vicinity of bedchambers."

"Nothing happened upstairs."

Something had happened. She'd progressed far beyond ninnyhood and entered wanton territory. "I can't hire you, Wright."

He shrugged. "Suit yourself. If you hear word from your brother contact me at St. Katharine Docks where I'll be making repairs on the ship *Angela*."

After he left, Beatrice collapsed into a chair. She knew it was for the best. He was simply too dangerous to her good sense . . . and to her heart.

"Has Mr. Wright gone?" asked Mrs. Kettle, returning with the tea tray and setting it on a table. "I do hope he's coming back?"

"He's not."

"Such a shame. He seems a most capable fellow, and so handsome, wouldn't you agree, Lady Beatrice?"

"I hadn't noticed."

Liar. It's all she'd thought about for weeks now. He'd truly gone this time, out of her life and her thoughts. And her dreams. He wasn't allowed to come back into those, either.

"Sit down, dearie. Have a nice cup of tea and read Mrs. Castle's letter."

The letter. Beatrice had almost forgotten about it. She allowed Mrs. Kettle to fuss over pouring her tea and bringing her a blanket for her knees to protect against drafts.

She opened the letter.

Dear Lady Beatrice,

I remember the day that you visited our bookshop so clearly. I watched from behind the door, unable to reveal myself. I remember that you spoke in hushed tones, as if you were in church. I recognized a fellow bibliophile. And that's why I've left you Castle's Bookshop. These books were like our children, and I have every faith that you will treat them with respect.

I've made many mistakes in my life, but marrying Mr. Castle was not one of them, even though that choice precluded me from being a part of your life.

I hope you will divine my meaning and that this Revelation of Love helps you to be brave, and not hide yourself away. Allow me to point the way.

I place my trust in you.

Your loving (secret) Aunt Matilda

What a strange choice of words. Revelation of Love, capitalized in that way. It was almost as if her aunt were trying to tell her something more with this letter, but Beatrice couldn't, for the life of her, figure out what.

The main intent of the letter was very clear. Keep the property in the family. Protect the precious collection of books. Even if it meant defying her mother and striking out on her own.

It was the same message she'd received from her friends and from Wright.

Finding a way to make her mother agree to allow her to renovate the bookshop into a clubhouse wouldn't be easy.

This house filled with ancient manuscripts and research books felt far more inviting than her brother's house in Mayfair. She wanted to stay here, to open those tantalizing crates of books, and transform the property into a clubhouse for her friends. A welcoming haven where women could meet to discuss goals, to nurture dreams, and to support one another, safe from society's scorn and censure.

Perhaps she'd been selfish turning down Wright's offer outright, just because he made her feel on edge and weak-kneed at the same time.

The bookshop required rescuing, even if she didn't.

Too late.

She'd already refused his offer, and he didn't strike her as a man who extended an offer twice. She'd have to take charge herself—find another carpenter, and consult with Isobel and with her brother's solicitor regarding Foxton's claim to the property. It was imperative to begin the renovations immediately, before Foxton had a chance to regroup and make good on his threats.

She gazed at the cracked leather spines of several early dictionaries she'd gathered from the shelves in the showroom. This was her chance to write a new chapter in her life, to claim a modicum of freedom within her mother's kingdom.

She wouldn't relinquish this chance without a fight.

Chapter Eight

*I*T HAD TAKEN four hours and a small army to ready Beatrice for tonight's ball at the Earl of Mayhew's home in St. James's.

She'd been bathed, and then powdered, perfumed, and wrapped in a robe to sit by the fire, dry her hair, and await the arrival of that most important of personages, the hairdresser.

The dowager duchess wasn't going to entrust the dressing of her daughter's hair to a mere lady's maid. She'd hired a private hairdresser direct from Paris to attend her daughter and create a style so elaborate that it would awe every person at the ball by sheer dint of complexity.

The hairdresser, a Monsieur Armoire, had parted Beatrice's hair into three sections, exclaiming in consternation at the unruliness of her curls, which he tamed into submission by combing through her long hair until her eyes watered. The two partings on the side were formed into glossy ringlets with curling tongs and the liberal application of pomade. The back section was pulled painfully by the roots and braided tightly, then wrapped atop her head with the ends of the long braids fashioned into a bow.

The whole braided, looped, and bowed creation was stuck with diamond pins in the shape of cupid's arrows. The final touch was a diamond *ferronnière* draped across her forehead with a central diamond drop that lay in the center of her brow and sparkled in the corners of her vision.

After her hair had been tortured, her body had been corseted within an inch of her life, and encased in a heavy gown of ivory silk brocade with a sheer overlay and voluminous gigot sleeves made of transparent gauze.

The low, wide bodice of the gown left her shoulders bare but encased her bosom in four layers of stiff lace ruffles that extended across the sleeves of the gown, rather like an Elizabethan ruff that had migrated from her neck to spread across her upper arms and décolletage.

The darling slippers of her mother's dreams completed the ensemble, done in the same ivory silk, which, to Beatrice's mind, was a ridiculous color for shoes. The slippers had pointed toes that pinched her feet and diamond clips that could prove hazardous to her hem.

When she was finally pronounced ready and led to the looking glass, Beatrice didn't recognize herself at all. She was an elegant, if bizarrely silhouetted, creature of her mother's invention, a sylph-like will-o'-the-wisp emerging from layers of creamy lace and topped by a stiff bow of red hair that bobbed when she nodded.

By this time they were late for the ball, so Beatrice was bundled into a carriage like a precious, breakable package and trundled along the London streets with her mother chattering about dance cards and eligible earls the entire way.

Her mother didn't seem to notice that Beatrice was silent as a tomb, perhaps mistaking her silence for awe at the transformation that had been accomplished, or even acquiescence to her mother's matrimonial aspirations.

She couldn't have been more wrong.

Beatrice spent the carriage ride running through the details of the plan she'd devised.

Her plan required subtle persuasive tactics, which had never been her strong suit, and strategic failure, which was something she excelled at.

If it worked, the plan would result in her mother allowing her to keep the bookshop, and sign it over to the league of ladies, and would allow Beatrice the freedom to inventory the crates of books and manuscripts at her leisure.

It would make these months in London infinitely more bearable if she could escape her mother for even a few hours every day. She might even complete some work on her dictionary in the sanctuary of the bookshop.

If her plan worked.

She was determined to make it work.

Upon arriving in the brightly lit ballroom that buzzed with conversation and laughter, Beatrice immediately set about accomplishing the strategic failure part of the plan. She insulted Mayhew's mother with an observation that she'd seen a similar centerpiece to the silver one on her refreshment table at the home of a grocer's wife, and trod upon the Duke of Marmont's toes as they danced. She managed to catch one of her diamond shoe clips on the Dowager Countess of Fletcher's hem, which ripped off a goodly portion of lace and caused an awkward scene.

Beatrice's conversation was alarmingly fast-paced and punctuated by nasally laughter that produced pained expressions from her dance partners. And the coup de grâce was accomplished when she managed to dip her enormous sleeves into the punch bowl, thereby staining the sheer fabric with a watery red splotch that wouldn't come out, no matter how hard her mother scrubbed at it in the lady's retiring room.

Her mother draped a lace shawl around Beatrice's shoulders and pinned it with a brooch, all the while pronouncing that it spoiled the effect of the bodice most egregiously.

Beatrice could barely restrain a self-satisfied chuckle. When would her mother reach her breaking point?

"My dance with Mayhew is at hand, Mama."

"I know," her mother said with a grim expression, grabbing Beatrice by the elbow and steering her, none too gently, toward a row of potted ferns.

"I thought I wasn't to hide behind the ferns, Mama."

"I want to speak with you. In private."

She must play this conversation perfectly. No tipping of her hand.

"Now listen to me, Beatrice." Her fingers tightened around her daughter's elbow. "Are you trying to humiliate me? When I said you needed to make more of an effort, I meant more of an effort at being agreeable and charming, *not* annoying and clumsy."

"I haven't read any books, or used one arcane word or mentioned my dictionary at all. I've danced with six eligible gentlemen of your choosing, and I've avoided the company of the timorous wallflowers hovering along the edges of the ballroom."

"You have followed all my rules but done so in a way that renders the rules meaningless."

"I'm sorry, Mama. I'm so distracted this evening. My mind is back at Castle's Bookshop with all of those glorious unopened crates of books."

Her mother gestured impatiently. "We'll have the crates brought to our house, though heaven knows where we'll keep more books. There are entirely too many books already."

"One can never have too many books, Mama. I didn't have time to do a thorough search of the premises—but there might be some very rare volumes that I wouldn't want just anyone handling—"

"Balls, Beatrice. Not books. Focus, please. You must at least pretend to be enjoying yourself while dancing with gentlemen."

"I can't enjoy myself when I'm worried I'll make the wrong step. I would be a more graceful and gracious dance partner if you would allow me to wear my spectacles. I have them in my reticule in the cloakroom."

"You don't need your spectacles. I'm here to guide you through the evening and into the arms of eligible gentlemen."

"It might help if I could actually see their faces instead of a blur with eyes. I might enjoy myself more."

"That matters not at all. Your duty is to smile and follow their lead. Men are looking for their own reflections. Always remember that, Beatrice. They want to see their strength, wit, and power reflected in your eyes."

Don't be beastly, Beatrice.

Smile. Be congenial. Hide your true nature. Be a mirror for others' glory. "Don't be difficult," said her mother.

"I'm not being difficult, I'm only distracted by the thought of all of those ancient manuscripts languishing in wooden crates and threatened by damp floorboards."

"Your father told me that there was some scandal attached to the bookshop though he would never tell me the specifics. If this buried scandal comes to light, I don't want it reflecting poorly on your reputation."

"It won't, Mama. I've decided to sign over the bookshop to the Knitting League, as our new clubhouse. If any scandal comes to light, it will be associated with our president, the Duchess of Ravenwood."

"I daresay duchesses are more able to weather scandal. Especially Ravenwood, since her reputation wasn't exactly spotless to begin with. But what of our solicitor? I told Greenaway to sell the property."

"No papers have been signed." Beatrice made her face as bland as possible. This next move was where the subtlety came into play. "You know, Mama, it might be easier to enter more fully into the spirit of these entertainments if I were allowed to explore my new inheritance."

Her mother searched her face. "I see. So that's what this is all about. I can garb you in finery, dress your hair in the latest fashion but I can't force you to be sociable, is that it?"

"Your words, Mama. Not mine."

"You want to strike a bargain."

"A bargain?"

"Don't act so innocent. You know that's what you're hinting at. You want to spend time in that dusty old bookshop, and if I let you do that, then you'll make more of an effort. Very well. What will it take, Beatrice? One hour a day? Two?"

Beatrice dropped the idea of subtlety. Her mother was far too perceptive, as well as being the master of bargaining.

"If you grant me two hours a day at the bookshop, I promise to be the most sweet-tempered and congenial lady in the room on every social call, at every ball, soiree, and musicale."

"Ha! I'll believe that when I see it."

"Try me, Mama. See how I sparkle. See how proud I make you."

The first notes of the waltz drifted into her ears. She was to dance with Mayhew, her mother's chosen target. The stakes were high . . . would she agree?

Her mother held her gaze for several more seconds, before heaving a decidedly un-duchess-like sigh. "Oh, very well. You win, Beatrice. When your schedule permits, you may spend a few hours going through those dusty crates of books. With adequate chaperonage, of course."

"Of course," Beatrice agreed eagerly. "There's a housekeeper, a Mrs. Kettle, a most motherly matron, who is present most days."

"The shop is closed I presume?"

"Closed and kept locked."

"You'll take one of our carriages, and the coachman will wait for you outside."

"Agreed." Beatrice couldn't believe her plan was actually working. "I won't disappoint you, Mama."

"Now is your chance to prove yourself. Go and dance with Mayhew." She practically shoved her out from behind the ferns.

Beatrice was prepared to dazzle now that she'd accomplished her goal.

Soon she was gliding across the floor in the arms of the golden-haired Earl of Mayhew. She remembered her mother's instructions and stared vacantly up at him, smiling sweetly and allowing him to control her every movement.

He blathered and blustered on and on about himself, and all she had to do was supply fresh subjects for his soliloquies, such as the bloodlines of his stables, his legendary prowess at sports and hunting, and his castle in Herefordshire.

His increasingly warm manner and attentions made it plain that if she played her cards right, she might very well have a chance at the unfathomable honor of becoming the Countess of Mayhew.

It would be one avenue away from her dear, well-meaning, overbearingly smothering mother.

No, it wouldn't. Not really.

As Lady Mayhew, she'd be expected to entertain, to fulfill her role as a society doyen, to turn a blind eye to her husband's indiscretions while maintaining a blameless reputation.

A whole new set of rules and expectations and social obligations would descend on her like a plague of locusts, eating away at her spirit and her dreams.

She'd seen it happen to girls who made advantageous marriages against their wishes. She'd seen the desperation in their eyes, the curtailment of any freedoms, the dulling of conversation and stilting of movements. She'd witnessed her own parents' marriage.

A marriage of social convenience where her mother gave up all of her own needs and desires in order to service her demanding and dismissive husband.

All Mayhew cared about was himself—all he wanted was the use of her more than generous dowry, and a meek, docile pool in which to view, like Narcissus, his own reflection.

After the dance, Mayhew delivered her back to her mother. "Lady Beatrice, I hope you will do me the honor of standing up with me again later in the evening?"

"I'd be most honored, my lord," replied Beatrice, with a pretty curtsy that made her mother smile brighter than the flickering candles.

Beatrice was swept into the arms of another eligible gentleman, and her mother gathered with her friends to gossip about the evening's developments.

Toward the end of the evening, Lady Millicent Granger, Beatrice's sworn enemy, arrived by her side as she stood for a moment, catching her breath after all the dancing.

"A few new feathers do not a swan make," said Lady Millicent in an undertone, maintaining a beatific expression on her lovely face. "You'll always be—"

"Beastly," said Beatrice, cutting her off. "So you've maintained all of these years since finishing school. One does wonder why, over the years, you couldn't think of more varied ways to insult me. I could suggest a plethora of more inventive invectives, should you be interested in expanding your vocabulary."

"As outlandish as ever, I see." Lady Millicent got to the point. "Mayhew is mine. Don't think that you can entice him with your dowry and your new French gowns."

"I don't see a ring on your finger." Beatrice didn't mind if Lady Millicent believed her pretense, though she had no intention of stealing her prize earl.

Her mother swooped in to rescue her from Lady Millicent, and they left the ball shortly thereafter.

"You were remarkably successful tonight, after our little chat, but it's better not to push our luck." Her mother hurried her into the carriage. "We'll keep your appearances brief. We'll leave them wanting more. I knew this was your year, Beatrice. I felt it. What did Lady Millicent want?"

"To warn me away from Mayhew."

Her mother settled into the carriage and wrapped her fur-trimmed cloak around her shoulders. "I was beginning to doubt you had the fortitude for this battle, and here you are becoming a triumph before my very eyes."

"I will try, Mama."

She had the fortitude. She'd do whatever it took to keep the shop and transform it into a clubhouse. Her aunt's legacy, and the wonderful collection of books that could be kept as a library for the use of club members, would be put to a worthy purpose. She wouldn't let anyone stand in the way of this dream. Not her mother, and certainly not predatory Mr. Foxton.

This time, the wallflowers were going to win.

Chapter Nine

"Do you ever think about it, Griff?" Ford didn't have to say what *it* was. His old navy friend Griffith knew. He'd been there.

"Course I do." Griffith continued coiling rope. They were on the deck of his fishing vessel, the *Angela*. Griff, as his friends knew him, was a grizzled old salt with deep lines grooved into his cheeks, a shock of untamed white hair, and an even wilder look in his piercing blue eyes. He'd retired from the navy a year ago and now fished for a living.

"Sometimes I can't sleep thinking about it," Ford said.

"That's when you find company to take your mind off things. If your body's too tired from bed sport, your mind can't betray you."

Ford stopped sanding the deck boards. "Haven't had much company lately."

"Problem with the flagpole, lad?"

"My pole's just fine. It's my mind that drags down."

"Happens sometimes."

They worked silently on their respective tasks. It was a cold, sunny day. Gulls wheeled overhead and sun shone on the back of his neck as he sanded the decking he'd replaced. Ford hadn't boarded a ship in six months. He'd missed the water . . . and he'd feared it.

"Why'd you never marry, Griff?"

His friend tied a bowline knot. "Never met the woman who could tie the Griffster down, though many have tried. Had a

sweetheart once, a feisty little brunette in Bristol with the round-
est, bounciest bum you ever did see."

"What happened to her?"

"Married my best friend while I was at sea."

"Oof." Ford bent back to his task of sanding the splinters from
the deck. The monotonous chore used the strength of his arms
but left his mind free to worry over events from his past.

"What'd they die for, Griff? Young Sal. Bent-nose Billy. Pretty
Tom. I can still hear Tom singing 'The Foggy, Foggy Dew' sometimes."

"You heard them read the vice admiral's letter. 'They died in
the service of their country, and in the cause of suffering hu-
manity.' There you have it. King and country. Bloody honor and
glory."

He'd seen their coffins, perforated with holes and filled with
bags of wet sand to make them sink, laid into the water covered
by the Union Jack.

He'd watched the sea swallow them.

Their man-of-war had limped from Greece to Malta, no longer
proud and gallant, but battered and torn with shot. He'd patched
her as best he could with lead and pieces of plank.

Once Ford had been as gallant as that man-of-war, filled with
a righteous sense of destiny, but after that brutal, bloody battle
there'd been a hole shot through his heart for every one of the
friends he'd lost.

He felt the weight of their deaths as bags of sand tied to his soul
until the balance shifted, dragged him down, until his soul was
sodden with death, consumed by it.

"The action in Greece was bad. I'm not saying you're not
right to think about it," said Griff. "I'm only saying there's no
use dwelling on it—that only leads to the madhouse. You're still
young, and now you're moving up in the ranks. Likely the last
time I'll have you on my boat, eh? Once you're an officer you
won't have time for the likes of me. You'll turn up your nose and
look the other way."

"That'll never happen and you know it."

"You're a bloody war hero, Ford. You saved lives."

"I can't even remember it."

It was all a blur when he looked back. The booming of cannons. Smell of scorched flesh.

Screams of his friends.

Staunching the leaks. Staunching the blood.

"Well, I remember it." Griff finished another knot. "You damn well saved my tough old hide."

Ford ducked his head back to his work. He should be proud of what he'd done, but all he felt was emptiness, a sense of being lost at sea, adrift without an anchor.

For some reason he thought about Lady Beatrice crooning to her beloved books, telling them she'd patch the roof and give them a nice safe home. He'd been serious about helping her battle his grandfather and keep the bookshop. But it was for the best that she'd turned him down. His dreams had been filled with her again last night.

She'd been expanding his vocabulary, and he'd been instructing her in the pleasures of—

"Look lively, mate," Griff said, shading his eyes with his hand. "There's a lady here to see you."

"A laddie?"

"A *lady*. She's got one of 'em big shiny carriages waiting, and she's wearing one of 'em big showy bonnets with ribbons and feathers flying in the breeze. She's waving at me."

He knew only one lady who wore big bonnets trimmed with ribbons and feathers.

Lady Beatrice Bentley.

Ford clambered up from his knees. Sure enough, there she was, wearing an enormous straw bonnet with red ribbons flapping in the breeze and copper curls coiling down her neck.

His dream made flesh.

She was out of place on the docks, her rich satin cloak gleaming in the afternoon sun, proclaiming *here be pockets for the picking* to all and sundry.

When she caught sight of him she waved, her white glove like a seagull flying against the sky.

He waved back.

"Already keeping fancy company, I see." Griff elbowed him in the ribs.

"Shut up." Ford brushed off the knees of his trousers, grabbed his coat, and ran a hand through his hair.

"Going to leave me high and dry?"

"Possibly. The lady's in quite a predicament. She inherited an old bookshop and she needs a carpenter in the worst way."

"Needs rescuing, does she?"

"She's Thorndon's sister, so she can afford to pay me a lot more than you, you old salt."

"Oh ho—the duke's sister. Isn't he your father's employer? Never a good idea to mix business with pleasure."

"That's not it at all. It's a job, nothing more."

Griff shrugged. "I see the way you're looking at her. Like you want to find out what's under that cloak."

"She's not my type. Too snobbish. Always lecturing me about something. It's her coin I'm after, nothing more."

Another shrug. "If you say so, my lad. If you say so."

BEATRICE HIKED THE hem of her bell skirts (her mother would surely wonder if she arrived home smelling of rotting fish—which was *not* a pleasant smell she was discovering) and picked her way across the docks.

She'd wasted two precious days trying to find a carpenter but to no avail. She'd enlisted the help of Hobbs.

"It's the strangest thing, Lady Beatrice," Hobbs had told her. "When I mention Castle's Bookshop, every carpenter quickly offers excuses for why they're too busy to take the job."

Foxton had made good on his threats.

Beatrice was here to eat humble pie.

As loath as she was to admit it, Wright was her best, and possibly only, hope. He'd seen her waving and was disembarking the ship, heading across the dock.

The sky today had decided to be a cheerful blue after weeks of rain. Freshly laundered white clouds drifted happily over the boat masts. The cries of gulls mingled with shouts from sailors, shipwrights, and other tradespeople.

"Watch yourself, missus," a man pushing a cart piled high with crates shouted as he nearly collided with her.

The sonnet bonnet, while helpful in maintaining distance from passersby, sadly limited her scope of vision.

Her gray silk cloak had seemed a prudent choice for visiting ship's carpenters, the most subtle of the clothing her mother had insisted on ordering for her this Season, but here its richness was out of place, the fabric shimmering and calling attention to her.

Wright strode toward her, confident and imposing. His hair was tousled by the sea breeze, and there was an uneven line of dark whiskers accentuating his angular jaw that gave him an even more forceful air. Did he steal everyone's breath away, or just hers? She looked around the bustling docks. There weren't many females here. She was the only one, and she was drawing everyone's attention.

"Good day, Lady Beatrice. These workman's docks don't see the likes of you very often. You're today's entertainment. We could put that gigantic bonnet on the ground and collect a coin for every stare."

She swiveled her head. Several shipwrights had stopped working to ogle her. When he saw her watching him, one of the men waggled his eyebrows at her.

"That's quite some headgear," said Wright. "How do you make your way forward if you can't see what's coming on the sides?"

"I'm supposed to have someone at my elbow at all times guiding the way. A governess, a maid, a footman, a family member."

"And yet you're here all alone."

"My carriage is waiting. Will you come for a ride with me?" The fewer people who saw her here, the better. She was going far outside her mother's sphere of what was allowable conduct for a lady.

"Right now?"

"Yes, right now. We need to speak in private. There's not a moment to lose."

A hopeful expression filled his eyes. "Have you heard from the duke?"

"No, not yet. I came to say that you were right."

"What was that?" He cupped his hand over his ear. "I didn't hear you."

"I said that you were right. My brother may be a duke, but Foxton's reach is wide and his pockets deep. He owns law officers, judges, fire and safety inspectors, and he helps govern the Worshipful Company of Carpenters. I've no idea how he spread the word so swiftly. I had my butler inquire with several carpenters, and when the bookshop was mentioned they slammed the door in his face."

"So you're in need of rescuing, is that what you're saying?"

He was going to make this difficult for her.

"I could use your help," she admitted through gritted teeth. "No carpenter, joiner, or builder in London, even the apprentices, is willing to risk angering Foxton. He's too powerful. Are you still brave enough to take him on?"

He cocked his head. "That depends."

"On what?"

"The prize money. I collect prize money for every enemy ship captured—and every bookshop renovated into a clubhouse for lady knitters."

"We'll discuss terms on the way to the shop."

For the first time, Beatrice realized that they would be alone in the carriage. No matter. There would be no kissing—imaginary or otherwise—while she was wearing such a wide-brimmed rogue-deflecting bonnet.

"My mate on the *Angela*—"

"Will be handsomely remunerated. Get in the carriage, Wright. There are too many people staring at me."

"It's the bonnet."

"Just get in the blasted carriage!"

"Tut-tut, Lady Beatrice. Such language." His grin was filled with devilry. "I never enter carriages with strange ladies."

She glared at him. "You'll want to hear my offer, I assure you. I can't force you into the carriage but my footmen could."

"Am I being kidnapped?"

"Get. In. The. Carriage."

He laughed. "All right, all right. You win, princess."

Chapter Ten

FORD CLIMBED INTO the carriage after Lady Beatrice. "I'm not sure there's room enough for me *and* that bonnet."

"It's ridiculous, I know."

He settled onto the seat, and a servant closed the door behind him. The carriage had luxurious red leather upholstery.

He was facing Lady Beatrice, but he couldn't see much of her expression under the brim of her bonnet, especially when she had her head turned. She appeared to be studying a spot on the wall several inches above his head.

Ford made himself comfortable and spread his arm over the back of the seat as the carriage rolled away from the docks. "Let me guess, your mother made you wear that bonnet."

"She threw out all of my more sensible millinery when I was away from the house yesterday, leaving me only the fashionable ones."

"I don't like it. I can't see your eyes when I'm talking to you."

"I think that's the point. My mother wants to hide as much of my face as possible."

He leaned in, squinting at the large white and gray roses adorning the bonnet. "Are there words printed on those roses?"

"Unfortunately, yes."

He bent forward and touched one of the paper roses, flattening it enough to read the words. "'Love is not love which alters when it alteration finds.'"

"It's trimmed with Mr. Shakespeare's sonnets. A desecration I did not condone."

"Live a little. Spread your wings. Take a risk. Defy your mother and refuse to wear the bonnet."

"Spoken like a man who does as he pleases. You don't know my mother. It's easier to go along with the flow than to attempt a barricade against the tidal wave of her maternal ambitions. I allow her to dress me, make my social engagements, bring me to balls, but I don't give her the things that matter most to me. My work. My ambitions. My future."

"Does your mother know you're alone in a carriage with me, Lady Beatrice?"

A slight tremor of her lower lip. "Not specifically. She does know that I'm visiting the bookshop. And that there will be a carpenter hired to perform the repairs necessary for the property to become a clubhouse."

"So you found a way to gain her permission. Well done."

"I struck a bargain with her—two hours a day at the bookshop in exchange for following her social schedule and being docile, decorous, and congenial to every titled gentleman who deigns to speak with me. The bookshop will be a small taste of freedom. I plan to make the most of it."

"You know that if I'm working in the shop there will be noise, and debris, and all of the other items on your list of my sins."

"I know. But you said there was little damage to the upper floors. I will have the crates of books moved to the reading room."

"Did you tell your mother that you were engaging the services of the most good-looking carpenter in all of London?"

"I may have neglected to tell her that I was hiring the most conceited rogue in all the world."

"We haven't discussed the terms yet. I'm not sure you can afford me."

She made a little incredulous huffing noise. "I'm quite sure that I can."

"And how will you obtain the funds?"

"Name your price."

"A word to wise ladies—never tell a rogue to name his own price."

"I can afford to pay you handsomely."

"A rogue might ask for something other than money."

She must be blushing by now, though the damned bonnet hid half her face from him.

"If you're insinuating that you would ask for favors of an . . . an amorous nature, let's just nip that idea in the bud and never let it flower again. We both know that you would never do that so you can stop teasing."

"Those rumors of my honorable nature could have been exaggerated."

"I'm willing to take a gamble. I have firsthand knowledge of your skills and the speed with which you complete difficult renovations. You know me to be the sister of a duke, and therefore solvent enough to satisfy your most outrageous salary request. Which is . . . ?"

The lady wanted a business arrangement. Very well, he could keep things strictly professional, and profitable in the bargain. He named an outrageous sum of money, more than he would earn in two years at sea.

She swallowed. "That is acceptable." She didn't even try to bargain lower.

"You'd pay me that much?"

"It's a high salary, but there was a small inheritance included with the property, and I intend to sell the collection of bawdy books, anonymously of course. You'll be paid half up front, and the rest after you complete the work. That is if you're able to do so. You have less than a fortnight now."

The sum would put his dream of owning property within reach. There was nothing else to hesitate about. Save enough money to buy his own plot of land and become a thorn in his grandfather's side at the same time. It was irresistible. He'd always enjoyed a challenge, and working long and hard was nothing new.

"I accept."

"Very good. I would ask that you follow a few simple rules, the first being that you will refrain from calling me princess."

"Whatever you say, pr—Your Ladyship."

"And I would ask that we keep our working relationship dispassionate and professional."

"That's not a problem for me, if it's no problem for you."

"No mention of kisses, unforgettable or otherwise."

"I can control my lips if you can control yours, Your Ladyship."

"And you're to wear a coat at all times."

"Can't do that last one. Carpenters don't wear coats. We'd split the seams out of all of them."

"I want you to remain respectable if you're in my employ. My mother might decide to visit the shop."

"Most ladies enjoy the view."

"Will you listen to yourself?"

"I'm only speaking an established truth."

"This is serious, Wright. Foxton wants this property, and I have a feeling he'll stop at nothing to attempt to purchase, or steal it, away from me. I will rely on you to function as a sort of guard, as well. Will you move into the premises?"

"Happy to. It will be far more comfortable than the room I'm sharing with Tiny right now. The giant doesn't leave much space for me."

"You may use Aunt Matilda's room. It's the largest and most well-appointed."

"Those pink velvet bed hangings will have to go. Not very manly."

"Remove any furnishings you please, the décor will have to be completely redone when the property becomes a clubhouse. I'm determined to save the shop from Foxton's avaricious clutches, Mr. Wright. I believe that the world needs a clubhouse to support the goals of ladies far more than it requires another polluting factory."

"Hear, hear."

"I view Foxton as a symbol of every man who has ever stood in the way of female goals and ambitions. Every man who attempts to control us, cut us down to size, and take our property and our very freedom."

He couldn't argue with that. Foxton was a symbol to him, as well. The villain who had exiled his parents to the countryside and stolen their futures away.

Ford and his grandfather shared a name, and they shared a blood connection, but that was where any similarities ended. Foxton was obsessed with money and power to the exclusion of all else. He was a monster who valued gold more than his own family.

This was Ford's chance to set up a blockade in the path of his grandfather's ruthless ambitions. And he'd be helping freethinking lady knitters in the process.

And he'd be spending more time with Lady Beatrice. Just like he'd dreamed about.

The dreaming stopped now.

"I swear to you that I'll do whatever it takes to keep Foxton from stealing the bookshop from you," he promised.

He'd sworn to his mother that he'd never reveal his blood connection to Foxton and therefore he couldn't tell the lady that he also had a personal motive for accepting her offer. Let her think he'd taken it solely for profit, and for the good report she would give her brother of his work.

Ford had vowed to never have his life or his fate controlled or owned by any man . . . there were no rules about bookish ladies.

Why would he say no? This was easy money. He'd have comfortable accommodations, a housekeeper to prepare his meals, a large bankroll, and he'd be impeding his grandfather's plans.

It was a winning proposition all around.

And the offer came from an employer who was a damn sight more pulchritudinous than old Griff.

Though her allure was more of a warning bell than an incentive. He must keep his attraction to the lady firmly under control at all times. This was a straightforward business proposition.

A duke's sister wouldn't be allowed to spend too much time on the Strand. She'd be out most days hobnobbing with other highborn ladies and gentlemen.

What could go wrong? If she did visit the shop, he'd be working and she'd stay well away from him for fear of besmirching her costly silk gowns.

"I have a rule as well, Lady Beatrice."

"Oh?" She inclined her head.

"Absolutely no bonnets trimmed with sonnets."

A faint smile hovered at her lips. "I'll never wear it again, Mr. Wright."

"You could never see it again, if you chose. What if a strong gust of wind blew it off your head? Then it wouldn't be your fault if it disappeared."

"My mother's choice of millinery, like her aspiration for my future, is bound tightly by stout ribbons and stifling social conventions."

"What if your maid had left the ribbons only loosely tied and they slipped undone through no fault of your own?"

He caught the edge of one rosy silk ribbon between his thumb and forefinger and tugged steadily until the bow beneath her chin came loose.

Chapter Eleven

$\mathcal{B}$EATRICE'S BREATH CAUGHT as he loosened her bonnet ribbons. If he removed her bonnet, there would be no barriers left between them.

Would that be so very terrible?

He untied the red silk ribbons until they hung freely down her neck and over her bosom.

She closed her eyes. She couldn't see much anyway because, predictably, her spectacles had gone murky, whether from his breath or hers. He was very near. Within kissing distance.

She'd just made him promise to never mention the subject of kissing.

You didn't say anything about actual kisses, you dolt.

The carriage lurched to a halt.

She was saved.

When they alighted, Wright lifted a finger to the air. "What a strong breeze there is today."

Before she knew what was happening, he'd plucked her bonnet off her head and flung it into the avenue, where it cartwheeled for a moment until it was squashed flat by carriage wheels.

She stared at him, openmouthed. "I can't believe you just did that."

"We agreed to follow the rules."

"Are you going to destroy articles of my clothing every time we meet?"

"Quite possibly. If you come to the bookshop while I'm working you'll encounter dust, debris, water . . . probably some rats I flush out of the basement. It might be best for you to stay away, at least for the first few days."

"Trying to be rid of me already. I'm only here for another half hour. I've used most of my allotment of hours. The coachman will wait for me here." She used her key this time to let them into the building.

They were met by a gloomy Coggins and a chipper offer of hot tea from Mrs. Kettle, which they politely declined.

Wright entered the front room. "I'll start bringing the crates upstairs. Where should I leave them?"

"You can place them in the reading room adjacent to the first-floor landing."

He stacked two crates, lifted the heavy load, and disappeared into the hallway.

Beatrice examined the titles on the shelves. She'd have to move the most ancient and rare volumes upstairs to the reading room, to protect them from Wright's dust and destruction. The remainder of the books would need to be covered with cloths.

Excitement bubbled up in her chest, giddy and sweet.

She owned these volumes. She owned this building.

She wasn't going to let anyone take this newborn freedom away from her.

WHEN FORD RETURNED downstairs, Lady Beatrice was still there. He'd assumed she'd be gone by now. He'd loitered upstairs for at least a quarter hour, stacking and restacking crates, and giving himself a stern talking-to about the divestment of bonnets from highborn ladies whose brothers held the fate of one's family in their hands.

The devil had made him do it. And the sight of her red hair radiant in the sunlight had been worth risking the fires of hell.

Not only was she still here, she was in the process of removing more articles of clothing.

The fire in the grate was doing an admirable job of heating the small room, but did she have to disrobe if she was only staying a few more minutes?

Ford nearly sprinted back upstairs, but he had a job to do. Crates to carry. No time to waste.

He'd simply have to ignore the lady, and the languid way she undid her smart blue coat. Button after brass button, fabric parting to reveal the lovely, and extremely impractical gown beneath. It was pale pink, with large puffed sleeves that ended in silk bows at her elbows, tied so tightly that he could see the mark they made on her skin.

Her elbow-length white gloves came off next.

As he repacked crates and stacked them together, he watched her from the corner of his eye. Why did it take so devilishly long to remove gloves? Each luminescent pearl button gave way to her fingers in a slow, tantalizing revealing of flesh.

She tugged one glove all the way off and draped it over her shoulder while she worked on the second one. The discarded glove dangled down her back, where his fingers wanted to roam.

Over her delicate shoulder blades, along the ridge of her spine, down to the sweet curve of her . . .

None of that. Lift some heavy crates and climb those steep stairs again in penance for forbidden thoughts.

When he returned, she was standing by the bookshelves with a dusty volume in her hands, her face rapturous as she turned pages.

"Are you inventorying or reading?" he asked.

"Just a few more pages," she murmured. "And then I'll go."

Why did fancy ladies cover up their hands and leave their chests so exposed? He approved of this bodice. It was edged in darker pink ribbon that might even match her . . .

Don't picture her nipples.

He groaned aloud.

"Is anything the matter?" she asked, glancing up from her book.

"Nothing," he muttered. He lifted more crates.

"What will you require for the renovations?" she asked him when he returned from his last trip.

"A full set of carpentry tools. Ladders. Oak floorboards to replace the damaged ones I remove."

She jotted it all down with a pencil and notepad she'd pulled from her bag. "Hobbs will have everything delivered tomorrow morning. I probably won't be able to come myself. I have a lamentably full schedule tomorrow."

"That's for the best. It will be chaos in this room when I knock out the wall between the showroom and the side parlor. This is no place for young ladies wearing costly finery. You wouldn't want to dirty your fine frock. And those flimsy slippers wouldn't protect your toes from much of anything."

"I quite agree. These heeled slippers make my ankles wobble precariously. I always wore sturdy footwear in Cornwall. The next time I visit the bookshop, I'll wear something more practical, I promise."

The next time she visited? He'd thought she'd give him a wide berth in the short time he had to complete the demanding job. "It might be best if you stayed away from the shop while I do the worst of the demolition and repairs."

"Ah . . . but you never let me have a moment's worth of peace in the library in Cornwall. Why should I humor you now?"

"This is an entirely different situation. You're the one employing me, and I'll finish more swiftly if I'm allowed to work unimpeded."

The last thing Ford needed when he was trying to finish a project swiftly was a privileged, opinionated lady telling him what to do, attempting to help, and making everything more difficult.

"Now you know how I felt in Cornwall, Wright. I'm sorry if my presence will incommode you but I bargained with my mother for the chance to escape her ministrations and spend time in the relative freedom of this shop, and I plan to be here as often as possible. I'll do my best not to disturb you."

If she kept removing her clothing in that unintentionally sensual way, there was small chance of that.

"Who knows? I might even be of use to you in your endeavors, Mr. Wright. I may not be broad of shoulder, but I know my mind to be a formidable tool. I shall read a reference book on the subject of carpentry and form my own opinions on the most efficacious and efficient methods for the swift transmogrification of this shop."

That sounded ominous. "How about if I don't tell you how to write a dictionary if you don't tell me how to carpenter."

"But you *did* tell me how to write a dictionary, don't you remember? You said it wouldn't be profitable unless it was fun."

Ford and his big mouth. "I was only joking."

"My friends agreed with you, and so there may be some merit to what you said. It's true that Samuel Johnson infused humor into his *Dictionary of the English Language*. For example, he defined a lexicographer as a 'harmless drudge that busies himself in tracing the original and detailing the signification of words.' It was his sly moments of humor that made his dictionary a success."

"I don't know anything about Samuel Johnson, but it's true that everything's better with laughter."

"I also find it interesting that your critique of my dictionary was based not on its unsuitability as a female pursuit, but on its lack of humor. Most people, my mother chief and foremost, belittle and criticize my endeavor on more conventional grounds."

"I don't see why females shouldn't write dictionaries. But I also don't see why they shouldn't write dictionaries that might make them some profit in the process."

She gave a sharp little nod. "Agreed."

"Just because you're taking my advice doesn't mean that I welcome your thoughts on carpentry. I have less than a fortnight and I know exactly how to accomplish what needs to be done. I won't require your help."

She shrugged. "Very well. But I'll still be here as often as possible to inventory the books and escape my mother."

She went back to perusing the bookshelves and he began examining the shop counter, to see how it was constructed.

She stole glances at him from under her lashes. Just as it had in Cornwall, her gaze made him want to impress her with his brute strength. He lifted a heavy oak lectern and moved it into the corner of the room. He'd have to move all the furniture out of the way when he knocked down the wall to enlarge the room.

She selected a book and curled up in a chair, tucking her feet underneath her. He imagined that was how she spent a good part of her days, and evenings, when her mother wasn't pushing her into society.

"I nearly forgot—I brought you this." She opened her silk handbag and pulled out a book. "It's the second in the Villeneuve series after *The Mad Marquess's Secret*. It's called *The Wicked Earl's Wishes*. I thought you might like to read this one since you appeared to enjoy the first in the series."

"It had its moments. Though I won't have time for reading."

"Keep it by your bedside. I have several copies so you needn't finish it before you leave London."

He accepted the book and it immediately fell open to a location about halfway through. He closed and opened it again. "Curious. It opens at the same place every time. Could this be your favorite scene?" He skimmed the page until he found what he was looking for. " 'Fair reader, the Earl of Wrothmore was a most wicked and profligate rogue, but when he kissed me there was nothing I could do but succumb to his embrace, for I craved the taste of his lips in much the same way as—' "

She snatched the book out of his hands. "The binding must have become damaged."

He held out his palm. "It was just getting good. I want to know what happens next."

"You can't start in the middle."

"I would never do such a thing."

She handed the book back. "I love Miss Villeneuve's stories, but the heroine in this one borders on too silly to live. She walks right into the devious snares set for her by the wicked earl."

"It sounded to me like she was enjoying their entanglement. And if there weren't any snares, there wouldn't be much of a plot. It would all be kissing."

"A subject we agreed to refrain from mentioning."

"I didn't mention it, I read it in your book, in your favorite chapter."

"Humph."

The clock in the hallway chimed and she startled. "I'm late. I must go. I'll have your supplies delivered tomorrow."

She grabbed her coat and gloves and ran for the door. She paused and turned back, her face lit by a smile. "Thank you, Mr. Wright."

Ford hadn't known he'd been waiting for her smile until that lopsided quirk of her lips caught his heart unawares and lifted it like a sail in a brisk headwind.

Chapter Twelve

ক 🌹 ক

BEATRICE HAD BEEN attempting to return to the bookshop for two days, but her mother had kept her trotting from one social engagement to the next, trailed by maids and modistes to refresh her appearance between engagements.

She was heartily sick of society and beyond ready for an afternoon of books and freedom.

When she finally managed to steal a few hours at the bookshop, a more than usually morose Coggins greeted her at the door.

"That carpenter you hired is smashing everything to pieces." Coggins took her bonnet and cloak.

The noise was deafening. "What's he doing in there?"

"Bringing the house down around our ears, that's what. We'll all be crushed and then that will be the end of us. All they'll find in the wreckage is some shattered china and my old bones."

"Where's Mrs. Kettle?"

"At her daughter's house. Wednesday's her off day."

The front room was utter chaos. The counter had already been reduced to splinters. Wright wielded a large hammer with both hands like Thor on the battlefield, smashing it against the inner wall that separated the showroom from the small side parlor. He'd already opened a huge jagged hole in the center of the wall.

Beatrice clapped her hands over her ears. "Wright!" she shouted, but he couldn't hear her.

He continued his demolition, heaving the blunt-edged hammer behind him and crashing it into the wall. Plaster and small slats of wood broke under the force of his blows. He could probably give the gentlemen she knew a run for their money on the cricket field. He'd knock the ball clear out of the green.

He'd thrown cloths over the bookshelves, but it wasn't nearly enough protection. He did everything hard and fast without consulting anyone but himself.

Crash!

One of the cloths slid off a shelf and books danced as if they'd come to life. A volume tumbled from the shelf and landed on the floor in a disarray that would be murderous to its binding.

There were fragile and ancient books in that collection. She had to make him stop hammering long enough for her to cover the books more securely. This was her house, and he must consult her on these matters.

"Wright!" she shouted.

He was too focused and intent on his task to hear her. She'd have to venture closer, to the hammer . . . and the rogue.

She was near enough to reach out and touch him, but he was still unaware of her presence.

She was fully aware of all six foot and more of him. Damp white linen clung to his arms and chest. Dark brown hair curled against his wide neck, and the muscles of his shoulders strained and bulged with every swing of his hammer.

"You should put more cloths on the books," she yelled. And while he was at it, he could wear more cloth himself instead of attacking her good sense with such a mouthwatering display of muscularity.

He paused midswing and spun around, hammer raised, chest heaving. "What?"

She could see that he had cotton stuffed into his ears to block out the noise. She pointed at the bookshelves. "More protection!"

"Already patched the leak in the ceiling and that was the real danger. Stand back now." He raised his hammer.

She grabbed hold of his solid biceps with both of her hands, physically stopping him from swinging. Too late, she realized the inadvisability of touching him.

The shock of contact lanced through her body, reaching her heart and setting it racing.

He looked down at her with a bemused expression.

She dropped her hands.

He was dirty—not just around the edges, ragged fingernails, and such. He was *really* filthy. Covered in dirt and plaster dust. Smudges across his cheek. He smelled like sweat and earth.

The men of her acquaintance smelled of hair pomade and brandy.

If he laid his hands on her, he'd leave dirty prints on the pale yellow gown her mother had chosen for her to wear today.

How would she explain *that*?

Still, she wasn't going to give an inch, even if he was holding an enormous hammer and towered over her like Vulcan in his forge.

He lowered the hammer to the floor and removed the cotton from his ears. "The books are adequately protected. It's you who looks the worse for wear. What's wrong, Lady Beatrice? Why such a cross expression?"

Blast. He was too perceptive. "Nothing. I'm fine."

"Then I still have half a wall to pulverize after which there will be a pint of ale with my name on it waiting for me at a dockside tavern."

"It's this dratted bargain with my mother." Beatrice's shoulders slumped. "It's working too well. It turns out that all I have to do is pretend to be someone else and suddenly everybody loves me."

For some reason admitting that brought her perilously close to tears.

For the past two days, she hadn't been herself at all. She'd been playing a role, and here she was in a space that was entirely free from her mother and the weight of all that pretending had crashed into her chest, just like Wright's hammer into plaster.

"So you're not a wallflower anymore."

"Regrettably. I preferred reading books behind the potted ferns. I hate being the center of attention."

"Why is that?" He regarded her steadily, his question asked in earnest, as if he truly wanted to know the answer.

She'd noticed that about him. When he asked her a question, he was genuinely interested in her response. There was nothing blasé or disinterested about him.

She was accustomed to speaking with wealthy lords and beautiful ladies who always appeared to be looking for someone more interesting to talk to.

Wright's conversation, while teasing and often infuriating, was directed wholly at her, and he listened to her when she talked. He was right there with her, not waiting for something better to come along.

It made her want to tell him the truth.

"The Earl of Mayhew is taking an interest in me when he never even knew I existed before now." She scuffed the toe of her boot against a pile of plaster chunks. "We'll be together at the opera house tonight, and I'll have to pretend to hang on his every vainglorious word. The entire world revolves around him, to hear him tell it. I have to listen to his self-aggrandizing stories and pretend to enjoy them because of the bargain I made with my mother, and I loathe myself every second I'm with him. I can't believe my mother wants me to marry the man."

A shadow passed across his face, or maybe it was just a smudge of dirt she hadn't noticed before.

"I've come here to escape lecturing mothers and pompous earls, if only for a few hours."

"Here." He held the wooden handle of the hammer toward her. "Take a swing. It'll make you feel better."

"I can't lift such a heavy hammer, I'm too small."

"You can lift a sledgehammer and you can swing it. Trust me."

He lifted her hand and wrapped it around the handle of the hammer. A tremor began in her belly like the fronds of an ostrich feather waving atop a bonnet.

He wrapped her other hand over the top until she held the hammer with both hands. It was warm from his touch and solid in her grip.

He moved behind her and his arms bracketed her elbows,

positioning her grip lower on the hammer. "Widen your stance. Bend your knees slightly."

Now she really wouldn't be able to lift it—not with his arms hugging her and turning her knees to jelly.

He removed her spectacles and set them high on a nearby shelf. "You don't need these. It's a large target and I wouldn't want your spectacles to fly off and be damaged."

He stepped away. "Now, aim for the wall."

She swung the hammer at the wall and only made the smallest of dents.

"Is that all you've got? You won't achieve much if you hit like a lady."

Like a lady.

She'd been behaving like a docile and decorous lady for three days now, and she was sick to death of the deception. She hefted the hammer and heaved with all her might. A chunk of plaster flew into the air on the other side of the large gash in the wall.

If her mother could see her now, her mouth would gape open. *Lady Beatrice, wielding a hammer is not a suitable activity for a lady. You'll damage your gown. You'll damage your reputation.*

"I don't care," Beatrice said aloud, answering the voice in her head. "I don't care about my reputation." She swung with everything in her soul. A larger chunk of plaster disintegrated beneath the blunt iron of the hammer.

"I'm not docile, or decorous, or obliging." With each word she blasted the wall.

"That's better. Now you've got the swing of it," Wright said.

Sweat dripped down the back of her gown. It would be ruined but she didn't care. All she wanted to do was obliterate her mother's voice in her mind. Drown it out forever.

"I'm Beastly Beatrice." She slammed the hammer into the wall again and again. The hole grew bigger. She blew her hair away from her forehead and redoubled her efforts. "I hate balls." She smashed another chunk. "And ball gowns. And puffed-up pillocks of earls."

"That's right. Break free and live a little!"

She raised the hammer again, pretending that she was one of the mighty Amazon warrior princesses that the Duchess of Ravenwood had given a lecture about to the League, and brought it down so forcefully that she stumbled backward.

He folded his arms around her, taking some of the weight of the hammer in his hands. "Easy there, tiger."

"I'm not a well-behaved lady," she said forcefully. "I'm prickly, bookish Beatrice."

"My friends call me Ford," he said, his voice rumbling low in her ears.

She rested against his solid chest. Were they friends now? They were certainly in intimate proximity. "I find that I like hammering, Ford. It's very freeing, isn't it?"

"Try doing it for a whole day. You might think otherwise. But, yes, smashing things can be liberating. That's why I gave you the hammer."

Did he know what his touch did to her? His breath tickling her neck, his arms around her. The heavy hard hammer in her hands and the large solid man behind her, cradling her gently.

Her breath coming in gasps from the exertion and from his nearness. She wasn't thinking anymore, only feeling.

The excited, hopeful feeling returned, fizzing in her chest like bubbles rising in a glass of champagne.

The joy of his solid arms around her, encouraging her to bring the walls down and do something for herself. Something to break away from her mother's control.

He smelled like sweat and the chalk-scent of plaster, with an underlying hint of evergreen cedar, like the scent of the hope chest that contained her wedding trousseau.

She'd watched him working, so strong and so free, and she'd wanted to possess that confidence, nurture it in her own heart.

All summer long she'd dreamed of kissing this man. She'd been thinking about kissing him for so long—her whole life, it seemed.

She'd seen him as an object, as a beautiful sculpture, bursting with muscles, bursting with life. Something completely beyond her reach, beyond her window, behind glass and at a distance.

He was within her reach now. He was right here, holding her, urging her to live a little.

She wanted to live *a lot*.

And so she dropped the hammer, turned to face him, and plastered her lips to his.

Chapter Thirteen

ONLY . . . HE DIPPED his head at the same time she was reaching for him, and so she missed his lips and planted a kiss on his nose instead.

Yes. She, Beatrice Bentley, imaginer of extraordinary kisses, completely missed the mark and smacked her lips against his nostril.

It was definitely one of the more humiliating attempts in the history of kisses. What had she been thinking?

The answer to that question was that she hadn't been thinking at all. She'd allowed herself to be carried away by his strong arms and his exhortations to do something unladylike.

She squirmed with embarrassment, attempting to extricate herself from his grasp, but he held her firmly about the arms.

"What was that?" he asked, his blue-and-gold eyes all confusion.

"Never mind what it was, I was . . . mistaken. I'm going to go upstairs now."

"Did you just try to kiss me?"

She struggled to free herself. "I was carried away with lifting hammers and smashing down barriers and I . . . I . . . oh."

Her last words were swallowed up by his lips descending and claiming hers in a kiss so devoid of awkwardness that it melted her knees like sealing wax.

His lips were gentle, yet firm, as he folded her more forcefully into his embrace, kissing her with sensual skill.

Here was the sunrise she'd imagined, her body heating from the inside out, the warmth spreading along unfamiliar routes: from the pit of her belly to the peaks of her breasts, and from the corners of her lips down her limbs to the tips of her toes.

Warm in strange places and cold in others. Her hands were cold. She had to warm them against his chest, slip them under his shirt collar to feel the beating of his heart.

He held her as if he'd never let her go, kissing her so long and so well that all of the clocks in England must have frozen, for time had stopped.

It was sweet, so very sweet.

And then it became something less controlled, something more wild than sweet.

His tongue slid along the edge of her lower lip, nudging her to open her mouth. He slipped his tongue inside her mouth and the warm places in her body caught fire, blazing into new awareness.

His hands reached for her hips and pulled her flush against him.

Kissing him was everything she'd imagined it to be and more. She wanted more.

He broke away and put her at arm's length. "Now you can go upstairs."

"Oh. Er." She dropped her gaze to his boots. "Yes, quite. Upstairs." Where she had crates to open and new words and worlds to discover.

"Now that you've been properly kissed, you'll be forced to concede that kisses are far more scintillating than archaic words."

Was that all this had been? A rogue proving a point, nothing more. "Ha!" She knew her smile was wobbly, but she couldn't let him see how shaken she was by the kiss. "I'll concede nothing of the sort."

He gave her a smoldering look. "Then you want more kissing? I thought I'd been hired to make renovations, but if it's kissing you want . . ."

"No, no, it's renovations, nothing more. Carry on, Wright." She waved her hand at the wall and backed away swiftly. Too swiftly. She stumbled against a chair and nearly toppled to the floor.

He was at her side in seconds, spectacles in hand. "You might need these."

"Thank you," she said briskly, donning her spectacles and clinging to the shreds of her dignity. "About what just happened . . ."

"Nothing happened. I was proving a point."

"Precisely." She laughed, but it sounded hollow and forced. "It didn't mean anything. It was merely a question mark and there's nothing left to discover. Full stop. Carry on with the renovations. You're doing God's work. Helping bookish ladies and bluestockings for decades to come."

She made an awkward exit and hurried upstairs.

Inside the reading room she inhaled deeply of the scent of scholarly tomes and unfinished dictionaries.

What in heaven's name was the matter with her? Here she was surrounded by a carefully curated selection of ancient manuscripts and books, and all she could think about was kissing Ford, when she should be reveling in the freedom to be as scholarly as she pleased.

She also meant to reexamine her aunt's letter. She felt certain that there was a hidden meaning she hadn't uncovered yet. Her aunt had been trying to tell her something about her inheritance.

Ford. She tasted his name on her tongue. The Old English noun meant a shallow place where water could be crossed. Used as a verb, if one forded a river, one crossed a body of water by walking along the bottom.

Either way, the diminutive of his name denoted a passage, a crossing from one shore to another.

A transition.

She knew what his name meant, but what had the kiss meant? When presented with an unfamiliar word, Beatrice always broke it down into small increments, searching for the Latin, French, Greek, Old English, or Germanic roots in order to piece together an educated guess as to the meaning.

She had no educated guess about what the kiss had meant. It hadn't been a frivolous or meaningless moment for her.

It had been a whole new vocabulary. A new language.

And it meant nothing to him. He kissed women all the time.

These alarming sparks of desire that he ignited in her were wholly uncharacteristic and should be dealt with immediately. She couldn't ignore them, because they kept returning, growing stronger and more heated every time they met. She must deliberately stamp them out, douse them with cold water, until all that remained was a lingering scent of smoke.

There could never be a conflagration.

FORD FELT LIKE smashing something so it was a good thing he had a sledgehammer in his hands and a wall to bring down.

What the bloody hell had just happened?

He'd never meant to kiss her. Yes, he'd been thinking about kissing her, but he was always thinking about that when she was around. She was such an alluring combination of primness and passion.

Tension coiled in his body. Desire. The memory of her soft backside against his groin. The way she'd turned in his arms and tried to kiss him.

She was just so damned tempting. He kept catching these glimpses of the sensual woman beneath her proper facade. Today he'd caught more than a glimpse. He'd seen her hammering down walls like a warrior princess.

He'd liked that glimpse of her power.

He liked the lady far too much.

She was this creature fashioned from silk and lace and ambition. A lady whose determination bolstered a soaring intellect, like a flying buttress supporting the spires of a cathedral.

He was a man who swung a hammer.

They were from disparate worlds. Kissing was off limits. Anything beyond kissing was never even to be imagined.

He'd given her the hammer as a way for her to vent some frustration.

And then she'd kissed him. Her kiss had been surprising, inexpert, and electrifying.

All it had taken was one application of her soft pink lips and she'd obliterated his restraint.

He swung the hammer so hard that plaster flew against the far wall.

She was a highborn lady, sister to a duke.

A duke whose good opinion and trust he required. Giving in to the desire to kiss her back had been wrong. And bad.

Bad and wrong and . . . glorious.

He dismantled the wall blow by blow, stopping only to wipe dust out of his eyes. When it was finished, he scrubbed his fist across his brow.

Stick to the plan. It was simple enough. He fixed up her property and left England on his new ship, knowing that he'd not only obstructed his grandfather's plans, but had made enough money to purchase a plot of land in the process.

When she got under his skin, he'd have to work harder to keep her out. And if she ever kissed him again, he'd remember all of the reasons why intimacy with the duke's sister was forbidden.

No more untying of ribbons and removing of bonnets.

No more holding of sledgehammers.

He'd like to show her how to hold other hard, solid things.

Mother of God . . . he needed a drink. The wall was gone, only jagged edges remained, rather like his state of mind.

He'd accomplished enough for the day. It would be best if he were gone when she came back downstairs.

"I COULD USE a pint. Or three." Ford settled onto a stool next to Griff at the Captain's Choice pub near the docks.

Griff caught the barmaid's eye and gestured toward Ford with his head. "Not going so well with your new employer? Should have stuck with me, lad. I may not be pretty, but I'm far less complicated and less likely to work you into knots."

There would be less peril involved in working for his old friend. They'd work hard until the task was complete, and then go out drinking.

End of story.

"I taught Beatrice how to use a sledgehammer today."

Griff nearly snorted ale through his nose. He wiped away the foam coating his bristly white whiskers. "Did you now? And did she enjoy holding your hammer?"

"Not *that* kind of hammer."

"What happened to the lady?"

"She smashed some plaster."

"No, I mean what happened to *Lady* Beatrice. Holding your hammer made her your special friend?"

Ford gulped his ale. Griff didn't miss a trick. "Not exactly."

They'd shared only one very long and scorching hot kiss.

He gazed into his mug, and all he saw was the moment when she'd pressed up against him and he'd nearly lost his damned mind with longing.

"Something happened. I can tell." Griff sipped his beer. "You've a guilty, tortured look on your face."

Ford swallowed half his ale in one long swig.

"Out with it," said Griff.

"We kissed."

"Oh ho! Gave her a good tongue lashing, did you, lad?"

"She kissed me first. I know." He hung his head. "That's no excuse. She's the duke's sister. I have to talk to him about the embezzlement on his estate—I don't want my father being blamed for timber going missing or profits disappearing. The last thing I need is for the duke to catch drift of me kissing his pampered sister. I'm an idiot."

"A blithering bilge-drinking lug-headed idiot. Next you'll be falling in love with the lass. Ahoy, Peg! Bring my friend another one to set his head on straight."

The buxom barmaid poured another for Ford, giving him a flirtatious smile along with the ale.

"I'm not falling in love with her." Ford pounded the ale and slammed his glass on the bar top. "Love is a choice, not an uncontrollable slide. There's no falling happening here. I'm standing firm and heading back out to sea."

"Sure you are."

Ford gave him a sidelong glance. "My parents talk about love that way." He stared at the scarred wood of the bar. "'We tumbled madly in love at first sight. My eyes met hers and I knew she was the one.'"

"Now isn't that sweet? My parents hated each other, far as I could tell."

"If my father had made a different choice, he would have continued as a respected builder in London, made a decent living, married a woman of his own class. My mother would have married well, someone of her higher station in life. Perhaps she wouldn't have loved the man, but she would have had all the comforts and luxuries she was entitled to from birth."

"Ah . . . but opposites attract, Ford my boy." Griff wiped his beard with his sleeve. "Tale as old as time. You're a workingman and she's a highborn lady. She swans around Mayfair, you sleep in a hammock on a ship. It's the forbidden fruit we want to pluck the most."

"Love is out of the question. Do you hear me? It's not going to happen. It can't happen. I won't let it."

His friend smirked. "Keep telling yourself that, mate, if it makes you feel more in control. Keep deluding yourself."

Ford didn't have the heart to voice any more denials, but he couldn't admit that there was even a sliver of truth in Griff's words. "She's at the opera tonight with some foppish Earl of Maypole."

"Maypole?" Griff snorted. "Sounds like a right tosser."

"No, it was Mayhew."

Griff's hand closed around Ford's forearm. "Mayhew. You certain that's the name?"

"That's the one—why, do you know him?"

"I do." He spat on the floor. "And he's not the sort you want near her if you care about her at all."

"Why?"

"'ere, Peg. Tell my friend about the Earl of Mayhew."

Peg approached, a look of contempt on her face. "Mayhew, that scum sucker. If he ever comes in here again, I 'ave ten good men will give him a thrashing he won't soon forget."

"What did he do?" Ford asked.

"Left my sister for dead, that's what he did. Threw her out like she was so much refuse. Him and his wealthy friends come to the public houses looking for sport. About a month ago, he took a liking to my sister. Nelly was a good girl, all sunshine and birdsong, she was. Until Mayhew forced himself on her. He set her up in a house, after that, promised to keep her, then threw her into the gutter." Peg wiped her nose with her sleeve. "Poor broken bird. She's gone back to Sussex, back to the farm."

"I'm sorry," said Ford. "He deserves more than a thrashing."

"His kind take what they want and never suffer the consequences," Griff said.

Ford's stomach roiled. This was the man Beatrice's mother wanted her to marry.

Over his dead body.

"Easy now." Griff laid a hand on Ford's shoulder. "You're about to crush that tumbler to splinters."

Ford glanced down at his hand. Griffith was right. He wanted to be crushing something else. Mayhew's windpipe. "I can't sit here while she's in danger, Griff."

"Lots of people crowding that opera house. She won't be in danger."

"Lots of shadowy corners, as well," Ford growled. "I've got to warn her away from him. What if he proposes to her tonight and she accepts? I can't stand the thought of Beatrice shackled to that cur for life."

"What are you going to do, burst into their box at the opera?"

"If I have to."

"That'll mean pistols at dawn, my boy. That's how the Fancy do things."

"I'm a crack shot."

"I know you are, lad. I know you are. But what were you just saying about highborn and low? It wouldn't be a fair fight. He'd find some way to cheat and you'd end up dead."

Ford jumped off his stool. "I don't care. I have to do something. I'm going to the opera."

"You're not dressed for the opera."

"My money's as good as theirs. I'll bribe my way in if I have to."

"One kiss and you're willing to fight to the death for her." Griff shook his head. "Oy, lad. You've got it bad."

Chapter Fourteen

"Was it a real kiss this time?" Viola whispered, her eyes sparkling in the gaslit opera box.

"Very real." Beatrice closed her eyes briefly, remembering the kiss. "Not imaginary in the least." She glanced at her mother, who was occupied with perusing the gathering crowd below their box, leaving Beatrice free to have a whispered conversation with her friend. "I kissed him first, but that was a disaster since I connected with his nose instead of his lips, and then he, seeking to rectify matters, gave me a proper kiss. Wrong choice of words. There was nothing proper about it."

Viola giggled. "Beatrice. I'm surprised at you."

"Of course it can never happen again." She knew that, but her traitorous mind kept imagining second kisses.

"Tell me all about it. Don't leave anything out."

The dowager duchess fit her opera glasses to her eyes, searching the crowd. "Where is Lord Mayhew? His mother promised that she would bring him to our box for an intimate tête-à-tête before the opera began."

"I'm sure he'll be along soon, Mama," Beatrice said loudly. Her mother was seated in a velvet chair at one end of the built-in wooden table made to hold refreshments and opera programs, and Beatrice and Viola were at the other end.

Beatrice rolled her eyes at Viola. "Ugh. Mayhew. He's been overly attentive lately."

"I don't see why not. You're a great success now and each new gown you wear is more beautiful than the last. This one with the embroidered roses with diamonds for dewdrops is quite the most gorgeous thing I've ever seen."

"It's dreadfully uncomfortable and very heavy."

"I wish I had a new gown to wear." Viola glanced down at her plain white muslin gown with its ordinary blue sash. Her father, a famous composer, was related to an earl by marriage, but a composer didn't generate much income when he was going deaf.

Due to her father's worsening infirmity, their income had been sorely reduced, and Viola had been forced to take employment as the music instructor to the Duke of Westbury's five sisters.

"Take some of my gowns," said Beatrice. "You're welcome to them. I must have two dozen new ones hanging in my rooms." She'd rather be wearing the same plain blue gowns she wore all summer in Cornwall.

"I don't think they would fit me. I have a much more ample bosom."

"The gentlemen won't mind if your bosom can't be fully contained," Beatrice said with a wink.

Viola giggled. "I think that kiss has changed you, Beatrice. You're much saucier now. I like the new you."

"I see him!" exclaimed her mother. "Beatrice, smile at the earl."

Beatrice dutifully glanced down into the crowd and pasted a smile on her face.

"He saw you," her mother reported. "He'll arrive soon, I have no doubt."

Oh, joy. She had summoned a conceited windbag of an earl. The very last thing in the world she desired.

Her mother's dearest friend, the Dowager Countess of Fletcher, arrived in a flurry of wavering ostrich feathers and the cloying scent of floral perfume.

"How are you, Lady Fletcher?" asked Beatrice.

"I'm very well, Lady Beatrice. You look lovely tonight, ladies."

Lady Fletcher settled into the empty seat next to Beatrice's mother. "And what are you plotting now, my dear dowager duchess? I heard Mayhew's name mentioned."

The two older ladies bent their heads together, laughing and chattering like magpies.

"My mother's been very secretive lately," Beatrice whispered to her friend. "She's plotting something, and I won't know what it is until the very last moment, so that I can raise as few objections as possible."

"Would you like me to make some inquiries to see if I can discover what she's up to? I'm supposed to go and say hello to the conductor from my father, before the opera begins."

"Would you? I'd like to know what her plans are, and there's no use simply asking her because she enjoys keeping me in the dark."

"It would be my pleasure. I'll be back." Viola slipped out of the box.

"Where's Miss Beaton going?" her mother asked.

"She promised her father that she would give his regards to the conductor of the orchestra."

"I do wish she'd take more care with her appearance. That gown must be two seasons old. I know her circumstances are reduced, but surely they can afford at least a few new gowns. The girl is not lacking in beauty, but her dowdy clothing will attract her no suitors of quality."

"Perhaps I'll give her one of my gowns."

"Absolutely not," said her mother sternly, her normally placid face settling into a frown. "I don't want her outshining you. Especially not at the costume ball next week."

Her mother and her friend went back to passing judgment on the clothing of the other attendees and repeating the latest gossip.

Beatrice would rather be anywhere else than sitting here waiting for Mayhew to come and talk about himself. Thankfully, he wouldn't stay long before going to his family box. She couldn't take much more of his inanity without allowing her true feelings of revulsion to show. He always smelled overpoweringly of spiced cologne. She knew from experience that she'd smell it in the air for a full half hour after he left the box and even taste it in her mouth. How she detested the overuse of scents.

Ford used nothing more than soap, yet he always smelled delectable. And tasted even better.

Talking about the kiss had made her remember it vividly.

The rough touch of his hand on her cheek, sliding over her chin. The taste of his lips on hers . . . his tongue coaxing her mouth to open. The possessive grip of his hands around her waist.

"Are you cold, dear?" asked her mother. "You're shivering. Here, take my wrap."

"It's the Parisian style of gown," said Lady Fletcher. "It doesn't cover the shoulders and bosom enough—she'll catch a chill."

This brought their conversation around to the subject of clothing, which would occupy her mother and Lady Fletcher until the performance began.

"I wonder what Miss Hind will be wearing tonight?" mused Lady Fletcher. "I heard that she dismantled her jewels and the diamonds were sewn to the bodice of her costume."

"I heard that the opera house hired several policemen to guard the jewels," Beatrice's mother replied. "There she is!"

The ladies trained their glasses on the entrance of the scandalous prima donna who was rumored to be having an affair with a member of the royal family.

Beatrice couldn't care less about jewels sewn on bodices.

All she wanted to do was relive forbidden kisses.

FORD WASN'T DRESSED for the opera but he didn't care. Women were still giving him appreciative glances as he made his way through the crowd. Normally he would have returned those glances, assessing any offers, but tonight there was only one woman he wanted to see—and she was floating above him, so far out of reach she may as well be on another continent.

He craned his neck to see her, wishing he had a pair of those little magnifying glasses on a stick that everyone was waving about. He stopped walking, and someone bumped into him and cursed in his direction.

Finally he located her box by searching for the glow of her red hair. She sat with her mother and another mature matron. As he watched, a fair-haired man wearing elegant black evening dress entered the box and bowed over her hand.

Mayhew.

The bastard was practically sticking his nose in her cleavage.

And Beatrice was smiling up at him, fluttering her lashes and laughing at something he'd said.

Ford's jaw locked, and white-hot resentment obliterated all rational thought. That vile abuser had the right to bow over her hand and Ford was stuck down here, powerless to do anything about it.

Ford glared at them with rising fury. His fists clenched.

He couldn't allow that man to propose to her. What if she bowed to the pressure from her mother, from society, and accepted him? His heart clenched along with his fists.

He didn't belong in this glittering world, but he wasn't going to stand down here like an impotent fool any longer.

He had to go up there and warn her.

He began pushing his way through the crowd. He didn't care if he had to fight his way to her door and oust Mayhew by the collar.

"Mr. Wright, is that you?" A soft touch on Ford's elbow drew his attention.

"It's Miss Beaton, don't you remember me? Why, whatever is the matter? You look ready to kill someone."

"I have to speak with Lady Beatrice. I have to warn her about something. Someone. I'm going up there to speak with her."

"My, that would cause quite a scene. You're not dressed."

"I'm wearing clothes."

"Not the right ones."

"I don't care about any of that. I have to talk to her."

"Mr. Wright, stop a moment. Listen to me. You can't charge in there. It will put everything in jeopardy—Beatrice, the future of the bookshop, your very life. If you care about her, if you want to continue your work, then you have to calm down and come with me. I know a back way. And there's an empty box at the end of the row."

Ford realized that Miss Beaton was on his side. "You'll bring her to me?"

"I'll find a way. It might take a little while. Once you're in the unoccupied box, you should try to relax. You might even enjoy some opera."

"I doubt that."

"Not an opera lover?"

"Don't know, and don't care."

"Don't dismiss what you haven't tried. Wait until you hear the Queen of the Night's most famous aria. It's fiendishly difficult. I hope the soprano is ready for all of that coloratura and the top F."

"I'm not here for the arias. I have to talk to Lady Beatrice."

"My, so impatient." She hit his arm playfully. "Don't worry, I'll give her the message."

"If you don't, I'm coming in."

MAYHEW HAD FINALLY left. Her mother and Lady Fletcher would gossip and play cards through the opera, stopping only to scrutinize the prima donna as she sang her arias.

Viola reentered the box and sat beside Beatrice. "I discovered two things," she whispered. "The first is that your mother has been spreading the rumor that Mayhew will propose to you at the costume ball at your house—and that you will accept."

Beatrice's temperature rose. "She's delusional if she thinks I'll accept a proposal from that bombastic braggart."

"The second is that there is a highly volatile and possessive rogue waiting for you in the empty box down the hall."

"Wright?" she whispered urgently, her heartbeat starting to gallop.

Viola nodded. "He says he has something urgent to tell you."

Beatrice's first thought was Foxton. He'd been back to the bookshop and made more threats. It must be dire if Ford had come here to talk to her.

Beatrice looked at her mother. She was absorbed in her game of cards. Mayhew had already visited and been promised the first dance at the costume ball, so her mother's goal for the evening had been achieved.

"Mama?"

"Yes?" Her mother didn't even glance up from her hand of cards.

"May Viola and I take a brief turn down the hallway and back? I'm feeling somewhat faint and would like a little exercise."

"Handsome earls do tend to make ladies feel dizzy," said Lady Fletcher with an insinuating smile.

"Yes, dear," her mother said distractedly. "Don't be gone too long."

Chapter Fifteen

"WHAT IS IT, Ford? What's so urgent?" Beatrice asked. He was a hulking shadow in the unlit and unoccupied box.

"Shh." Ford pulled her inside and drew the curtains, enclosing them in darkness and red velvet. "We can't let anyone see us."

"I know that. I'm taking quite a risk coming here. I only have until the end of this aria. Viola is keeping watch outside. Is it Foxton? Did he return to the shop?"

"It's not Foxton."

"It's not? Then it must be Mrs. Kettle or Mr. Coggins. Has something happened to one of the servants?"

"It's not the servants." He grasped her shoulders. "It's Mayhew. I don't want you talking to him."

"Mayhew?" She laughed softly. "Is that all? He's harmless."

"No, he's really not. I don't want you talking to him, laughing at his jokes, gazing up at him, or allowing him to stare down your bodice. And you definitely can't marry the man." He let go of her shoulders. "That is all. You may go back now."

Her jaw dropped. "Seriously? And here I thought you had something truly important to say. You came all the way here . . ." She sniffed the air. "From the pub, if I'm not mistaken, to tell me what I can and can't do." She tossed her head. "I get quite enough of that from my mother, thank you very much."

"You don't understand. I've just heard a story about Mayhew that would make your blood run cold. He's dangerous."

"What story?"

"I was in a pub by the docks and a barmaid told me that Mayhew had . . . violated her sister. He lured her with promises and
then cast her away like a soiled glove."

Her stomach dropped. "He can't get away with that."

"He already has. Happens all the time. Wealthy men treat the
dockside taverns as their hunting grounds. Promise me you won't
marry him. Promise me."

"Or . . . ?"

"Or I'll . . ."

"You'll what?" She rested her hand on his chest. "You'll kiss me
into acquiescence?"

Now why had she said that?

He narrowed his eyes. "No more kisses. That was a mistake."

"Obviously."

"I was going to say that I'd burst into his opera box and drag
him out by his collar and give him a drubbing."

"I'm disappointed in you, Ford. Do you honestly think I would
be featherbrained enough to marry someone like Mayhew?"

"I don't know, Beatrice. I saw you flirting with him, laughing
up at him." His hands curled into fists by his sides. "I saw him
staring down your bodice."

"I'll have you know that this is the latest fashion." She wriggled
her bare shoulders.

His jaw muscles twitched. His gaze made her feel shivery and
powerful. She liked being able to make his jaw clench.

"You're jealous." She poked a finger into his chest. "Ford Wright,
notorious rogue, is jealous."

"Damnation, Beatrice. I'm not jealous. I don't want to see you
shackled to a heartless abuser. I'm furious with your mother for
considering him as a worthy suitor for you."

"He's an earl."

"That doesn't make any difference. He preys on innocents. He
ruins and discards barmaids for sport."

"I didn't know about that. It's unconscionable."

"You're sheltered from the knowledge of such things."

"It's wrong to keep women in ignorance."

"I'm telling you now—he's a base-minded rotter who isn't worthy to even breathe the same air as you."

"I truly had no intention of accepting his proposal. I'm not going to accept any proposals. I'd have no talent for marriage, none whatsoever. I don't want anyone telling me what I can and can't do. I'm going to be a confirmed spinster by next summer, and I'll spend the rest of my life at Thornhill House."

"A spinster? You don't strike me as a candidate for spinsterhood."

"All I want to do is return to Thornhill. My brother told me I could live there as long as I liked."

"Find a gentleman who values your intellect and wants to see you succeed at your dictionary."

"Don't make me laugh. Marriages in my set are usually matches of convenience, designed to enrich fortunes and better social standings. My mother and father were certainly not a love match."

"But you want a love match. Those novels you read all have happy endings."

"I used to be a romantic until I realized that all the titled gentlemen of London want is my dowry."

"You're going to fall for some verse-spewing fop and settle in London to produce a large family of bespectacled literary geniuses."

"Never." She gave a little nod. "I'll never marry."

"Even so, why not stay in London? You have friends here, and family, and now you have a property of your own. Give lectures, fill the library with more books from your brother's estate."

"I can't stay in London. My life is all planned out."

"Deviate, take a different road, try a new path."

"My dictionary and my writing are my priorities. My words will live on after me. The dictionary will be my legacy. Lady Beatrice Bentley, the noted etymologist."

"Sounds like you're writing your epitaph, but you're young, for God's sake. Too young to bury yourself in Cornwall."

"It's not some passing whim, Ford. Retiring from London and moving to Cornwall is the choice I've made. I haven't found a way to tell my mother yet, but I'll have to find the courage to do so very soon."

"Why are you so afraid to live?"

"I'm not your rehabilitation project, Ford. You can't paint a new coat of confidence on me and transform me."

"I don't want to change you." He cupped her cheek with his hand. "I didn't know that you felt that way. I assumed that your protestations were only surface deep. You can marry, just don't marry Mayhew."

"Thank you very much."

"I'm not trying to tell you what to do. I'm . . . damn it, I care what happens to you. I don't want to see you hurt. You're so vibrant and intelligent. I wouldn't want anyone to take away your power. Promise me that you'll never be alone with Mayhew."

"I promise."

Somewhere below them a soprano voice soared into the heavens on a run of trilling notes.

Beatrice was acutely aware of how close they stood. How they were shielded from prying eyes, here in the heart of London, with music swelling around them.

Desire didn't follow any rational order or purpose.

When he was near, she wanted to touch him. Be closer to him. Listen to his voice, because it made her skin sensitive, made her body thrum and throb.

Really, there was no more delicate word for the sensation. A throbbing in hidden places, a tingling awareness of her body . . . and his.

He was a forceful blur in the darkness. A warm wall of man, heating her through her clothing.

Her hand still rested on his chest, perilously close to his heart.

His thumb stroked her cheek.

Viola was waiting for her beyond the curtain. The aria would end soon.

This was a risky game. Alone in the velvety darkness with Ford. This was about danger and it was about possessiveness.

He'd come running to the opera house to warn her about Mayhew.

He kissed her and she met him halfway, closing her eyes and surrendering to her desire. His lips caressed hers. He hadn't removed her spectacles and they felt like a barrier, so she removed them and slipped them into her pocket.

His hands moved to her waist and he pressed her closer until their bodies met.

She tasted ale on his tongue, sweet fruit with a hint of bitterness.

He cared about her. He urged her to take risks.

She wanted to take this risk, seize and savor it.

Perfectly suspended in this moment up above the crowd, above the drama being enacted on the stage, up near the rafters where the notes reverberated in a different way, where the soaring high notes felt like they were reaching for her, trying to find her, and when they did the beauty of it made her want to cry.

The orchestra and the singers were all here for her pleasure. Everyone was there to give her joy. Ford, most of all.

He dipped his head to her bodice and kissed the tops of her breasts. She tilted her head back against the wall.

This. She wanted this.

She arched her back, offering herself to him.

FORD'S BREATHING WAS ragged, his mind gone blank. He hadn't meant for this to happen, all he'd wanted to do was warn her about Mayhew, but now he had his lips inside her bodice.

He'd read her diary entry, felt the pain emblazoned in the words written by a young girl who had been ridiculed and bullied. The knowledge rolled through him like a summer squall on calm seas: this eloquent, lovely woman standing in front of him had no idea how exquisite she was.

He could show her.

He kissed the edge of her corset, touching his lips to the soft swell of her breasts. Her breathing quickened and her heart beat faster beneath his lips. Fingertips massaged the back of his neck in soft circles.

She had small breasts, perfect for her slight figure, framed by creamy silk with a pink bow in the middle and seed pearls sewn into the bodice edging, so fine, so delicate.

His fingers shook as he traced the bow.

He glanced up and she smiled at him.

That lopsided smile and the warmth in her hazel eyes was his undoing.

He tugged her bodice down, it required only a slight movement, and gorgeous nipples appeared over the edge of the silk.

Soaring cascades of tremulous notes spilled around them. The soprano sounded like she was singing about life, about death, about love.

He lowered his head and took one of her nipples between his lips, sucking gently. Her small gasp was more beautiful music than the aria.

Kissing her gave him so much pleasure, made his blood pump through his body, made him hard and ready. He felt more alive than he had in years. He had a clear and present purpose: give Beatrice pleasure. Make her body quiver and her heartbeat quicken.

Make her moan his name, the soft sound swallowed by the shimmering aria.

The last notes hovering in the air around them, fading to silence . . . no . . . just a moment longer.

She took a stuttering breath. "I—I must go."

He helped her rearrange her bodice.

And then she was gone.

And he was back in the darkness. Adrift and alone.

Chapter Sixteen

THE INVITATIONS KEPT arriving. Her mother was ecstatic, treating each new card that arrived as a small triumph in her grand scheme to marry Beatrice off in style.

Beatrice hadn't anticipated that upholding her end of the bargain would make her quite this popular. Apparently the combination of dowry-plus-newly-docile was potent enough to send her straight to the top of everyone's social calendars.

She hadn't found any time to visit the bookshop in the last few days.

I won't require your help, Ford had said, but she knew he hadn't really meant it. He was there all alone, racing against a very strict deadline. He must be working night and day, repairing roof tiles and removing damaged floorboards.

She thought about him all the time.

About their kiss in the opera house. About his lips doing those wicked things. His hot breath against her skin, lips closing around her . . .

Don't think about the opera.

They'd been alone in the darkness, swept away by the passionate music. He'd only done what a Ford was born to do. She'd known he was a rogue, and an incorrigible flirt, when she'd hired him.

In order to maintain a proper and businesslike relationship, she must play her part more convincingly. The prim, unassailable spinster. The role she'd chosen in life.

As long as she kept any irrational desires locked away there was no reason to avoid the bookshop. Besides, she wanted to give Ford the good news. Her brother's solicitor and Isobel had confirmed that because the property was not entailed, and because Beatrice was unmarried and had reached her majority, she owned the bookshop and could dispose of it as she pleased. Greenaway had begun drawing up the documents that would transfer the title to the ladies league for use as a clubhouse.

Perhaps Foxton had given up and moved on to another property, though she highly doubted that he would simply disappear. He owned the vacant buildings on either side of the bookshop, which could prove problematic.

Her best hope was to sign the shop over to the League, remove every trace of the bawdy books, and complete the renovations swiftly, before Foxton made his next move.

Coggins was too old and frail to be of much help, and Ford required an assistant. She might not be especially strong, but she'd learned how to swing a sledgehammer with gusto.

She was determined to make herself useful.

This morning she'd risen early, before her mother awoke, and taken a shirt and a pair of trousers from her absent brother Rafe's adjacent apartments. She'd left her mother a note saying she would be inventorying books at the bookshop and would be back in time to be made presentable for this evening's entertainments.

She arrived at the bookshop before the sun had taken its coffee and decided to put on a bright face. Ford had removed the sign above the door. Beatrice had liked the sign with its fairy-tale castle and mysterious woods. Without the sign this was just a building, nameless like the empty buildings next door.

Not empty for long.

She and the ladies would have a plate inscribed for the door with the name of their club and the year of dedication. A name that was less about knitting, but not so radical as to reveal their true purpose to the world.

She let herself in with her key. The shop was quiet save for the bell announcing her arrival. Coggins appeared wearing a nightcap and rubbing his eyes. "Lady Beatrice?" he croaked. "What time is it?"

"Time for carpentering." She marched into the entrance hall and he locked the door behind her.

"Mr. Wright is still abed," he informed her.

"Perfect." She'd be hard at work when he came downstairs. "I need a quick start to my day. My mother owns the second half of it and I'm determined to own the first. Is Mrs. Kettle in?"

"Not yet. She never arrives until later." He yawned. "I'll make you some coffee. Could use some myself."

"I need tools, Coggins."

"Tools, milady?"

"Hammers, and nails, and such things."

"Mr. Wright left a bucket of tools in the front room."

"Excellent."

She changed her clothing in Mrs. Kettle's little sitting room under the stairs. It was a difficult feat to wrestle out of her gown and corset with no maid, but she managed it. She put on the shirt, tucking it into the trousers. Rafe was slimmer in the hips—the trousers were quite close fitting.

Lady Beatrice Bentley. Displaying your limbs. Shameful!

She banished her mother's voice. She had no jurisdiction here. This was Beatrice's domain. She could wear trousers, wield a hammer, revel in her new library, and do it all on her own terms.

When she emerged, Mr. Coggins stared at her, his brows closing into one straight line.

"Do stop staring, Coggins. You don't expect me to carpenter in my frilly gown, do you?"

He handed her the coffee. "What's the world coming to?" he mumbled. "Ladies in trousers. I'm going back to bed."

She sipped her coffee and opened *Practical Carpentry, Joinery, and Cabinet-making* by Peter Nicholson, written "for the use of workmen" with "fully and clearly explained" instructions.

She turned to the chapter entitled, "Flooring for First-Rate Houses."

So these rotting floorboards in the showroom were nailed on top of the joists. But which type of construction was it? She'd have to rip up a floorboard to determine the structure beneath.

She found a hammer in the bucket. This one was much smaller than the one they'd used for knocking down the wall. It had a metal head set crosswise on a wooden handle. The curved end was obviously meant to pry things apart. But how to insert it beneath the board? And, once inserted, how did one succeed in dislodging the board?

What felt like hours later, but was probably only ten minutes, Beatrice's back ached and her knees hurt from kneeling on the floorboards.

She'd only managed to pry up one small wedge of timber. "Come loose, damn you despicable board!"

"Cursing at it won't help," said a deep voice over her head.

Ford. She glanced up and then quickly back down again. Sunlight kissed the angular contours of his face. The smile teasing his lips demolished her resolutions to remain impassive and industrious.

"What do you think you're doing?" he asked.

"Proving you wrong."

"About what?"

"I've received definitive confirmation that I own the property and will be able to sign it over to the league of lady knitters. Therefore, it's of the utmost paramountcy that we finish repairing the property swiftly so that Foxton can't claim it's in a state of hazardous dereliction. You said you wouldn't require my help, but since we can't hire another carpenter as your assistant, I believe I may be of use. I understand the basic principles of floor joists and floorboards." She frowned at the board she'd been attempting to remove. "At least I thought I did."

"What in the name of God are you wearing?"

She smoothed her palm over the front of the shirt. "My brother Rafe's clothing. He's not in London so he won't miss it."

His gaze raked the length of her body leaving her feeling exposed, and uncharacteristically feminine. If he was going to stare at her so boldly, she'd take an inventory of her own.

He looked delicious enough to spoon into her coffee. Dark hair tousled, loose white shirt open at the neck, sunlight softening the hard angles of him, the stern set of his lips and the sturdy plane of his shoulders.

"You look good in trousers," he said.

The compliment startled her. She'd expected him to order her to change back into her feminine frills and march upstairs to the reading room where she belonged.

She wiped a damp palm on the sturdy fabric of the trousers. "My friend India, the Duchess of Ravenwood, wears trousers when she goes on archaeological digs. And when she infiltrates all-male societies. I find I quite like the freedom they afford. I may never wear a gown again."

"I liked the gown you were wearing at the opera." His eyes did that smoldering thing where the blue warmed up and his lids closed halfway.

She'd been determined not to bring up the subject of what happened at the opera. It seemed best to pretend it hadn't happened. But if he were going to be cavalier about it, she'd answer in kind. "I recall you rather liked sliding it down my shoulders."

She tried to imitate his smoldering look, but feared she probably looked as though she were trying to blink a speck of dust out of her eye.

He folded his arms over his chest and the motion brought his muscles into swelling prominence. "Shall we talk about what happened at the opera? I went there to warn you . . . and we ended up . . ."

She swallowed. She was still on her knees, and he was standing over her like temptation incarnate. "Kissing again. I was there. But you must know that opera has that effect on people. The music is so transporting that it has a tendency to provoke people to fits of passion."

"It was the opera, was it?"

"Quite." Prim, proper, and purposeful. "I'm not here for conversation, Ford. I'm here for woodworking." She held up the carpentry book like a shield against all of that virility. "I have a book. *Practical Carpentry* by Mr. Peter Nicholson."

"Very well." He dropped to a squat beside her. "What has Mr. Nicholson taught you about removing damaged floorboards?"

"There are several figures and diagrams and an explanation of the system of floor joists. It says that these large strong timbers I've uncovered are called girders and—"

"Put the book down, Beatrice."

"Pardon?"

"I know this will be difficult for you, but you can't remove floorboards while holding a book. Put down the book."

She lowered the book.

"Not everything in life revolves around books. Some things must be learned through practical application."

"I'm willing to learn."

"First of all, you don't have the right tool for the job. You can't use a hammer alone. You need a crowbar." He searched the bucket of tools and lifted a long flat metal tool with a curved fork at one end. "This is designed to use for leverage. You insert it under the board and lift enough to maneuver the hammer in, like so. See, the nail is standing proud now, and you can easily remove it with the claw end of your claw hammer."

He demonstrated the motion and the nail popped free.

"Oh, so that's how it's done. May I try?"

He handed her the crowbar and the claw hammer, and she practiced the movements he'd taught her. She managed to pry the board loose and remove a nail with less difficulty this time.

"Very good. I'll join you after I have my coffee."

She set to work, feeling very industrious now, humming bars of Mozart as she pried and denailed the boards. It was difficult, but it wasn't impossible, with the proper tools.

Ford returned and began moving down the opposite row of

water-damaged floorboards. He removed boards much faster than she did, but that was to be expected.

He reached her quickly, setting to work on the adjacent floorboard, their elbows almost touching.

"There's something so satisfying about the ping of the nails as they slide free, isn't there?" Beatrice asked. "And then when a whole board is removed—it's visible progress. It makes me want to continue just for the satisfaction of reaching the end."

"Try doing this for a whole day in the hot sun on the deck of a ship. You might not like it so much."

"I'm sure it can become tiresome. But then again smiling at loathsome earls at balls is irritating to no end."

They worked in tandem for a few minutes, the sound of their breathing mingling with the ping of nails and the scraping of metal against wood. "Doesn't your father want you to stay in Cornwall and take over as carpenter to my brother?"

"Of course he does. I'm his only child."

He didn't elaborate. Very well, she'd have to pry the information out of him like he was a nail stuck in a board.

"Why did you choose the Royal Navy instead of taking over your father's position?"

"I left home after an altercation with my father. I was young and hotheaded. I wanted to see the world. That village was too small for me. Still is."

"What did you argue with your father about?"

He sat back on his heels. "If you must know, the fight was about your father, the late duke. He rarely visited the estate in person, but when he did, he made his presence known. He visited our cottage one evening. He was screaming at my father about something and I wanted my father to stand up to him, but my father bowed and scraped and apologized until I flew into a fit of temper. I insulted the old duke, who left in a rage, vowing to have us thrown off his lands."

He bent back to his work, his hammer ripping nails free, as

he spoke of his past. "My father tried to force me to apologize to the duke but I refused. We had a huge fight. He told me that I needed to be realistic, to learn my station in life, and I told him he needed to grow some . . ." He paused, his breathing ragged.

"Bollocks," she said primly. "Germanic at root, from the Old English *beallucas*, meaning testicles, deriving from words that mean leather bag, balls, nuts—"

"That's quite enough etymology, Beatrice." He smiled briefly, but his face soon clouded over again. "I ran away to the docks and didn't return to Cornwall for three years."

Beatrice set down her hammer. She wanted to reach out and touch him, but stopped herself just in time. "My father, the cause of your flight from home, died when I was fourteen. I barely knew him. He was this menacing presence lurking around the edges of my life, disapproving and aloof. How old were you when you ran away?"

"Fifteen. Brash, hotheaded, believing I was invincible." He gave a short laugh. "I was a handful, and I had to fend for myself on ships full of rough and ready sailors. What were you like at fifteen?"

"Even more awkward than I am now, though that's difficult to believe, I know. My mother tried her very best to polish me to gracefulness, but I was all knobby knees, sharp elbows, and even sharper opinions. I've never been particularly decorous or feminine."

"You have an economy of motion that I prefer to grace. You're doing very well at removing this flooring."

Her heart warmed at his praise. She resumed working. "Fifteen can be a challenging year. My brother Drew, the duke, was kidnapped at the age of fifteen and it changed him. I was only a small child at the time so I didn't know him well, but I knew that he used to pick me up in his arms and kiss my cheek and after the kidnapping he became distant and withdrawn. I later learned that he lost himself in London's underworld, searching for oblivion in unhealthy pleasures. After our father died, he retreated to

Thornhill House and I barely saw him anymore. I wanted to follow him to Cornwall. I worshipped him."

"Your brother's a fair and honorable man. I remember when he
arrived to live at Thornhill. My father wrote to me that the old duke
was dead and the new one had taken an interest in the estate. His
system of crop rotation has done wonders. He's increased profits
for his tenants exponentially and everyone is very loyal to him."

"Except Gibbons, it would seem."

"Gibbons never had to worry about where his next meal would
come from. He's made of the same stuff as Foxton—greedy and
grasping."

"What does your mother think about you sailing around the
world? She must miss you."

"There's always a letter from her waiting for me at every port.
Some of my fellow sailors spend all their pay on the fleeting
pleasures available around the docks, but I like to visit as many
new sights as possible so that I can write back to my mother and
describe it for her."

"Aha!" Beatrice waved her hammer in the air. "I've found a vulnerability in that rogue's armor of yours."

"I doubt that."

"You love your mother."

"Every man should love their mother. She gave them life."

"I mean that you *really* love her."

"I'm not ashamed to admit it. She'll be coming to London next
week to see me off on my next voyage."

"It must be painful for her to visit London if she was disinherited."

"She only comes here once a year. She meets with her estranged
sister in secret. I've never even met my aunt, or my young cousins
who live here. Our family was sundered and the two sides can
never be rejoined."

"Well, even so, I think you were lucky to be raised in a family where there was genuine love and feeling. My parents shared
nothing but a name and a house."

"You had every luxury and privilege."

Beatrice plucked a nail free, welcoming the physical exertion. It kept her from becoming too wistful. She had a specific task, and her heart wasn't to perform too many maudlin meanderings.

"What are luxuries when there's no love?"

"Spoken like a lady who's never had a Christmas morn with no gifts to unwrap."

"I would have traded my expensive gifts for a Christmas-tide filled with love and laughter. My father was always absent. When he was home, it was worse than when he wasn't. And while my mother loves me, it's a smothering kind of love that seeks to change me. I'm never good enough. In the same way that we're transforming this bookshop, my mother wants to make me more conventional and presentable. All I want to do is retire to Cornwall and work on my dictionary. What's so terrible about a solitary life surrounded by books?"

"Sounds a little lonely, that's all."

"I could never be lonely surrounded by books." She'd said the same thing to her friends, and she'd meant it, but now she wasn't as certain.

Would it be lonely? Was she making a mistake?

WHEN FORD HAD seen her walking alone in Cornwall, he'd thought she held herself aloof because she believed she was above everyone else.

But now he knew better.

She'd chosen to isolate herself because of the pain of her child-hood, and because her mother had attempted to place her inside a box. No one could grow and be happy inside a box.

It flew in the face of everything he thought he knew about the privileged and perfect lives of highborn ladies.

She wasn't holding herself apart now.

She was down here with him in the wood shavings and plaster dust, working hard, and disarming him with her probing questions and the flashes of her infrequent smile.

"I'd like to meet your mother," Beatrice said softly.

Ford nearly struck his thumb with a hammer. Those were dangerous words.

He made a noncommittal sound in the back of his throat. This conversation was heading for rocky shoals.

He'd thought that she'd hammer her thumb or drive a splinter beneath her nail and that would be the end of it. He hadn't considered the possibility that a highborn lady who'd never done a real day's work in her short, pampered life would actually learn to denail boards.

But she'd taken to it easily, learning to move the length of the board and not attempting to lift it free until all of the nails were loosened.

And she looked altogether too enticing working alongside him, wearing those skintight trousers that hugged every one of her slight curves. He could see the shape of her breasts, small and round, under the thin cotton of her shirt. Her hair was tied into a simple knot that could be easily undone. He longed to see her hair unbound, tumbling around her shoulders and glowing in the morning sun.

She worked with a fierce look of concentration on her face, biting her lower lip as she pried a board up in intervals along the length until she arrived at the end.

She picked up the board with both hands and lifted, shimmying it from side to side.

He moved to help her, their shoulders touching. The board lifted clear, and Ford threw it onto the growing pile. They wouldn't have to replace the whole floor, only the water-damaged boards.

He pulled a tool belt out of the bucket. "This frees up your hands and ensures that all of your tools are at the ready. Lift your arms."

She set down her hammer and lifted her arms. He resolutely ignored the swell of her breasts while strapping the leather belt around her waist. "It's too big of course." He cinched it as tight as it would go. "But it'll stay up. Your hammer goes here." He showed her the loop made for the hammer, and she slid it into place.

"How clever. I love it." She threaded the crowbar through another loop. "Shall we continue?"

Was there any sight more arousing than a beautiful woman wearing a leather tool belt?

Not that he'd ever seen such a sight before. This would be his new benchmark for arousing sights.

Without thinking, because his hands knew what to do and he always kept busy, he began helping her pry another board loose.

They worked side by side, finding the rhythm that worked best, she taking the first nails and moving down the row while he lifted the board, making it easier for her.

She was dirty and disheveled, but there was a new kind of smile on her face, a less guarded one. It made him want to smile back.

It was such a disconcerting sight, this lady with a capital "L" working with him, down on her knees, in the dust and dirt.

He'd never worked with a woman before, much less a woman wearing tight trousers that strained over her rounded bum every time she bent over.

Their hands kept brushing accidentally on purpose.

She paused for a moment, wiping her brow. "It's hard work."

"But it's an honest profession. I come from a long line of carpenters. My father, and his father before him. Most of them were house builders. I'm the first to join the navy as a carpenter."

His father's hands were these large gnarled things, swollen and battered. Bruises under the nails. They would be his hands soon enough.

"I've never been on a boat before," she said.

"Now that's an experience. Standing on the deck of a ship, the vast ocean on every side and you floating in a tiny speck of wood, iron, and pitch—the only thing between you and the briny depths. It's an awful lot of faith we put in the craftsmanship of man when we go out for months at a time."

"An awful lot of faith in *you*, Ford. Have you seen battles?"

"One. And one was enough. I emerged unscathed when others died. They say I saved lives."

"You're very resourceful."

"I'm the man you want to have around in case of an emergency. I think about that sometimes. What if there was a flood, or something catastrophic happened, and civilization was upended. I'd be the one who survived."

"There's a word for that—apocalypse, from Church Latin, *apocalypsis*, meaning revelation. Though that generally refers to the end of the world."

"I'm not talking about the world ending. I'm talking about some catastrophic natural event that returned civilization to the wilderness. I'd be the one with useful skills. Real skills. Noblemen wouldn't survive without their servants and their silver tea sets. I never rely on others to do for me. I don't need anyone or anything."

"I would find a way to survive. Just look at how I'm learning to remove floorboards."

"You're surprisingly useful."

"Thank you."

"All right, tell me this, if you were washed ashore on a desert island and you could only take one item with you, what would it be?"

"Are you assessing my likelihood of survival?"

"Yes."

She pulled a few more nails before answering. "I'd bring a book."

"Ha." Ford laughed. "Typical."

"Well, what would you bring?"

He grabbed his father's invention from his tool belt and flipped it open. "This versatile tool. It's all I'd need."

Beatrice held out her hand and he handed her the tool. "It's ingenious. I wonder that your father hasn't patented it—didn't Isobel say something similar?"

"My father is a dreamer. He's always concocting these wild schemes, inventing these tools. He's always so certain that the next one will be the one that earns him a fortune. But they all come to naught. And he's just a carpenter on your brother's land. He owns nothing of his own and has no capital for patent applications. This one is his best invention, though."

Ford placed no trust in dreams or schemes. He believed only what he saw, what he touched with his hands. He was a self-made man.

"I would use the blade to carve wooden spears to use for defense, and to catch wild game and fish to eat. This tool is all I'd need to build us shelter. It even has a fork so that you could eat the food I provided."

"Oh, so now we're stranded on the desert island together?"

"That's right. And the only thing your book would be good for would be to start a fire."

"That's not true. I didn't tell you which book I'd bring with me."

He raised his brows. "Well?"

"A desert island survival guide." Her smile was triumphant.

"Being stranded on an island with me might not be so bad. I'd teach you how to swim, how to spear a fish."

"How do you know I don't know how to swim?"

He raised his brows higher.

"You're right," she admitted. "I don't know how. Ladies aren't taught many practical skills. Do you know how to swim?"

"I'd better. I'm a sailor."

"Isn't the water dreadfully cold?"

"Not off of Greece. Before the war for Greek independence began, my mates and I would sometimes have time for a swim."

He stopped working, remembering the hazy, sun-dappled pleasure of it. "The sun painted a sparkling trail across the water that seemed to lead directly to me, water like glass, waves rolling and then breaking closer to shore. I was far out, where land was only a line on the horizon. I dipped my head underwater, and what I heard was a profound silence. It's peaceful out there, and you float, and your feet could never touch the bottom, and there's a fear in that but also a freedom."

"In Cornwall I liked to stand on the cliffs and watch the waves battering the land. I certainly never felt the desire to be tossed about in those stormy seas."

"Too cold to swim off that coast. I prefer Greece. Or maybe our desert island."

"It does sound enchanting. Though I'd have to bring paper, pens, and ink to continue my dictionary."

"No dictionaries on our desert island. No pens and ink. You'd have to chisel your words onto stone, write on the side of a cave, memorize your words and pass them down to your children."

"I'm not going to have any children."

He lowered his hammer. "How do you know that?"

"Because I'm never going to marry. Have you forgotten?"

"I haven't forgotten. You'd have no talent for it. You wouldn't want anyone telling you what to do."

"That's it." She wrenched a section of board out too hard and the wood split down the middle. "Drat. You won't be able to salvage this one."

"Happens sometimes. Don't worry. But if you're tired you should take a rest."

"Why don't you rest, as well? We could have a cup of tea. Mrs. Kettle isn't here yet but I think I could manage."

"I have to finish—this floor isn't going to replace itself. I never leave a job half-finished."

And he never sat around sipping tea with his work partners. Or dreaming about being stranded on desert islands together.

Because his work partners had never been slim-hipped young ladies in tight trousers that left little to the imagination.

And her shirt left even less unseen. She would have to choose a threadbare linen shirt, one that had been laundered so many times it was as fine as silk.

He could clearly see her nipples. He was too busy looking at them to watch what he was doing. He lifted a board so forcefully that it flew up and smacked him in the forehead.

"Ford! What did you do that for? Here, come and sit down." She took his hand and led him toward a chair. "You're bleeding."

He wiped the blood away from his forehead with his shirtsleeve. "It's only a scratch."

"I won't have you injured on the job. Sit," she said, pointing at a chair. "I won't be a moment."

She returned with a basin of water and a clean cloth and proceeded to clean the wound on his brow. Every swipe of the cloth afforded him a delectable view of her breasts.

They were directly at eye level as she wiped the blood from his hair. He sat on his hands to stop from pulling her close and popping one of those nipples into his mouth, tonguing her through linen.

"You have bits of wood in your hair," she observed.

"And you have smudges of dirt on your cheeks and nose."

She patted his forehead dry with a cloth.

"Enough, Beatrice." He caught her wrist. "It's just a scratch."

"So you're allowed to come charging into the opera house and tell me I can't marry Mayhew, but I'm not allowed to care for your injury?"

"You're not allowed to care. Full stop."

"You can't stop me."

Chapter Seventeen

*B*EATRICE CARED. S*HE* couldn't help herself.

He was strong and confident and yet she sensed vulnerability at the heart of him, that fifteen-year-old boy who'd run away from home and joined the navy, unwilling to serve her father. He'd wanted to see the world, strike out on his own, and he had and now he was back in England.

He was here with her, making her dream of giving the ladies a clubhouse a reality.

And giving her freedom in the process.

He put his arms around her waist and pressed his cheek against her chest.

Her heart skipped wildly. She cradled his head in her arms, resting her chin on top of his head.

"Beatrice, don't care for me. I'm leaving London."

"I know you're leaving. I've always known that. I'm leaving London, as well. But we're here together, right now."

She wanted to be close to him and she felt no shame about it.

This new space they were creating together, had muffled the stern, castigating voices in her mind.

Here Beatrice smashed plaster and ripped nails from boards. She listened to her own voice.

And what her voice was telling her was this: grab this moment with both hands, don't be frightened, don't think too much. Reach for this liberty, this newfound power, and hold on tight.

He pulled her into his lap, settling her against his hard body.

He unbuckled the leather tool belt and it fell to the floor with a clattering sound.

He removed her spectacles and set them safely on a shelf. His hands moved to the back of her head, fumbling with hairpins, and then she felt the soft sweep of her hair falling around her shoulders.

"You don't know how long I've wanted to do this." He drew a shaky breath, his fingers massaging the back of her neck. "In Cornwall, your hair was like a beacon in that library window, a warmth I wanted to seek, a fire to guide my way."

"I watched you from the library window all summer," she whispered.

"I know. I saw you watching. It made me work harder and faster."

He flexed his arm and she ran her fingers over the curve of his muscle, experiencing a thrill at the breadth of him, the sheer strength and controlled ferocity. "I saw you lifting those enormous beams, and I thought about how you could lift me so easily. Lift me into your arms."

He rose from the chair with her in his arms, carrying her to a bookshelf and pressing her up against the books. There was nowhere for her hands to rest except on his shoulders.

He wrapped her legs around his waist, and she curled around him like a rose climbing up a stone wall.

His body was solid where hers was soft, and she wanted his strength for her own.

His hands cupped her bottom, holding her up, anchoring her against his hard length. She felt weightless. She shook her hair out and it fell down her back. His lips sought her neck, nibbling and teasing the sensitive flesh behind her ears.

Chipping away at her control.

"Kiss me," she commanded.

He brought his lips to hers, a questing kiss, tender and restrained.

A contrast to the iron grip of his hands holding her immobile, the crush of his body against hers.

"Kiss me harder. I'm not fragile," she said.

He growled deep in his throat, and it was a sound of desire and frustration. His kiss turned rougher. The stubble along his jaw scratched her face. He parted her lips with his tongue and kissed her possessively.

His fingers played over her collarbone, before sliding lower, flirting with the top of her breasts.

His hands had calluses not only on the tips of his fingers but in the middle of his palms.

Large, capable hands, toughened by work and weather. She'd seen what those hands could accomplish, what his body could do, the way he attacked life with certainty and skill.

His teeth nipped at her lips, tasting her, and she mimicked the movement, sucking his lower lip between her teeth. His tongue teased her lips open, delving inside her, filling her and making her hungry for more.

He sank to his knees, bringing her with him, laying her down on the exposed floorboards.

"Beatrice," he moaned into her hair. "You'll be the death of me."

FORD ATTEMPTED TO rein himself in but the contrasts were too dramatic—the softness of her skin, the satin of her lips, and the roughness of the wooden floor.

Beatrice with her brilliant red hair spread around her, spilling over that borrowed shirt the color of parchment, like the pages of a book he'd yet to open. A story he'd give his life to read.

No trespassing! This was the exact circumstance he'd sworn never to enact. This was history repeating itself. The carpenter and the lady.

This was wrong.

This was right.

He could kiss her forever on the floor, in the dust, cushioning her head with his arm.

Filling his hands, his mind, his mouth.

There was no right or wrong. There was only kissing. Only Beatrice.

"Ford," she breathed, her voice throaty.

He liked the way she said his name, from one side of her mouth, saying it in a way that was different from any other person who'd ever said it before.

"Ford . . . you're . . . it's . . ."

"I know. It's so good, Beatrice." He kissed her hungrily. "So good."

"No. Ford." She broke away. "You're . . . pressing on me and I think . . . there may be a nail sticking up from the floor."

He rolled off her immediately. "I'm so sorry. Are you hurt?"

She laughed ruefully as he helped her rise to a seated position. "Not hurt. It was only . . . slightly uncomfortable."

"I shouldn't have laid you on the floor like that. It was wrong of me."

"Ford." She touched his arm.

He tried not to feel the pleasure of her touch, not to react to it.

"I didn't want you to stop kissing me. I just didn't want to get a puncture wound and die a horrible death from blood poisoning."

Of course he had to stop kissing her. He never should have kissed her in the first place.

The moment was lost. Gone forever. He was a fool.

There was a right and a wrong and this was wrong. Coggins could have walked in on them at any moment and received an eyeful.

"We can't. Not here. We can't. Ever." His breathing jagged, his words not making sense.

"You're not speaking in complete sentences, Ford."

He stumbled to his feet and offered her his hand. "Beatrice, you deserve so much better than this. I don't know what I was thinking."

"You weren't thinking and neither was I."

"So much for keeping things businesslike."

"I don't think it's possible for us to be strictly business associates. We always wind up doing the most wildly inappropriate things."

"We have to make a pact. Absolutely no more kissing."

She took a deep breath. "Where are my spectacles?"

He handed them to her and she hooked the wires over her ears. "I can maintain control of my lips if you can," she said.

"It might be easier to maintain control if you remained upstairs in the reading room. Don't you have crates to unpack?"

"I do. I only wanted to help with the renovations."

"And you did. Thank you. But I'll take it from here. You'll have your clubhouse, at least the rudimentary configuration, before I depart. You may come for a final inspection with your friends in one week's time. I'll go up to the roof now and finish patching the shingles."

He needed to clear his head.

She bound her hair back into a tight knot at the nape of her neck and jabbed it with the pins he handed her. "I'll go upstairs, then." She avoided his gaze, gathering her carpentry book and leaving the room.

The memory of her legs twined around his hips while he kissed her up against the bookshelves followed him up the ladder and out onto the roof.

He balanced atop the slate tiles, staring out over the rooftops of London and over the river that led to the docks, to where his ship would arrive soon, the path he'd chosen.

One thing he knew for certain: Lady Beatrice Bentley was trouble.

Flame-haired, nimble-fingered, tool-belt-wearing trouble.

She made him laugh. She was intelligent and talented.

She looked incredible in a tool belt.

But forbidden things were always alluring. And what was alluring as well was that she needed his help to best Foxton and keep this property.

Being her knight in sawdusty trousers was exhilarating.

Ford had a personal stake in her victory. Personal because it was a way to wrest control back from his grandfather. But at some point, he'd begun caring more about helping Beatrice find her freedom than being a thorn in his grandfather's side. This could be a haven for her. She didn't have to retreat to the countryside. Why shouldn't she live here if she wanted to escape her mother? It wasn't a grand house, but he could make it a perfect bookish retreat for her.

She'd asked him why he hadn't become an architect, and something inside him had reawakened. Some long dead ambition to not only build and repair structures, but to design them, as well.

But dreaming larger was perilous. They were from entirely different social classes. Her brother was his father's employer.

Ford needed Thorndon to take his warning seriously and avert all suspicion from his father in the matter of the missing profits on the Thornhill estate. The duke wouldn't be inclined to feel kindly toward Ford if he found out that he'd been kissing his refined, innocent sister.

If Ford's intentions weren't honorable, and how could they be when dallying with him would ruin her life, then he had no business becoming intimate with Beatrice, in conversation or up against bookshelves.

Finish the renovations, speak with Thorndon, and get the hell out of London, away from her searching questions and her luminous eyes.

Chapter Eighteen

*I*T HAD BEEN nearly a week since Beatrice had visited the bookshop. She hadn't been back to unpack the crates of books, and she hadn't discovered the hidden meaning in her aunt's letter. Her mother had kept her busy running from one social engagement to the next, but there was another reason Beatrice had stayed away.

She needed to inventory these feelings she was having for Ford. File them away into tidy little lots. Make them more manageable and less confusing, and hopefully be rid of them for good.

This evening she was attending a meeting of the Mayfair Ladies Knitting League at the Duchess of Ravenwood's apartments.

Fern, the duchess's maid, served red wine in dainty glasses. Normally they drank brandy or sherry out of teacups, but today their newest member, Lady Henrietta Prince, had brought wine for them to taste from her ancestral cellars.

Beatrice drained her glass in one swallow and held it out for more.

Wine-fueled oblivion. Perhaps intoxication might help her forget the sensual scenes that filled her mind's eye. Ford lifting her, carrying her across the room in his strong arms, setting her against a bookshelf and covering her with his body.

She'd wrapped her limbs around his hips and felt his hardness pressing against her . . .

"This vintage is meant for sipping, Lady Beatrice," admonished Lady Henrietta, her full lips pursing. "You won't experience the complexity if you gulp it like that."

"I'm not here for the complexity—I want the sweet oblivion."

"What are you trying to forget?" asked Viola.

"My life."

"Is it your mother again?" Viola asked with a sympathetic smile. "What's she done this time?"

"Ahem, ladies." Isobel brought her gavel down upon the lectern. "I call this meeting of the Mayfair Ladies Knitting League to order. Let the record show that there are"—Isobel glanced around the room—"four ladies present this evening. Our president, the Duchess of Ravenwood, is still absent, though we expect her back soon from Egypt. Is anyone taking notes? Where's Miss Finchley?"

"She had a little explosion in her chemistry lab today," Viola said.

"Is she all right?" asked Beatrice. Miss Ardella Finchley was one of the sharpest minds she knew, but tended to be vague on the practical details of life. Her gloves were always mismatched, and her stockings always had a run.

"She's unharmed. But she's staying home to try and scrub the foul odor away before her mother returns from the Continent."

"I'll take the notes," Viola volunteered.

"Thank you, Viola. Now, let's all welcome Lady Henrietta Prince to our ranks."

Lady Henrietta was so beautiful it almost hurt to look at her, with her mahogany hair and ruby red lips. "I was invited to attend this meeting by Miss Beaton. Thank you very much ladies for having me. I understand that though this is a knitting society there is little needlework involved?"

"Quite right," said Viola. "The society was envisioned by myself and Lady India, now the Duchess of Ravenwood, after she decided to infiltrate the Society of Antiquaries in a male disguise. We conceived of this secret society as a gathering place for all females, no matter their origin or station in life, who've been barred from joining societies they should by rights be eligible to join because of their talents or achievements."

Beatrice held up a knitting basket stuffed with yarn, while

maintaining her grip on her wineglass with her other hand. "We always have our knitting baskets at the ready, in case of an unexpected arrival. We maintain the ruse of being a charitable organization. Which we are, of course. We donate blankets and garments to foundling hospitals. We just don't make those blankets ourselves."

"We purchase them," said Isobel with a grin.

"I'm honored to be in on the secret," said Lady Henrietta. "I share your enthusiasm for achieving goals. I've been managing my elderly father's estate for him. My family came to England from France in the seventeenth century, and my distant relative brought grape vines with him and planted them. No one expected them to thrive in British soil, but they did, and we've been producing wine for the family cellars ever since. Now I propose to bring this wine to a larger market."

"I'm no judge of wine," said Beatrice, "but as far as I'm concerned, you have every expectation of success. This is delicious."

And it made her braver, and less questioning.

Perhaps it hadn't been *so* bad that she'd goaded Ford into kissing her. Maybe it wasn't a terrible thing that she'd loved it so much.

Perhaps she wasn't too much of a ninny.

"I'm very glad you approve of the wine. Of course I can't let anyone know that there's a woman behind the venture. I use my father's name when I write letters to potential distributors and restaurateurs. Why should being female preclude me from being an entrepreneur? I say, smash down the barriers."

Lady Henrietta took her seat to vigorous applause from the ladies.

Beatrice had to set her wineglass down for that, but she immediately picked it up again.

"We welcome you to our ranks, Lady Henrietta, and we look forward to supporting your venture in whatever way we can. As for me," said Isobel, "I'm attending a School of Law in disguise as my brother."

"A daring deception," said Lady Henrietta.

"And I'm finishing my father's symphonies," said Viola. "He's gone almost completely deaf. I haven't had much time for composing these days. I'm the music instructor to the Duke of Westbury's sisters. They are to perform in a music recital very soon and the duke expects them to shine, but I'm inclined to despair."

"You can't let them take all your energy and creativity, Viola. You must carve some time out for yourself," said Isobel.

"I know." Viola sighed. "But they're such a handful. Enough about my woes. Beatrice, tell us about the progress on the new clubhouse."

"I'm pleased to report that I have secured a site for our new clubhouse, ladies. We will no longer meet here, but at our own property on the Strand. It's a modest building, but it will see us through several years of expansion. It's the former premises of Castle's Bookshop and has been bequeathed to me by my aunt Matilda Castle. I'm in the process of working with our solicitor to sign the property over to the League."

"Our very own clubhouse." Lady Henrietta clapped her hands. "What a prodigious achievement."

"When I inherited the building it had a leaky roof, rotting floorboards, and rats in the basement, but I hired a carpenter and he's nearly finished renovations. Soon we'll be able to have a tour."

"How is Mr. Wright?" asked Viola.

"He's . . . busy."

"He's a handsome brute," said Isobel.

"What he looks like hardly signifies," said Beatrice. "It's what he can do for us."

"Describe him to me," said Lady Henrietta, pouring another round of wine for everyone.

"He has a nose," said Beatrice. "And two eyes. He's always looking at a lady as if he's mentally undressing her."

"He only looked at you like that, Beatrice," said Viola.

Isobel's lips quirked. "And I must say that you returned the favor, Beatrice."

"And what was it like to kiss him?" Viola asked.

"Hold a moment." Lady Henrietta nearly spilled her wine. "You kissed him?"

"Viola." Beatrice fixed her friend with a stern look. "You weren't supposed to mention it."

"Well?" Isobel prompted. "What was it like?"

Beatrice closed her eyes. "It was like discovering a new word. Rolling the unfamiliar syllables around on your tongue, searching for meaning only to find that it resists all attempts at classification. Instead, this word changes you, makes you redefine yourself. Like a medieval alchemist, its goal is transmutation. Everything he touches turns golden. Dreamlike."

"Oh dear," said Viola.

Beatrice opened her eyes to find all three ladies gazing at her with the same worried expression.

"That wasn't just a kiss." Isobel pointed her wineglass at Beatrice. "You're halfway in love with him."

"Don't be ridiculous," said Beatrice. "Enough talking about men. Let's find a new name for the league, since we'll be moving out of Mayfair soon."

"A very good idea," said Viola. "What about The Muses Society. It's innocuous enough that it won't call too much attention to us, while we would know that it meant we were each other's muses."

"I like that." Isobel placed her chin on her fist. "But it might be too commonly used? I was thinking something a little more daring. What about . . . The Virago Club."

"I see where you're going with that, Isobel," Beatrice said. "You want to reclaim the word, just as the bluestockings did. But I think the colloquial usage is too negative. Even though the Latin means exemplary and heroic qualities, everyone associates the word with the definition put forth by Mr. Johnson, which ended with the unfortunate summation, 'an impudent turbulent woman.'"

"I'd like to keep my position as music instructor," Viola said. "I don't want to reveal our true purpose to the world just yet."

"Why should we have to hide under the cover of domestic

pursuits?" Isobel asked. "The world is changing and perhaps, if we reveal our ambitions, we may speed it along."

Beatrice didn't think the world was ready to allow females to attend schools of law, but if anyone could clear that new pathway for women, it would be Isobel. "Let's revisit the matter of the name at another meeting. We'll put it to a vote. There's a piano for you to play at the clubhouse, Viola. You can go there to compose your works without fear of being overheard."

"This is splendid news," said Viola.

"There's also a courtyard in back that may be used in fair weather by the Duchess of Ravenwood for training ladies in the art of self-defense. My sister-in-law, Mina, will also be helpful in that department. And we will have a lending library replete with books of interest to females, with particular attention paid to female authors."

"Bravo," said Lady Henrietta.

"The property comes with a jovial and competent housekeeper who thinks tea cures all ails and is under contract through next year but will most likely wish to continue her employment," Beatrice continued. "As well as a rather dour octogenarian man of all work who, I may gently suggest, might be past the age for a well-compensated retirement to the countryside. There's only one obstacle to our plans, ladies, and it's a large one."

"There's always an obstacle to a lady's goals," observed Lady Henrietta.

"A London builder and developer named Foxton wants the property. He owns the buildings on either side and plans to join them into a manufactory. He visited the shop while I was there and was most unpleasant. He's been quiet lately but I don't trust his silence. He's plotting something."

"We won't let him take it from us," said Isobel.

"We'll find a way to keep it," Viola agreed.

Beatrice rose from her chair. She raised her wineglass in grand elocutionary style. "It's utterly imperative that we don't allow Foxton to win. I own the bookshop. He can't have it. He's a symbol, that's what he is. A symbol of every man that's ever stood in our way, denigrated our goals, told us to stay home, or tried to take away our freedom."

"Huzzah," the ladies cried, rising to their feet and raising their glasses.

The meeting concluded shortly thereafter due, in no small part, to the wine running out.

Beatrice offered to give Viola a ride home in her carriage.

"Have you guessed the secret meaning your aunt was hinting at in her letter yet?" Viola asked.

"I still haven't. Her language was so odd. She wrote, 'I hope you will divine my meaning and that this Revelation of Love helps you to be brave, and not hide yourself away.' Revelation and love were capitalized."

"Like the title of a book."

Beatrice stared at her friend. "What did you say?"

"Capitalized as if they were the title of a book."

"Viola, that's the answer. There's a fourteenth century manuscript that's gone missing. We know about it because there were copies made in the seventeenth century. The title was *Revelations of Divine Love*. I don't know why I didn't think of it until now."

"Perhaps it was the wine."

"It was you, Viola. I must visit the bookshop."

"What, now?"

"It's only half-nine. My mother won't be home for hours. I can't wait to find out if my theory is correct. I don't know why my aunt would keep such a treasure hidden, but she must have had her reasons."

"I'd go with you, but father has been feeling ill lately and he'll worry if I'm not there to prepare his medicines."

Beatrice squeezed Viola's hand. "Don't forget what we said in the meeting. You're always taking care of everyone else and never finding time for yourself."

"It's all right. I'm used to it. Are you sure it's a good idea to visit the bookshop? Won't Mr. Wright be there?"

"I doubt it. After finishing his work he likes to share a libation with his sailor friend at a dockside tavern. Don't give me such a suspicious look. I'm not going there for kisses, I'm on the hunt for an ancient manuscript."

BEATRICE LET HERSELF in with her key.

All was dark and quiet in the shop. Coggins didn't answer the bell. He must have already retired for the evening and was probably snoring soundly.

She hung her cloak and bonnet in the entrance hall. Removing her gloves, she lit the candle in a small lantern to carry with her as she moved through the darkened house.

Ford had been busy since her last visit. She could barely remember where the shop counter used to be. He'd laid new flooring seamlessly over the entire room, the oak gleaming like honey in the candlelight.

She imagined the spacious room as it would look when it was the clubhouse's central meeting place. There'd be a table large enough to gather around, with stately high-backed chairs for each member. She'd place cozy velvet armchairs by the fireplace, for reading and fireside chats. It would be warm and welcoming, and filled with books and laughter.

All was quiet on the stairs. Just as she'd suspected. Ford was out carousing with Mr. Griffith and the lads, holding court in a noisy pub, the focus of every barmaid's attention.

She pictured him leaning back in a chair, boots planted firmly on the floor, his shirt collar loosened to reveal his muscular neck and a hint of broad chest. The barmaids couldn't stop staring at him. They poured ale into glasses until it sloshed over the sides and spilled over the bar top.

She climbed the stairs, holding her candle ahead of her. It was preferable that he wasn't here. Her mission was to search Aunt Matilda's private chambers for the *Revelations* and be home in bed before her mother's return.

Chapter Nineteen

FORD HAD BEEN reading one of the books from the hidden side of the shelves. Things had just been getting good. Bodices ripping. Buttons popping.

And then he heard the footsteps in the hallway. He'd assumed it was one of the servants passing by, until Beatrice barged into his bedroom.

A few seconds later and she would have walked in on him pleasuring himself.

Why hadn't he locked the door? He hadn't realized there was trouble on the forecast tonight.

"Ford!" Her hand shook and the lantern she held wavered, casting flickering light over her wide eyes and astonished expression. "I thought you'd be out drinking with your sailor friend."

He covered his groin with the book, as his underclothing hid only so much. "I'm too tired to go to a pub, Beatrice. I worked extremely hard all week long."

"The progress is astounding."

"You hired the right man for the job. I work fast and I work hard . . . and I enjoy my well-earned rest. What are you doing here? Shouldn't you be prancing around ballrooms with prattling dandies?"

"I just attended a meeting of the Mayfair Ladies Knitting League, and one of our new members is opening a wine cellar in London and she gave us some wine to test."

"How much wine?" he asked suspiciously.

"Oh, a few glasses. I'm perfectly in possession of my faculties."

"Then you'll realize that it's never a good idea for a young lady to enter a rogue's bedchamber at night and you'll march right back down those stairs."

When she didn't move, he growled, "Now."

"I'm not here for you, Ford. I'm here for ancient manuscripts."

"Whatever you're searching for can wait until tomorrow morning." He would have bundled her out the door by now but he couldn't stand up yet. Not until his arousal subsided.

"No, it can't. If I'm right about my interpretation of my aunt's letter, then I could own one of the very first works authored by a woman in English!" Her head swiveled as her gaze swept the room. "I know the *Revelations of Divine Love* is hidden here somewhere. It's a fourteenth-century book of mystical devotions written by the anchoress Julian of Norwich. The original manuscript has been lost, but there were several copies made which have been seen or heard of from time to time, but never found." She rounded on him, her eyes shining. "I had a feeling that Aunt Matilda was speaking in code in her letter. She obviously feared that someone was going to try to steal the manuscript after her death. She couldn't entrust it to anyone but me. I'm the one she chose."

Ford let go of the book for a moment to rub at his eyes. "What's it going to take to get you to leave?"

"A quick search for the book and then I'll be on my way." She waved an elegant hand toward the bed. "And then you may slumber."

"In her letter, my aunt says, 'I hope you will divine my meaning and that this Revelation of Love helps you to be brave, and not hide yourself away. Allow me to point the way.'"

Ford groaned. "Very well. Let's consider that literally. Is she pointing at anything in her portrait?"

"The portrait! I hadn't thought of it." She approached the bed, lifting her candle to the painting. "She's looking downward, but her chair and her knees are pointed"—she turned her head—"to her writing desk. The manuscript could be secreted there." She hastened to the desk and set down her lantern.

All of this wide-eyed racing around the room and breathless exclaiming was not helping Ford's situation. He still couldn't leave the chair.

She searched through the desk drawers and then bent over the desk, pointing her round backside in his direction. She slid forward until her bum was in the air and her head pointed toward the floor. Her toes lifted and dangled a few inches above the floor.

Definitely not helping.

"What are you doing?" he asked, his voice strangled and thin.

"The book . . . could be hidden . . . behind the desk," she said, her voice muffled by the desk. She moved her hands over the back of the desk. "You could . . . help me, you know."

No, he couldn't. Unique lost manuscripts were all very good, but what he had in his sights was a unique and very present woman in the exact position that he'd fantasized about—over a desk, her feet swinging off the floor as he rolled up her skirts and feasted his eyes on the contours of her body before running his hands . . .

He was having very, very bad thoughts.

He pressed down on the book in his lap.

He closed his eyes. Think about the most nonerotic thing imaginable.

Dukes.

Dukes who were elder brothers of bookish ladies.

Dukes who held the fate of one's family in their hands.

She turned her head toward him, spectacles askew and bosom squashed against the hard wood surface. "Nothing back here. Perhaps there's a hidden drawer beneath the desk?" Her toes hit the floor and she dropped to her knees in front of the desk. "I can't find anything."

"Usually valuable possessions are hidden in safes."

"That's it! Help me lift the portrait—there could be a hidden safe behind it."

She was so focused on finding this book that she wouldn't notice anything untoward about his anatomy. As long as she didn't glance down.

He rose on unsteady legs and lifted the portrait off the wall, setting it carefully aside. He dragged his hands over the wall. "Nothing."

She gave a frustrated sigh. "The bookshelves?"

"They don't swivel. I tried them."

"The glass! It could be behind the looking glass."

He searched behind the large, gilt-framed mirror. "Nothing."

"I was certain we'd find it in her bedchamber." She plopped down on the bed with a frown on her face. "It's somewhere else in the house, then."

"We can't search the entire house right now. It's late, Beatrice."

"It's not that late. My mother won't be home for hours yet."

She sat on the edge of his bed, her hair escaping its pins and her cheeks flushed with pink. "Do you have any wine?" she asked.

"I think you've had enough wine. And I only have whisky."

"I've never tried whisky before. Did you know that the word comes from the Gaelic word *uisgebeatha*, meaning 'water of life'?"

"It's sustained me over the years, but I'm not pouring you any. And it's time for you to leave."

"What were you reading when I arrived? *The Wicked Earl's Wishes*?"

"Never mind what I was reading. We haven't found the ancient manuscript so it's time for bed." Separate beds. In separate houses.

At opposite ends of a social gulf.

They reached for the book he'd set on the bed at the same time. Beatrice won. She held it up to the lamp. "*The Ups and Downs of a Woman of Pleasure*. Is it any good?" she asked with a saucy smile.

"Ungh . . ." And now she was sitting on his bed and reading a naughty book.

Good lord. Ford didn't know if he could take much more of this, and he didn't have another book to place over his groin. Hopefully she didn't notice his predicament . . .

She noticed. Her eyes widened behind her spectacles.

He placed his hands over his groin. "I was having a private moment before you arrived."

"Apparently." She flipped the page. "My goodness. Is that . . . is that *done*?"

Don't ask her what. Don't do it, Ford. "Is what done?"

"He's underneath her skirts. He's kissing her . . . in unexpected places. *Gamahuching*. It must be from French, but the Latin roots don't suggest any vulgar associations. What an interesting word. Some words have unknown etymological origins, which always pose a challenge."

And Ford was dead. Heart stopping, palms gone clammy *dead*.

The woman was talking about *gamahuching*. As long as she didn't ask for a practical application to help her better understand the word, everything would be fine.

Just breathe, Ford. In. Out.

"Perhaps I could include a few unexpected words in my dictionary. It might be a way to increase the readership." She skimmed through more pages. "How fascinating."

A lock of wavy hair fell over her cheek as she read. She brought a finger to her lips and moistened it before turning another page.

Ford followed the line of her finger into her mouth. Tip of her finger touched by tip of her tongue.

He wanted her so badly.

Someone had to have some sense of propriety around here. He lunged for the book and slammed it closed. "Enough reading."

His voice sounded faint, like it was an echo coming back to him from a long tunnel.

"It was just getting interesting." She smiled sweetly, with a hint of challenge that made him even harder. "You told me to live a little. To take risks."

"This wasn't what I meant."

"At our meeting tonight, my friends and I spoke of our passions and goals. Lady Henrietta Prince wants to sell the wine she produces on her family estate. I'm working on my dictionary. Viola is completing her father's symphonic works for him because he's going deaf, and Isobel is attending a school of . . ." She clapped her hand over her mouth. "I'm not supposed to be telling you any of these secrets. The point I'm trying to make is that I'm ardent about learning new words. And I find that I'm developing a passion not only for discovering their origins, but for putting them into practice."

She couldn't be suggesting what he thought she was suggesting.

She dropped her gaze to his lips, and her voice turned sultry. "I've heard that some things can't be learned from books. They must be learned by practical application."

Firelight licked her hair and danced in her eyes. If he touched her, she'd incinerate him.

He wanted nothing more than to drop to his knees and service her so well she moaned his name.

"Unless . . ." She bit her lip. "Unless you don't wish to teach me?"

Teaching her carnal lessons was all he'd been thinking and dreaming about since he first glimpsed her staring at him from the library window.

The hesitation in her voice and the wavering uncertainty in her eyes wrung emotion from some part of him he hadn't even known existed.

All he longed to do was prove to her that she was the most tempting, most alluring woman he'd ever met.

He closed his eyes for a beat. When he opened them, he'd shoved any qualms as far down in his chest as they would go. She'd said she was in full possession of her faculties. Her words weren't slurred or her movements erratic.

The lady knew precisely what she was asking.

"You truly don't know how lovely you are. How desirable."

He knew how to repair broken things, how to build things to

last, shore up support. He couldn't take away her scarring childhood years. It was all a long time ago.

But he could show her how attractive she was.

"You don't have to pretend to be someone else. You don't have to change or hide yourself away." He dropped to his knees. "You're you, Beatrice. And you're perfect."

He pushed her skirts up her limbs, revealing the sweetest most sensual pink garters he'd ever seen and slim, elegant legs he wanted to wrap around his waist. "You're not like anyone else and you're extraordinary."

He lifted her ankles in turn and untied her boots. "I want you. I've wanted you since I first saw you." He kissed the hard little knot of her anklebone and trailed his lips up her silk stockings.

"Oh," she breathed. "Ford."

That was a good start, but he wanted to hear her moan his name, cry out with pleasure.

Her drawers were easily untied and loosened enough to slide to her ankles. He threw them aside.

He placed his hands on her knees and parted her legs, sliding them open. "Do you ever touch yourself, Beatrice?" He slid his fingers along her inner thighs. "Here?"

Her body quivered as she shook her head vehemently. "No. Never."

"You don't live in your body. You live here." He reached up to touch her forehead.

"My body hasn't always been the safest of places."

"Do you want me to touch you?"

"Yes," she whispered, "I want you to show me what that word meant."

He stroked his hands over her thighs. "If you want me to stop, all you have to do is say so." He wanted her to know that. He caught her gaze and held it.

She nodded. "I understand. I'm in control."

"That's right. You control what I can do to you. I want to kiss you so badly." He brushed a finger softly over her core. "I want to give you pleasure."

He kissed his way up her thighs, stopping to revel in the satin and ribbons of her garters.

His prick pulsed against the bed, stiff and swollen, but he wasn't in any hurry. This wasn't about him.

He licked the edges of her sex softly, teasing her. She squirmed but she didn't stop him.

He slid his hands under her bum and squeezed a delicious handful in each palm.

She gave a soft gasp as he spread the lips of her sex with his tongue, licking around the edges only. He waited a few seconds, building the anticipation, before covering her with his lips and flicking his tongue softly, so softly, over her.

Honeysuckle on his tongue. Desire coursing through his veins.

Her hands drifted to rest on his head. He pulled her forward on the bed and hooked her legs over his shoulders until most of her weight rested on him. It would be better for her that way if she didn't have to support herself, if she could relax and let him do all of the work.

He stilled, listening, ready to stop if she wanted him to stop.

Her fingers dug into his hair, over his scalp, and she opened her thighs wider, guiding his head back into place.

He smiled before resuming his work.

She sighed and quivered beneath his tongue.

This was something he knew how to do. Something he was skilled at. It didn't matter if they were from different worlds. Here in the firelight, with his head between her thighs, they were perfectly matched.

He was the one who would make her come, give her a climax that would ripple through her body in waves of intense pleasure.

He was the man for the job.

Her thighs trembled and she angled up into his mouth, her hands in his hair, guiding his movements. His Beatrice wasn't shy. She said what she meant, and she took her pleasure in the way that was best for her.

THIS YEARNING WAS still new to Beatrice, for to feel desire one had to feel desirable. It was human nature to want reciprocity.

She'd wanted Ford since she saw him from her library window. She hadn't known precisely what she wanted; she hadn't possessed the vocabulary to express the specifics of her appetites.

This. She'd wanted this.

Sinful and wild, his tongue stroking her, teasing her softly and steadily. Stoking the heat in her belly.

His lips doing things that she couldn't see, could only feel. His talented hands shaping her, molding her, urging her deeper into abandon.

Her spectacles had fogged over a long time ago. She removed them and placed them on the bedside table.

She ran her hands over his head, his broad shoulders, holding on to those steely muscles.

Holding on as he kept going, as he lapped at her gently.

It didn't feel invasive, or wrong. It was shocking, of course, but it was also exquisitely right.

Blood rushed to unfamiliar places, time slowed, and pleasure came sharply into focus.

Body asserting control now, responding to the skill of his lips.

She had no doubt that this was an act that humankind had discovered early on and perfected over centuries. Just because her mind had never invented it, because she'd lived a chaste and sheltered life, didn't make it depraved. She'd thought of kissing mouths, and she'd thought about his tongue inside her mouth, but now his tongue was . . . down there. Beneath her skirts.

Producing the most heavenly sensations.

Would he suffocate under there?

He knew precisely what he was doing. She was in experienced hands.

Her body instinctively knew that pleasure was coming, and soon. A few more soft, languorous swipes of his tongue and . . .

He held her tightly. She held her breath.

The beginning of pleasure, soft notes at first and then louder, more insistent ones, pleasure spilling around and inside her and her inner muscles fluttering.

The sensation was already waiting for her. All she had to do was allow it to take her.

She imagined that she was floating in a warm ocean, the one he'd told her about, the sun lighting a sparkling path down her body from the crown of her head over her throat and belly, between her legs and down to the tips of her toes.

She didn't want to break the spell, the mellow, sun-dappled feeling in her belly, still warming her.

She listened and what she heard was stillness, the absence of thought, of worry.

No need to define what she was feeling. All she had to do was float, weightless, and allow the pleasure to flood her body until it subsided, and her heartbeat slowed.

He emerged from her skirts.

She was suddenly shy.

"Well?" He wiped his lips with his sleeve. "Did that satisfy your curiosity? It's done. And done well, I might add."

"Arrogant rogue." She laughed shakily. "I'm satisfied."

"Then my work here is finished." He smiled teasingly. "I think you'll sleep well tonight." He held out his hand.

She didn't want to leave yet. "There was another word." She slid closer to him and whispered the word she'd read in his ear.

His face went still.

"Will you teach me that one, as well?" she asked.

She slipped her hand across his chest, over his heart and down the center of his abdomen.

Feeling brave, she moved lower. She dipped her hands underneath his undergarments and her fingers closed around something long, hard, and cylindrical.

"Got a big tallywhacker, 'ave you?" she asked in a guttural male voice.

He choked on a laugh. "It's above average."

"I have nothing to judge you against, that's all."

"You'll have to trust me on this one."

She did trust him.

She trusted him enough to allow him to see the woman she was becoming. Wilder. More free. A woman who lived inside her body, as well as her mind.

His staff rose to meet her touch, growing harder and thicker with each stroke of her fingers.

"Does he like to be touched?"

He made a strangled noise that Beatrice took for a yes. She circled the head with her fingertips.

His hand closed over hers, guiding her around his stiff length and showing her how to move up and back down.

Soon she had learned the correct method, judging by the quickness of his breathing and the soft moans he made.

They lay side by side on the bed. He reached between her thighs and she parted her legs.

As she stroked him, he touched her in slow, luscious circles.

His lips sought hers in a long, slow kiss. His hand covered hers, gripping more forcefully, showing her that he wanted more pressure. He began to move in her grip, thrusting with urgent movements.

"That feels so good, Beatrice," he gasped.

She strengthened her grip, matching his movements. He made low noises deep in the back of his throat as he reached his pleasure, bucking into her hand and collapsing against her, the weight of his body pinning her to the bed.

She smiled into his hair.

He lifted his shirt off and wiped his phallus and her hands clean, before covering himself with his undergarments.

"That was amazing. Beatrice, you are . . ."

"Highly distracting to the virile rogue?" she supplied.

"Highly addictive." He kissed her neck, nipping her with his teeth. She squeaked and he nipped harder, nibbling his way from her throat to her sensitive nipples.

"Ready to learn more new words?" he asked, with a devilish glint in his eyes.

His fingertips brushed over her again. There. And sensation rippled through her belly.

"Again?" she gasped.

"Again," he commanded, shifting his hand so that his palm covered her mound, rocking gently over her in slow, deliberate circles.

She tensed. "No, I'm . . . not . . . I couldn't."

This one was quieter than the other, more of a mellow ripple than a flood of pleasure.

She laughed, delighted by her body. "I had no idea I could do that again. Ford?"

"Yes, Beatrice?"

"If we were stranded together on a desert island, I'd want to do *this* every day."

His laugher brushed her ear, soft and low. He kissed her earlobe, then her lips, his tongue slipping inside her mouth.

Tendrils of longing curled inside her again, threatening to burst into blossom, rose petals on her tongue, perfumed by desire.

"You'd spend so much of your time scratching dictionaries onto cave walls that we wouldn't have time for *this*," he finally replied.

"I would make time. Dictionaries aren't everything. Sometimes life needs to be experienced, instead of written about."

"You could read aloud to me from your dictionary while I pleasured you," he suggested wickedly.

"But then you wouldn't be listening."

"And you wouldn't be able to keep reading."

"Is that a challenge, rogue?"

"It's a certainty. If I wasn't so tired, I'd take you up on it."

"Another time," she said lightly.

He stopped smiling and flopped to his back beside her.

She'd said the wrong thing. Brought reality into the room with them. There couldn't be another time.

They weren't on a desert island. They were in a bed in a house not far from the house where she lived with her mother.

And somewhere, a ship was moving closer, coming to take him away.

Beatrice laid her head against his chest, listening to the sound of his heartbeat. A few more moments within the circle of his arms.

A few more moments within the walls of this impossible dream.

"I read your diary entry, Beatrice."

She lifted her head. "My diary?"

"You left a torn-out diary entry in the book you lent me."

What was he talking about? "I didn't mean to give you any of my writing."

"I know. I started reading the page and I knew immediately that you hadn't meant to give it to me so I stopped. You were describing overhearing your mother's conversation with the doctor about your inability to form a proper smile because of your palsy."

"I can't believe I left that in the book I gave you." She hid her face from him.

"Beatrice." He lifted her chin. "Don't be ashamed. Your words were painful to read but they made me know you better."

She saw no pity in his eyes, only understanding. If there had been even a hint of pity she would have left his bed immediately.

Instead, she answered a strange inner call to divulge more secrets.

"I remember that night so well. The doctor had been there with his metal instruments, stretching my mouth apart, probing and invasive. He'd prescribed a type of sling to wear around my head, to pull the side of my face into position. It was supposed to train my face to behave more normally. It was humiliating."

"There wasn't anything less invasive they could do?"

"It was all useless. My mother lived in a world patched together from false hope and quackery. That night I had a stomachache and I couldn't find my nurse, and I walked downstairs and my mother and father were arguing. I pressed my ear to the door of the study. My father said that I was a damned cripple. That no one would ever love me."

He cradled her in his arms, stroking her back lightly with his fingers. She nestled closer to his warmth.

"My mother was sobbing. 'My poor girl,' she said, 'she can't even smile. How will she ever attract a mate?' I ran back to my bed. That was the moment that I knew I'd never be the daughter my parents had wanted. I was hurt and angry. I didn't understand."

He didn't say anything. He just stroked her shoulders comfortingly.

"There was one physician that I liked. A kindly older man, very distracted and mumbling, but he suggested a healing exercise that I actually enjoyed. He said that reading aloud from dictionaries might help me with the ability to realize and feel facial movements. I progressed from memorizing dictionaries to wanting to create them. I learned all of these new words and I delighted in using them."

He kissed the top of her head.

She pressed her cheek against his chest. He was so warm and strong. "I retreated into my mind. It was safer there. My mother couldn't follow me into my scholarship. I decided that if I couldn't be whole of body, I'd become mighty of mind. But my intellectual prowess and odd turns of phrase didn't make me any friends at boarding school. There was one girl, Lady Millicent Granger, who decided I was secretly laughing at all of them and thought myself to be superior. She gave me the nickname Beastly Beatrice."

"She sounds like the beastly one."

"After my debut, I swiftly learned to shut my mouth, keep my head bent over a book, and hide behind the potted ferns. I became an expert at disappearing. That's what I was doing when you met me in Cornwall. Hiding from my mother. Trying to find a moment of peace to be myself."

He rose onto his elbow. "Look into my eyes, Beatrice. Do you see a reason to hide?"

His eyes were a shadowy blue in the firelight, his gaze steady and focused on her.

She could talk to him about this vulnerability. The young girl she'd been, angry and confused. "I've developed a tough skin. Nothing bothers me anymore."

"Your skin doesn't feel tough to me." He swept his fingers over her cheek. "It's soft as the underside of willow bark."

"I'm on the margins of society and I prefer to stay there. A spinster in my library in Cornwall."

"I think it would be a shame if you retreated to Cornwall forever, buried by towering stacks of books. Your bright light hidden away."

"If I'm hiding behind my books, you're hiding behind your charm. The jokes you make, the way you tease, and flirt and throw bonnets under carriage wheels. All of that posturing and bravado, it can't possibly be natural all the time. Everyone is sad sometimes, everyone hurts. You're no exception. And I'm not going to be hiding. I'm going to be free to be as scholarly as I please without fear of ridicule. Being a spinster doesn't have to mean a miserable existence. I might even take a lover, like Aunt Matilda did."

He coughed. "Take a lover?"

"A likely candidate might come along. Or I could place an advert in the *Village Crier.* 'Bookish spinster seeks fun-loving rogue for amorous adventures. Only highly skilled applicants need apply.'"

"You're not serious."

"Why, am I shocking you? Someone like you might climb through my library window one day."

"Someone like . . . me."

"Handsome. Roguish. The strong silent type. Someone like you would make a perfect lover. You'd never kiss and tell."

"Are we talking about your future . . . ? Because it sounds like you might be talking about this bed."

"And why not? By now you've learned that I'm not a conventional thinker. I don't follow the commonly held belief that a female must protect her virtue at all costs, that her virginity is her most precious possession. It's a double standard, one that comes at a cost to women. Men are encouraged to be promiscuous while women are taught to be virtuous. How can those two coexist peacefully? It seems to me, and to the other ladies of my society, that this is a dangerous standard to uphold."

"Lord, protect us from freethinking knitters."

"What would I be saving my virtue for? I don't plan to marry. And my friend the Duchess of Ravenwood has an excellent pamphlet detailing how to avoid unwanted conception."

He sat upright. "Now just wait a moment. If it's a lover you want, you don't have to advertise in the *Village Crier.*"

"Are you applying for the position? I know we only have a few days left together, but that's ideal for both of our purposes. I wouldn't want a lover moping about. What if you became enamored of me? Highly inconvenient to a scholarly female's grand plans to publish a dictionary."

"Ah . . . I rather thought it might be you who became enamored of me. There's where the danger lies."

"I'm willing to gamble with my emotions. Inside these walls I can be myself. Bolder. Freer. I can live life on my own terms, and I want to experience as much of that as possible. You bring it out in me. When I go back to my brother's house, I shrink back inside myself. Within these walls we belong together."

"But this isn't real life, Beatrice. This is a fairy tale we're telling ourselves. There would be real-life consequences."

"Perhaps. Or, perhaps not. It could be a beautiful memory we treasured forever. Sleep on it," she said lightly. "We'll talk tomorrow."

She kissed him in parting, then, because she had to return to her brother's house.

And she kissed him in greeting, because she'd met the new version of herself within these walls. This bookshop was a world unto itself. The rules she'd lived her life by didn't apply here.

And maybe, just maybe, they could find a way to be together.

Chapter Twenty

WHAT HAD SHE done?

Beatrice groaned into her pillow.

She hadn't drunk *that* much wine. Her head ached, though. Perhaps she'd imbibed a little more than she'd thought. The wine had loosened her natural inhibitions and then she'd become intoxicated on pleasure, on closeness. She'd opened up to Ford, told him secrets she'd sworn never to reveal.

About her childhood. About her friends.

Things she'd never confessed to anyone before. It had felt right in the moment but now she wasn't so sure. He was boarding a ship in a matter of days, so why had she told him so much about her past? And all of that audacious talk about taking a lover . . . what had come over her?

Her cheeks flamed as she remembered what he'd been reading and how she'd opened the book and read that particular passage about . . .

She burrowed deeper under her pillow.

What had happened between them last night was far beyond the boundaries of propriety—she wasn't delusional enough to attempt to convince herself it had been anything other than scandalous.

In society's eyes she was now ruined. Fallen. Downcast and lost forever.

She should be ashamed of what had happened but she wasn't.

Being with him last night had been revelatory. But she must remember that the bonds of intimacy between them had formed because they'd been working together toward a common goal.

Not because of any harebrained notions of love, or of a future together. She wasn't *that* much of a ninny. She wasn't ashamed of what they'd done on the bed. That had been delightful.

She was angry with herself for allowing him inside her heart. And for revealing her friends' secrets. She'd sworn an oath to the sisterhood not to reveal their true goals until it was agreed upon by the group.

She'd told him Viola's secret, and she'd been about to reveal Isobel's daring deception. She'd betrayed the trust of her fellow members of the League. How could she have done such a thing?

Viola and Isobel would attend her mother's costume ball tonight, and Beatrice would have to tell them what she'd done. She also wanted to be able to assure them that she'd sworn Ford to secrecy.

She must return to the bookshop and swear him to silence, for her friends' sake.

"My dear, are you ill?" Her mother sailed into the room, accompanied by the scent of violets and hair powder. "Why are you lazing abed? We have much to do before the ball tonight. First a round of morning calls, and then we will supervise the final touches in the ballroom before beginning your toilette."

"I'm feeling a little under the weather this morning."

Her mother sat on the bed and laid a cool hand on Beatrice's forehead. "You do feel slightly hot. You mustn't be ill. Not today of all days. You must look your best tonight. I'll send for Dr. Merton. He'll have something to ease the pain."

"No doctors, Mama." She'd had enough of doctors to last a lifetime. "I'll feel better after I have a rest and a bite to eat. You go on the calls, Mama. I'll be fresh as a daisy when you return."

Her mother stood up. "Very well. I expect to see you rosy-cheeked and bright-eyed when I return. That's an order."

Beatrice had two hours at most. She waited until her mother

left before dismissing her maid and dressing herself in one of her plain blue gowns and a pair of sturdy boots.

IT WAS A brisk day, and the walk through Mayfair and Pall Mall toward the Strand did Beatrice good. As she arrived at the book-shop, she noticed a carriage standing near the front door. As she fit her key to the lock, the carriage opened and Mr. Foxton alighted.

"Lady Beatrice," he said, lifting his hat. "I was here to see Mr. Wright, but it seems he's gone out."

"Whatever you have to say to Wright, you may say to me," she said coldly. "I own this property."

"Do you, though?"

"And just what are you insinuating by that question?"

"Why don't we discuss this inside?"

Beatrice bristled at the way he took ownership, inviting her to enter her own building. She pushed past him and hung her bon-net on a hook. It was market day and Mrs. Kettle and Coggins would be out purchasing provisions. Since Ford was gone as well, Beatrice was alone with Foxton.

Though he'd leave swiftly; she'd make sure of that.

"I can't offer you tea, Mr. Foxton, but I expect this isn't a social call. Say what you have to say." She hugged her arms over her chest and remained standing.

Foxton's gaze traveled over the front room. "I see you've made good on your promise to renovate the shop."

Afternoon sun played over the grain of the new oak flooring, highlighting blond and red strands. "Mr. Wright doesn't waste time. Now tell me why you're here, Mr. Foxton."

"Lady Beatrice, I had hoped that you and I might come to an amicable agreement as concerns the fate of this property. Since you persisted in reneging on the original agreement to sell me the property, I had to take matters into my own hands."

"I never made any agreement with you."

"Your solicitor's promise."

"Which is not the same thing at all."

"A point which has been rendered meaningless by what I'm about to tell you."

The gaunt, older man bared his teeth in a wolfish smile. "You don't own this bookshop, Lady Beatrice, and therefore its disposition is not a matter under your control."

"I beg your pardon?"

"While you have been tearing out counters and replacing floorboards, I had my lawyers do some research. It seems that the late Mr. Castle left the bookshop to his wife without scouring his family tree for any more appropriate male relation upon which to bestow his legacy. A Mr. Leonard Castle has come forward, and he has a legitimate claim to the property and to the inheritance. The matter of his claim could be tied up in the courts for months, if not years, I'm afraid."

Beatrice sat down in a chair, her mind refusing to accept that he'd found a way to defeat her. "You say this Mr. Leonard Castle came forward, but what you really mean is that you dug him up."

"If you want to dress it in those terms, Lady Beatrice. Someone's going to sell me the property, either you, or Leonard Castle. If you sell it to me right now, before he's made his claim, then you can keep the proceeds and I'll ensure that he goes away quietly."

"I know that you want to tear down these buildings and build a manufactory. But surely you see that a clubhouse would be far better for the Strand than another polluting factory. Such an eyesore might force the neighborhood into decline."

"Your definition of decline is my vision for progress, Lady Beatrice."

"You mean that once the neighborhood declines, you can open more factories. Profit in the name of progress."

"I don't understand why you've developed such a sudden attachment to a neglected property with an unsavory reputation. Surely your mother doesn't approve."

"She doesn't approve, but my brother, the Duke of Thorndon, is returning from the Continent soon and he's always been very generous to me. Do you want to pit yourself against a duke, Mr. Foxton?"

He was becoming angry. She read it in the set of his shoulders, even though he was as cold and expressionless as always. His fury was betrayed in the grip of his hand on his walking stick, the knuckles turning white. "Is that a threat, Lady Beatrice?"

She stood, squaring her shoulders and standing as tall as she was able. She had a sudden longing for Ford to be at her side, his wide shoulders a bulwark and a protection.

She must face down Foxton on her own.

She inhaled sharply. "My brother will stand behind me in this. You thought I would be easily manipulated, easily purchased. Now that you find me to be intractable, you're grasping at loose straws. But if it's a legal battle you want, then I'll be happy to give it to you."

Inside, she was shaking and her heart was pounding, but she stood her ground, unwilling to give an inch.

Foxton's face reddened and he pounded his stick on the floor. "You're what's wrong with womanhood these days, Lady Beatrice. Female intellects should be occupied with gentle, nurturing concerns. This mistaken grasping for independence and authority, this attempt to topple the natural order of things, is a dreadful travesty."

"Good day, Mr. Foxton. This conversation is over."

"I'll see you in the courts, Lady Beatrice."

The door slammed behind him and Beatrice sank into a chair, her limbs trembling with fear and anger. Even though she'd bravely dismissed him, the news of another potential heir had taken the wind from her sails. She knew from speaking with Isobel that the courts rarely sided with females over males when it came to inheriting property.

The door opened and Ford walked into the room carrying a heavy stack of boards and whistling a tuneless song. He stopped whistling when he saw her. Setting the boards down against the wall, he walked toward her, concern flooding his eyes. "Beatrice, what's wrong?"

"Foxton was here."

He dropped to his knees in front of her chair and grasped her hands. "Did he threaten you? Harm you in any way?"

"No. Yes. My head aches. I can't think."

"Which is it, no, or yes?"

"He told me that he found a distant male relation of Mr. Castle's who has some claim to the property. He threatened legal action that could tie up the ownership of the building for months or years."

She hung her head. "It's all over, Ford. They'll find a way to steal the property."

He stroked her hands. "It's not over. Not by half. He can't just come in here and talk to you like that. How long ago did he leave?"

"He left in a carriage and you won't overtake him. I handled it, Ford. I stood up to him. I didn't give an inch or let him see my dismay."

"I'm sure you were ferocious." He dipped his head to try to catch her eye. "Feeling a little under the weather, are we?"

She nodded.

"Wine always seems like a good idea in the moment, but sometimes the next day can be a challenge. Here, let me prepare you a remedy." He stood and offered her his hand.

She allowed him to pull her to her feet and lead her into the kitchen.

"Sit," he commanded.

She sat at the worn kitchen table and rested her elbows on the solid wood.

"Here's my remedy for a case of crapulousness." He handed her a glass. "A teaspoon of bicarbonate of soda mixed into a large glass of water. Drink up."

The mixture didn't look appetizing, but she drank it down.

"He won't stop until he owns this property, Ford. Isobel always says that the laws are firmly on the side of males when it comes to the ownership of property."

He took a seat across the table from her. "You don't know that this person has a credible claim."

"All of the work you've done. The dreams I allowed myself to dream. All of it could be for nothing."

"You fell in love with this house, with the idea of freedom from your mother's control."

"It's just a house. Four walls and a roof."

"A roof that doesn't leak now. Walls that will stand the test of time. I've made sure of that."

Beatrice sighed. "It's foolish to fall in love with a house. I thought we could make something beautiful, a lasting legacy, but we were only passing through. We're already memories, Ford. Already ghosts."

"Don't say that. It's not like you to just give up on your goals. This is your house, and it will be a welcoming haven for women to support each other's ambitions."

"About that. Ford, I shouldn't have told you Viola's secret."

"That she's finishing her father's symphonies?"

"Shhh." Beatrice placed a finger to her lips. "It's a secret. If word got out that Mr. Beaton wasn't composing the symphonies anymore, no one would pay him for them, and the audiences would disappear. Please promise me that you won't tell a soul."

"I would never betray your trust."

"Thank you. I'm sad that my ladies won't have a new clubhouse, after all."

"You can't take Foxton's word for anything. You'll have to verify this distant relation's claim for yourself."

"My brain isn't working properly today, though this tonic is improving things considerably. I didn't think I'd drunk too much wine, but perhaps . . ."

He met her gaze. "Yes, perhaps it was the wine. I didn't know you'd had so much."

"It wasn't the wine." How could she tell him what she needed to say? That she'd fallen in love with more than the bookshop. That she didn't want him to leave.

So many things to say and all of them sounded wrong in her head.

Everything seemed so bleak now. Foxton could find a way to take the shop. And Ford . . . hadn't put his arms around her yet.

"I only have a few small odds and ends to finish," he said. "I'll be finished by tomorrow."

"You may as well stop working. If the bookshop isn't mine, or if the ownership is under review, then there's no point in your completing the renovations. I'll still pay you, of course."

"It's not about the payment. I never leave a job half-finished. It's not in my nature. I've got to keep my hands busy."

"You may as well just leave." It would be better if he left. Seeing him again was only prolonging the inevitable pain of their parting.

"Don't lose heart. Let's pay this potential heir a visit. With my muscle and your pocketbook, we should be able to find a way to influence him."

Beatrice brightened. "I hadn't thought of that."

"I'm sorry I wasn't here when Foxton arrived. I hate that you had to face him alone."

"It's all right. I'm accustomed to being alone."

FORD WAS SEETHING. He didn't care about the vow he'd made to his mother any longer. It was time he paid his grandfather a visit. He couldn't allow him to threaten Beatrice, steal her dreams away.

"I'll be damned before I allow you to lose this property. You'll have your clubhouse for revolutionary lady knitters. And we'll find that ancient manuscript your aunt hid. I promise you that."

She smiled wanly. "Don't make promises you can't keep."

His jaw clenched tightly. "We'll find a way."

"I appreciate your optimism and I hope you're right."

"I made you something, Beatrice. I didn't have a chance to show you yesterday when you . . . visited me. Will you come upstairs with me?"

He led her upstairs to the reading room and opened the door. She entered, and spun slowly, observing the changes he'd made.

"Ford," she said wonderingly. "You built these for me?"

"I thought you might need a few more shelves for all of those books piled next to your bed," he said, his voice gone gruff. "I made them from the floorboards we pulled up together."

She ran a finger over the smooth wood. Her eyes shone behind her spectacles. "They're absolutely beautiful. I love them. And the desk?"

"I found that in the basement and brought it upstairs. It's a good size for you, I think." He'd placed the desk against the window. She'd said that would be a fine view for writing.

He'd laid out a brass inkpot he'd found, and several quill pens. He'd even found a stack of fresh manuscript paper and arranged it in the center of the desk.

"Ford." Her voice trembled. "I don't know what to say."

He hoped she wasn't going to cry. He felt suspiciously close to tears himself. He never cried. Not even when his friends had died. He wasn't about to start being sentimental now.

"I thought you could use the desk to work on your dictionary when you visit London. Perhaps other lady authors will use this desk, as well. Is that Daphne Villeneuve still alive?"

"She's very secretive. No one knows her true identity."

"I can imagine scintillating, bestselling etymological dictionaries being finished in this room," he said. "I also boxed up all of the naughty books and placed them in the basement. I may have kept one or two for myself."

"It's perfect, Ford." She wrapped her arms around his shoulders and hugged him. "All of it."

Startled, he stood there like a fool for a few moments, before returning the embrace. "I'm glad you like it."

"Like it? It's the most marvelous thing anyone's ever done for me."

"It was nothing."

It felt so right to hold her, fold her into his arms. He hadn't meant to make her cry. He scuffed his boot against the molding. "I had an idea last night, after you left."

She pulled back a little. "About the manuscript?"

"Yes. But I have to show you, and it's upstairs in the bedroom."

The unspoken words hovered there. Could they trust themselves to go into the bedroom together?

"You think you know where to find it?" she asked.

"I think you'll know, when you see what I show you."

"Then what are we waiting for?" She grabbed him by the hand and practically dragged him up the stairs. He laughed. When the lady was on the scent of an ancient manuscript, nothing got in her way.

When they arrived in Aunt Matilda's bedchamber, he brought her to the portrait. "Remember that her letter said 'let me point the way' and you took it literally to mean that her body was pointing in that direction?"

"Yes. Go on."

"Well, I thought, she's reading a book. Perhaps there are words somewhere on the book that might give us a clue."

"Of course! Why didn't I think of it?" She pushed her spectacles up the bridge of her nose and peered at the book in her aunt's hands. "She's reading the *Revelations*. I didn't notice because it was written in Latin instead of Old English. And the letters look like a recent addition—the paint strokes are fresher. And beneath the title"—she bent forward—"it says in French, *une chamber avec vue*. A room with a view."

She grabbed hold of his arm. "Ford. We have to go back to the reading room. The view of the Thames and the steps leading down to the river."

She raced back down the stairs. He'd known she would cleverly put it all together.

What an intellect. It made him want to kiss her in the worst way.

But they were on the hunt for an ancient manuscript.

When they entered the room, he pushed the desk out from the wall and dropped to his knees in front of the window, searching the floorboards for cracks. Almost immediately, he found what he was looking for. He pulled his trusty versatile tool out of his pocket and opened it to the blade.

He scraped around the edges of the board, working it loose, and then pried it up with the flat of his blade. It lifted easily. He reached his hand inside the exposed cavity and found the wrapped parcel.

He brought it out and handed it to Beatrice.

She accepted it with an expression of awe, holding the bundle as if it were an infant. "My treasured one, you've found a good home. I'll take care of you."

Ford couldn't take much more of her sweet words and the joy in her eyes. He made a show of replacing the board and moving the desk back into place.

"I don't even want to unwrap it yet, Ford. I want to live in this moment of discovery forever."

He wanted to unwrap her. She was too lovely in the morning sun, holding her precious book.

She set the wrapped parcel carefully onto the shelves he'd built her. "Ford, we'll find a way to keep this property, I know we will." She touched his cheek lightly.

"Beatrice, when you say we'll find a way to keep this property, it sounds like you think we could have a future together." He placed his hand over hers. They stood like that for a few seconds, their hands joined, their gazes locked.

"When I'm here with you in this house, I believe that anything is possible," she replied softly.

He kissed her fiercely, reveling in her sweet scent and the softness of her skin. The blazing intellect that burned through her words and the bravery with which she faced the world.

The mingling of their lips was nearly desperate, close to bruising, a driving urge to imprint themselves, to make this memory last forever.

She was wearing the same blue gown she'd worn in Cornwall, simple and pretty. "I like this one of your gowns the best."

"It's my favorite, as well."

"And this hairstyle is so easy to undo," he said in a husky voice, following his words with action.

Her red curls bounced over her shoulders, beckoning his fingers.

They were probably going to run back up those stairs in a few seconds.

"Beatrice? Where are you?" A high-pitched voice intruded into their idyll.

She jerked away from him, her face panic-stricken. "My mother!"

He dropped his arm from her waist. They stared at each other, frozen, for the space of a few seconds, and then they both began to move.

Pins back in her hair. His shirt tangling as he hastily fastened the buttons. The sound of footsteps on the stairs and another call of "Beatrice?"

"Mrs. Kettle and Coggins must have returned and they let my mother in," she whispered. She touched her lips, which were pink and swollen. "She can't see me like this."

"No," he said grimly. "She can't. You'll have to hide. Quickly, under the desk."

Chapter Twenty-One

BEATRICE CROUCHED BENEATH the desk. Her mother entered the room.

Don't look down, Mama.

"Have you seen my daughter? She left a note that she'd be here, and the housekeeper told me she was upstairs."

"Good day, Your Grace," Ford said smoothly. "I'm sorry, I didn't hear you calling as I was hammering these shelves." He held up a hammer. "Lady Beatrice was here, but she left shortly before you arrived. I think she said she was going to visit a Miss Mayberry."

"That's back in Mayfair. I wonder why she didn't take the carriage today. I don't like her walking when she's feeling ill. She must have slipped away without the servants seeing her. Are you the carpenter my daughter employed?"

"Stamford Wright." He bowed. "At your service. Would you care for a tour of the improvements I've made on the first level?"

Beatrice's nose tickled; it was dusty beneath the desk. She was going to sneeze. *Oh lord.* She held her nose and tried breathing through her mouth.

"I don't want a tour, Wright. I want you to return to Mayfair with me," the dowager duchess said.

"Pardon me?"

"I'm hosting a costume ball this evening and everything is in a shambles. I had a set piece designed for Lady Beatrice, and it's completely unstable and not fit to be seen. I want you to come and fix it for me."

"Er . . ."

"It's only for an hour. I'll hear no protests. My daughter can spare you for an hour. Come along." Her mother always did get what she wanted.

They left the room together, and Beatrice listened until the carriage wheels crunched away before emerging from her hiding place.

That had been entirely too close of a thing.

WHEN SHE ARRIVED home, Hobbs informed her that her mother wanted her in the ballroom. "Such a to-do, Lady Beatrice," he said as he took her pelisse and bonnet. "This ball will truly be a memorable occasion."

Her mother was in the ballroom, standing over Ford's shoulder as he fitted wheels onto a wooden cart of some sort. "Beatrice! You're here at last. Come and see! This is what I've been planning."

She approached, pretending to feign surprise at seeing Ford. "Mr. Wright?"

"I borrowed him for an hour. The other carpenter ruined everything, and Wright is doing an admirable job on the repairs."

He caught Beatrice's gaze for a brief moment before returning to his work.

Seeing him made her blush, thinking of what they'd been about to do.

Her mother caught her hand. "Well, I see the fresh air has done you good, you look blooming."

"Mother, what is this?"

It appeared to be an elaborate bed in front of a painted backdrop depicting a lush meadow filled with flowers and birds. The bed was mounted on a wooden frame that curved up at the sides, and the entire affair was set atop four wheels.

"It's your bower, Your Ladyship," said Ford.

"Isn't it beautiful?" her mother exclaimed rapturously.

"Why does it have wheels?"

"Because you're going to be rolled into the ballroom, reclining upon your bower. Oh, how I wish your brothers would be here. I would have them roll you in. As it is, I'll have to use footmen. Mr. Wright, I request that you attend tonight to make certain there are no mishaps with the wheels."

"She's lighter than a feather, Your Grace," Ford said, "and I'll build these wheels to last. Never fear."

"Excellent. That's exactly the reassurance I needed to hear." She pulled Beatrice toward the arrangements of red hothouse roses arranged at intervals along the walls. "Aren't they lovely?"

"Surpassingly." She plucked a red rose.

"Don't do that, my dear. You'll spoil the arrangement."

"What is my costume to be, Mama? You still haven't told me."

"You'll see soon enough. Mrs. Adler will arrive any moment now. And how was Miss Mayberry?"

Beatrice stared blankly for a moment before remembering Ford's story. "Ah, er, she's doing well. She'll be here tonight."

"What will her costume be?"

"I believe she's attending as the scales of balance."

"Well that should be interesting. Such a strange girl, Miss Mayberry. Almost totally lacking in feminine graces."

It was disconcerting seeing Ford inside her brother's house. He looked as confident and commanding as ever. He never changed, no matter the setting.

She wanted to go to him. Pull him upstairs to her room to show him the pile of books by her bedside. He'd built her those bookshelves, and she couldn't help thinking that perhaps he'd been trying to tell her something with his gift.

"Are you listening, Beatrice?"

"I'm sorry, Mama, what were you saying?"

"I was not at all satisfied with the way you waltzed at the last ball we attended. Your steps were very poorly executed and your carriage was insufficiently erect."

Beatrice thought she heard a soft snort of laughter from Ford's direction. Yes, her mother had said erect. The man had a filthy mind.

And so did she, when it came to rogues who had been about to carry her into bedrooms.

"I'll do better tonight, Mama."

"It's your carriage and the position of your neck the critics will be scrutinizing. Mr. Wright," called her mother. "Do you waltz?"

Ford turned. "I know how to waltz. But I don't care for dancing."

"Overcome your distaste and help me, Wright. This is an urgent matter."

"Mother," Beatrice said, "he doesn't want to waltz, and neither do I. I'm rather tired. May I go upstairs?"

"Not yet. I want to see you waltz. Every detail must be perfect tonight." She sailed over to Ford. "Mr. Wright, indulge me for a moment. Come to the center of the floor"—she led him out by the hand—"so that I may show my daughter the correct posture for the waltz."

Beatrice nearly broke into laughter when she saw the expression of helpless horror on Ford's face as her mother positioned his arms to her liking and then stepped into them . . . and led him into a waltz.

"Now see, Beatrice," her mother said. "Observe how the angle of my head makes my neck appear longer. Very nice, Wright. You'll do much better for dancing practice than Hobbs, and that's certain. Are you watching, Beatrice?"

Beatrice chuckled softly. "I'm watching."

Ford glowered at her as he spun around the dance floor with her mother in his arms.

"There, now, it's your turn," said her mother breathlessly, curtsying to Ford and stepping away.

Ford held out his hand. "Lady Beatrice," he said in his low, compelling voice. "May I have this dance?"

Her mother clapped her hands. "That's perfect, Wright. Join in the spirit of things."

The laughter died on Beatrice's lips. All of the smolder had flared back to life in Ford's eyes. Couldn't her mother see it? He was practically devouring her with his gaze.

The temptation in that simple question was too much to resist.

Yes, I'll dance with you. I'll take you to my bed. I'd board a ship with you, if you asked me in that wicked way.

"I would be honored, Mr. Wright." She walked to him, holding his gaze.

She handed him the red rose she'd plucked and he tucked it into a buttonhole of his coat.

"Now, take her in your arms, Wright. And Beatrice, lift your chin, you look like a turtle. And arch your back slightly, there, that's better . . . One, two, three. One, two, three."

Her mother's voice receded into the background. All that existed was Ford's hand on her waist, his fingers closed around hers.

I'm sorry, she mouthed.

"Don't be," he whispered in her ear. "I'm enjoying myself."

She breathed the sweet scent of the rose. What would her mother do if Beatrice and Ford ended this waltz with a searing kiss?

Probably collapse on the floor and have to be wheeled out on that bower.

Hobbs came into the room and handed her mother something, and she left with him.

Ford slipped his hand lower, over her hip. The impact of that possessive gesture hit her full force in the chest. Yearning filled her heart.

He stroked his thumb over her palm. "So soft."

She felt both fearless and tentative, the new Beatrice, the one who waltzed with her lover in her mother's ballroom.

She wanted to run her hands over his bare flesh. She wanted to be shaped by him, in return.

"How's my favorite little sister?" a gruff voice asked.

Beatrice dropped Ford's hand and spun around. "Drew!" She raced toward her brother, arms outstretched, and flung herself into his embrace. "You're back!"

"Beatrice, sweetheart. Let me look at you." She laughed as her brother held her at arm's length. "What's happened while I've been away? You're positively glowing."

Beatrice glanced at Ford, who had moved back to his work and taken up his hammer. "I've been busy."

"I can't wait to hear all about it."

"Where's Mina?"

"She's feeling a bit off—went upstairs with mother. She'll be down soon. What's all this?"

"Rehearsals for the costume ball tonight."

"Tonight?" Drew groaned loudly. "Dear God, no."

"Afraid so. And you know you'll be expected to attend as the guest of honor. In fact, you'll probably have to wheel me into the ballroom on that ridiculous contraption over there."

"What the devil is that?"

"A mobile bower."

"Wright? Is that you?" Drew asked. "What are you doing here?"

Ford stopped hammering at the floral bower and bowed. "Your Grace."

"Thought you'd be back at sea by now," said Drew. "And your father, is he fully recovered?"

"Back on his feet and already repairing the mews."

"I'd expect no less. So you're in London and my mother found out and hired you?"

"Actually, Lady Beatrice hired me."

A puzzled frown appeared on Drew's face. "Hired you, for what?"

Beatrice hooked her arm into her brother's elbow. "So many things have happened since you've been away. I inherited a bookshop from Aunt Matilda—did you know about her?—and Mr. Wright has been helping me repair the roof and patch the flooring. He's done a wonderful job! It's going to be the new clubhouse for the Mayfair Ladies Knitting League, that is if another prospective heir doesn't win his dubious claim."

"I've been gone too long." There were mauve shadows under her brother's eyes and new lines around his mouth.

"My ship arrives day after next," Ford said. "Before I leave London, I'd like to speak with you on a business matter, Your Grace, but it can wait until tomorrow, after you've reunited with your family."

"Why don't you join me in the billiard room? I could use a drop of something to calm my stomach. Still feel as though I'm standing on the deck of the ship."

"I know the feeling," Ford replied.

The dowager appeared at that moment. "Andrew, my love, you can't take my carpenter away. Not when I've just found him. The bower will be complete by tonight, won't it, Mr. Wright?"

"Of course, Your Grace."

"Wright, you'll attend the ball as my guest," Drew said. "I'll invite some naval officers. It will do your career good to be seen hobnobbing with dukes."

"That's very kind of you," said Ford stiffly, his back straight. "I don't own any formal wear."

Drew clapped him on the back. "It's a costume ball, so you can wear anything you like and I won't take no for an answer. You'll be my guest. And he'll keep an eye on the bower, Mother. He'll make sure everything goes smoothly. Wright always gets things done. Now about that drink . . ."

Drew winked at Beatrice and then steered Ford out of the room.

Beatrice knew that Ford had been waiting to talk to her brother. It had been his goal all along. Now that the shop was renovated and her brother had returned, he really had no reason to remain in London.

As her mother chattered about costumes and dance cards, Beatrice couldn't help thinking that tonight might be the last time she ever saw Ford.

The thought pierced her heart, leaving a pain that was almost physical.

If he attended the ball tonight, she'd be expected to ignore him while lavishing attention on people she was at best indifferent to, and at worst loathed passionately.

She could never ignore Ford.

The seed of an idea began to germinate in her mind. A proper lady was supposed to wait for a gentleman to ask her to dance.

But Ford was no gentleman, and Beatrice no longer followed the rules of propriety.

Chapter Twenty-Two

THORNDON WAVED AWAY his servants and poured Ford a brandy. They sat in comfortable chairs by a roaring fire and the duke loosened his cravat.

"It's an unexpected pleasure to see you, Wright. And it's wonderful to be back in England."

"Did you have a good tour?"

"It was . . . thrilling. Glorious. Exhausting. Couldn't be anything else with a bride like Mina. My brother got into a spot of difficulty and we . . . Mina and I . . . let's just say it wasn't much of a tranquil honeymoon. As I said, I've been gone too long. I feel as though I've been neglecting my estate. How are things at Thornhill? I can't wait to see the faded old beauty again."

"That's what I wanted to speak with you about. The great house is very well—I finished the renovations and even progressed further."

"Thank you. I was lucky to have your services."

"The house is in fine repair, but I'm afraid I have some bad news. I discovered something disturbing during my time there. I think your land agent and your solicitor are in league to skim profits away from Thornhill, and possibly your other properties, as well. Several things just didn't add up while I was there."

Thorndon sat up straighter and set down his brandy. "That's a serious accusation. Do you have any proof?"

Ford hadn't brought the bill of sale with him that he'd pilfered from Gibbons's desk. "I can present you with proof tomorrow. It's a bill of sale for timber from your estate. Some of it was to be used on Thornhill, some to be distributed to the tenants for repairs, and some purchased by townsfolk. I calculate that Gibbons only recorded half of what was sold."

Thorndon tossed back his brandy. "Thank you for bringing this to my attention."

"I didn't want my father to be cast into suspicion if the truth came out another way, as he's responsible for the logging on your estate. I think they took advantage of his injury to sell for their own profit. And I suspect they've been in league for years, and not just undercounting the sale of the timber."

"This is disheartening. Gibbons is a distant relation and I trusted him completely. I'll launch a full investigation." He poured more brandy. "And I won't blame your father. He's never given me any cause to doubt his absolute integrity. I like and value him and I like you, Wright. You're a good man."

"Thank you. So are you."

"Even though I neglected my estate."

"I didn't say that."

"You didn't have to . . . I heard it loud and clear. As I said, I like you." Thorndon set down his glass. "But if you're toying with my sister's affections, if you've hurt her in any way, I'll cheerfully kill you."

Ford blinked. The transition from amiable to murderous had been so sudden. "Your sister is in no danger from me."

Was that true? Ford wasn't so sure anymore. When they waltzed around the ballroom today he'd indulged in the wild fantasy that they might find a way to conquer the barriers of class that stood between them.

And here was her brother making certain that those barriers were solidly in place.

"Good. Then we understand each other?"

"Completely." Ford was a good man, but he wasn't good enough for the duke's beloved little sister.

Thorndon refilled Ford's glass. "Let's drink to Thornhill."

"To Thornhill."

A tall, fair-haired man with a pronounced limp walked into the study. "Pour me a glass, Thorny."

"Rafe, you reprobate," said Thorndon. "Where have you been? We've been halfway across Europe searching for your sorry arse."

"Here. There." The duke's brother waved vaguely with his hand. "Hand over that bottle. I've a dreadful feeling that I might be sobering up for the first time in weeks."

"That's not an answer, and you know it." Thorndon poured his brother some brandy. "Rafe, this is Mr. Wright, the son of my lead carpenter at Thornhill."

"Pleased to meet you, Wright." Lord Rafe nodded his way. "Beatrice is looking well. Must be in love, silly goose. Women only get that shiny look in their eyes when they have some poor fellow in their sights. Who's the lucky man?"

Ford shifted in his chair. It was probably time to leave now that he was outnumbered.

"Earl of Mayhew, I think I heard mother say?" said Thorndon.

Ford couldn't stay silent at that. "She's not marrying Mayhew."

Both brothers turned to stare at him.

"Oh?" asked Thorndon, raising one thick, black brow.

"That is, Mayhew's not fit to marry her," he clarified. "The man's a heartless debaucher. I know it from a friend."

"I agree with you there, Wright," said Lord Rafe. "Mayhew's rotten, and that's putting it mildly. Wouldn't allow Beatrice to marry him."

"I'll have a chat with our mother," said Thorndon. "Tell her to set some other poor fellow up in her sights."

Ford cleared his throat. "Thank you for the brandy, Your Grace. I'll leave you and your brother to talk. I believe your mother requires me back in the ballroom for more repairs."

Thorndon held his gaze for a long moment before nodding. "I'll see you tonight at the ball, Wright. I'll send you one of my old costumes. We're much of a height and build."

Ford should feel relieved. The duke had taken his warning about his land agent seriously, Ford's naval career might receive a major boost tonight, and he had completed the renovations on the bookshop.

But instead he felt hollow. None of it mattered if Beatrice lost the bookshop . . . and he lost Beatrice.

"You've changed, Beatrice." Mina cocked her head. "There's something different about you. You're looser somehow, less guarded. You don't hold yourself with such stiffness and formality."

"And you're looking lovely as ever, Mina." Her sister-in-law had the dainty features and fair hair of a porcelain child's doll, but her delicate appearance belied her dynamic, resourceful, and powerful character.

"I feel like a lumbering elephant. Have you noticed how swollen my ankles are? Drew hasn't even noticed yet. He can be dense sometimes, the big lug."

"Noticed what?"

"That I'm with child."

"Oh, Mina. How marvelous!"

"Is it? Because so far it's been endless bouts of nausea and swollen extremities."

"Why haven't you told Drew yet?"

"I wanted to be sure. It could have been seasickness. But your mother took one look at me and she knew. So now I have to face the facts."

"You're not happy about it?"

"I don't know what I am. Of course I'm happy, but I feel so out of control of my body. It's doing these strange things. And my emotions keep seesawing from one extreme to the next."

"Once you tell Drew you'll feel better. Then he'll have to rub your feet and fetch you whatever delicacies you desire."

"He already does that. I have him well-trained."

"Mina." Beatrice laughed. "I missed you."

"Did I hear my name?" asked Drew, entering the parlor. He bent to kiss his wife on the cheek.

"I see your mother is up to her old tricks. Hosting balls in the hopes of finding mates for her remaining children," said Mina.

"Nothing can stop Mama when she has her heart set on something," Beatrice agreed.

"I hear she wants you to marry the Earl of Mayhew?" asked Drew.

"Not going to happen," Beatrice replied vehemently. "I've been meaning to set her straight on that count but she keeps avoiding the subject."

"Glad to hear it. Because I just had a very bad report about the earl from Wright." Drew settled on the sofa next to Mina and draped his arm around her shoulders. "You were dancing rather closely with Wright when I walked into the ballroom."

"Mama was making me practice my waltzing."

"I remember when you met Mr. Wright in Cornwall." Mina's lips lifted in a smile. "You told us that he was the most annoyingly arrogant man in the world and that he thought he was God's gift to womankind."

"He does have a very high opinion of himself," said Beatrice, "but he lives up to his reputation."

Her brother narrowed his eyes. "I hope you are referring to his reputation as a formidable builder, and not as an inveterate rogue."

"As a builder, of course," she said sweetly. "I can't wait to show you the bookshop I inherited. Although there's a ruthless man, Mr. Foxton, who covets the property so that he can build a factory, but we're not going to allow him to steal it. He's found a distant relation to make a claim, but Ford, that is Mr. Wright, and I are going to visit this so-called heir and—"

"Have you and Wright been spending a lot of time together?" Drew asked, the suspicion deepening in his eyes.

Beatrice kept her mouth closed. She couldn't be goaded into revealing her feelings so easily.

"I don't want to see you hurt, Beatrice," said Drew, his gaze softening.

"I'm not going to be hurt." Though she might be confused. She'd had her life all planned out, and now she felt like something might be missing.

"Do you love him?" asked Mina, never one to mince words.

"We can't be together so what's the use in using labels like that? He's leaving London soon and our mother would never approve of a match between us." And Ford had made no indication that he was thinking about marriage.

And Beatrice would never marry. Though she might share one dazzling waltz with a handsome rogue this evening. A waltz that could lead to . . . other things.

Mina and Drew exchanged a worried look. "I think that might be a yes, Drew."

"Beatrice, I know that love can come out of nowhere and blindside you. It happened to me." He stroked Mina's shoulder. "You lit a fuse that blew a ragged hole in my heart, Mina. I've never stopped marveling that you found me."

"I was given a duke dossier and your name was at the top, my dear."

Beatrice had heard the full story of their initial animosity and subsequent courtship many times, and it never failed to make her smile.

"I only caution you to be careful," said Drew. "Men like Mr. Wright aren't the type to settle down with one woman. And you're right about our mother's disapproval. She has her heart set on you making a titled match."

"I don't intend to marry, you know that," said Beatrice. "I'm enduring a few more balls and then I'll move back to Cornwall. That is, if you'll still have me?"

"Of course we will. You may stay there as long as you like," said Drew.

"Forever?"

"Forever. Just don't adopt seven cats and start talking to ghosts," Mina said.

"I might, at that."

Their conversation turned to Thornhill House. She'd successfully deflected their concern for her. She was genuinely glad to see them, and it made her happy, but seeing them openly professing their love had set her heart aching again.

Wishing for impossible things.

Chapter Twenty-Three

"Mother—what am I supposed to be?" Beatrice asked later that evening, after she'd been costumed for the ball.

"Why, Psyche, of course. I thought you'd recognize it immediately, being such a learned Greek scholar. Psyche was a princess so beautiful that the goddess Venus became jealous and exacted her revenge by—"

"Yes, I know the myth of Psyche and Cupid. It's quite a salacious one though, isn't it? Lots of tribulation and more than the usual amount of violation."

"Yes, but thankfully there's a happy ending. Psyche becomes immortal, and she and Cupid are married in the heavens. It's ever so romantic."

Not really. Not if one factored in the violating Cupid did in the name of love. Better him than the beast, he reasoned. But it was violation, all the same. Not wanting to argue about the twisted plotlines of Greek mythology, Beatrice decided to let that one lie.

She plucked at the diaphanous yellow skirts. "What I want to know is . . . why am I covered in butterflies?"

"White butterflies to symbolize purity. You are my pure, sweet girl. You've always been so very virtuous, held yourself so aloof. You will be like a butterfly tonight. You will climb down from your bridal bower and flit here and there, darting amongst the guests."

"Mama, please. I don't flit."

"Try to flit, darling. Do try." Her mother took her hands. "For me."

Beatrice was doing all of this for her mother. Agreeing to wear the gown, be wheeled in on this confounded contraption. Wear the yellow gown and butterflies in her hair.

But she drew the line at *flitting*.

"And are these actual dead butterflies glued to this blindfold you want me to wear?"

"Mrs. Adler assures me that the glue will hold and not one fragile wing will tatter. Of course you mustn't venture too close to the candles."

"Am I combustible?"

"Mrs. Adler did say that the glue was highly flammable, but there's nothing to worry about. She's a genius. I didn't have the heart to tell her that you misplaced her masterpiece of a bonnet before you'd even had a chance to wear it in public."

"You know this is a blindfold, not a mask?"

"Psyche was kept blindfolded so she wouldn't see her monstrous bridegroom—and then your Cupid will appear from the crowd and replace your blindfold with this mask." She removed Beatrice's spectacles and placed a yellow silk mask studded with diamonds and edged by more white butterflies on her face, tying it with a bow at the back of her head.

"Is Lord Mayhew my Cupid? If so, I need to talk to you about something—"

"Not now, Beatrice. Not now. I have so many preparations to make. All you have to do is recline upon your bower and look beautiful. You look so lovely tonight. You make me so proud." Her mother wiped a tear away from her eyes with a lace-edged handkerchief.

Beatrice had pined to hear those words as a child, but tonight they left her hollow.

"Your mask slipped, darling. Make sure it's tightly secured."

And there it was. *You look beautiful.* And then, *Make sure you stay covered.*

Her mother left the room.

Beatrice sat on the bower in her cheerful yellow gown with its army of chaste butterflies.

She didn't feel very bright and cheerful. All of this pretending to be docile, chaste, and decorous was beginning to be ridiculous. After what she'd done with Ford, the freedom and abandon she'd experienced, she didn't want to pretend anymore.

She wanted to be truly herself from this moment forth.

"Knock, knock," a voice called and Isobel and Viola entered the room.

Isobel was dressed all in gold silk. She raised her arms, showing Beatrice the gold chains and round gold basins attached to her wrists. "I do love a costume that precludes me from being able to dance, for fear of knocking some poor bloke about the head with a gold scale."

Beatrice chuckled. "And what are you, Viola?"

"You can't tell?" Viola did a little twirl. "I'm a viola, of course. Can't you see the scrolls and strings I painted on this old gown?"

"Now that you mention it I do see some squiggles."

"We smuggled in a bottle of Henrietta's wine," said Viola. "We thought you might require fortification."

A lump rose in Beatrice's throat. She loved her friends. "Thank you."

"Oh dear. What is that thing you're sitting on?" Viola asked.

"It's meant to be my bridal bower," she said glumly. "I'm Psyche. And no doubt my mother told Mayhew to come dressed as Cupid. I'm to be wheeled into the ballroom on this thing."

"And your gown is . . . well, it's . . . words fail me," Isobel said.

"Instead of a Grecian robe, my mother has imagined me as some sort of yellow burst of sunshine, dripping with glass beading and butterflies. I think I'm going to blind everyone. Pass me some wine."

"I brought glasses." Isobel pulled three glasses out of her reticule.

"I'm supposed to wear this blindfold." Beatrice held up the silk cloth. "She doesn't want anyone seeing my face until the very last moment."

Viola sighed. "I'm sorry, Beatrice."

"My mother . . . I love her but . . ."

"It's always difficult with mothers," said Isobel. "They want the best for us but can't seem to truly *see* us."

"She told me that I looked beautiful, and then, in the very same breath, told me to keep my mask tightly secured. Those two things can't exist together anymore. I don't want to stay covered, hidden away. Not anymore. I want to be me."

She sipped her wine. "Perhaps I should spill red wine all over this gown."

"Then they'd think you were supposed to be the female version of Bacchus," said Isobel.

"You could roll out clutching a wine bottle," said Viola. "Perhaps we could find a cluster of grapes."

"And we could dress one of the footmen in a Roman toga and have him lolling at your feet. You could feed him grapes."

"Ladies," said Beatrice. "While I appreciate your enthusiastic efforts to cheer me up, the fact of it is that this gown is hideous, I look ridiculous in it, and wine won't improve anything."

"Wine improves everything," said Viola, taking a large sip from her glass.

"Mr. Wright is here," said Beatrice.

"What, here at the ball tonight?" asked Viola.

"My brother invited him."

"How does that make you feel?"

The butterflies sewn on her mask migrated to the inside of her belly. "It feels like I've walked over the edge of the ninny cliff and plummeted into the lovelorn abyss."

"Oh. Beatrice." Viola sat next to her on the bower. "Have you finally admitted it?"

"I don't think I can hide it anymore."

"Then don't," said Isobel, always so pragmatic.

"But he's leaving soon. And I knew that, of course I knew that. But I continue to have these irrational dreams that he decides to stay, and that my mother magically transforms into someone who would allow me to be happy."

"Does he make you happy?" asked Isobel softly.

"He does." She hadn't meant to admit any of this, but her friends were so dear to her and she was tired of suppressing her emotions.

"Maybe you can find a way to be together," said Viola, ever the romantic.

"There's another obstacle thrown in our path, ladies. Foxton visited the shop today and threatened me with the possibility of another heir to challenge my ownership of the property."

"We'll fight him," said Isobel. "We'll fight him to the death! He doesn't know about me, for example, or my access to legal records."

"Why are men so threatened by the idea of allowing women to have any power?" asked Viola.

"Ford . . . Wright suggested that we pay this potential heir a visit." Beatrice sighed. "And there's the problem of Mayhew. I'll never marry him, obviously, but I haven't found a way to inform my mother that all of her hopes are in vain."

"Your mother lives in a fantasy world," said Viola. "She thinks that if she sets the stage and writes the script, that you'll learn to speak your lines like an obedient girl and accept the handsome prince, and live happily ever after."

"Poor Mama," said Beatrice. "She's in for a rude shock. You know, I've been thinking. We women are all so critical of ourselves. We're too plump, or too thin. Too tall, or too short. Our hair is too curly, or too straight. We live in a society that rewards conformity to a strict set of physical standards and an even more rigid set of rules for proper behavior. We have these unpleasant thoughts running round and round in our minds. Wouldn't it be revolutionary if we decided to love ourselves exactly the way we are?"

"I'll drink to that," said Viola, clinking her glass against Beatrice's.

"I have an idea," said Beatrice. "My mother won't like it, but it's not about her." As she told her friends what she was planning, they nodded enthusiastically and offered helpful suggestions.

"Your mother will probably never let you speak to us again after this," said Viola.

Her friends helped her with the transformation, keeping the maids from the room and watching for her mother.

No one disturbed them and soon Beatrice was ready.

"Are you certain that you want to do this?" Isobel asked her solemnly.

"I've never been more certain of anything in my life," Beatrice replied. "I've decided to stop hiding for the benefit of others. I intend to be wholly me."

She inhaled, held the breath for a moment, and exhaled, thinking of Ford. He'd given her this idea. Casting her bonnet into the street, praising her choice of gown in Cornwall, and telling her to break free from her mother's control.

To breathe. To be fully present. To take risks and live life to the fullest. Unburdened by shame or by fear.

She was tired of the bonnets and the blindfolds.

It was time to emerge from her chrysalis.

The costume Thorndon had given him fit Ford perfectly.

Tight black trousers, shiny black boots, a white shirt with lace at the throat and cuffs, a long black silk cape with a high collar, and a black tricorn hat.

A black silk mask that tied at the back of his head completed the highwayman costume.

Ford didn't give one goddamn about London high society and its exclusionary and frivolous entertainments, but he did care about Beatrice, and how she saw him. In this mask he was a mysterious marauder, come to steal her breath away.

He strode through the crowded ballroom with his customary swagger, and every highborn lady in the room followed him with glittering eyes behind their masks.

Sorry, ladies. I'm here for one woman, and one woman only.

And she was going to be wheeled into this ballroom on a bed atop a wooden platform laden with flowers, fruit, and birds like some sacrifice to the gods.

But he'd be the one to claim her, if only for one waltz. For one night.

He'd show everyone in this room, and Mayhew in particular, that the lady was his, and his alone. And, let's be honest, he wanted to steal a kiss on the balcony.

And another.

As many as he could. He was well and truly addicted to Lady Beatrice Bentley.

"Admiral, this is the man I was telling you about, Stamford Wright." Thorndon approached with a naval officer in tow. "Wright, this is Admiral Sir Francis Emsworth."

"Wright. You're about to sail on the HMS *Boadicea*, I hear?" asked the admiral.

"Sir, yes, sir."

"You look an able-bodied sailor, Wright. We require stalwart men in the Royal Navy. I tell you what I'll do—I'll see about having you posted to a first-rate three-decker. How does that sound? You'd see more action that way."

More action. More bodies to feed the roiling cauldron of the sea.

Maybe his own body weighted down by cannonball shards and growing seaweed in his hair at the bottom of the ocean.

"That sounds brilliant, sir. I'm honored."

"Pretty ladies here tonight, Thorndon. And you can't tell which one is your wife and which one your mistress with all of these masks, eh?"

Thorndon didn't crack a smile. He was dressed in a similar costume to Ford, with a black cape with a red silk lining, but no tricorn hat. "I have no mistress and never will. One woman is all I can handle."

The admiral shrugged. "To each his own."

"What are you supposed to be, Your Grace?" Ford asked.

Thorndon pulled his black silk cape over his face with one arm. "I'm a bloodthirsty vampire. Now where is that pretty wife of mine? I want to bite her neck."

Thorndon and the admiral left.

Ford intended to stay right here in the center of the throng, ready for Beatrice's grand entrance. The moment had arrived. A hush fell over the crowd as the orchestra began a dreamy melody with lots of quivering notes from the violins.

Soon Beatrice would glide through the doors, hidden at first by the high sides of the bower, and then she would rise in her glittering silk gown with her hair towered high and probably stuck all over with flowers and feathers, and, who knew? Perhaps an actual bow and arrow. Ford wouldn't put anything past that mother of hers.

He was here to applaud her triumph, and he wanted her to see him watching.

The rolling wooden bower appeared with Miss Mayberry and Miss Beaton pushing it from behind, trailed by some very confused looking footmen.

They wheeled it into the center of the ballroom, and the footmen opened the hinged sides of the platform to reveal Beatrice reclining in her boudoir, propped up on one elbow.

She plucked an apple from the basket of fruit and took a large bite.

The room went completely silent.

The dowager duchess emitted a high squeaking sound.

Beatrice smiled that breathtaking, lopsided smile of hers, and stepped down from her bower with the aid of her friends.

Instead of a frothing silk ball gown, she wore the simple blue dress. The one he liked the best.

Her hair was loose and long. She looked like a dreamy Arthurian maiden from a painting in a museum, coppery red curls rioting over her shoulders and down nearly to her waist.

She held the apple in one hand, and a book in the other.

She wore no mask, and her spectacles caught and reflected the light from the chandeliers overhead. She held her head high, regal as any princess, as she stepped forth, setting the apple down but keeping the book.

"Greetings," she said, nodding to a guest. "How are you this evening, Lady Livingstone?"

It came to him in a blinding flash. This wasn't the costume she was meant to be wearing.

She'd thrown her mother's elaborate costume away. She was taking a stand. Drawing a line in the sand.

This was Beatrice in all of her bookish glory.

And Ford wanted to fall at her feet.

He began applauding, loudly, wanting her to know that he understood the purpose of her performance and he celebrated her choice. At first it was just him standing there, clapping his hands, but then Thorndon joined in the applause.

Once the duke was clapping, everyone had to join in.

Thorndon gave him a brief smile as the applause swelled.

Beatrice met his gaze from across the room. She gave him a smile, and his heart expanded to fill his entire body.

She was too gorgeous, his Beatrice. The one with ink stains on her fingers and books in her pockets.

He'd been deluding himself since the day he met her.

She was the reason he'd agreed to work on the bookshop—not his grandfather.

When she'd visited him at the docks in that travesty of a bonnet that blinkered her from the world, he'd thrown it away, and latched on to her like a life preserver in a stormy sea.

Cold, unwelcoming London had grown a heart, and that heart beat inside a woman brave enough to defy her mother in public. Bold enough to claim this ballroom as her own.

She'd claimed his heart from the very first moment he saw her.

Chapter Twenty-Four

"Well that went as well as could be expected, I'd say," said Viola.

"Is my mother still breathing?" asked Beatrice.

"Mina is there with her, offering her a glass of punch," Isobel reported.

"That tall masked highwayman started clapping and then everyone joined in. I think you have a mysterious admirer, Beatrice."

"Not mysterious." She'd known him instantly. No mask could hide those handsome features, that chiseled jaw, those mismatched blue eyes.

He'd applauded and her heart had soared into the chandeliers. He'd been swallowed up by the crowd but she knew he was there, and that he cared for her, and she meant to find him and claim him for a waltz.

"It's Mr. Wright, isn't it?" asked Viola, her eyes dancing. "He makes a dashing highwayman. Maybe he'll throw you over his shoulder and kidnap you."

That would be fine with Beatrice. She was still walking on air, her heart speeding with the knowledge of what she'd done. She felt powerful and more than a little drunk, even though she'd only touched her lips to the wine.

She took her friends' arms. "Shall we, ladies?"

"We shall," they said in unison.

They walked through the crowded room, arms linked and heads held high.

"That was quite the entrance, Bea." Rafe kissed her on the cheek. He wore a green Robin Hood costume with a peaked cap stuck with a jaunty feather. "Wouldn't have missed that performance for the world. I gather that's not the costume you're meant to be wearing?"

"Not even close," she replied.

"Her other costume was much more elaborate, Lord Rafe," said Viola.

"Good evening, Miss Beaton." Rafe made a flourishing bow. "Miss Mayberry." He doffed his cap for Isobel, who performed the briefest of curtsies in return. She'd always disapproved of Rafe's wild, and purportedly criminal, ways.

Beatrice searched the crowd for Ford. His tricorn hat shouldn't be difficult to find.

"Looking for someone, Bea?" Rafe asked.

"A certain tall, dark, and handsome highwayman, perhaps?" Viola asked.

Beatrice noticed a young girl wedged between the potted ferns and the wall. "I think we have another wallflower to befriend." She nodded toward the girl, who looked truly miserable, the feathers on her straw bonnet drooping to match her forlorn expression.

"A new recruit!" said Viola.

"Ladies," Rafe said with a bow. "I have an assignation with a brandy bottle."

"He hasn't changed at all," said Isobel, watching Rafe walk away. "It's a shame he's such an inebriate. He has a fine head on his shoulders but it's always sloshing with brandy."

The three of them headed for the ferns.

"Good evening," said Beatrice.

"Oh. Good evening," said the girl, glancing around to make sure they were addressing her.

"I used to hide exactly in that spot during balls," said Beatrice. "We won't all four fit, though."

"I suppose n-not," the girl stammered, her cheeks turning beet red.

"I'm Lady Beatrice Bentley, and this is Miss Beaton and Miss Mayberry. Might I know your name?"

"I'm Lady Philippa Bramble. This is only my second ball. I'm new to London. Thank you for inviting me, Lady Beatrice."

"You don't mean that. You're having a terrible time."

"I was until I saw you emerge in your spectacles holding your book. It was splendid. I love your costume. I wish I could wear a simple gown instead of this hideous creation."

"What are you meant to be?" asked Viola.

"I'm not quite sure." Lady Philippa glanced down at her dress with a woeful expression. "I think I'm meant to be a shepherdess?" She wore a straw bonnet and a wide, ruffled gown all in white. "Though I feel more like the sheep."

Beatrice laughed. "You don't like balls. It's all right, you can admit it."

"I don't like speaking to strangers, present company excluded. I'm no good with conversation. I'd rather be anywhere else, really."

"I like you, Lady Philippa," said Beatrice. "Isobel, do you have one of our cards?"

Isobel extracted a card from the small reticule she had looped around her wrist by a silken cord. "Come to the next meeting of our ladies society. You'd be most welcome."

"Th-thank you. Though I don't know how to knit."

"That won't be a problem," Viola assured her.

Beatrice caught sight of Ford near the refreshment table. "Ladies, I think I'll just go and have a glass of punch."

Viola followed her gaze. "A long, tall glass."

Beatrice hurried across the room, but people kept stopping her to offer insincere flattery. Luckily, she didn't see her mother. That was a conversation she dreaded.

When she finally made it to the refreshments, Ford had disappeared again. Frustrated, she stood on her tiptoes, searching the room for a tricorn hat.

A head of blond curls suddenly blocked her vision. "Lady Beatrice," Mayhew said, "I was told you would be garbed as Pysche. See? I'm your Cupid."

He preened for her in his fawn-colored tights and white toga. "I have a quiver of arrows waiting to pierce your heart."

"Mayhew," she said icily.

"You look flushed. Why don't we take some air." He placed his hand on the small of her back and steered her toward the nearby balcony door.

Beatrice dug her heels against the waxed ballroom floor. "I don't want to. I'm looking for a friend."

"A brief conversation, my lady." He caught her eye and raised one eyebrow. "There's something I want to ask you."

Beatrice's heart sank. She'd always known she'd have to refuse Mayhew at some point. There was no use hiding from this onerous duty. "Very well. A brief conversation."

He led her through the balcony doors. It was a cold evening and Beatrice shivered. "Very brief, Lord Mayhew."

He dropped to one knee in front of her and attempted to take her hand, which she promptly snatched away. "Lady Beatrice, you must know what I'm about to ask you."

"I have a sinking suspicion."

"Our mothers have arrived at an understanding."

"Have they?"

"And now it's up to us to fulfill their fondest hopes and desires. I agree it will be an excellent match. I'm willing to overlook your eccentricities, and you'll be gaining the most sought-after groom in all of London."

Beatrice couldn't stand the smug smile on his face. Her shoulders shook with rage. He actually thought he was doing her a favor.

"Lord Mayhew, let me be extremely clear. I would never marry you. Not in a million years."

"Pardon me?" An expression of disbelief descended over his face. "I must not have heard you correctly." He rose to his feet gracefully, towering over her while storm clouds gathered in his eyes.

Beatrice threw back her shoulders. "I know what you did to that barmaid, Mayhew. And I'm sure she's not the only innocent you've debauched and discarded."

His face blanched. "I've no idea what you're talking about. I was told that you would accept my proposal of marriage."

"You were told wrongly, then."

"You won't have a better offer."

"There couldn't possibly be a worse one."

"Now see here, you drab little eccentric, you should be thanking me." He propped his hand against the doorframe, effectively blocking her path back to the ballroom.

She'd broken her promise to Ford that she would never be alone with Mayhew. But she'd thought she'd be safe at her mother's ball, on the balcony only a short distance from the crowded ballroom filled with laughing, dancing people.

"Let me go back to the ballroom," she said evenly.

"Not until you agree to be my wife."

"That's never going to happen."

"I need your dowry and you're going to give it to me."

"Oh, now we get to the heart of it. I'm only a dowry to you. You'll never have me or my money, Mayhew."

"I'll have both. You know it's the thing to do. You'll come round."

"The lady refused your proposal. Now leave," said a gruff voice.

Ford. Coming to her rescue again.

Chapter Twenty-Five

BEATRICE WANTED TO applaud Ford, as he'd applauded her in the ballroom. He was every inch the highwayman, appearing suddenly in a whirl of black silk and flashing ice blue eyes set off by his black mask.

"Leave this ball right now or I'll break your nose and blood will drip all over that dainty white toga," he growled.

"I'd call you out if I knew your name, sir," said Mayhew.

"And I'd kill you from any distance, with any choice of weapons," Ford replied.

Beatrice shivered, from the night air and from the lethal edge in Ford's voice. She had no doubt that he could make good on that threat.

"You'd better leave, Mayhew," she said. "Before you do something truly stupid. No one's seen any of this. You can leave now with your nose intact."

"I can't believe I ever entertained the thought of marrying you." Mayhew adjusted his wig and shook out the folds of his toga.

"I'll be warning every lady of fortune I know about you," said Beatrice. "You won't find your bountiful dowry here, Mayhew."

"Leave," Ford said. "Now. While you can still walk."

Mayhew glared at them, and then edged his way toward the door.

When he was gone, Beatrice took a long, quivering breath.

Ford framed her face with his hands. "Did he hurt you?"

"No."

"Gods, Beatrice." His forehead touched hers. "Don't ever do that again."

She laid her hands over his. "I won't, I promise. I didn't think he'd be audacious enough to threaten me at my mother's ball."

"Men like him lash out like wounded animals when their pride is at stake. I lost you for a moment in the crowd. I was searching everywhere for you."

They stood like that, foreheads and hands touching. His lips were so close to hers.

"I have to go back inside."

"I know." Ford grinned. "So this is a costume ball. A bunch of fops running around in tights and curly wigs."

"Isn't it ridiculous? And I'm the Princess of the Wallflowers. My mother will be livid. You should have seen the costume she wanted me to wear. It was stuck all over with actual dead butterflies."

"I gather that the change was a surprise?"

"An unwelcome one for my mother. I'm always disappointing her and tonight I decided to do so in an ostentatious and irrevocable manner. Thank you for applauding."

"Of course. I understood the statement you were making. You look enchanting."

Her skin heated despite the cold air. "I really do have to go back inside. But I was hoping, that is . . . would you do me the honor of waltzing with me?"

He smiled. "Wallflower princesses don't follow the rules of propriety, I see."

"Propriety? I don't even know what the word means."

"Then allow me to recommend an excellent etymological dictionary by a studious lady I know . . ."

They entered the ballroom together, but before they reached the dance floor Lady Millicent intercepted them.

She flicked her gaze up and down Beatrice's gown. "And what are you supposed to be?"

"I'm a wallflower," said Beatrice.

Lady Millicent laughed. "I know that, silly. Why would you

wear an old gown like that to a ball? No one's going to want to dance with you." She turned to Ford. "Aren't you the dashing highwayman? Do I know you? You may steal me away for a waltz if you like."

"I'm spoken for," said Ford, taking Beatrice's hand.

They walked to the dance floor, leaving Lady Millicent gaping after them.

"She looks like a trout," said Ford.

Beatrice giggled. "She does, rather."

"You know that's my favorite gown of yours?"

"I know. You told me."

The waltz began and Ford took her into his arms. This time they had an audience. Everyone in the room was staring at them.

"No one knows who I am," Ford said. "Except your family."

"You're my mysterious highwayman."

"And you're my wallflower."

His hands were so large and capable. They built her bookshelves, defended her from harm, and sent desire racing through her body.

"I love you, Ford," she whispered.

SHE'D SAID THE words. Now it was his turn.

But if Ford said those words, everything would change. He'd have to admit that he believed there was a way for their two worlds to collide, to overlap. When there was none.

And yet she was waltzing with him in plain sight of her mother, for everyone to see.

Yes, he wore a mask, but she didn't. Not anymore.

"You don't have to say anything, Ford. Because I know you love me, too." Her smile sliced through his clothing and lodged in his heart.

"And how do you know that, princess?"

"Because you built me those shelves and you arranged that writing desk for me to use." She gave a little shrug of her shoulders. "It's quite easy to interpret."

"You think you know everything, do you?"

"My mother's always telling me not to be a know-it-all, but I just can't help myself. A Wallflower Princess can always tell when a highwayman loves her."

There was no use denying it. She'd stolen his heart.

He squeezed her hand. "You're right." There, he'd admitted it . . . in a way.

"I know that you don't want some socially acceptable version of me. With you I'm joyously myself—or not joyously—I won't pretend anymore. I don't have to be the perfect daughter my mother wants me to be. You helped me see that, Ford."

Her smile was light shimmering on the ocean.

A stone temple built to the gods, where he could shelter from every storm.

"Beatrice," he whispered, like a prayer. Like a poem.

A line from a song that stayed with you, that came to mind when you saw the sun set orange and fierce over a turbulent sea.

They were building something here, something good and strong.

But was it strong enough to weather the storms ahead?

The waltz ended, and Thorndon arrived to claim his sister for the next dance. He threw a look at Ford that could only be described as thoroughly suspicious.

Ford backed away. He'd had his one dance. It was time to leave.

He'd vowed to go speak with his grandfather, to find a way to convince him to allow Beatrice to keep the shop. He had no idea how he would find the leverage to make the old snake crawl back to his hole, but he'd damn well do it, or die trying.

He was going to make this right. Perhaps if Beatrice had her clubhouse, if what they'd created together was hers to keep, they could find a way to build a life together.

He was about to leave the duke's house when a footman approached him. "Mr. Wright?"

"Yes?"

"The dowager duchess would like a word with you. In her chambers."

Chapter Twenty-Six

"*I* SHOULD HAVE KNOWN." The dowager duchess paced in the center of her pink-and-white boudoir. "I should have known when my daughter showed such an interest in that dusty old bookshop. Ever since your appearance in her life she's become a completely different person. You've been corrupting her. Who do you think you are, Wright? You're nothing. You're no one."

Ford bore the onslaught of her contempt in silence.

Life was always attempting to bring him to his knees, but he always landed on his feet.

He clenched his jaw. The dowager just kept talking, spewing forth insults and hurling abuse, so finally he broke into the tirade. "I love your daughter."

When the words left his lips, he knew them to be true. He loved her and he didn't care who knew it.

"Love. What do you know about love? My son said that you have a reputation as a rogue. You're nothing but a common fortune hunter with delusional aspirations."

Thorndon must be in on the campaign to be rid of him, then.

The duke had warned him away from his sister, and introduced him to the admiral as a method of ensuring that Ford left England.

His mother's method of driving Ford away was far less subtle.

"I know your kind, Wright, but the fact that you would aim so high is incomprehensible to me."

"I'm not a fortune hunter. I don't care about her dowry."

"Of course you'd say that. To think that my son trusted you, and your father, and this is how you repay him?"

The mention of his father chilled his blood. The dowager and her son held all of the cards here. "It was only a waltz."

"What else has happened? Is she ruined?" Her cheeks were mottled with pink. "If she's compromised, the duke will have to call you out."

"She's not ruined. I give you my word."

His mind had gone numb. His heart was breaking.

What had he been thinking? Poetry and sunsets. Fairy tales and happy endings.

Weathering storms.

This was a blast of Arctic wind so deadly that it might freeze his bollocks off.

Beatrice's mother didn't just disapprove of him, she loathed him, and all his fortune-hunting kind, as she was happy to inform him over and over again.

"She was supposed to marry an earl," she wailed. "Mayhew left in a fury. Said a man dressed as a highwayman had gravely insulted him. I wonder that he didn't call you out."

She definitely wanted to see him at the wrong end of a pistol. Ford was beginning to wonder if she'd pull a firearm on him herself.

"Your Grace, there are things you don't know about the Earl of Mayhew. He has a cruel and heartless past."

"Heartless, you say. Do you know what is heartless? Attempting to steal away my only daughter under my very nose. I've been so blind. I knew she was acting differently, but I thought she'd finally decided to see reason. When all the while she was with you at that bookshop, being seduced. You are the cruel one, Wright."

"I haven't coerced her in any way. We didn't mean for this to happen."

"We. There is no we, Wright. Lady Beatrice is the daughter of a duke. You are a nobody. And your kind always has a price."

She stalked to a writing desk. "How much? Will twenty thousand be enough?"

His heart hardened to ice and broke off inside his chest.

Beatrice's mother was attempting to pay him to leave. "I would never take your money."

"Don't be stupid, Wright. You'll never have her fortune. This is the best you'll do. Take the money and leave. Never attempt to contact Lady Beatrice again."

Take the money and leave London. Never contact me again.

His stomach heaved. The exact words his grandfather had said to his mother when she'd taken Ford to London with her when he was eight.

The harsh, remembered shame of it.

He wasn't going to stay here and listen to any more of this vitriol. "I will never take your money."

He left the duke's townhouse without once looking back.

The waltz he and Beatrice had shared this evening had only been a lie they were telling themselves. They could never find a way to be together.

If she left the comfortable bosom of her family, if she lost her mother's respect and affection, she'd regret it for the rest of her life and she would grow to resent him.

And the duke could ruin Ford's family so easily. Take away his father's livelihood, his home.

No matter how much he cared for Beatrice or how he'd begun picturing a life with her, he'd always be the fortune hunter in her mother's eyes.

Highborn ladies had family fortresses built around them to keep the riffraff away—even ladies as unconventional as Beatrice.

The best thing he could do for Beatrice, and for his parents, was to leave. He'd pack his things and sleep on Griff's boat tonight.

His mother arrived in London tomorrow to meet with her sister and to see Ford off.

He had a path to follow.

At the moment that path led to a bottle of whisky and a night in the cramped quarters of a ship.

FORD WAS MISSING. Beatrice couldn't find him anywhere.

She'd noticed that he hadn't even looked at any other women tonight. He'd been focused on her. Attuned to the true meaning of her costume.

He'd been there in her moment of need. A larger-than-life avenger.

Dangerously threatening one moment and tenderly teasing the next.

When she was in his arms, it was a safe place. Not because he would defend her physically, though that had been thrilling, but because he knew her. He knew the young girl who'd written that journal entry and then torn it out, hidden it away in a book, in the same way that she'd buried her emotions.

She'd fought against her attraction to him from the moment she'd seen him outside her library window. She'd resisted the temptation to care about him, but it was impossible to resist any longer.

She had a choice to make: she could be a spinster who'd only experienced life in the pages of books.

Or she could seize this opportunity to live, even if the risks were enormous.

But how did one broach the subject of ravishing? *I'd like you to debauch me, please?*

Or maybe *she* should offer to ravish *him*?

There was only one way to find out which method worked the best. Her mother had gone to bed after taking a sleeping powder, and the household was quiet.

It was four o'clock in the morning.

And she had a rogue to ravish.

Chapter Twenty-Seven

"Ford." Beatrice knocked on the windowpane. "Ford!"

The window opened. "Beatrice? What on earth . . . ?"

"Let me in, it's freezing out here."

He leaned over the windowsill and lifted her by the armpits into the room where a lovely fire was blazing in the grate.

"How did you get up here?"

"There was a ladder against the side of the house."

"Your hands are like ice." He rubbed her hands between his. "You could have fallen to your death. Why didn't you just take the stairs?"

"Now where would the fun be in that?" she asked with a wink. "I wanted to surprise you."

She unclasped her cloak and it fell to the floor. She moved to the fireplace. She had to say this next part quickly, before she lost her nerve. She didn't turn around, speaking into the flickering flames. "I'm here for ravishing, Ford. And before you tell me that's a bad idea, I want to say that I've thought it all through very carefully."

He made not a sound. She'd shocked him into silence.

"I want to be with you tonight, Ford. Tonight and . . . always. You don't have to say anything, just listen. I know what I'm saying and I know what I'm doing."

He remained silent.

She rushed ahead, her face hot from the fire. "You handed me that hammer, and I know you were asking me to demolish more than plaster. You wanted me to be able to express my anger and to listen to my inner voice. I finally know that I'll never be able to please my mother, or society, or the world, and so now I can do what pleases me. And what pleases me is to be with you."

Why wouldn't he speak? She turned around. And that's when she saw it.

The trunk, packed and ready by the door.

She hadn't even noticed when she arrived—Ford had his coat on, and his boots.

"You're leaving?"

He bowed his head. "Yes."

"Right now?"

"It's for the best."

"But . . . why? Without saying goodbye to me?"

His face was impassive and stubborn. "I was always leaving, Beatrice."

"I know that. I . . . I didn't think you'd leave without saying farewell."

"You know I want to stay, Beatrice. You also know that I can't. Your mother, your family, this entire society would never approve of a match between us."

"Oh, so now you care about the rules of propriety?"

"This thing between us, this thing we've been building, it wouldn't survive the storm of scandal. I'd be labeled a fortune hunter and you'd be labeled as ruined, lowered, even lost."

"I don't care."

"You don't care now, but what about two years from now. Ten? When your mother still won't speak to you, when you've lost the life you knew."

"But we renovated this house together, and we found ourselves in the process. Now you'll throw me away like you threw my bonnet into the street because I don't suit you anymore? You said that you never leave a job unfinished. What about us? Don't leave us unfinished."

"I've done what I was contracted to do."

She couldn't believe he was saying these cold, heartless things. It was so sudden, almost like he was a different person. Not even a hint of that charming, smiling rogue. "I thought . . . I thought you cared. Why did you build me those bookshelves?"

"I built you the bookshelves because I want you to be happy. I think you should live here in London instead of retiring to Cornwall. Don't deprive the world of your light."

To go from such happiness, such bliss, to this nightmare.

She had knowingly walked into this trap, just like one of Daphne Villeneuve's heroines.

She'd walked right in, drunk on newly discovered power. Intoxicated by his kisses and the tenderness she'd thought she'd seen in his eyes.

Now his eyes held only anguish. She had to know what had happened to transform him so completely.

Something had happened.

"During our waltz you said you loved me . . . well, you didn't really say it but you agreed when I said it, and now it's as though a wall of thorns sprang up to cover your face, your eyes."

"I saw reality, Beatrice. I saw the disparity between our worlds. You would grow to resent me if I tore your family apart. Your mother would never accept me and to have that rift be my fault—you might think it's worth the pain now, but I know from experience that my mother never healed completely."

"Our situation is different. You're not your father, Ford."

No, HE WASN'T his father. And that meant he wasn't going to selfishly and blindly claim her love no matter the cost. Beatrice's mother had made it very clear that she considered him to be totally unworthy of her precious daughter.

He refused to be the wedge driven into her family that split it apart, sundered mother from daughter.

He couldn't allow history to repeat itself.

He hated himself even as he spoke the words, but he had to do this. He must be harsh. "These two weeks were only a fantasy, Beatrice. A fairy tale with no basis in reality. I don't belong in your world and you don't belong in mine. I have to leave."

"You don't. You don't have to leave."

"My mother arrives in London in a matter of hours. My ship departs in a matter of days."

This was the most difficult thing he'd ever done in his life. His whole body and mind screamed for him to stay. Sweep her into his arms.

He turned away from her stricken face and wounded eyes and shouldered his trunk. "Goodbye, Beatrice."

He walked downstairs quickly. He had just opened the door when a tall shape shoved past him and entered the room.

Ford's entire body stiffened. "A bit early for a call, isn't it, Foxton?" He'd kick his grandfather out onto the street before he'd let him discover Beatrice in the house with him at this early hour.

He had to force him to leave before any hint of Beatrice's presence in the house was revealed. He prayed that she stayed upstairs.

"I'll own this property soon enough," Foxton said.

"I wouldn't be too sure about that."

Coggins arrived finally, rubbing sleep from his eyes. "Should I throw him out, Mr. Wright?"

"Go back to bed, Coggins. Mr. Foxton is leaving."

Coggins glared at Foxton before shuffling back the way he'd come.

"Why so eager for me to leave?" Foxton asked. "Could it be because you have a certain highborn visitor who arrived on foot and climbed a ladder into your bedchamber?"

Damn. She'd been wearing a cloak. She could have been anyone. "I ordered a fancy lady from Covent Garden. I left that ladder there for her."

"Distinctive color of hair, your ladybird."

"You may have dug up another heir, but Lady Beatrice has powerful friends in high places to contest the claim."

"I'm sure she does."

"You're leaving." He grabbed his grandfather by the collar and bodily moved him toward the door. "I've been meaning to have a talk with you. We'll do it at a place of my choosing."

"Roughing up your own grandfather?"

That stopped Ford cold. "You knew?"

"You didn't think I'd put it together? You have your father's eyes . . . and his peasant hands."

"Ford?" Beatrice's soft voice. She stood in the doorway. There were tear streaks on her cheeks. He'd done that. He hated himself.

"My, what have we here?" Foxton chortled. "I've caught two birds with one stone."

"Ford—what did he mean about roughing up your grandfather?" Beatrice asked.

"You haven't told her?" Foxton exploded into nasty laughter.

Ford wanted to strangle him.

"That's right, Lady Beatrice. He's my grandson. Though I disinherited his mother long ago, and I don't acknowledge her bastard."

"I'm not a bastard," said Ford.

"You were conceived out of wedlock. Your father seduced my innocent daughter. I would have sent her to the countryside to give birth and she could have adopted you out, but she had the ludicrous idea in her head that she was in love with her seducer. I couldn't understand it—a girl who'd been given every opportunity, every privilege and still she rebelled."

"They loved each other."

"Stamford. How pathetic that Joyce named you after me. Such a transparent bid for reconciliation. She wanted my money, you see. Because your father couldn't support her."

Beatrice advanced on Ford, eyes sparking with fire. "Is it true? Is he your grandfather?"

"Yes, but I can explain everything."

"You lied to me. I thought you wanted to help me, to help the ladies. I thought you were helping me out of kindness, out of love for this house, love for . . . for me." Her voice broke and he fought the impulse to throw his arms around her and kiss away her tears.

"I did want to help . . . I do . . . If you'll allow me to explain," he said.

"You think he loves you, Lady Beatrice?" Foxton gave a mirthless laugh. "Fortune hunters don't fall in love. His father married my daughter thinking that I would allow her to keep her dowry. Like father, like son."

"That's not true. Beatrice, you know me."

"Do I? Ford . . . do I know you?"

"A lovers' quarrel, how tragic," said Foxton. "He didn't tell you that he was helping you renovate the property because he wanted revenge on me?"

"I didn't want revenge before, but now I do," Ford said bitterly. "I want you to know you can't own everyone and everything. You won't force her out of this house, the way you forced my mother out and cut her off mercilessly."

"But you see, I can own everything and everyone." His smug voice made Ford want to smash something. "If you run home, Lady Beatrice, you'll be there before your mother rises and all of this can be forgotten."

"If I sell you the property," she said.

"That's right. Clever girl."

"You can't control her," Ford ground out. "You don't even rule your daughters. Every year they meet in secret, defying your decrees, clinging to their love for one another in the face of your tyranny."

Foxton frowned. "They do?"

Too late, Ford realized his mistake. He'd spilled his mother's secret in the heat of anger, and his aunt would surely pay the price.

"They haven't met for years," he lied.

"You're lying. You said they met every year. Is it soon?"

His mother's coach would be arriving in London in a matter of hours.

"I don't think you two quite realize what this means," said Foxton. "Now I have further ammunition. It's plain for anyone to see that you're lovers. If you don't sign this property over to me, Lady Beatrice, I'll have Mr. Wright expelled from the navy."

"You couldn't do that," said Beatrice.

"Try me. And if that threat isn't enough, I'll inform your mother of what I saw here. And I may inform the scandal sheets, as well. I don't think your little knitting society would survive the taint of such a salacious scandal, do you?"

"You won't get away with this, Foxton," Ford said.

"I think I will. The choice is up to you, Lady Beatrice. Your reputation. His career. All I want is this property. I just don't understand why that's so difficult for you to comprehend. I'm building a factory here and there is nothing you can do to stop me. Nothing. Do you hear me? I'm willing to let this man sail away. I'm willing to let you continue being a debutante. I'll keep your dirty little secrets."

He twisted free of Ford's fist. "You have until noon today to make your decision, Lady Beatrice. I'll return with the papers for you to sign."

He walked out the door with one last smug smile.

Beatrice clutched the doorframe. "Ford, were you using me? Was this only about seeking revenge on your grandfather?"

"You have to believe me when I say that I never wanted revenge. I honestly wanted to help you defeat him, because I could see that he was attempting to curtail your joy, in the same way that he stole my mother's by cutting her out of the family."

He saw the doubt in her eyes and it nearly killed him.

"How could you lie to me this whole time?" she asked. "You don't care about me at all."

She refused to look at him. All the light had gone from her eyes.

"That's not true, but I don't expect you to believe me. He has us over a barrel. I don't care about my career, but your reputation." He ground his teeth together. "I won't allow you to be ruined."

"It's not my reputation I care about, but he's right. If word of my ruination spreads, the ladies league will be tainted by association.

I need to think. And you need to leave." She fled the room and ran upstairs.

He slammed his fist against a chair back. He hated feeling helpless.

Everything was broken. Would he ever regain her trust? All of this was because of him. Without him, Foxton would have no further leverage over her.

He'd ruined everything.

He had to explain himself to Beatrice. He ran up the stairs after her.

Chapter Twenty-Eight

BEATRICE LAY FACEDOWN on her aunt's bed when Ford entered the room.

He approached warily. "Beatrice? May I say something?"

She didn't reply, but inched over to the right side of the bed. He sat down next to her on the bed, pulling a pillow into his arms.

She'd rolled onto her side, facing the wall, not him.

"My father's name is Jonas Wright," he began. "He was Foxton's lead carpenter, supervising all of his new construction, earning a good salary in the process. And then disaster struck—the ill star rose. He fell in love with Foxton's eldest daughter, Joyce, and she returned his affections."

She'd made no sign that she'd heard him use one of her etymology lessons. He forged ahead. "My parents eloped to Gretna Green without Foxton's blessing and he ruthlessly cut my mother out of the family, transferring all of his hopes to his second born daughter, Phyllis, the aunt I've never met. Over the years he's remained immovable, refusing to even acknowledge that his eldest daughter exists, with no regard for the lives he ruins and the pain he causes."

She flipped onto her back, staring at the ceiling.

At least she hadn't told him to leave yet.

"My father is an honest, hardworking man who can fix anything, build anything. But he was never able to mend the hole inside my mother's heart that formed when she lost her family, her inheritance, and her very identity. I told you about her misfortune but I wasn't able to divulge that Foxton was my grandfather."

"Why couldn't you tell me?"

"I'll come to that. My parents built a simple life together in Cornwall, but throughout my childhood I saw my mother smile through half-shed tears. Saw her forced to wear twice-turned gowns, and eat watery turnip soup for supper. Her hands became cracked and red from doing the washing, and her spirit lowered living in the shadow of the great house, when she should have had a fine residence of her own."

"Her experience must have had some bearing on your own rebellion against becoming one of the duke's servants."

"Yes. I wanted more from life for myself . . . and for my mother. When I was eight years old, she brought me with her to London. We visited a stately house in Regent's Park. We were admitted into a study and I saw an old man sitting behind a desk. He had the same light gray eyes as my mother. I wasn't scared of him. I was curious. Why had my mother brought me here?"

Beatrice turned onto her side and looked at him for the first time since he'd entered the room. "Go on."

"They had a conversation while I explored the study, spinning globes and opening cigar boxes. I caught words here and there. At one point they were talking about me so I listened more closely. My grandfather called me a bastard. Said he wanted nothing to do with me. My mother replied that I was his only grandson and asked how he could be so heartless as to extend his censure to me, an innocent child. She asked him to pay my way to boarding school. She said that it was a drought year, that there wasn't enough to eat, and she had lost another baby. I didn't understand everything they were saying, but I remember those words. *Bastard. Heartless. Drought. Lost baby.*"

"Ford." Her hand drifted onto his forearm. "What a terrible thing to overhear."

"The next thing I knew, this man behind the desk with the steel gray eyes was waving something at my mother, something he'd written. 'Take the money, and leave London,' he said. 'Never contact me again.' My mother pleaded with him. I remember I hated hearing the beseeching tone in her voice, one I'd never heard her use before. I rushed to her side and held her hand. I told my grandfather that we didn't want his stupid old money. Then he turned those cold eyes on me and he told my mother to get the bastard out of his sight."

Beatrice pulled him down beside her on the bed until they lay side by side. She placed her hand over his heart. He didn't allow himself to hope. He only had to finish telling her this story; he didn't know what would happen next.

"My mother took his money and promised never to contact him again, or even speak his name. She made me swear, after we left, that I would never tell anyone about their meeting and I was never to mention my grandfather, even though we shared a name. As I grew older, I understood the meeting better. I felt the shame of it more keenly. It was wrong to take his hush money. His blood money."

"She was only doing what she had to do for her family. For her child."

"I forgave her, but I never forgave him. He doesn't deserve my compassion."

"No, he doesn't." Her finger traced the line of his jaw. "I understand why you kept silent, Ford. You swore not to reveal the connection."

"It was an oath I swore long ago but it's been part of my life for so long I couldn't . . . I couldn't go against it."

She reached for his hand and wove her fingers into his. She stroked her thumb over the center of his palm. "You don't have to run away. Stay here with me. Tell me more stories."

He relaxed against her, into the warmth of her body, the pulse of her wrist, the understanding in her eyes.

"When your mother . . ." His throat constricted, remembering the awful conversation. The hatred in her mother's eyes.

The disheartenment and shame descended again, driving away the small shreds of blue sky beginning to appear through the clouds in his mind.

"What did she do, Ford? Tell me what she did."

"After your brother claimed you for a dance, your mother brought me upstairs and she offered me twenty thousand pounds to leave London immediately and never contact you again."

Her nails bit into his palm. "She didn't."

"She did. She told me that she knew my kind, that I was a common fortune hunter. She said a lot of other things, none of them good. I told her I'd never touch her money and I walked out. It was . . . it brought everything back to me. The day my mother brought me to see my grandfather. The hush money. Money meant to silence, to humiliate. To put me in my place." His jaw locked so tightly he might never be able to open it again.

"I'm so sorry, Ford. I can't believe she would do something like that. It's unconscionable."

He sighed. "She's only trying to protect you, Beatrice. You have everything to lose. Your bookshop, your reputation, your fortune. Your mother. I refuse to be the author of all of that loss."

"What if I want to write my own story? What if I'm willing to risk everything?" She rolled toward him, pressing her cheek against his cheek. "I couldn't even allow myself to acknowledge that I wanted to kiss you. I had to imagine myself as a fictitious heroine before I could even give myself permission to express my desire. I've been living at a remove from life, at a distance, living within my head instead of my heart. You make me feel, Ford. Feel everything—joy, pain, love, sorrow."

She kissed his cheek. "Pain and love go hand in hand. I struggled against loving you. I battled to keep myself removed from my emotions, but pain and risk are part of life. We can't outrun suffering, or love. I love therefore I suffer. Because I could lose you. Because you could walk out this door and onto your ship and I would never see you again. Love brings struggle and strife, Ford, but it also brings joy and freedom and endless possibilities."

She was wiping something off his cheeks with her thumbs. He must be crying. But he never allowed himself to weep, to be vulnerable.

There was a first time for everything.

"You've changed me, Ford. When I showed my true self to the world at the ball, that was . . . because of you, because of the way you challenged me to live my own life. To discover myself, expose myself, my true self, without fear of rejection when the inevitable laughter arrived. It took courage. And what I'm doing right now, uncovering myself for you . . ."

She sat up and slipped one sleeve of her blue gown off her shoulder. "Exposing myself for you . . ." The other sleeve fell. Her hands moved to the top of her bodice and she slid it down her body.

It was nearly unbearable, the tension of that last half inch, the fabric clinging to her nipples, ready to fall and show him everything he craved so badly. His cock hardened and his mouth went dry.

She looked down at her exposed breasts, and then she looked at him and smiled. She was a highly intelligent woman. She didn't make this offering easily or glibly.

This was Beatrice at the height of her power and Ford was in awe of her—absolutely in awe of this woman.

"Beatrice," he moaned. He drew her into his embrace, sliding the gown off her small, perfect breasts and lowering his mouth, taking her nipple between his lips, tonguing it with swirling strokes.

"This takes courage, Ford," she said, curving her body to meet his tongue. "Are you brave enough to meet me halfway?"

She was everything he desired.

He could no longer picture leaving her, resuming the life he'd left behind when he agreed to renovate her bookshop.

That life didn't exist anymore. It didn't fit anymore.

When their bodies coupled, he knew that it would change him. This was a journey into the unknown.

She smelled like fresh night air and apple blossoms.

He rubbed her neck muscles, wanting to ease her tension.

Why did she have to be so very beautiful? Hair like flame. Skin smooth as silk. Trusting eyes. He kissed the base of her neck and flicked his tongue over the pulse beating wildly there.

She sighed, fitting herself more firmly against him.

Too much fabric between them. Remove skirts and petticoats. She flung her spectacles onto the bedside table, eagerly returning to his embrace.

Linger on the silken ribbons of her garters. Trail his fingers along her inner thighs and listen to her breath catch. Watch her eyes close as firelight flickered across her face.

Touch her sex with the tip of his finger, gently opening her, reveling in her wet heat. Sinking his finger inside to the knuckle.

He could deny her nothing. He would give her everything.

Including his heart.

He removed all of her clothing, and his, until they were naked together. He stroked his hands all over her, everywhere he wanted to roam.

No area forbidden. No signposts warning him away. They would find their way together through this uncharted territory.

The curve of her belly, and the soft hair between her legs, a mahogany reddish color, not as fiery as her head.

Holding her gaze as he dipped his fingers inside her wet heat.

He built kiss upon kiss, guiding her toward ecstasy.

He loved the halo of coppery curls spread against the white sheets. Those rosy-tipped nipples begging for his lips again, cheeks flushed and eyes lit by desire.

Take. Drink deep. Give.

Starry sky over the prow of a ship. Journey into the unknown.

He kept his fingers inside her as he kissed her breasts, and moved lower, shifting down the bed until he could taste her again.

She held still, tensing, as he lapped at her sex softly and slowly. He used his free hand to stroke her belly, quieting the muscles there.

She relaxed against the bed, giving herself to the pleasure.

Hearing her soft moans and feeling her clench around him as she climaxed gave him an intense pleasure. After her crisis she lay limply against the bed. His cock throbbed.

She opened her eyes.

"Still want ravishing?" he asked.

"Very much so."

Tongue to tongue, hot blood now, fire in his veins. He shifted his weight onto his hands. He pushed forward gently, pausing to give her time to adjust, listening intently for any cry of displeasure, of pain.

When he was fully buried inside her, he began to move, rocking deeper. It was everything he'd imagined.

"Beatrice, it feels so good. I never want to leave." He splayed her thighs wider and reached beneath them to cup her firm little bottom with his palms, guiding her into his rhythm.

"Then don't, Ford. Don't leave." She kissed him fiercely and held on to his neck, right there with him, matching his movements. It was too much. Pleasure built and clamored for release and he slowed a moment, prolonging the sensation.

Her arms twined around his neck, their sweat mingled, her hair damp and spiraling around her face. Breasts crushed beneath his chest, cushioning him, pleasure building in his bollocks.

All of this was familiar.

All of this he knew, and knew well.

How to give and take, when to ease off, allow his partner to breath, and when to ride hard, racing for the finish line. He'd had many of these moments before—the soaring plateau before the plunge into pleasure—but this felt different.

The stars on this horizon were thicker, closer together, covering the sky with pinpricks of light.

This welling of emotion wasn't supposed to roll over him every time he kissed her soft lips. His heart wasn't supposed to clench along with the muscles of his abdomen as he thrust deeper inside her heat.

Tears weren't supposed to escape his eyes as her sex clasped him, squeezed him, in a warm embrace as if she'd never let him go.

He stopped and took her face in his hands. He stared into her eyes and she gazed boldly back, and the look in her eyes was the most beautiful, tender, terrifying thing he'd ever seen.

"Beatrice, I love you," he whispered, emotion roughening his voice to gravel.

She smiled, her eyes shimmering with tears. "I love you, too, my rogue."

She moved against him. Tentatively at first, just a slight rolling of her hips, sheathing and unsheathing an inch of him at a time.

Her face changed, grew more focused. She furrowed her brow, biting her lip, setting the pace.

All he had to do was be fully present with her. Hold firmly to his control. Not allow himself to go over the edge.

"Oh, oh, *my*," she said on a sigh, and her inner muscles gripped and released and gripped again.

"Yes, Beatrice," he moaned. Now he could ravish her.

He took her with deep strokes, joining their bodies together to make something wholly new.

BEATRICE WOUND HER legs around Ford's hips and dug her fingernails into the solid muscle of his shoulders as they moved together.

Her body had a new purpose. Build and be built.

Love and be loved.

He used his body with the same focus and skill he applied when he used his tools. He demanded equal participation; she had no chance of keeping any part of herself hidden away.

She owned this house—she wouldn't let Foxton take it away— and now for the first time, she owned her body. It was hers to give. Not a burden, a gift.

This body with its damaged nerves and eager mind. This body with its urges and desires and responses.

How could a man with roughened, callused hands touch her

so gently? There was no more potent combination. He sawed and hammered and built things, repaired roofs and refinished floors. But when he touched her, it was with reverence, a whisper of a caress, butterfly wings on her lips, the brush of a rose against her inner thighs.

And then this.

She'd never imagined this. These long, slow strokes, filling her, joining them as one.

She tilted her head back, unable to see the portrait clearly but knowing it was there. She had a feeling her scandalous aunt would approve of these wanton goings-on in her bed.

The pace of his movement increased and she held on to his sweat-slick shoulders, twining her legs around his taut bum and holding on for dear life.

He was going to drive this bed halfway into the wall.

He was going to drive her insane. "Ford," she moaned. "I'm yours. Make use of me."

He growled against her throat, filling her again and again until, with one last mighty stroke, he collapsed against her chest, crushing her against the bed as pleasure took him.

His breathing slowed. He slipped out of her body. He threw the coverlet over them and encased her in his strong arms.

"Ford?"

"Mmm?"

"I have to wash up." He lifted his arm and she hopped off the bed. She threw one of his shirts over her head and went to the washroom and bathed between her thighs with shockingly cold water.

When she crawled back into bed, he'd moved onto his side so she held him from the back, her face pressed against the hollow of his shoulder blade, her arm circling his torso, hand over his sternum. She felt his heart beating beneath her palm, strong and steady. "Are you asleep, Ford?"

He turned and cradled her in his arms, folding her head against his neck. "I may have been dozing."

"If you stay here in London, you'll lose your naval career. All those things you told me about being at sea, swimming in the ocean, the pride you take in your work, in keeping the ship in top shape—all of that is your freedom. I don't want to take it away from you."

"I painted a rosy picture of my life at sea. There are other aspects to that life. Dark, painful memories. It's not all sparkling seas and frolicking in the surf. I know my experience of war was mild compared to other conflicts, but sometimes I wake up gasping for air and drenched in sweat. I lost friends, too many friends, to the one battle I saw in Greece. And even the enemies . . . I still see their bodies falling into the ocean. Each one a millstone around my neck. My job was to keep our ship afloat, and I fulfilled my duties with flying colors . . . but at what cost? We lost half our crew. I'll never be rid of those memories. I was already having doubts about going back, but I couldn't see any other path. I can see now that I've been running away my whole life and what I was looking for was always around the corner, over the next horizon. But I've found what I was searching for." He kissed her lips. "You."

"We'll find a new path together."

He kissed the top of her head. "But first we have to find a way to save this clubhouse."

"We will, I know we will."

"My mother's arriving at the coaching inn soon and I must be there to meet her, but I'll return after that. I have to warn her that I revealed to Foxton that she secretly visits with her sister."

"And I need to go home and confront my mother about what she did."

"She thought she was acting in your best interests."

"I know. And I'm prepared to face her anger." She kissed him. "Let's meet back here in three hours. Foxton said he'd return at noon. That will give us time to decide on a plan, on the best path to take."

He cupped her cheek with his palm. "I don't want to leave you,

Beatrice. Even for a few hours. There's so much to talk about, so much to decide."

"And what about ravishing?" she asked, with a roguish wink.

He gave her the answer to that question with a passionate kiss that left her breathless, and left little doubt about his intentions for the future.

There would definitely be more ravishing.

Chapter Twenty-Nine

BEATRICE FOUND HER mother propped up by pillows in her bedchamber.

"Why, Beatrice?" her mother wailed. "Why humiliate yourself, and me, in such a public fashion?" Her head dropped back against her pillows. "I can see the scandal sheets." She painted a headline in the air. "'The Wallflower's Revolt.'"

"I didn't mean to hurt you."

"Why didn't you just tell me you didn't want to wear the gown?"

"It was a last moment decision. I've been meaning to talk to you. I was only going along with your plans to soften the blow. I thought that if I failed yet again, you might let me go more easily."

"Let you go? But Beatrice, where would you go if not into marriage?"

"I never had any intention of marrying."

"You've always been difficult."

"I've always been different. At the ball I embraced that difference. I celebrated it."

"Did you have to celebrate it quite so openly? I've been very tolerant, Beatrice. Until now."

"Mother, you will feel more free if you allow me my independence. You've been living your life through mine. You're not dead yet. You could remarry. You could build a new life."

"What a strange thing to say to your mother when you just told me you have no intention of marrying."

"I said I'd *had* no aspirations toward matrimony. Now I have hopes and I have dreams."

"No, Beatrice. Don't do this." Her mother clutched a pillow against her chest. "Don't do this to me."

"You had a conversation with Stamford Wright in this very room recently. How could you offer him money to leave?"

"He's nobody."

"He's the man I love."

"Society forgives men when they make an imprudent marriage. They won't forgive you."

"How is it any different?"

"Men hold the power in this world, Beatrice. And the men with money most of all. They set their own rules."

"I've decided to break the rules."

"If your father were alive he'd put a swift stop to this madness. He'd have something to say about his only daughter throwing her life away."

"He'd say what he always said. That I was a cripple, that I was deficient and unlovable."

"You heard him say those terrible things?"

"Of course I did, Mama. He shouted them. And I absorbed his words and I believed them. Until I met Ford and decided to start living my life, instead of watching it from a distance. There's pain in this world, and there's joy. I'll taste both, but I won't hide from life anymore."

Her mother turned her face away. "So you love him?"

"With all my heart."

"And you're ruined?"

"Utterly."

"Oh, Beatrice. My little girl." Her mother started crying then, and it broke Beatrice's heart to hear her sobbing.

"Can you be happy for me, Mama?"

"I should never have allowed you to go to that bookshop."

"Probably not."

"I was going to announce your engagement to Mayhew at the

ball. Oh," she moaned, pressing her fingers to her eyes. "This is a nightmare."

"Mayhew's not a worthy suitor, mother. He is a known degenerate."

"He's an earl, Beatrice. Once upon a time, I'd hoped you might wed a duke, as I did. But an earl would have sufficed."

"And was your marriage so blissful that you wanted the same for me?"

"My marriage with your father may not have been a loving one, but he provided all of the material comforts and protection that any lady could ask for."

"I don't want the same things you want, Mama. You think you can mold me in your image, that the heavy pendulum of societal mores and expectations will move me into my proper place."

"We all have our duties to fulfill."

"But I was never able to fulfill mine, was I, Mama? I've never been your perfect daughter. I can't even smile. How am I to attract a mate?" She used her mother's own words, the words she'd overheard her saying. The words she'd written in the diary entry that Ford had read.

"Why can't you see that everything I've done has been for your own good?" asked her mother. "It will break my heart if you are cast out from society."

"There are many kinds of happiness, Mama. Aunt Matilda was happy."

"She was scandalous. I wasn't even allowed to speak to her. My Beatrice, I don't want you to suffer. I don't want you to become an outcast." Tears slid down her mother's cheeks, and Beatrice moved closer to her bedside and wiped them away with a clean handkerchief. "I wasn't able to protect you. Not when you were a baby, when they pulled you out of me with their metal instruments and marred your face. And not now, when you're making such an enormous mistake. Consider the consequences of your actions."

"Mama," Beatrice said gently. "I know you want the best for me, but you must allow me to lead my own life. It's my life."

Her mother turned away. "Perhaps I've pushed you too hard. Pushed you away."

"We'll find a way through this. We'll find a way to forgive each other."

Her mother sighed. "The scandal sheets won't be forgiving."

"They never are."

"Your friends will cut you."

"Not if they're my true friends."

"So you'll marry that man?"

"His name is Ford, Mama. And yes, I'll wed him if he asks me."

Her mother sat up. "He hasn't asked you yet? What's wrong with the man? He ruins you and doesn't offer you the protection of marriage?"

"We haven't arrived at that conversation yet." It was time to change the subject, distract her mother. "Rafe looked well at the ball."

"He did." Her mother perked up. "He's not limping as much now. Do you think he took an interest in any young ladies last night?"

"I'm sure the young ladies took an interest in him," said Beatrice. "Now that he's back in London he'll be the most eligible bachelor, besides Westbury, that is."

"That's true. I could plan another ball in Rafe's honor."

Beatrice hid a smile. "Our family will survive this scandal, Mama."

"I only wanted life to be easy for you. I wanted you to become a countess so no one could laugh at you anymore."

"Let them laugh. At least they're laughing, and not crying. Now dry your tears, Mama."

Her mother sighed heavily. "You've always been headstrong. You've never listened to me, not really. I don't know why I thought matters of the heart would be any different."

FORD EMBRACED HIS mother in the yard of the coaching inn.

"Why, Ford, what's wrong?" She'd always been able to read his mind.

"Come inside and I'll explain." He lifted her small trunk, waving the porter away, and carried it into the coaching inn. When they were seated in her rooms and she'd splashed water on her face and taken some refreshment, Ford sat down beside her.

"There's no easy way to say this. I made a mistake. I hope you can forgive me."

"Of course, my darling, I would forgive you anything."

"You can't meet with Phyllis while you're here. You should return to Cornwall immediately."

"Why, what's wrong?"

"I told grandfather that you two were secretly meeting."

"Ford! Why would you do such a thing?"

He ran a hand through his tangled hair. It had been a long night and morning. "Pride. Anger. I was lashing out because I wanted to hurt him—he was so hateful. Sitting there, lording it over Beatrice and me."

"Lady Beatrice? Ford, slow down. Your poor mother can't read your mind."

"And all these years I thought that you could." He smiled at her. "You know Lady Beatrice from Thornhill House."

"Thorndon's sister, yes."

"She recently inherited a bookshop and hired me to renovate it into a clubhouse for her friends. Grandfather covets the property. He wants to tear it down and build a garment manufactory."

"I see. None of this surprises me, I suppose. I saw that you had developed an interest in Lady Beatrice in Cornwall. I didn't think anything would come of it. And my father being cruel . . . well, that's nothing new." She gave a bitter little laugh. "And now that he knows I've been defying his decrees, he'll find a way to stop me from seeing my own sister."

"I'm sorry, Mother."

"It's not your fault. I knew that there was the risk I could be caught, that Phyllis and I would have to stop meeting like this. She's been trying to convince me to talk to him in person. She has some silly idea that reconciliation could be staged at this late date. I've no such illusions."

"Nor I. Mother, he's truly a monster."

"He knows who you are?"

"We locked horns."

"Enough about my father. I want to hear about you and Lady Beatrice." Her expression turned hopeful. "Is there to be a wedding?"

"We haven't had that conversation yet. We spoke of finding a path together. It's . . . complicated. We're from such different stations in life."

"What on earth are you saying? Marrying you would be the greatest prize any girl could hope to win."

"Ha! Spoken like my mother. We have to consider this with clear heads and do what's right. Falling in love outside of your social class carries a heavy cost. Just look at you and Father."

"Where did you arrive at such a wrongheaded notion? A heavy cost. Pshaw. Love is the best thing that ever happened to me."

"Watching you, Mother. The years of deprivation. Watching you let out your hems, your hands reddened and roughened, watching you smile but seeing the sadness born of deprivation lingering in your eyes."

"My dear boy." She touched his hand. "You've always been sensitive to emotions. I'm sorry if I allowed you to see that sadness, but please believe me when I say that I wouldn't change one second of my life. I love your father completely and without reservation. I love him even more today than I did when I first saw him."

"Yes, but that doesn't change the fact that you gave up everything to be with him, and your life has been immeasurably more difficult because you married him."

"I'd give it all up again in a heartbeat. True love, a love that is real and undeniable, only comes along once in a lifetime if ever, and if it finds you then you must seize it with both hands."

"She's sister to a duke, Mother. A duke who holds power over our family."

"I don't care if she's a princess of royal blood. You're more than worthy of her," she said fiercely.

Ford smiled. "Again. Spoken like my mother."

"You're a good man, Ford. I'm proud of the man you've become. Strong, honorable, hardworking. And so very handsome." She ruffled his hair.

"Stop."

"Well, it's true. I can't understand why every girl in London hasn't tried to snap you up."

"Oh, they've tried, all right."

"And so very modest," she teased.

"I know that I'm worthy of her, that's not the question. It's only that I have nothing to lose, nothing I couldn't rebuild. And she has everything to lose. Her reputation, her life of luxury. Her family's approval and love."

"Do you love her?" she asked, her eyes solemn.

Ford nodded. "I do."

"And does she love you?"

"For some reason, she says that she does."

"Then it's quite simple. Ask her to marry you, and figure everything else out later."

"Simple, you say. There's the small matter of finding a way to defeat grandfather first. He's threatened to tell the newspapers about a compromising situation he found us in last night."

"Sounds like my father. I have utter faith in you, Ford. You can fix anything. Build anything. Just like your father."

Hope surged in his heart. Could it be that simple?

"You know, I've never formally met Lady Beatrice," said his mother.

"Come with me to the bookshop."

"What are we waiting for?"

"We'll have to send word to Phyllis, warn her that Grandfather knows about your meetings."

"Let's bring her to the bookshop, as well. We can all have a chat together. I'm tired of meeting in secret. It's time to take a stand."

"You know? There seems to be plenty of that going around."

Chapter Thirty

WHEN BEATRICE ARRIVED at the bookshop later that morning, she found Ford sitting in the parlor with a woman who had to be his mother and another lady who looked enough like him that she immediately knew it had to be his aunt.

They were drinking a pot of Mrs. Kettle's excellent tea, and being plied with biscuits and offers of a hearty breakfast by the worthy housekeeper.

Beatrice realized she hadn't eaten anything since the ball last evening. Her stomach growled.

"Good morning," she said as she entered the parlor. "I'm famished."

"Beatrice." Ford jumped up from his chair and took her by the hand. "This is my mother, Joyce, and my aunt, Mrs. Phyllis Gilbert." He led her to a seat and placed a cup of strong tea in her hands, and brought her a plate piled high with biscuits. When she'd taken some refreshment, she felt much improved.

"So you're the mysterious young lady in the tower who bewitched my son," said Mrs. Wright. She had dark wavy hair, gray eyes, and the same sharply angular jaw as Ford.

"Mrs. Wright, I'm sorry we haven't met before. Ford told me that you wished you could have met me in Cornwall. I'm afraid I was very preoccupied with my work."

"That's quite all right, Lady Beatrice."

Ford's aunt smiled. "What a lovely shade of hair you have, Lady Beatrice. It quite lights up a room."

"Doesn't it, though?" Ford flashed his roguish grin and Beatrice's heart melted.

A memory of last night rolled through her mind. Anchored by his solid body to the bed, soaring on pleasure's wings. She hid a blush by drinking more tea. The steam from the tea made her spectacles nearly opaque.

Or perhaps it was the memories.

"I hear that our father is giving you problems with this property," said Mrs. Wright.

"He's been quite . . . challenging."

"You needn't mince words. He's relentlessly ambitious. He loves gold, and gold alone," Ford's mother said.

Mrs. Gilbert nodded in agreement. "So many times I've wished that his heart would soften. He was born on the streets, you know. Born to a fallen woman and raised in a cruel workhouse. He turned his back on that life forever, on poverty and destitution, want and hunger. So when he turned his back on his own daughter, on you, my dear Joyce, when he cut you out of his life, and out of mine, it was because of his horror of poverty and his greed for wealth."

Ford glanced at his mother. "You never told me about his past."

"It doesn't make much difference when you judge him solely by his actions," his mother replied. "But I try to see the good in everyone, and I understand why my father is the way he is."

"It makes me understand him better, as well," Beatrice said thoughtfully.

"At times I've thought I sensed a mellowing in him," said Mrs. Gilbert. "He keeps a miniature portrait of Joyce that he had painted on the occasion of her sixteenth birthday. I've seen him take it out sometimes, when he thinks no one is watching."

"He still loves you," Ford said to his mother.

"I believe he does," his aunt agreed. "But he's too set in his ways and too stubborn to admit it. I think, no, I'm certain, that he knows he did wrong. But too many years have passed, and his pride keeps him from reaching out and making amends."

"I saw no signs of softness or empathy in him during our interactions," Ford said.

"You don't know him as I do," his aunt said. "I've always thought that if I could bring Joyce and Father into the same room, that blood would bring them together, would overcome the prejudices that keep his heart closed. It's my fondest dream for you, Joyce and Ford, to know my daughters. And Papa should acknowledge his only grandson."

"What if there was a way to bring Foxton and Mrs. Wright together in this very room?" asked Beatrice.

Ford's mother startled, nearly dropping her teacup. "Is he coming here?"

"You didn't tell her?" Beatrice asked Ford.

He shook his head. "I was waiting for you."

"He'll be here in a matter of hours," Beatrice said gently.

Mrs. Kettle, who had overheard that last comment, clutched at her heart. "Mr. Foxton is coming here? What does he want?"

"He wants to steal the property," Beatrice said. "He believes he's found another heir to challenge my inheritance. A Mr. Leonard Castle."

"Never heard of him," said Mrs. Kettle. "Foxton. That ogre of a man. He'll stop at nothing."

Mrs. Gilbert reached for her sister's hand. "Are you willing to give my idea a try, Joyce?"

Ford's mother turned anguished eyes on her son. "Do you want me to try? Perhaps . . . perhaps we could soften him. Convince him to build his factory elsewhere."

"I don't think that will happen," said Ford. "He's too cold-blooded and heartless."

Beatrice ate another biscuit. "Ford, you told me that you couldn't understand how the world would ever be at peace when families are so uncivil to one another. Well, here's my belated answer to that. I believe that love is stronger than hate. I believe that there is hope for even the hardest of hearts." She set her teacup down. "This is a battle against enmity and bitterness, and love and compassion are our best weapons."

Ford gazed into her eyes. "You think you can soften his heart."

"We can try."

"If anyone can do it, you can," he said.

"With help from his daughters." Beatrice smiled at Ford's mother and aunt. "Never underestimate the power of women gathered together for a common goal."

"And never underestimate carpenters, Lady Beatrice," said Ford's mother. "They always find a way to repair what's broken."

The shop bell tinkled and Coggins's voice was heard. "Your Grace, an unexpected pleasure."

Which *Your Grace*? Beatrice's and Ford's gazes met.

"Wright," said a loud male voice. "Where are you? We need to talk."

"My brother," Beatrice said. "Come and join us, Drew," she called.

Her brother stalked into the room, glancing around at the gathering with growing confusion. "What's going on here?"

"Drew, this is Mrs. Wright, Ford's mother, and Mrs. Gilbert, his aunt. Now sit down and have a cup of tea."

Mrs. Kettle offered the duke a chair. "It's very good tea, Your Grace, if I do say so myself."

"How do you do, ladies?" Drew said.

"Your Grace," replied Mrs. Wright. "A pleasure."

Drew's eyes rested on Ford. "I want to talk to you, Wright. Tea can wait."

"Happy to," Ford replied easily. "Why don't we go into the front room and leave the ladies to their tea?"

The shop bell rang again.

"Now who can that be?" Beatrice asked.

She recognized the female voices instantly. "Isobel, Viola," she cried, running to greet her friends.

FORD STOOD AWKWARDLY in the front room with Thorndon as Beatrice and her friends chattered their way down the hall toward the parlor.

The duke cleared his throat. "I gather from the presence of your mother that your intentions are honorable, Wright, and I don't have to murder you today?"

"I hope not, Your Grace. And, yes, my intentions are entirely honorable."

"That's a relief."

"May I hope for your blessing, Your Grace?" He held his breath. So much hinged on the words that followed.

"Beatrice loves you, that's plain to see, and I want her to be happy. So there's the end of it. Is there any brandy in this house? I've had one devil of a night." His eyes were red-rimmed and dazed. "I just had the most extraordinary news from my wife. I'm going to be a father, Wright."

"Congratulations, Your Grace. I've got a strong Irish whisky, will that do?"

"That'll do. Pour me a stiff glass."

Ford's spirits lifted as he went upstairs in search of the whisky bottle he'd packed into his trunk. The duke might not approve of the match, but he wouldn't stand in their way. And he wouldn't ruin Ford's father.

Ford glanced into the reading room. The ancient manuscript still sat on the shelf, covered in cloth. He hadn't opened the parcel, as he knew Beatrice would want to be the one to unwrap her treasure first.

Ford was hoping to have the pleasure of removing Beatrice's clothing while she unwrapped the book. The thought sent desire coursing through his body.

He brought the parcel upstairs with him and laid it next to the bed.

"I'm going to be a father," the duke repeated when Ford returned. His eyes held a mixture of excitement and terror.

"I'll leave you with the bottle, Your Grace," Ford said. "You look like you could use a nice quiet drink by the fire."

He left Thorndon in the front room with the whisky and a blazing fire in the grate, and went back to the parlor.

The room was filled with women.

Mrs. Kettle buzzed about, happy as a bee in a clover field, dispensing tea to all and sundry. Beatrice and her friends had their heads together, and were all talking at once.

His mother and aunt were talking quietly.

Nothing for it but to brave the tide of femininity.

"There's the handsome highwayman," said Miss Beaton. "You caused quite a stir last night."

"Not as much as Beatrice did with her wallflower costume," said Miss Mayberry.

"I think it was about equal. Especially when you two waltzed, and it was clear for everyone to see that you were enamored of one another." Miss Beaton sighed and clasped her hands together. "It was so romantic."

Speaking of romance, Ford had a question he needed to ask Beatrice, now that he was certain the duke wouldn't stand in their way. It did make things easier, but there were still so many obstacles in their path. He wanted Beatrice to answer his question with her eyes wide open; fully aware of the extent of the risk she'd be taking.

He went to her side and bent close to her ear. "Come upstairs with me for a moment," he whispered.

"Not yet, rogue. We're devising a plan. Foxton has no idea what's in store for him."

"If he proves difficult, we have knitting needles." Miss Beaton brandished a pair of needles. "And we know how to use them."

"We're not going to use weapons of any kind," said Beatrice. "We're going to vanquish him with kindness."

"And tea," said Mrs. Kettle. "A nice piping hot cup of tea."

"Or we could lock him in the cellar," said Ford. "With the rats."

"I thought you got rid of those," said Beatrice.

"I can always bring up more from the river."

"I think our plan is better," she said.

"He's only one man, and we're an army," Miss Mayberry said, standing and giving him a salute.

The shop bell rang. Coggins creaked past them, muttering about all of the comings and goings.

"Another of your friends?" Ford asked Beatrice.

"I don't think so. Unless it's my mother . . . ? There's still an hour before Foxton's arrival."

"Mr. Foxton," they heard Coggins say in an affronted tone. "I'll thank you to moderate your language. There are ladies present in this house. Far too many ladies."

"Oh no!" Beatrice's brow wrinkled. "He's early."

"Then it's the cellar," Ford said roughly. "I'll tie him up. Mrs. Kettle, where can I find some rope?"

Beatrice swatted his arm. "No brute force. Kindness, remember? Now, ladies, Ford and I will meet him in the front room, and then you will play your parts, as we discussed."

Her friends and his mother and aunt all nodded.

"Come with me," she said.

Ford had a bad feeling about this. Foxton had given him absolutely no indication, not one glimmer of hope, that his heart could be thawed.

"Well?" Foxton asked when Ford and Beatrice entered the room. "Have you decided to finally sign this property over to me?"

The duke was sitting in a high wingback chair, hidden from Foxton.

"I haven't," said Beatrice.

"You're going to agree to leave us alone, instead," Ford said.

"Not a chance, Wright."

"We know about your childhood, Mr. Foxton," Beatrice said. "We know that you were raised in a workhouse. It must have been a harsh and a brutal upbringing. I can understand why you wish to better yourself, but what I can't understand is why you would want to build a factory that mistreats children."

"Pardon me?" Foxton staggered before righting himself with his walking stick. "I've no idea what you're talking about, Lady Beatrice."

"She's speaking about compassion, Grandfather. About understanding and forgiveness."

Foxton glowered at them, his face a venomous mask. "We have no further business here. I'll go straight to the newspapers, and I'll see you in court."

He turned to leave, but Ford's mother and aunt headed him off at the doorway.

"Phyllis?" Foxton staggered again. "What are you doing here? What's going on? And . . . Joyce?"

"Good day, Father," said his mother, her lower lip trembling. She and her sister clasped hands, blocking his exit path.

"Lady Beatrice, I demand to know what's happening here," Foxton shouted.

The duke suddenly leapt out from behind the chair, brandishing the now half-empty whisky bottle menacingly. "You demand nothing from my sister!"

Ford caught him by the elbow before he reached Foxton. "Allow your sister to work her magic, Thorndon," he murmured. "Trust her methods."

"Allow me to explain, Mr. Foxton," said Beatrice. "Your daughters are here because it's high time that you faced the consequences of your actions."

Ford moved to stand beside her. "It's time that we stood up to you."

"This is outrageous. I want no part of it. Stand aside, Phyllis. Let go of Joyce's hand and let me pass."

Ford could see that it wasn't working. Foxton's heart was a shriveled thing that no amount of compassion could bring back to life.

But there was one heart in this room that was filled to bursting with love.

His own.

And if he didn't ask Beatrice his question soon, he might explode. And was there any better way to illustrate the awesome power, and potential peril, of love than a proposal?

He dropped to one knee on the oak floor that they'd worked on together. "Beatrice. Before this goes any further, I need to ask you something."

WHAT WAS FORD doing? This wasn't the plan. "Not now, Ford," she whispered urgently. "I'm about to make my speech."

"Let me make a speech first."

"I'm leaving," said Foxton.

"No, you're not." His daughters linked arms, standing in front of the doorway.

"Is it happening?" asked Isobel and Viola, appearing in the doorway. "Is it our turn?"

Tears gathered behind Beatrice's eyes. Blast. This wasn't at all how she'd wanted the scene to go. Everyone must be staring at them, but all she could see was Ford.

The sunflower in his eye. His powerful shoulders.

"Mr. Wright is down on one knee," Viola whispered. "Hush now."

"Lady Beatrice Bentley, you make me believe that love is stronger than hate. That good can triumph over evil. That a carpenter can find love with a lady. I swear to you that I will work my fingers to the bone to give you the life you deserve."

"And what life is that?" she asked.

"A life where you never want for anything, a large house and a commodious carriage. Perhaps not so grand as what you're accustomed to, but something you can be proud of."

"Is that what I want?" She clicked her tongue against her teeth. "Ford, I thought you knew me better. You're talking about some Beatrice you've created in your mind. A princess on a pedestal. That's not me at all. We could live in a one-room cottage and I'd be happy."

"But where would you put all of your books?"

"Well, perhaps a one-room cottage with a large library attached?"

"You'll need money to buy paper and ink."

"True. But those aren't extravagant requirements."

"I may not be able to keep you in diamonds, but I want to keep you in the best ink, the finest quills, and the thickest paper."

"And I want to be by your side, ripping up floorboards, patching roofs, and learning how to use more tools. I want to build beautiful things with you, Ford. A life. A . . . family. Four walls and a roof that doesn't leak, and you. That's all I require."

"Beatrice, would that truly be enough?"

"More than enough."

"Isn't this a touching scene," said Foxton with a sneer.

"Hush, Father," said Ford's aunt.

Ford reached for her hand. "Lady Beatrice Bentley, in front of these gathered witnesses, will you do me the honor of becoming my wife?"

"It had best be a hasty wedding," said Foxton. "They're lovers. I caught them here early this morning."

"Quiet, Foxton," Isobel commanded. "You're not allowed to speak. You're trespassing on the premises of the Mayfair Ladies Knitting League, or whatever we decide to name this clubhouse."

"We have knitting needles," said Viola. "And we've been taught to use them in unusual and painful ways."

Beatrice's spectacles were becoming fogged by tears and emotion. She wiped them on her skirts. Ford rose from the floor and set her spectacles back on her face.

The soft brush of his fingers on her cheek sent ripples of desire through her entire body.

"Ford Wright, I love you because you threw my bonnet into the road," she said with a catch in her throat.

"It didn't suit you," he replied.

"Fear didn't suit me. I was afraid to truly live. I was going to retreat from life, bury myself in an early grave, and then you came along. You challenged me at every turn and you made me see that I wanted to live. Truly be alive. Taste life and love and all that it has to offer."

Ford smiled at her, his eyes beginning that slow smolder that made her knees weak. "And you came along and expanded my vocabulary . . . and taught me how to love in the process."

"Well, Beatrice . . . are you going to answer his question?" asked Drew.

"Oh. I forgot to answer." She brought Ford's hand to her lips and kissed each one of his hardworking knuckles. "Yes, you arrogant rogue. I'm yours. Now and forever."

"Hoorah!" Viola cried.

"Oh, my dear ones, I'm so very glad to hear it," said Mrs. Kettle, who stood with Mr. Coggins, watching from beyond the doorway.

"Just you wait," said Coggins. "Something'll go wrong, yet."

"Don't think this is over," Foxton growled. "You'll be hearing from my lawyers. Phyllis, let's go."

"No," said Ford's aunt. She tightened her grip on her sister's hand. "No, Father. I'm not leaving. Not without Joyce. You can't keep me from my sister any longer. I love her too much. We've lost too much time already."

"Father," said Ford's mother. "I forgive you. Can we move forward from here?"

"I forgive you, as well," said Ford. "I know now that you had a harsh and unforgiving upbringing."

Foxton shook his walking stick at them. "Stop forgiving me. I don't want your forgiveness. Phyllis, we're leaving."

"Or what, Father? You'll disinherit me, as well? Cut me and your granddaughters out of your life? You can't build enough walls to keep all of us out."

"I believe that there's a heart beating inside your chest somewhere, Mr. Foxton," said Beatrice. Finally, she could give her speech. "I don't believe we ever lose our capacity for love. We can bury it, or it can be stolen away, or it can atrophy, over time. But it's always there inside us, waiting to be remembered. Waiting to blossom."

Mrs. Kettle chose that moment to arrive with a tea tray. "Now everyone, if you'll all have a seat, I'll serve the refreshments now. Mr. Foxton, please be our honored guest."

"Pah," he said. But he took a seat.

Mrs. Kettle poured him some tea. "Here you go, love. A nice cup of tea."

Foxton accepted the cup. "I see you've all united against me."

"Not against you, Father," said Phyllis. *"For* you. We are your family. We love you."

"Love. The root of all evil," said Foxton.

"I believe you mean money," said Beatrice. "For the love of money is the root of all evil."

"I meant love," said Foxton. "It doesn't make the world go round, it turns it inside out. Turns sensible people into fools."

"That's how I felt, Grandfather," said Ford. "Until I met Beatrice."

"That's what I thought, as well," said Drew. "Until I met my Mina. I'm going to be a father." He grinned from ear to ear. "Can you believe that?"

"That's wonderful, Drew!" Beatrice cried.

Viola clasped her hands together. "Congratulations, Your Grace."

"Father," said Ford's aunt. "Have you considered that this could be the fulfillment of all your ambitions?"

Foxton's eyes narrowed. "Can't say that I have."

"You've always wanted someone in your family to marry into the nobility. And now it's coming to pass. Your status will be greatly elevated by association with a duke."

Foxton's brow wrinkled. "I suppose I hadn't considered it in that light."

"And not just any duke," said Drew. "Me. You're not a fortune hunter, are you Wright?" he asked suddenly, as if he'd just remembered to ask the question. "My mother seems to think you are."

"I'm a carpenter," said Ford, "and a damn good one."

"I suppose I'll have to employ you now," muttered Foxton.

Had Beatrice heard him correctly? "I think your grandfather just offered you a job," she whispered to Ford.

He grinned. "I think he did."

"I still don't see why you can't have your clubhouse somewhere else, Lady Beatrice," Foxton said with a loud harrumph. "I have other suitable properties, you know."

"My aunt wanted me to keep this property in the family," said Beatrice. "And my friends will be the beneficiaries of her bequest."

"Lady knitters." Foxton glared at Isobel and Viola.

Viola shook her knitting needles at him.

"Does this Mr. Leonard Castle have a valid claim, Mr. Foxton?" Isobel asked.

Foxton shrugged his bony shoulders. "I didn't think we'd have to find out. I thought Lady Beatrice would fold more easily."

"I'll take that as a no, then. The prosecution rests," said Isobel.

Beatrice gave her a loving smile.

Foxton set his cup on a side table. As he attempted to rise, he nearly lost his balance.

Both of his daughters immediately rushed to his side, taking his arms.

"Don't fuss, don't fuss," he said testily, but he didn't try to pull his arms away from them.

They helped him rise. "Let's go home, Father," said Ford's aunt. "This has been enough excitement for one day I should think." She smiled warmly at Beatrice. "Thank you, Lady Beatrice. For everything."

Ford's mother approached. "It was lovely to meet my future daughter-in-law. I'm looking forward to a nice long conversation very soon."

Beatrice nodded. "I'd like that very much."

"I'd better go back to Mina," said Drew. "She said she had a craving for ripe strawberries coated in sugar and dipped in cream, though where I'll find strawberries in London, in winter, lord only knows."

One by one, everyone left, giving their excuses and their congratulations, until she and Ford were left alone.

"He's not going to transform overnight, but I'd say it's a promising beginning," she said.

He nuzzled her cheek. "Now will you come upstairs with me? I'm hoping to unwrap you while you unwrap that ancient book."

She started. "The *Revelations*."

"You completely forgot about your ancient book, didn't you? I have that effect on bookish ladies."

They climbed the stairs together and Beatrice's heart soared higher with every step. She was about to make a momentous discovery for womankind, if she was right about the book.

And she was about to taste pleasure again in the arms of a rogue.

Her very own rogue.

Chapter Thirty-One

BEATRICE UNTIED THE parcel with trembling fingers. She parted the folds of the cloth to reveal the leather-bound manuscript she'd been longing to see. "It's the *Revelations of Divine Love*, Ford."

"Why would your aunt leave it hidden beneath the floorboards?"

"Perhaps this will explain." She lifted a sheet of parchment from the book. It was a letter from her aunt. "She says that she acquired the manuscript in a box of ordinary religious texts that had been stored in the attic of an estate in Kent. This could be a very rare fifteenth century copy, or a copy made in the mid-seventeenth century, she's not sure which. She was growing ill and didn't dare trust it to anyone's care for analysis, for fear it would be stolen."

"And so she left it for you to find, knowing you would treat it with love and respect."

"I can't believe it." She opened the book gingerly and examined the color of the dark curving ink letters. "Either way, it's extremely valuable. It belongs in a museum, though I'll make use of it first. After I finish my dictionary I'll move on to a study of female authors. How thrilling to own an intact copy of the earliest known work written by a woman in English."

"It's one of a kind. Just like you, Beatrice."

"I can't wait until we open the clubhouse. It will be a haven for those females who feel ostracized, or silenced. For the ambitious ladies who want to succeed at endeavors normally relegated solely to men."

"I'm honored to have aided in creating this sanctuary. I'm humbled by it."

"It's not finished yet. I have a long list of projects for you. Why don't we purchase the buildings on either side from your grandfather and transform them, as well?"

"Using your money," he said, a shadow crossing his face.

"Yes. Why not? Just because I'm a woman you won't accept my money? The gentlemen I know accept large dowries as a right."

"I'm not a fortune hunter."

"Don't be so hardheaded. I'll purchase the buildings, and you can renovate them. And I won't have to pay you anymore for your services."

He grinned. "I hadn't thought about it like that."

"I have a way with words."

"And I have a way with kisses. Beatrice?"

"Yes, my rogue?"

"Put down that book."

She folded the cloth back around the manuscript.

He kissed her then, tumbling her back onto the bed and covering her with his powerful frame.

"Damn you, Ford. You reduce me to a puddle of quivering ninnyhood." She wrapped her arms around his neck. "And do you know? I'm quite happy about that."

"I don't usually admit these things, my love, but you make me weak at the knees."

"I do?"

"Mmm. Especially when you whisper archaic words in my ear."

"*Crapulous*," she whispered. "*Slubberdegullion. Quodlibetificate.*"

He groaned. "Stop, temptress."

"*Sesquipedalian*. That's me. It means 'having the tendency to use long words.' Here's one you might like—*apodysophilia*, the feverish desire to undress."

"I do like that one."

"And here's another you might like—*dodrantal*. It means 'nine inches in length.'"

"I think you just added another inch, or two," he growled. "I once had a lady teach me some wooing words. Let's see if they work. Beatrice, your eyes are lambent. Your lips are sapid. And your figure is pulchritudinous."

"Ford." She beamed at him. "You remembered."

"I remember everything. Seeing the glow of your hair in the library window and wanting so badly to talk to you, to walk with you to the sea. Hand in hand."

His lips teased the edges of her mouth. "Thinking that you really, really loved words and wondering what it would be like to have that passion directed at me."

He slid a hand down her bodice, cupping one of her breasts in his palm.

"Handing you that sledgehammer that weighed nearly as much as you did and watching you smash the plaster to dust. Something came loose inside of me then, Beatrice. I think that's when I knew that I was seriously in trouble."

"That's when I knew I was . . . falling in love," she said, her voice breathy because he was doing very wicked things to the tips of her breasts with his tongue. "When I held your hard hammer."

A snort of laughter. He lifted his head. "I was completely lost when I walked into the room and saw you wearing those trousers that you had no idea hugged every one of your curves."

"I had some idea."

"You were cursing at that stubborn floorboard, just like you castigated me during our arguments."

"You're stubborn."

"I know. But you found a way to pry my heart free from its moorings. And I'm so glad that you did."

He kissed her then, ravishing her lips until her mind filled with longing and her body craved his touch. But she had one more thing to show him.

She reached into the specially designed pockets of her blue gown. "I thought you might like the third book in the series."

"'*The Dangerous Duke's Desires*,'" he read.

"Turn to page one hundred," she instructed.

"Are we going to act out your favorite passage? I like the sound of that."

"Just open the book."

"What's this?" He pulled something fragile and red from between the pages.

"The rose you gave me in the library in Cornwall. I told myself I was keeping it as a talisman to ward away swooning tendencies and imaginary kisses from arrogant rogues. But really I kept it for much more sentimental reasons. I knew then, as I know now." She traced the line of his strong jaw. "You're the rogue that stole my heart."

LATER, WHEN THEY both gleamed with sweat and he was quite breathless, Ford decided to broach the subject of desks.

"I've had a fantasy about you ever since we first met, Beatrice."

"Oh? Do you want me to teach you more words?"

"I want to teach you about desks."

"Desks? I know all about those. I use them every day."

"Not in this way, you don't."

"Oh," she said in a knowing tone. "You don't mean writing on desks."

"I mean ravishing."

She gave him a saucy smile and hopped out of bed. "How does this work?"

His heart began pounding. "Bend over the desk, princess."

She bent over the desk, just as she had that night when she visited his room. But this time she was entirely naked.

And entirely his.

"When you arrived in this room the other night and slid over this desk with your pert bottom in the air. Gods, I wanted to . . ." He positioned himself behind her. "I wanted to do this."

He buried his length inside her, watching the globes of her bottom shiver with each thrust.

She moaned, tossing her hair over the desk. "I didn't . . . know that I was . . . being so provocative."

She wiggled her bum and tilted her chin back toward him. The look in her eyes was pure sensuality, and it was all over for Ford.

He wrapped an arm around her waist and rocked inside her until he exploded, moaning her name like a prayer.

SEVERAL HOURS LATER, they lay entwined on the bed, enclosed by pink velvet curtains and surrounded by love.

"Ford?"

"Yes, my wallflower?"

"Have you exhausted the limits of your excessive virility?"

"Maybe."

"Then we can talk."

"We can always talk, Beatrice. Always."

"I thought I was making the difficult choice by retreating from society, but this is the more difficult decision. Taking the risk of loving a rogue."

"I'm a one-woman rogue. I'm all yours. Risk-free."

He kissed her. He'd never get enough of being able to kiss her whenever he felt like it. "What will you name this new clubhouse?"

"We couldn't decide on a name at the last meeting. Isobel suggested the Virago Club, but I thought that was too negative. Viola offered the Muses Society, because we're our own muses, but that's too commonly used."

"What about the Boadicea Club?"

"The name of your ship?"

"She was going to take me away from you. It would be fitting if she were also the reason for our union."

She tilted her head to one side. "You know what? I love that idea. Boadicea was a warrior queen. And her name means 'victory.'"

She traced a bead of sweat down his chest. "I'm glad that you're not threatened by powerful and intelligent women, Ford. I'm glad I don't have to be weak for you to feel strong."

"You make me stronger, Beatrice. You reinforce me. I want to be the roof over your head, the floor beneath your feet. It feels like . . ." He brought her hand to his lips and kissed her fingertips one by one. "It feels like when I have a floor to lay down, and all of the boards fit together seamlessly. We fit together, Beatrice."

She rolled on top of him and brought her knees to either side of his hips. "We do, don't we?"

"Again?" he asked, a little breathlessly.

"Again," she said, rocking toward him and brushing her nipples against his chest.

His hands bracketed her hips. "Beatrice," he groaned. "You're going to be the death of me."

"I hope not, not when our life together is just beginning."

"I can't wait to see what's in store for us."

Soon they were flying toward the stars on the horizon again.

She was a new beginning.

She was his haven.

His heaven.

Epilogue

❧ 🌹 ❧

THE DEDICATION CEREMONY for the Boadicea Club, Strand, was attended by no less than four dukes, a grand number for any occasion.

Almost enough to quell the persistent rumors that this new clubhouse was a secret hotbed of revolutionary females plotting to overthrow the right and proper patriarchal order of British society.

The assembled members of the society looked just like ordinary ladies, not bloodthirsty warrior queens, the gathered crowd confirmed. Although Lady Beatrice Wright, who had made a marriage of unequal social rank to the handsome and virile carpenter standing by her side, Mr. Stamford Wright, was seen to be out of doors *without a bonnet*, though it was a sunny day that teased her copper hair to flame.

The Dukes of Banksford, Ravenwood, and Thorndon flanked the stone entranceway with their vivacious duchesses, while Westbury, who held the dubious honor of being the Most Eligible Duke in London, made a rare daytime appearance in the company of his unmarried sisters.

Two elegant and poker-faced dowager duchesses were in attendance to lend gravitas to the occasion. This solemnity was undermined by the antics of the Duke of Banksford's twins, a tall lad and a girl who should have known better, darting in and out of the crowd, playing hide-and-seek with their young brother, a sturdy little boy with surprisingly quick legs.

Another rather shocking circumstance was that the Duchess of Thorndon, a new mother, refused to entrust the care of her infant daughter to the affronted nurse who trailed after them, determined to have her charge back.

All in all, if the crowd was hoping for scandal and rabble-rousing speeches from deranged bluestockings, they left disappointed.

"Ladies and gentlemen supporters," Beatrice began, smiling at her friends and family. "We are gathered here to dedicate this club-house to the achievement of women in the arts and sciences and in the area of entrepreneurship, and to the goals of education and sisterhood. It is fitting that the name Boadicea was chosen, the name of a legendary queen and warrior, and a name meaning 'victory'. We have much to overcome—partiality, prejudice, custom, and ignorance. The members of our society have already achieved many milestones. May we celebrate those achievements, and move ever onward toward our goals."

"I'm confused," said Beatrice's mother as they entered the club-house together. "I thought this was a knitting society?"

"There's some needlework involved. Miss Finchley knit this blanket." Beatrice saw her mother seated in a comfortable chair near the fire. "Here, let me tuck it over your knees, there's a chill in the air."

The fact that her mother was here at all gave Beatrice great joy. Her mother hadn't fully accepted Ford into the family, but at least she no longer pretended that he didn't exist.

Ford caught her eye from across the room and Beatrice's heart skipped a beat. He looked so handsome today, but she couldn't wait to get him back to their house and reveal the taut, muscled flesh beneath that tailored suit.

They'd renovated one of the buildings next door into a modest, yet extremely comfortable, home.

Isobel and Rafe were arguing about something in a corner. And Viola was surrounded by a chattering crowd of the Duke of Westbury's sisters.

Lady Henrietta Prince was talking to the society's newest recruit, Lady Philippa Bramble, who had revealed some surprising ambitions when she attended her first meeting.

Even though they'd christened the society with a new name, Beatrice and her friends still weren't at liberty to fully divulge the extent of their activities. Isobel, in particular, would never be allowed to graduate from law school if her sex were revealed.

Mrs. Kettle, who had decided to stay on as housekeeper to the club, couldn't possibly make enough tea for everyone, but she was very happy to try. And Mr. Coggins, who hadn't yet agreed to retirement, was seen to smile by Viola, though no one would quite believe it.

Ford's grandfather attended, but only briefly. He complained loudly about all the profit wasted, but privately, she knew he was pleased with his grandson for marrying into the nobility. Beatrice was still certain that Foxton's business practices were less than humane, but she and Ford, and Ford's mother and aunt, were wearing him down, little by little, and he would come round to their way of thinking eventually.

Beatrice smiled happily as she walked around the room, making sure a good time was had by all. Who would have thought that she'd be living in London, hosting large social gatherings, one year earlier when she was cloistered in the library at Thornhill?

After the festivities ended, she and Ford walked back, arm in arm, to their adjacent home.

"Come and see what I've been working on while you've been writing your dictionary these past weeks, my love." He took her downstairs to his basement workshop.

"A cradle? Ford, isn't that putting the cart before the horse, so to speak?"

"It's for Tiny," he laughed. "I had a letter that his Eliza is expecting. I'll send it back to Cornwall with my mother."

His mother had been splitting her time between Cornwall and London now that she was reconciled with her father.

He winked at her. "Though it wouldn't be the worst thing to have a young Ford running around. He'd be a handsome little devil."

"Or a young Beatrice wearing spectacles and memorizing dictionaries."

"Or one of each."

"Perhaps. One day. We have time to try, my rogue."

"Would you like to try right now? Down here on top of this pile of cedarwood shavings?"

"Malapert rapscallion. Scurrilous scoundrel."

"You like scoundrels. We're far more interesting than other men."

She kissed him then, to show him just how much she loved scoundrels.

She kissed him with the fragrance of cedar around them, reminding her of his handiwork.

His large, capable hands shaping her waist.

She loved his work-roughened hands.

She loved him. More than she'd ever thought it was possible to love.

Their love was strong and solid and true.

Built to weather storms. Built to stand the test of time.

Acknowledgments

As ALWAYS, I must heap gratitude upon my amazing agent, Alexandra Machinist, and my peerless editor, Carrie Feron. I'm so very thankful for the entire dynamic and dedicated team at Avon, especially Pam Jaffee, Asanté Simons, Jes Lyons, and Guido Caroti, who perfectly captured Beatrice and Ford for this dreamy cover. All of my love to my husband, Brian, and to my extended family in Alaska, Utah, and Wisconsin. The Bookish Belles Facebook group sustains me with cat memes and virtual hugs. Hope to meet more of you in person someday! This book is my love song to you, dear reader. This one is for the lifelong bookworms with out of control TBR piles. The readers suffering from book hangovers, and swooning over their latest book bf/gf. Thank you for believing in HEAs. Thank you for being you.